FIRESPELL

PRAISE FOR THE
DARK ELITE NOVELS

FIRESPELL

"Chloe Neill has written an incredible cast of characters and her heroine, Lily, has a wonderful engaging voice. . . . Fans of urban fantasy, paranormal, and young adult will definitely want to pick this one up and lose themselves in the magical underground that is Chicago."
—Fresh Fiction

"If you crave a story full of intrigue, mystery, magic, and a bit of romance, then this is your book."
—Bookstack

"Exciting teen urban fantasy."
—Genre Go Round Reviews

"In a genre laden with boarding school dramas, how can one possibly stand out? Ask Chloe Neill. She did an excellent job of making *Firespell* stand out above all the others. How? you may ask. By writing exceptionally interesting, fun characters."
—Pure Imagination

HEXBOUND

"Neill continues building her urban fantasy geared toward tweens and teens featuring a slightly different take on magic...will appeal to fans of series like the *Blood Coven* [*Vampires*]."
—Monsters and Critics

"The Dark Elite series is absolutely gripping and definitely a page-turner. I could not resist this book and read it quickly. If you haven't picked up this series, you need to. This is one book that will rock your reading world."
—Books with Bite

continued . . .

THE
DARK ELITE

FIRESPELL

and

HEXBOUND

CHLOE NEILL

NEW AMERICAN LIBRARY

NEW AMERICAN LIBRARY
Published by New American Library,
a division of Penguin Group (USA) Inc.,
375 Hudson Street, New York, New York 10014, USA
Penguin Group (Canada), 90 Eglinton Avenue East, Suite 700, Toronto,
Ontario M4P 2Y3, Canada (a division of Pearson Penguin Canada Inc.)
Penguin Books Ltd., 80 Strand, London WC2R 0RL, England
Penguin Ireland, 25 St. Stephen's Green, Dublin 2,
Ireland (a division of Penguin Books Ltd.)
Penguin Group (Australia), 250 Camberwell Road, Camberwell,
Victoria 3124, Australia (a division of Pearson Australia Group Pty. Ltd.)
Penguin Books India Pvt. Ltd., 11 Community Centre,
Panchsheel Park, New Delhi - 110 017, India
Penguin Group (NZ), 67 Apollo Drive, Rosedale, Auckland 0632,
New Zealand (a division of Pearson New Zealand Ltd.)
Penguin Books (South Africa) (Pty.) Ltd., 24 Sturdee Avenue,
Rosebank, Johannesburg 2196, South Africa

Penguin Books Ltd., Registered Offices:
80 Strand, London WC2R 0RL, England

Published by New American Library, a division of Penguin Group (USA) Inc. *Firespell* and
Hexbound were previously published in separate Signet mass market editions.

First New American Library Printing (Double Edition), August 2011
1   3   5   7   9   10   8   6   4   2

Firespell copyright © Chloe Neill, 2010
Hexbound copyright © Chloe Neill, 2011
All rights reserved

 REGISTERED TRADEMARK—MARCA REGISTRADA

Set in Granjon • Designed by Elke Sigal

Printed in the United States of America

PUBLISHER'S NOTE
These are works of fiction. Names, characters, places, and incidents either are the product of
the author's imagination or are used fictitiously, and any resemblance to actual persons, living
or dead, business establishments, events, or locales is entirely coincidental.
   The publisher does not have any control over and does not assume any responsibility for
author or third-party Web sites or their content.

"Chicago—a city where they are always rubbing a lamp, and fetching up the genii, and contriving and achieving new impossibilities."

—Mark Twain

1

They were gathered around a conference table in a high-rise, eight men and women, no one under the age of sixty-five, all of them wealthy beyond measure. And they were here, in the middle of Manhattan, to decide my fate.

I was not quite sixteen and only one month out of my sophomore year of high school. My parents, philosophy professors, had been offered a two-year-long academic sabbatical at a university in Munich, Germany. That's right—two years out of the country, which only really mattered because they decided I'd be better off staying in the United States.

They'd passed along that little nugget one Saturday in June. I'd been preparing to head to my best friend Ashley's house when my parents came into my room and sat down on my bed.

"Lily," Mom said, "we need to talk."

I don't think I'm ruining the surprise by pointing out that nothing good happens when someone starts a speech like that.

My first thought was that something horrible had happened to Ashley. Turned out she was fine; the trauma hit a little closer to home. My parents told me they'd been accepted into the sabbatical program, and that the chance to work in Germany for two years was an amazing opportunity for them.

Then they got quiet and exchanged one of those long, meaningful looks that really didn't bode well for me. They said they didn't want to drag me to Germany with them, that they'd be busy while they were there, and that they wanted me to stay in an American school to have the best chance of going to a great college here. So they'd decided that while they were away, I'd be staying in the States.

I was equal parts bummed and thrilled. Bummed, of course, because they'd be an ocean away while I passed all the big milestones— SAT prep, college visits, prom, completing my vinyl collection of every Smashing Pumpkins track ever released.

Thrilled, because I figured I'd get to stay with Ashley and her parents.

Unfortunately, I was only right about the first part.

My parents had decided it would be best for me to finish high school in Chicago, in a boarding school stuck in the middle of high-rise buildings and concrete—not in Sagamore, my hometown in Upstate New York; not in our tree-lined neighborhood, with my friends and the people and places I knew.

I protested with every argument I could think of.

Flash forward two weeks and 240 miles to the conference table where I sat in a button-up cardigan and pencil skirt I'd never have worn under normal circumstances, the members of the Board of Trustees of St. Sophia's School for Girls staring back at me. They interviewed every girl who wanted to walk their hallowed halls—after all, heaven forbid they let in a girl who didn't meet their standards. But that they traveled to New York to see me seemed a little out of the ordinary.

"I hope you're aware," said one of them, a silver-haired man with tiny round glasses, "that St. Sophia's is a famed academic institution. The school itself has a long and storied history in Chicago, and the Ivy Leagues recruit from its halls."

A woman with a pile of hair atop her head looked at me and said slowly, as if talking to a child, "You'll have any secondary institution in this country or beyond at your feet, Lily, if you're accepted at St. Sophia's. If you become a St. Sophia's girl."

Okay, but what if I didn't want to be a St. Sophia's girl? What if I wanted to stay home in Sagamore with my friends, not a thousand miles away in some freezing Midwestern city, surrounded by private-school girls who dressed the same, talked the same, bragged about their money?

I didn't want to be a St. Sophia's girl. I wanted to be me, Lily Parker, of the dark hair and eyeliner and fabulous fashion sense.

The powers that be of St. Sophia's were apparently less hesitant. Two weeks after the interview, I got the letter in the mail.

"Congratulations," it said. "We are pleased to inform you that the members of the board of trustees have voted favorably regarding your admission to St. Sophia's School for Girls."

I was less than pleased, but short of running away, which wasn't my style, I was out of options. So two months later, my parents and I trekked to Albany International.

Mom had booked us on the same airline, so we sat in the concourse together, with me between the two of them. Mom wore a shirt and trim trousers, her long dark hair in a low ponytail. My father wore a button-up shirt and khakis, his auburn hair waving over the glasses on his nose. They were heading to JFK to connect to their international flight; I was heading to O'Hare.

We sat silently until they called my plane. Too nervous for tears, I stood and put on my messenger bag. My parents stood, as well, and my mom reached out to put a hand on my cheek. "We love you, Lil. You know that? And that this is what's best?"

I most certainly didn't know this was best. And the weird thing was, I wasn't sure even she believed it, considering how nervous she sounded when she said it. Looking back, I think they both had doubts about the whole thing. They didn't actually say that, of course, but their body language told a different story. When they first told me about their plan, my dad kept touching my mom's knee—not romantically or anything, but like he needed reassurance, like he needed to remind himself that she was there and that things were going to be okay. It made me wonder. I mean, they were headed to Germany for a two-year research sabbatical they'd spent months applying for, but despite what they'd said about the great "opportunity," they didn't seem thrilled about going.

The whole thing was very, very strange.

Anyway, my mom's throwing out, "It's for the best," at the airport wasn't a new thing. She and dad had both been repeating that phrase over the last few weeks like a mantra. I didn't know that it was for the best, but I didn't want a bratty comment to be the last thing I said to them, so I nodded at my mom and faked a smile, and let my dad pull me into a rib-breaking hug.

"You can call us anytime," he said. "Anytime, day or night. Or e-mail. Or text us." He pressed a kiss to the top of my head. "You're our light, Lils," he whispered. "Our light."

I wasn't sure whether I loved him more, or hated him a little, for caring so much and still sending me away.

We said our goodbyes, and I traversed the concourse and took my seat on the plane, with a credit card for emergencies in my wallet, a duffel bag bearing my name in the belly of the jet, and my palm pressed to the window as New York fell behind me.

Goodbye, "New York State of Mind."

Pete Wentz said it best in his song title: "Chicago Is So Two Years Ago."

Two hours and a tiny bag of peanuts later, I was in the 312, greeted by a wind that was fierce and much too cold for an afternoon in early September, Windy City or not. My knee-length skirt, part of my new St. Sophia's uniform, didn't help much against the chill.

I glanced back at the black-and-white cab that had dropped me off in front of the school's enclave on East Erie. The driver pulled away from the curb and merged into traffic, leaving me there on the sidewalk, giant duffel bag in my hands, messenger bag across my shoulder, and downtown Chicago around me.

What stood before me, I thought as I gazed up at St. Sophia's School for Girls, wasn't exactly welcoming.

The board members had told me that St. Sophia's had been a convent in its former life, but it could have just as easily been the setting for a gothic horror movie. Dismal gray stone. Lots of tall, skinny windows, and one giant round one in the middle. Fanged, grinning gargoyles perched at each corner of the steep roof.

I tilted my head as I surveyed the statues. Was it weird that nuns had been guarded by tiny stone monsters? And were they supposed to keep people out . . . or in?

Rising over the main building were the symbols of St. Sophia's—two prickly towers of that same gray stone. Supposedly, some of Chicago's leading ladies wore silver rings inscribed with an outline of the towers, proof that they'd been St. Sophia's girls.

Three months after my parents' revelation, I still had no desire to be a St. Sophia's girl. Besides, if you squinted, the building looked like a pointy-eared monster.

I gnawed the inside of my lip and scanned the other few equally gothic buildings that made up the small campus, all but hidden from the rest of Chicago by a stone wall. A royal blue flag that bore the St. Sophia's crest (complete with tower) rippled in the wind above the arched front door. A Rolls-Royce was parked on the curved driveway below.

This wasn't my kind of place. This wasn't Sagamore. It was far from my school and my neighborhood, far from my favorite vintage clothing store and favorite coffeehouse.

Worse, given the Rolls, I guessed these weren't my kind of people. Well, they *used* to not be my kind of people. If my parents could afford to send me here, we apparently had money I hadn't known about.

"This sucks," I muttered, just in time for the heavy double doors in the middle of the tower to open. A woman—tall, thin, dressed in a no-nonsense suit and sensible heels—stepped into the doorway.

We looked at each other for a moment. Then she moved to the side, holding one of the doors open with her hand.

I guessed that was my cue. Adjusting my messenger bag and duffel, I made my way up the sidewalk.

"Lily Parker?" she asked, one eyebrow arched questioningly, when I got to the stone stairs that lay before the door.

I nodded.

She lifted her gaze and surveyed the school grounds, like an eagle scanning for prey. "Come inside."

I walked up the steps and into the building, the wind ruffling my hair as the giant doors were closed behind me.

The woman moved through the main building quickly, efficiently, and, most noticeably, silently. I didn't get so much as a hello, much less a warm welcome to Chicago. She hadn't spoken a word since she'd beckoned me to follow her.

And follow her I did, through lots of slick limestone corridors lit by tiny flickering bulbs in old-fashioned wall sconces. The floor and walls were made of the same pale limestone, the ceiling overhead a grid of thick wooden beams, gold symbols painted in the spaces between them. A bee. The flowerlike shape of a fleur-de-lis.

We turned one corner, then another, until we entered a corridor lined with columns. The ceiling changed, rising above us in a series of pointed arches outlined in curved wooden beams, the spaces between them painted the same blue as St. Sophia's flag. Gold stars dotted the blue.

It was impressive—or at least expensive.

I followed her to the end of the hallway, which terminated in a wooden door. A name, MARCELINE D. FOLEY, was written in gold letters in the middle of it.

When she opened the door and stepped inside the office, I assumed she was Marceline D. Foley. I stepped inside behind her.

The room was darkish, a heavy fragrance drifting up from a small oil burner on a side table. A gigantic, circular stained glass window was on the wall opposite the door, and a massive oak desk sat in front of the window.

"Close the door," she said. I dropped my duffel bag to the floor, then did as she'd directed. When I turned around again, she was seated behind the desk, manicured hands clasped before her, her gaze on me.

"I am Marceline Foley, the headmistress of this school," she said. "You've been sent to us for your education, your personal growth, and your development into a young lady. You will become a St. Sophia's girl. As a junior, you will spend two years at this institution. I expect you to use that time wisely—to study, to learn, to network, and to prepare yourself for academically challenging studies at a well-respected university.

"You will have classes from eight twenty a.m. until three twenty p.m., Monday through Friday. You will have dinner at precisely five o'clock and study hall from seven p.m. until nine p.m., Sunday through Thursday. Lights-out at ten o'clock. You will remain on the school grounds during the week, although you may take your exercise off the grounds during your lunch breaks, assuming you do not leave the grounds alone and that you stay near campus. Curfew is promptly at nine p.m. on Friday and Saturday nights. Do you have any questions?"

I shook my head, which was a fib. I had tons of questions, actually, but not the sort I thought she'd appreciate, especially since her PR skills left a lot to be desired. She made St. Sophia's sound less like boarding school and more like prison. Then again, the PR was lost on me, anyway. It's not like I was there by choice.

"Good." Foley pulled open a tiny drawer on the right-hand side of her desk. Out of it she lifted an antique gold skeleton key—the skinny kind with prongs at the end—that was strung from a royal blue ribbon.

"Your room key," she said, and extended her hand. I lifted the ribbon from her palm, wrapping my fingers around the slender bar of metal. "Your books are already in your room. You've been assigned a laptop, which is in your room, as well."

She frowned, then glanced up at me. "This is likely not how you imagined your junior and senior years of high school would be, Ms. Parker. But you will find that you have been bestowed an incredible gift. This is one of the finest high schools in the nation. Being an alumna of St. Sophia's will open doors for you educationally and socially. Your membership in this institution will connect you to a network of women whose influence is international in scope."

I nodded, mostly about that first part. Of course I'd imagined my junior and senior years differently. I'd imagined being at home, with my friends, with my parents. But she hadn't actually asked me how I felt about being shipped off to Chicago, so I didn't elaborate.

"I'll show you to your room," she said, rising from her chair and moving toward the door.

I picked up my bag again and followed her.

St. Sophia's looked pretty much the same on the walk to my room as it had on the way to Foley's office—one stone corridor after another. The building was immaculately clean, but kind of empty. Sterile. It was also quieter than I would have expected a high school to be, certainly quieter than the high school I'd left behind. But for the click of Foley's heels on the shining stone floors, the place was graveyard silent. And there was no sign of the usual high school stuff. No trophy cases, no class photos, no lockers, no pep rally posters. Most important, still no sign of students. There were supposed to be two hundred of us. So far, it looked like I was the only St. Sophia's girl in residence.

The corridor suddenly opened into a giant circular space with a domed ceiling, a labyrinth set into the tile on the floor beneath it. This was a serious place. A place for contemplation. A place where nuns once walked quietly, gravely, through the hallways.

And then she pushed open another set of double doors.

The hallway opened into a long room lit by enormous metal chandeliers and the blazing color of dozens of stained glass windows. The walls that weren't covered by windows were lined with books, and the floor was filled by rows and rows of tables.

At the tables sat teenagers. Lots and lots of teenagers, all in stuff that made up the St. Sophia's uniform: navy plaid skirt and some kind of top in the same navy; sweater; hooded sweatshirt; sweater-vest.

They looked like an all-girl army of plaid.

Books and notebooks were spread on the tables before them, laptop computers open and buzzing. Classes didn't start until tomorrow, and these girls were already studying. The trustees were right—these people were serious about their studies.

"Your classmates," Foley quietly said.

She walked through the aisle that split the room into two halves, and I followed behind her, my shoulder beginning to ache under the weight of the duffel bag. Girls watched as I walked past them, heads lifting from books (and notebooks and laptops) to check me out as I passed. I caught the eyes of two of them.

The first was a blonde with wavy hair that cascaded around her shoulders, a black patent leather headband tucked behind her ears. She arched an eyebrow at me as I passed, and two other brunettes at the table leaned toward her to whisper. To gossip. I made a prediction pretty quickly that she was the leader of that pack.

The second girl, who sat with three other plaid cadets a few tables down, was definitely not a member of the blonde's pack. Her hair was also blond, but for the darker ends of her short bob. She wore black nail polish and a small silver ring on one side of her nose.

Given what I'd seen so far, I was surprised Foley let her get away with that, but I liked it.

She lifted her head as I walked by, her green eyes on my browns as I passed.

She smiled. I smiled back.

"This way," Foley ordered. I hustled to follow.

We walked down the aisle to the other end of the room, then into another corridor. A few more turns and a narrow flight of limestone stairs later, Foley stopped beside a wooden door. She bobbed her head at the key around my neck. "Your suite," she said. "Your bedroom is the first on the right. You have three suitemates, and you'll share the common room. Classes begin promptly at eight-twenty tomorrow morning. Your schedule is with your books. I understand you have some interest in the arts?"

"I like to draw," I said. "Sometimes paint."

"Yes, the board forwarded some of the slides of your work. It lends itself to the fantastic—imaginary worlds and unrealistic creatures—but you seem to have some skill. We've placed you in our arts track. You'll start studio classes within the next few weeks, once our instructor has settled in. It is expected that you will devote as much time to your craft as you do to your studies." Apparently having concluded her instructions, she gave me an up-and-down appraisal. "Any questions?"

She'd done it again. She said, "Any questions?" but it sounded a lot more like "I don't have time for nonsense right now."

"No, thank you," I said, and Foley bobbed her head.

"Very good." With that, she turned on her heel and walked away, her footsteps echoing through the hallway.

I waited until she was gone, then slipped the key into the lock and turned the knob. The door opened into a small circular space—the common room. There were a couch and coffee table in front of a small fireplace, a cello propped against the opposite wall, and four doors leading, I assumed, to the bedrooms.

I walked to the door on the far right and slipped the skeleton key from my neck, then into the lock. When the tumblers clicked, I pushed open the door and flipped on the light.

It was small—a tiny but tidy space with one small window and a twin-sized bed. The bed was covered by a royal blue bedspread embroidered with an imprint of the St. Sophia's tower. Across from the bed was a wooden bureau, atop which sat a two-foot-high stack of books, a pile of papers, a silver laptop, and an alarm clock. A narrow wooden door led to a closet.

I closed the door to the suite behind me, then dropped my bag onto the bed. The room had a few pieces of furniture in it and the school supplies, but otherwise, it was empty. But for the few things I'd been able to fit into the duffel, nothing here would remind me of home.

My heart sank at the thought. My parents had actually sent me away to boarding school. They chose Munich and researching some musty philosopher over art competitions and honors society dinners, the kind of stuff they usually loved to brag about.

I sat down next to my duffel, pulled the cell phone from the front pocket of my gray and yellow messenger bag, flipped it open, and checked the time. It was nearly five o'clock in Chicago and would have been midnight in Munich, although they were probably halfway over the Atlantic right now. I wanted to call them, to hear their voices, but since that wasn't an option, I pulled up my mom's cell number and clicked out a text message: "@ SCHOOL IN ROOM." It wasn't much, but they'd know I'd arrived safely and, I assumed, would call when they could.

When I flipped the phone closed again, I stared at it for a minute, tears pricking at my eyes. I tried to keep them from spilling over, to keep from crying in the middle of my first hour at St. Sophia's, the first hour into my new life.

They spilled over anyway. I didn't want to be here. Not at this school, not in Chicago. If I didn't think they'd just ship me right back again, I'd have used the credit card my mom gave me for emergencies, charged a ticket, and hopped a plane back to New York.

"This sucks," I said, swiping carefully at my overflowing tears, trying to avoid smearing the black eyeliner around my eyes.

A knock sounded at the door, which opened. I glanced up.

"Are you planning your escape?" asked the girl with the nose ring and black nail polish who stood in my doorway.

2

"Seriously, you look pretty depressed there." She pushed off the door, her thin frame nearly swamped by a plaid skirt and oversized St. Sophia's sweatshirt, her legs clad in tights and sheepskin boots. She was about my height, five foot six or so.

"Thanks for knocking," I said, swiping at what I'm sure was a mess beneath my eyes.

"I do what I can. And you've made a mess," she confirmed. She walked toward me and, without warning, tipped up my chin. She tilted her head and frowned at me, then rubbed her thumbs beneath my eyes. I just looked back at her, amusement in my expression. When she was done, she put her hands on her hips and surveyed her work.

"It's not bad. I like the eyeliner. A little punk. A little goth, but not over the top, and it definitely works with your eyes. You might want to think about waterproof, though." She stuck out her hand. "I'm your suitemate, Scout Green. And you're Lily Parker."

"I am," I said, shaking her hand.

Scout sat down on the bed next to me, then crossed her legs and began to swing a leg. "And what personal tragedy has brought you to our fine institution on this lovely fall day?"

I arched a brow at her. She waved a hand. "It's nothing personal. We tend to get a lot of tragedy cases. Relatives die. Fortunes are made and the parentals get too busy for teen angst. That's my basic story. On the rare but exciting occasion, expulsion from the publics and enough money for the trustees to see 'untapped potential.'" She tilted her head as she looked at me. "You've got a great look, but you don't look quite punk enough to be the expulsion kind."

"My parents are on a research trip," I said. "Twenty-four months in Germany—not that I'm bitter about that—so I was sentenced to lockdown at St. Sophia's."

Scout smiled knowingly. "Unfortunately, Lil, your parents' ditching you for Europe makes you average around here. It's like a home for latchkey kids. Where are you from? Prior to being dropped off in the Windy City, I mean."

"Upstate New York. Sagamore."

"You're a junior?"

I nodded.

"Ditto," Scout said, then uncrossed her legs and patted her hands against her knees. "And that means that if all goes well, we'll have two years together at St. Sophia's School for Girls. We might as well get you acquainted." She rose, and with one hand tucked behind her back and one hand at her waist, did a little bow. "I'm Millicent Carlisle Green."

I bit back a grin. "And that's why you go by 'Scout.'"

"And that's why I go by 'Scout,'" she agreed, grinning back. "First off, on behalf of the denizens of Chicago"—she put a hand against her heart—"welcome to the Windy City. Allow me to introduce you to the wondrous world of snooty American private schooldom." She frowned. "'Schooldom.' Is that a word?"

"Close enough," I said. "Please continue."

She nodded, then swept a hand through the air. "You can see the luxury accommodations that the gazillion dollars in tuition and room and board will buy you." She walked to the bed and, like a hostess on *The Price Is Right*, caressed the iron frame. "Sleeping quarters of only the highest quality."

"Of course," I solemnly said.

Scout turned on her heel, the skirt swinging at her knees, and pointed at the simple wooden bureau. "The finest of European antiques to hold your baubles and treasures." Then she swept to the window and, with a tug of the blinds, revealed the view. There were a few yards of grass, then the stone wall. Beyond both sat the facing side of a glass and steel building.

"And, of course," Scout continued, "the finest view that new money can buy."

"Only the best for a Parker," I said.

"Now you're getting it," Scout said approvingly. She walked back to the door, then beckoned me to follow. "The common room," she said, turning around to survey it. "Where we'll gossip, read intellectually stimulating classics of literature—"

"Like that?" I asked with a chuckle, pointing at the dog-eared copy of *Vogue* lying on the coffee table.

"*Absolument*," Scout said. "*Vogue* is our guide to current events and international culture."

"And sweet shoes."

"And sweet shoes," she said, then gestured at the cello in the corner. "That's Barnaby's baby. Lesley Barnaby," she added at my lifted brows. "She's number three in our suite, but you won't see much of her. Lesley has four things, and four things only, in her day planner: class, sleeping, studying, and practicing."

"Who's girl number four?" I asked, as Scout led me to the closed door directly across from mine.

Her hand on the doorknob, Scout glanced back at me. "Amie Cherry. She's one of the brat pack."

"The brat pack?"

"Yep. Did you see the blonde with the headband in the study hall?"

I nodded.

"That's Veronica Lively, the junior class's resident alpha girl. Cherry is one of her minions. She was the brunette with short hair. You didn't hear me say this, but Veronica's actually got brains. She might not use them for much beyond kissing Foley's ass, but she's got them.

The minions are another story. Mary Katherine, that's minion number two—the brunette with long hair—is former old money. She still has the connections, but that's pretty much all she has.

"Now, Cherry—Cherry has coin. Stacks and stacks of cash. As minions go, Cherry's not nearly as bad as Mary Katherine, and she has the potential to be cool, but she takes Veronica's advice much too seriously." Scout frowned, then glanced up at me. "Do you know what folks in Chicago call St. Sophia's?"

I shook my head.

"St. Spoiled."

"Not much of a stretch, is it?"

"Exactly." With a twist of her wrist, Scout turned the knob and pushed open her bedroom door.

"My God," I said, staring into the space. "There's so much . . . *stuff.*"

Every inch of space in Scout's tiny room, but for the rectangle of bed, was filled with shelves. And those shelves were filled to overflowing. They were double-stacked with books and knickknacks, all organized into tidy collections. There was a shelf of owls—some ceramic, some wood, some made of bits of sticks and twigs. A group of sculpted apples—the same mix of materials. Inkwells. Antique tin boxes. Tiny houses made of paper. Old cameras.

"If your parents donate a wing, you get extra shelves," she said, her voice flat as week-old soda.

"Where did you get all this?" I walked to a shelf and picked up a delicate paper house crafted from a restaurant menu. A door and tiny windows were carefully cut into the facade, and a chimney was pasted to the roof, which was dusted in white glitter. "And when?"

"I've been at St. Sophia's since I was twelve. I've had the time. And I got it anywhere and everywhere," she said, flopping down onto her bed. She sat back on her elbows and crossed one leg over the other. "There's a lot of sweet stuff floating around Chicago. Antiques stores, flea markets, handmade goods, what have you. Sometimes my parents bring me stuff, and I pick up things along the way when I see them over the summer."

I gingerly placed the building back on the shelf, then glanced back at her. "Where are they now? Your parents, I mean."

"Monaco—Monte Carlo. The Yacht Show is in a couple of weeks. There's teak to be polished." She chuckled, but the sound wasn't especially happy. "Not by them, of course—they've moved past doing physical labor—but still."

I made some vague sound of agreement—my nautical excursions were limited to paddleboats at summer camp—and moved past the museum and toward the books. There were lots of books on lots of subjects, all organized by color. It was a rainbow of paper—recipes, encyclopedias, dictionaries, thesauruses, books on typology and design. There were even a few ancient leather books with gold lettering along the spines.

I pulled a design book from the shelf and flipped through it. Letters, in every shape and form, were spread across the pages, from a sturdy capital *A* to a tiny, curlicued *Z*.

"I'm sensing a theme here," I said, smiling up at Scout. "You like words. Lists. Letters."

She nodded. "You string some letters together, and you make a word. You string some words together, and you make a sentence, then a paragraph, then a chapter. Words have power."

I snorted, replacing the book on the shelf. "Words have power? That sounds like you're into some Harry Potter juju."

"Now you're just being ridiculous," she said. "So, what does a young Lily Parker do in Sagamore, New York?"

I shrugged. "The usual. I hung out. Went to the mall. Concerts. TiVo *ANTM* and *Man vs. Wild*."

"Oh, my God, I *love* that show," Scout said. "That guy eats everything."

"And he's hot," I pointed out.

"Seriously hot," she agreed. "Hot guy eats bloody stuff. Who knew that would be a hit?"

"The producer of every vampire movie ever?" I offered.

Scout snorted a laugh. "Well put, Parker. I'm digging the sarcasm."

"I try," I admitted with a grin. It was nice to smile—nice to have something to smile about. Heck, it was nice to feel like this boarding school business might be doable—like I'd be able to make friends and study and go about my high school business in pretty much the same way as I could have in Sagamore.

A shrill sound suddenly filled the air, like the beating of tiny wings.

"Oops, that's me," Scout said, untangling her legs, hopping off the bed, and grabbing a brick-shaped cell phone that was threatening to vibrate its way off one of the shelves and onto the floor. She picked up the phone just before it hit the edge, then unpopped the screen and read its contents.

"Jeez Louise," she said. "You'd think I'd get a break when school starts, but no." Maybe realizing she was muttering in front of an audience, she looked up at me. "Sorry, but I have to go. I have to . . . exercise. Yes," she said matter-of-factly, as if she'd decided on exercise as an excuse, "I have to exercise."

Apparently intent on proving her point, Scout arched her arms over her head and leaned to the right and left, as if stretching for a big run, then stood up and began swiveling her torso, hands at her waist. "Limbering up," she explained.

I arched a dubious brow. "To go exercise."

"Exercise," she repeated, grabbing a black messenger bag from a hook next to her door and maneuvering it over her head. A white skull and crossbones grinned back at me.

"So," I said, "you're exercising in your uniform?"

"Apparently so. Look, you're new, but I like you. And if I guess right, you're a heck of a lot cooler than the rest of the brat pack."

"Thanks, I guess?"

"So I need you to be cool. You didn't see me leave, okay?"

The room was silent as I looked at her, trying to gauge exactly how much trouble she was about to get herself into.

"Is this one of those, 'I'm in over my head' kind of deals, and I'll hear a horrible story tomorrow about your being found strangled in an alley?"

That she took a few seconds to think about her answer made me that much more nervous.

"Probably not *tonight*," she finally said. "But either way, that's not on you. And since we're probably going to be BFFs, you're going to have to trust me on this one."

"BFFs?"

"Of course," she said, and just like that, I had a friend. "But for now, I have to run. We'll talk," she promised. And then she was gone, her bedroom door open, the closing of the hallway door signaling her exit. I looked around her room, noticing the pair of sneakers that sat together beside her bed.

"Exercise, my big toe," I mumbled, and left Scout's museum, closing the door behind me.

It was nearly six o'clock when I walked the few feet back to my room. I glanced at the stack of books and papers on the bureau, admitting to myself that prepping for class tomorrow was probably a solid course of action.

On the other hand, there were bags to be unpacked.

It wasn't a tough choice. I liked to read, but I wasn't going to spend the last few waking hours of my summer vacation with my nose in a book.

I unzipped and unstuffed my duffel bag, cramming undergarments and pajamas and toiletries into the bureau, then hanging the components of my new St. Sophia's wardrobe in the closet. Skirts in the blue and gold of the St. Sophia's plaid. Navy polo shirt. Navy cardigan. Blue button-up shirt, et cetera, et cetera. I also stowed away the few articles of regular clothing I'd brought along: some jeans and skirts, a few favorite T-shirts, a hoodie.

Shoes went into the closet, and knickknacks went to the top of the bureau: a photo of my parents and me together; a ceramic ashtray made by Ashley that read BEST COWGIRL EVER. We didn't smoke, of course, and it was unrecognizable as an ashtray, as it looked more like something you'd discover in the business end of a dirty diaper. But Ashley made it for me at camp when we were eight. Sure, I tortured her about how truly heinous it was, but that's what friends were for, right?

At the moment, Ash was home in Sagamore, probably studying for a bio test, since public school had started two weeks ago. Remembering I hadn't texted her to let her know I'd arrived, I flipped open my phone and snapped shots of my room—the empty walls, the stack of books, the logoed bedspread—then sent them her way.

"UNIMPRESSED RR," she texted back. She'd taken to calling me "Richie Rich" when we found out that I'd be heading to St. Sophia's—and after we'd done plenty of Web research. She figured that life in a froufrou private school would taint me, turn me into some kind of raving Blair Waldorf.

I couldn't let that stand, of course. I sent back, "U MUST RESPECT ME."

She was still apparently unimpressed, since "GO STUDY" was her answer. I figured she was probably onto something, so I moved back to the stack of books and gave them a look-see.

Civics.

Trig.

British lit.

Art history.

Chemistry.

European history.

"Good thing they're starting me off easy," I muttered, nibbling on my bottom lip as I scanned the textbooks. Add the fact that I was apparently taking a studio class, and it was no wonder Foley scheduled a two-hour study hall every night. I'd be lucky if two hours were enough.

Next to the stack of books was a pile of papers, including a class schedule and the rules of residency at St. Sophia's. There wasn't a building map, which was a little flabbergasting since this place was a maze to get through.

I heard the hallway door open and shut, laughter filling the common room. Thinking I might as well be social, I blew out a breath to calm the butterflies in my stomach, then opened my bedroom door. There were three girls in the room—the blonde I'd seen in the library and her two brunette friends. Given Scout's descriptions, I assumed the blonde was Veronica, the shorter-haired girl was Amie, the third of my new suitemates, and the girl with longer hair was Mary Katherine, she of the limited intelligence.

The blonde had settled herself on the couch, her long, wavy hair spread around her shoulders, her feet in Amie's lap. Mary Katherine sat on the floor in front of them, her arms stretched behind her, her feet crossed at the ankles. They were all in uniform, all in pressed, pleated skirts, tights, and button-down shirts with navy sweater-vests.

A regiment of officers in the army of plaid.

"We have a visitor," said the blonde, one blond brow arched over blue eyes.

Amie, whose pale skin was unmarred by makeup or jewelry except for a pair of pearl earrings, slapped at Veronica's feet. Veronica rolled her eyes, but lifted them, and the brunette stood and walked toward me. "I'm Amie." She bobbed her head toward one of the bedrooms behind us. "I'm over there."

"It's nice to meet you," I said. "I'm Lily."

"Veronica," Amie said, pointing to the blonde, "and Mary Katherine," she added, pointing to the brunette. The girls both offered finger waves.

"You missed the mixer earlier today," Veronica said, stretching out her legs again. "Tea and petits fours in the ballroom. Your chance to meet the rest of your new St. Sophia's chums before classes start tomorrow." Veronica's voice carried the tone of the wealthy, jaded girl who'd seen it all and hadn't been impressed.

"I've only been here a couple of hours," I said, unimpressed by the attitude.

"Yeah, we heard you weren't from Chicago," said Mary Katherine, head tilted up as she scanned my clothes. Given her own navy tights and patent leather flats, and the gleam of her perfectly straight hair, I guessed she wouldn't dig my Chuck Taylors (the board of trustees let us pick our own footware) and choppy haircut.

"Upstate New York," I told her. "Near Syracuse."

"Public school?" Mary Katherine asked, disdain in her voice.

Oh, how fun. Private school really *was* like *Gossip Girl*. "Public school," I confirmed, lips curved into a smile.

Veronica made a sound of irritation. "Jesus, Mary Katherine, be a bitch, why don't you?"

Mary Katherine rolled her eyes, then turned her attention to her cuticles, inspecting her short, perfectly painted red nails. "I just asked a question. You're the one who assumed I was being negative."

"Please excuse the peanut gallery," Amie said with a smile. "Have you met everybody else?"

"I haven't met Lesley," I said. "I met Scout, though."

Mary Katherine made a sarcastic sound. "Good luck there. That girl has *issues*." She stretched out the word dramatically. I got the sense Mary Katherine enjoyed drama.

"M.K.'s just jealous," Veronica said, twirling a lock of hair around one of her fingers, and sliding a glance at the brunette on the floor. "Not every St. Sophia's girl has parents who have the cash to donate an entire building to the school."

I guess Scout hadn't been kidding about the extra shelves.

"Whatever," Mary Katherine said, then crossed her legs and pushed herself up from the floor. "You two can play Welcome Wagon with the new girl. I need to make a phone call."

Veronica rolled her eyes, but swiveled her legs onto the floor and stood up, as well. "M.K.'s dating a U of C boy," she said. "She thinks he hung the moon."

"He's pre-law," Mary Katherine said, heading for the door.

"He's twenty," Amie muttered after Mary Katherine had stepped into the hallway and closed the door behind her. "And she's sixteen."

"Quit being a mother, Amie," Veronica said, straightening her headband. "I'm going back to my room. I suppose I'll see you in the morning." She glanced at me. "I don't want to be bitchy, but a little advice?"

She said it like she was asking for permission, so I nodded, solely out of politeness.

"Mind the company you keep," she said. With that gem, which I assumed was a shot at Scout, she walked to Amie. They exchanged air kisses.

"Nighty night, all," Veronica said, and then she was gone.

When I turned around again, Amie was gone, her bedroom door closing behind her.

"Charming," I muttered, and headed back to my room.

It was earlier than I would have normally gone to sleep, but given the travel, the time change, and the change in circumstances, I was exhausted. Finding the stone-walled and stone-floored room chilly even in the early fall, I exchanged the uniform for flannel pajamas, turned off the light, and climbed into bed.

The room was dark, but far from quiet. The city bustled around me, the thrum of traffic from downtown Chicago creating a backdrop of sound, even on a Sunday night. Although the stone muffled it, I wasn't used to even the low drone of noise. I had been born and bred amongst acres of lawns and overhanging trees—and when the sun went down, the town went silent.

I stared at the ceiling. Tiny yellow-green dots emerged from the darkness. The plaster above me was dotted with glow-in-the-dark stars, I assumed pasted there by a former St. Sophia's girl. As my mind raced, wondering about tomorrow and repeating my to-do list—find my locker, find my classes, manage not to get humiliated in said classes, figure out where Scout had gone—I counted the stars, tried to pick out constellations, and glanced at the clock a dozen times.

I tossed and turned in the bed, trying to find a comfortable position, my brain refusing to still even as I lay exhausted, trying to sleep.

I must have drifted off, as I woke suddenly to a pitch-black room. I must have been awakened by the closing of the hallway door. That sound was immediately followed by the scuffle of tripping in the common room—stuff being knocked around and mumbled curses. I threw off the covers and tiptoed to the door, then pressed my ear to the wood.

"Damn coffee table," Scout muttered, footsteps receding until her bedroom door opened and closed. I glanced at the clock. It was one fifteen in the morning. When the common room was quiet, I put a hand to the doorknob, twisted it, and carefully pulled open the door. The room was dark, but a line of light glowed beneath Scout's door.

I frowned. Where had she been until one fifteen in the morning? Exercise seemed seriously unlikely at this point.

That mystery in hand, I closed the door again and went back to bed, staring at the star-spangled ceiling until sleep finally claimed me.

3

My bedroom was cold and dark when the alarm—which I'd moved next to the bed—went off. Not nearly awake enough to actually sit upright, I fumbled for the OFF button and forced my eyes open. My stomach grumbled, but I didn't think I was up for food. I already had butterflies—the combination of new school, new classes, new girls. Questionable high school cafeteria fare probably wasn't going to help.

After a minute of staring at the ceiling, I glanced over at the nightstand. The red light on my phone flashed, a sign that I had messages waiting. I grabbed it, flipped it open . . . and smiled.

"SAFE & SOUND IN GERMANY," read the text from my mom. "FIGHTING JET LAG."

There was a message from Dad, as well, a little less businesslike (which was pretty much how it worked with them): "HAVE A HOT DOG FOR US! LV U, LILS!"

I smiled, closed the phone again, and put it back on the nightstand. Then I threw off the covers and forced my feet to the floor, the stone cold even beneath socks. I stumbled to the closet and grabbed a robe, then grabbed my toiletries and a towel, already stacked on the bureau, prepped and ready for my inaugural shower.

When I opened my bedroom door, Scout, already in uniform (plaid skirt, sweater, knee-high pair of fuzzy boots), smiled at me from the common room couch. She held up the *Vogue*. "I'll read about skinny chicks in Milan. When you get back, we'll go down to breakfast."

"Sure," I mumbled. But halfway to the hallway door, I stopped and glanced back. "Were you exercising until one fifteen this morning?"

Scout glanced up at me, fingers still pinched around the edge of a half-flipped page. "I'm not admitting whether I was or was not exercising, but if you're asking if I was doing whatever I was doing until one fifteen, then yes."

I opened and closed my mouth as I tried to work out what she'd just said. I settled on, "I see."

"Seriously," she said, "it's important stuff."

"Important like what?"

"Important like, I really can't talk about it."

The room was silent for a few seconds. The set of her jaw and the stubbornness in her eyes said she wasn't going to budge. And since I was standing in front of her in pajamas with a fuzzy brain and teeth that desperately needed introducing to some toothpaste, I let it go.

"Okay," I said, and saw relief in her eyes. I left her with the magazine and headed for the bathroom, but there was no way "exercise" was going to hold me for long. Call it too curious, too nosy. But one day after my arrival in Chicago, she was the closest friend I had. And I wasn't about to lose her to whatever mess she was involved in.

She was on the couch when I returned (much more awake after a good shower and toothbrushing), her legs beneath her, her gaze still on the magazine on her lap.

"FYI," she said, "if you don't hurry, we're going to be left with slurry." She looked up, her countenance solemn. "Trust me on this—you don't want slurry."

Fairly confident she was right—the name being awful enough—I dumped my toiletries in my room and slipped into today's version of the uniform. Plaid skirt. Tights to ward off the chill. Long-sleeved button-up shirt and V-neck sweater. A pair of ice blue boots that were shorter but equally as fuzzy as Scout's.

I stuffed books and some slender Korean notebooks I'd found in a Manhattan paper store (I had a thing for sweet office supplies) into my bag and grabbed my ribboned room key, then closed the door behind me, slipping the key into the lock and turning it until it clicked.

"You ready?" Scout asked, a pile of books in her arms, her black messenger bag over her shoulder, its skull grinning back at me.

"As I'll ever be," I said, pulling the key's ribbon over my head.

The cafeteria was located in a separate building, but one that looked to be the same age as the convent itself—the same stone, the same gothic architecture. I assumed the modern, windowed hallways that now linked them together were added to assuage parents who didn't want their baby girls wandering around outside in freezing Chicago winters. The nuns, I guessed, had been a little more willing to brave the elements.

But the interior of the cafeteria was surprisingly modern, with a long glass wall overlooking the small lawn behind the building. The yard was tidy, inset with wide, concrete paving stones, tufts of grass rising between them. In the far corner sat a piece of what I assumed was industrial sculpture—a series of round metal bands set atop a metal post. *Ode to a Sundial*, maybe?

Having perused the art, I turned back to the cafeteria itself. The long rectangular room was lined with long rectangular tables of pale wood and matching chairs; the tables were filled with the St. Sophia's army. After ten years of public school diversity, it was weird to see so many girls in the same clothes. But that sameness didn't stifle the excitement in the room. Girls clustered together, chatting, probably excited to be back in school, to be reunited with friends and suitemates.

"Welcome to the jungle," Scout whispered, and led me to a buffet line. Smiling men and women in chef gear—white smocks, tall hats—served eggs, bacon, fruit, toast, and oatmeal. These were not your mom's surly lunch ladies—these folks smiled and chatted behind sneeze guards, which were dotted with cards describing how organic or free-range or unsteroided their particular goods were. Whole Foods must have made a fortune off these people.

My stomach twitching with nerves, I didn't have much appetite for breakfast, organic or not, so I asked for toast and OJ, just enough to settle the butterflies. When I'd grabbed my breakfast, I followed Scout to a table. We took two empty chairs at one end.

"I guess we were early enough to avoid the slurry?" I asked.

Scout nibbled at a chunk of pineapple. "Yes, thank God. Slurry is the combination of everything that doesn't get eaten early in the round—oatmeal, fruit, meat, what have you."

I grimaced at the combination. "That's disgusting."

"If you think that's bad, wait until you see the stew," Scout said, nodding toward a chalkboard menu for the week that hung on the far end of the room. "Stew" made a lot of appearances over the weekend.

Scout raised her glass of orange juice toward the menu. "Welcome to St. Sophia's, Parker. Eat early or go home, that's our motto."

"And how's the new girl this morning?"

We turned our gazes to the end of the table. Veronica stood there, blond hair in a complicated ponytail, arms cradling a load of books, Mary Katherine and Amie behind her. Amie smiled at us. Mary Katherine looked viciously bored.

"She's awake," I reported. That was mostly the truth.

"Mmmm," Veronica said in a bored tone, then glanced at Scout. "I hear you're friends with someone from Montclare. Michael Garcia?"

Scout's jaw clenched. "I know Michael. Why do you ask?"

Veronica glanced over her shoulder at Mary Katherine, who made a sound of disdain. "We spent some time together this summer," she said, glancing at Scout again. "He's cute, don't you think?"

I couldn't tell if they were trying to fix Scout up, or figure out if she was crushing Michael so they could throw his interest in Veronica back at her.

Scout shrugged. "He's a friend," she said. "Cute doesn't really figure into it."

"I'm glad you think so," Veronica said, smiling evilly at Scout, "because I'm thinking about inviting him to the Sneak."

Yep. There it was. I didn't need to know what the "Sneak" was to figure out her game—stealing a boy from under Scout's nose. If I'd had any interest in Michael, it would have been hard for me to avoid clawing that superior look right off Veronica's face. But Scout did good—she played the bigger girl, crossing her arms over her chest, her expression bored. "That's great, Veronica. If you think Michael's interested in you, you should go for it. Really."

Her enthusiasm put a frown on Veronica's face. Veronica was pretty—but the frown was not flattering. Her mouth twisted up and her cheeks turned red, her features compressing into something a little less prissy, and a little more ratlike—definitely not attractive.

"You're bluffing," Veronica said. "Maybe I will ask him."

"Do you have his number?" Scout asked, reaching around for her messenger bag. "I could give it to you."

Veronica practically growled, then turned on her heel and headed for the cafeteria door. Mary Katherine, lip wrinkled in disgust, followed her. Amie looked vaguely apologetic about the outburst, but that didn't stop her from turning tail and following, too.

"Nicely done," I complimented.

"Mmm-hmm," Scout said, straightening in her chair again. "See what I mean? TBD."

I lifted my eyebrows. "TBD?"

"Total brat drama," she said. "TBD is way too much drama for me, especially at seven thirty in the morning."

Drama or not, there were questions to be answered. "So, who's Michael Garcia? And what's Montclare?"

"Montclare is a boys' private high. It's kind of our brother school."

"Are they downtown, too?"

"In a roundabout way. They have more kids than we do—nearly four hundred—and their classrooms are scattered in the buildings around the Loop."

"What's the Loop?"

"It's the part of downtown that's within a loop of the El tracks. That's our subway," she added in an elementary-teacher voice.

"Yes," I responded dryly. "I know what the El is. I've seen *ER*."

Scout snorted. "In that case, you'd better be glad you're hooking up with me so I can give you the truth about Chitown. It's not all hot doctors and medical drama, you know." She waved a hand in the air. "Anyway, Montclare has this big-city immersion–type program. You know, country mouse in Gotham, that kind of thing."

"They clearly don't have a Foley," I said. Given what I knew of her so far, I guessed she wouldn't let us out of her sight long enough to "immerse" ourselves in Chicago.

"No kidding," Scout agreed. She pushed back her chair and picked up her tray. "Now that we've had our fill of food and TBD, let's go find our names." Although I had no clue what she was talking about, I finished my orange juice and followed her.

"Our names?" I asked, as we slid our trays through a window at the end of the buffet line.

"A St. Sophia's tradition," she said. I followed her out of the cafeteria, back into the main building, and then through another link into another gothic building, which, Scout explained, held the school's classrooms.

When we pushed through another set of double doors and into the building, we found ourselves in a knot of plaid-clad girls squealing before three rows of lockers. These weren't your typical high school lockers—the steel kind with dents on the front and chunks of gum and leftover stickers on the inside. These were made of gleaming wood, and there were notches cut out of both the top and bottom lockers, so they fit together like a puzzle.

An expensive puzzle, I guessed. Slurry or not, St. Sophia's wasn't afraid to spend some coin.

"Your name will be on yours," Scout shouted through the din of girls, young and old, who were scanning the nameplates on the lockers to find the cabinet that would house their books and supplies for the next nine months.

Frowning at the mass of squirmy teenagers, I wasn't sure I understood the fuss.

I watched Scout maneuver through the girls, then saw blond hair bobbing up and down above the crowd, one arm in the air, as she (I assumed) tried to get my attention.

Gripping the strap of my messenger bag, I squeezed through the gauntlet to reach Scout. She was beaming, one hand on her hip, one hand splayed against one of the top lockers. A silver nameplate in the midst of all that cherry-hued wood bore a single word: SCOUT.

"It says 'Scout'!" she said, glowing like the proud parent of a newborn.

"That's your name," I reminded her.

Scout shook her head, then ran the tips of her fingers across the silver plaque. "For the first time," she said, her gazing going a little dreamy, "it doesn't say 'Millicent.' And only juniors and seniors get the wooden lockers." She bobbed her head down the hall, where the lockers switched back to white enameled steel with vents across the front—the high school classic.

"So you've upgraded?"

Scout nodded. "I've been here for four years, Lil, squeezing books into one of those tiny little contraptions, waiting for the day I'd get wood"—I made an admittedly juvenile snicker—"and G-Day."

"G-Day?"

"Graduation Day. The first day of my freedom from Foley and St. Sophia's and the brat pack. I've been planning for G-Day for four years." She rapped her knuckles against the locker as girls swarmed around us like a flock of birds. "Four years, Parker, and I've got a silver nameplate. A silver nameplate that means I'm only two years from G-Day."

"You really are a weirdo."

"Better to be myself and a little odd than trying to squeeze into some brat pack mold." Her gaze suddenly darkened. I glanced behind us, just in time to see the brat pack moving through the hall. The younger St. Sophia's girls—awed looks on their faces—moved aside as Veronica, Amie, and Mary Katherine floated down the hall on their cloud of smug. That they were only juniors—still a year from full seniority—didn't seem to matter.

"Better to be yourself," I agreed, then looked back at Scout, who was still massaging her nameplate. "Do I get a locker?"

"Only the best one," she snorted, then pointed down. LILY was inscribed in Roman capital letters on a silver nameplate on the Utah-shaped locker beneath hers (which was shaped more like Mississippi).

"If your stinky gym sock odor invades my locker, you're in deep, Parker." Scout slipped her own ribboned room key from her neck and slid the key into the locker. It popped open, revealing three shelves of the same gleaming wood.

She faked a sniff. "This is the most beautiful thing I have ever seen in my life. Such luxury! Such decadence!"

This time, I snorted out loud. Then, realizing the locker bay was beginning to clear out of students, I poked her in the arm. "Come on, weirdo. We need to get to class."

"You have to stop the compliments, Parker. You're making me blush." She popped extra books into her locker, then shut the door again. That done, she glanced at me. "They probably will be expecting us. Best we can do is honor them with our presence."

"We're a blessing, really."

"Totally," she said, and off we went.

Our lockers arranged (although I hadn't so much as opened mine—there was something comforting about having my books in hand), I used the rest of our short walk through the main corridor of the classroom building to our first class—art history—to drag a little more information out of Scout. Thinking it best to hit the interesting stuff first, I started with Veronica's breakfast-hour ploy.

"So," I said, "since you didn't answer me before, I'm going to try again. Tell me about Michael Garcia."

"He's a friend," Scout said, glancing at the room numbers in-scribed on the wooden classroom doors as we passed. "*Just* a friend," she added before I could ask a follow-up. "I don't date guys who go to Montclare. One private school brat in the family is enough."

There was obviously more to that story, but Scout stopped in front of a door, so I assumed we'd run out of time for chatting. Then she glanced back at me. "Do you have a boyfriend back home?"

Well, we were out of time for chatting about *her*, anyway. The door opened before I could respond—although my answer would have been "no." A tall, thin man peered out from the doorway, casting a dour look at me and Scout.

"Ms. Green," he said, "and Ms.—" He lifted his eyebrows expec-tantly.

"Parker," I filled in.

"Yes, very well. Ms. Parker." He stepped to the side, holding the door open with his arm. "Please take your seats."

We walked inside. Much like the rest of the buildings, the class-room had stone floors and walls that were dotted with whiteboards. There were only a couple of girls at desks when we came in, but as soon as Scout and I took a seat—Scout in the desk directly behind mine—the room began to fill with students, including, unfortunately, the brat pack. Veronica, Amie, and Mary Katherine took seats in the row be-side ours, Amie in the front, Veronica in the middle, Mary Katherine behind them. That order put Veronica in the desk right next to mine. Lucky me.

When every desk was taken, girls began pulling notebooks or lap-tops from their bags. I'd skipped the laptop today, thinking I had enough to worry about today without adding power outlet locations and midclass system crashes to the list, so I pulled out a notebook, pen, and art history book from my bag and prepared to learn.

The man who'd greeted us, who I assumed was Mr. Hollis, since the name was written in cursive, green letters on the whiteboard, closed the door and walked to the front of the room. He looked pretty much exactly like you'd expect a private school teacher to look: bald, corduroy slacks, button-up shirt, and corduroy blazer with leather patches at the elbows.

Hollis glanced down at his podium, then lifted his gaze and scanned the room. "'What was any art but a mould in which to imprison for a moment the shining elusive element which is life itself?'" He turned and uncapped a marker, then wrote "WILLA CATHER" in capital letters below his name. He faced us again, capping and uncapping the marker in his hands with a rhythmic click. Nervous tic, I guessed.

"What do you think Ms. Cather meant? Anyone?"

"Bueller? Bueller?" whispered a voice behind me. I pushed my lips together to bite back a laugh at Scout's joke as Amie popped a hand into the air.

When Hollis glanced around before calling her name, as if hoping to give someone else a chance, I guessed Amie answered a lot of questions. "Ms. Cherry," he said.

"She's talking about a piece of art capturing a moment in time."

Hollis's expression softened. "Well put, Ms. Cherry. Anyone else?" He glanced around the room, his gaze finally settling on me. "Ms. Parker?"

My stomach dropped, a flush rising on my cheeks as all eyes turned to me. Didn't it just figure that I'd be called on during the first day of class? I was more into drawing than talking about art, but I gave it a shot, my voice weirdly loud in the sudden silence.

"Um, moments change and pass, I guess, and we forget about them—the details, how we felt at that moment. You still have a memory of what happened, but memories aren't exact. But a painting or a poem—those can save the heart of the moment. Capture it, like Amie said. The details. The feelings."

The room was quiet as Hollis debated whether I'd given him a good answer or a pile of nonsense. "Also well put, Ms. Parker," he finally said.

My stomach unknotted a little.

Apparently having fulfilled his interest in seeking our input, Hollis turned back to the whiteboard and began to fill the space—and the rest of the hour-long period—with an introduction to major periods in Western art. Hollis clearly loved his subject matter, and his voice got high-pitched when he was really excited. Unfortunately, he also tended to spit the little foamy bits of stuff that gathered in the corners of his mouth.

That wasn't the kind of thing you wanted to see right after breakfast, but I had at least one other form of entertainment—Mary Katherine had this really complicated method of twirling her hair. I mean, the girl had a *system*. She picked up a lock of dark hair, spun it around her index finger, tugged on the end, then released it. Then she repeated the process. Twirl. Tug. Drop. Twirl. Tug. Drop. Again and again and again.

It was hypnotizing—so hypnotizing that I nearly jumped when bells rang fifty minutes later, signaling the end of class. Girls scattered at the sound, so I grabbed my stuff and followed Scout into the hallway, which was like a six-lane interstate of St. Sophia's girls hurrying to and fro.

"You've got to figure out how to merge!" Scout said over the din, then disappeared into the throng. I hugged my books to my chest and jumped in.

4

A little more than three hours later, we left art history, trig, and civics behind and headed again for the cafeteria.

"Grab a bag," Scout said when we arrived at the buffet line, and pointed at a tray of paper lunch bags. "We'll eat outside."

I'd been a vegetarian since the day I'd hand-fed a lamb at a petting zoo, only to be served lamb chops a few hours later, so I grabbed a bag labeled VEGGIE WRAP and a bottle of water and followed her.

Scout took a winding route from the cafeteria to the main building, finally pushing open the double doors and heading down the sidewalk. I followed her, the city street full of scurrying people—women in office wear and tennis shoes, men nibbling sandwiches on their way back to the office, tourists with Starbucks cups and glossy shopping bags.

Scout pulled an apple from her bag, then nodded down the street and toward the right. "We can't go far without an escort, but I'll give you the five-dollar block tour while we eat."

"I'm not giving you five dollars."

"You can owe me," she said. "It'll be worth it. Like I said, I've been here since I was twelve. So if you want to know the real deal, the real scoop, you talk to me."

I didn't doubt she knew the real scoop; she'd clearly been here long enough to understand the St. Sophia's procedures. But given her midnight disappearance, I wasn't sure she'd pass on "the real scoop" to me.

Of course, the most obvious fact about St. Sophia's didn't need explaining. The nuns who built the convent had done a bang-up job of picking real estate—the convent was right in the middle of downtown Chicago. Scout said they'd moved to the spot just after the Chicago Fire of 1871, so the city grew up around them, creating a strip of green amidst skyscrapers, a gothic oasis surrounded by glass, steel, and concrete.

One of those glass, steel, and concrete structures stood directly next door.

"This boxy thing is Burnham National Bank," Scout said, pointing at the building, which looked like a stack of glass boxes placed unevenly atop one another.

"Very modern," I said, unwrapping my own lunch. I took a bite of my wrap, munching sprouts and hummus. It wasn't bad, actually, as wraps went.

"The architecture is modern," she said, taking a bite of her apple, "but the bank is very old-school Chicago. Old-*money* Chicago."

I definitely wasn't old school or old money (unless my parents really did have way more cash than I thought), so I guessed I wasn't going to be visiting the BNB Building any time soon. Still, "Good to know," I said.

We walked to the next building, which was a complete contrast to the bank. This one was a small, squat, squarish thing, the kind of old-fashioned brick building that looked like it had been built by hand in the 1940s. PORTMAN ELECTRIC CO. was chiseled in stone just above the door. The building was pretty in an antique kind of way, but it looked completely out of place in between high-rises and coffee shops and boutique stores.

"The Portman Electric Company Building," Scout said, her gaze on the facade. "It was built during the New Deal when they were trying to keep people employed. It's kind of an antique by Loop standards, but I like it." She was quiet for a moment. "There's something kind of . . . honest about it. Something real."

A small bronze marker in front of the building read SRF. I nodded toward the sign. "What's 'SRF'?"

"Sterling Research Foundation," she said. "They do some kind of medical research or something."

With no regard for the employees or security guards of the Sterling Research Foundation, Scout made a beeline for the narrow alley that separated the SRF from the bank. I stuffed the remainder of my lunch back into my paper bag and when Scout signaled the coast was clear, glanced left and right, then speed-walked into the alley.

"Where are we going?" I asked when I reached her.

"A secret spot," she said, bobbing her head toward the end of the passageway. I glanced up, but saw only dirty brick and a set of Dumpsters.

"We aren't going Dumpster diving, are we?" I glanced down at my fuzzy boots and tidy knee-length skirt. " 'Cause I'm really not dressed for it."

"Did you ever read *Nancy Drew*?" Scout suddenly asked.

I blinked as I tried to catch up with the segue. "Of course?"

"Pretend you're Nancy," she said. "We're investigating, kind of." She started into the alley, stepping over a wad of newspaper and avoiding a puddle of liquid of unidentifiable origin.

I pointed at it. "Are we investigating that?"

"Just keep moving," she said, but with a snicker.

We walked through the narrow space until it dead-ended at the stone wall that bounded St. Sophia's.

I frowned at the wall and the grass and gothic buildings that lay beyond it. "We walked around two buildings just to come back to St. Sophia's?"

"Check your left, Einstein."

I did as ordered, and had to blink back surprise. I'd expected to see more alley or bricks, or Dumpsters. But that's not what was there. Instead, the alley gave way to a square of lush, green lawn filled with pillars—narrow pyramids of gray concrete that punctured the grass like a garden of thorns. They varied in height from three feet to five, like a strange gauntlet of stone.

We walked closer. "What is this?"

"It's a memorial garden," she said. "It used to be part of the convent grounds, but the city discovered the nuns didn't actually own this part of the block. Those guys did," she said, pointing at the building that sat behind the bank. "St. Sophia's agreed to put in the stone wall, and the building agreed to keep this place as-is, provided that the St. Sophia's folks promised not to raise a stink about losing it."

"Huh," I said, skimming my fingers across the top of one nubby pillar.

"It's a great place to get lost," she said, and as if on cue, disappeared between the columns.

It took a minute to find her in the forest of them. And when I reached her in the middle, she wasn't alone.

Scout stood stiffly, lips apart, eyes wide, staring at the two boys who stood across from her. They were both in slacks and sweaters, a button-down shirt and tie beneath, an ensemble I assumed was the guy version of the private school uniform. The one on the right had big brown eyes, honey skin, and wavy dark hair curling over his forehead.

The one on the left had dark blond hair and blue eyes. No—not blue exactly, but a shade somewhere between blue and indigo and turquoise, like the color of a ridiculously bright spring sky. They glowed beneath his short hair, dark slashes of eyebrows, and the long lashes that fanned across those crazy eyes.

His eyebrows lifted with interest, but Scout's voice pulled his gaze to her. I, on the other hand, had a little more trouble, and had to drag my gaze away from this boy in the garden.

"What are you doing here?" she asked them, suspicion in her gaze.

The boy with brown eyes shrugged innocently. "Just seeing a little of Chicago."

"I guess that means I didn't miss a meeting," Scout said, her voice dry. "Don't you have class?"

"There wasn't a meeting," he confirmed. "We're on our lunch break, just like you are. We're out for a casual stroll, enjoying this beautiful fall day." He glanced at me and offered a grin. "I'm guessing you're St. Sophia's latest fashion victim? I'm Michael Garcia."

"Lily Parker," I said with a grin. So *this* was the boy Veronica talked about. Or more important, the boy Scout had avoided talking about. Given the warmth in his eyes as he stole glances at Scout, I made a prediction that Veronica wasn't going to win that battle.

"Hello, Lily Parker," Michael said, then bobbed his head toward blue eyes. "This is Jason Shepherd."

"Live and in person," Jason said with a smile, dimples arcing at each corner of his mouth. My heart beat a little bit faster; those dimples were killers. "It's nice to meet you, Lily."

"Ditto," I said, offering back a smile. But not too much of a smile. No sense in playing my entire hand at once.

Jason hitched a thumb behind him. "We go to Montclare. It's down the road. Kind of."

"So I've heard," I said, then looked at Scout, who'd crossed her arms over her chest, the universal sign of skepticism.

"Out for a casual stroll," she repeated, apparently unwilling to let the point go. "A casual stroll that takes you to the garden next door to St. Sophia's? Somehow, I'm just not buying that's a coincidence."

Michael arched an eyebrow and grinned back at her. "That's because you're much too suspicious."

Scout snorted. "I have good reason to be suspicious, Garcia."

Michael's chocolate gaze intensified, and all that intensity was directed at the girl standing next to me.

This was getting pretty entertaining.

"You *imagine* you had a good reason," he told her. "That's not the same thing."

I glanced at Jason, who seemed to be enjoying the mock debate as much as I was. "Should we leave them alone, do you think?"

"It's not a bad idea," he said, brows furrowed in mock concentration. "We could give them a little privacy, let them see where things can go."

"That's a very respectful idea," I said, nodding gravely. "We should give them their space."

Jason winked at me, as Scout—oblivious to our jokes at her expense—pushed forward. "I don't understand why you're arguing with me. You know you have no chance."

Michael clutched at his chest dramatically. "You're killing me, Scout. Really. There's chest pain—a tightness." He faked a groan.

Scout rolled her eyes, but you could see the twitch in her smile. "Call a doctor."

"Come on, Green. Can't a guy just get out and enjoy the weather? It's a beautiful fall day in Chicago. My amigo Jason and I were thinking we should get out and enjoy it before the snow gets here."

"Again, I seriously doubt, Garcia, if you're all that concerned about the weather."

"Okay," Michael said, holding up his hands, "let's pretend you're right. Let's say, hypothetically, that it's no coincidence that our walk brought us next door to St. Sophia's. Let's say we had a personal interest in skipping lunch and showing up on your side of the river."

Scout rolled her eyes and held up a finger. "Oh, bottle it up. I don't have the time."

"You should make time."

"Guys, eleven o'clock," Jason whispered.

Scout snorted at Michael. "I'm amused you think you're important enough to—"

"*Eleven o'clock,*" Jason whispered again, this time fiercely. Scout and Michael suddenly quieted, and both glanced to where Jason had indicated. I resisted the urge to look, which would have made us all completely obvious, but couldn't help it.

I gave it a couple of seconds, then stole a glance over my shoulder. There was a gap in the pillars through which we could see the street behind us, the one that ran parallel to Erie, but behind St. Sophia's. A slim girl in jeans and a snug hoodie, the hood pulled over her head, stood on the sidewalk, her hands tucked into her pockets.

"Who is that?" I whispered.

"No—why is she here?" Jason asked, dimples fading, his gaze on the girl. While her face wasn't visible, her hair was blond—the curly length of it spilling from her hood and across her shoulders. Veronica was the only Chicago blonde I knew, but that couldn't be her. I didn't think she'd be caught dead in jeans and a hoodie, especially not on a uniform day.

Besides, there was something different about this girl. Something unsettling. Something *off*. She was too still, as if frozen while the city moved around her.

"Is she looking for trouble?" Michael asked. His voice was quiet, just above a whisper, and it carried a hint of concern. Like whether she was looking for trouble or not, he expected it.

"In the middle of the day?" Scout whispered. "And here? She's blocks away from the nearest enclave. From *her* enclave."

"What's an enclave?" I quietly asked. Not so quietly that they couldn't hear me, but they ignored me, anyway.

Jason nodded. "Blocks from hers, and much too close to ours."

In the time it took me to glance at Jason and back at the girl again, she was gone. The sidewalk was as empty as if she'd never been there at all.

I looked back and forth from Scout to Michael to Jason. "Someone want to fill me in?" I was beginning to guess it was pointless for me to ask questions—as pointless as my trying to goad Scout into telling me where she'd gone last night—but I couldn't stop asking them.

Scout sighed. "This was supposed to be a tour. Not a briefing. I'm exhausted."

"We're all tired," Michael said. "It was a long summer."

"Long summer for what?"

"You could say we're part of a community improvement group," Michael said.

It took me a minute to realize that I'd been added back into the conversation. But the answer wasn't very satisfying—or informative. I crossed my arms over my chest. "Community improvement? Like, you clean up litter?"

"That's actually not a bad analogy," Jason said, his gaze still on the spot where the girl had been.

"I take it she was a litterbug?" I asked, hitching my thumb in that direction.

"In a manner of speaking, yes, she was," Scout said, then put a hand on my arm and tugged. "All right, that's enough fond reminiscing and conspiracy theories for the day. We need to get to class. Have fun at school."

"MA is always fun," Jason said. "Good luck at St. Sophia's."

I nodded as Scout pulled me out of the garden, but I risked a glance back at Michael and Jason. They stood side by side, Michael an inch or two taller, their gazes on us as we headed back to school.

"I have so many questions, I'm not sure where to start," I said when we were out of their sight and hauling down the alley, "but let's go for the good, gossipy stuff, first. You say you aren't dating, but Michael obviously has a thing for you."

Scout made a snort that sounded a little too dramatic to be honest. "I didn't just *say* we aren't dating. We are, *in fact*, not dating. It's an objective, empirical, testable fact. I don't date MA guys."

"Uh-huh," I said. While I didn't doubt that she subscribed to that rule, there was more to her statement, more to her and Michael, than she was letting on. But I could pry that out of her later. "And your community service involvement?"

"You heard—we clean up litter."

"Yeah, and I'm totally believing that, too."

That was the last word out of either of us as we slipped through the gap between the buildings, then back onto the sidewalk, and finally back to St. Sophia's. In the nick of time, too, as the bells atop the left tower began to ring just as we hit the front stairs. Thinking we needed to hurry, I nearly ran into Scout when she stopped short in front of the door.

"I know this is unsatisfying," she said, "but you're going to have to trust me on this one, too."

I arched an eyebrow at her. "Will there come a day when you'll trust me?"

Her expression fell. "Honestly, Lil, I hope it doesn't come to that."

Famous last words, those.

There were three more periods to get through—Brit lit, chemistry, and European history—before I completed my first day of classes at St. Sophia's. Maybe it was a good thing I hadn't had much of an appetite for lunch, because listening to teachers drone on about kinetic energy, *Beowulf,* and Thomas Aquinas on a full stomach surely would have put me into a food coma. It was dry enough on an empty stomach.

And wasn't that strange? I loved facts, information, magazine tidbits. But when three, one-hour-long classes were strung together, the learning got a little dullsville.

My attention deficit issue notwithstanding, I made it through my first day of classes, with a lot of unanswered questions about my suitemate and her friends, a good two hours of homework, and a ravenous hunger to show for it.

And speaking of hunger, dinner was pretty much the same as breakfast—a rush to the front of the line so Scout and I weren't stuck with "dirty rice," which was apparently a combination of rice and everything that didn't get eaten at lunch. I appreciated the school's recycling, but "dirty rice" was a little too green for me. I mean that literally—there were green bits in there I couldn't begin to identify.

On the other hand, it definitely reminded you to be prompt at meal times.

Since we were punctual and it was the first official day of school, the smiling foodies served a mix of Chicago favorites—Chicago-style "red-hot" hot dogs, deep-dish pizza, Italian beef sandwiches, and cheesecake from a place called Eli's.

When we'd gotten food and taken seats, I focused on enjoying my tomato- and cheese-laden slice of Chicago's finest so I wouldn't pester

Scout about our meeting with the boys, her "community improvement group," or her midnight outing.

Veronica and her minions spared us a visit, which would have interrupted the ambience of eating pizza off a plastic tray, but they still spent a good chunk of the dinner hour sending us snarky looks from across the room.

"What's with the grudge?" I asked Scout, spearing a chunk of gooey pizza with my fork.

Scout snuck a glance back at the pretty-girl table, then shrugged. "Veronica and I have been here, both of us, since we were twelve. We started on the same day. But she, I don't know, took sides? She decided that to be queen of the brat pack, she needed enemies."

"Very mature," I said.

"It's no skin off my back," Scout said. "Normally, she stays on her side of the cafeteria, and I stay on mine."

"Unless she's in your suite, cavorting with Amie," I pointed out.

"That is true."

"So why this place?" I asked her. "Why did your parents put you here?"

"I'm from Chicago," she said, "born and bred. My parents were trust fund babies—my great-grandfather invented a whirligig for electrical circuits, and my grandparents got the cash when he died. One trickle-down generation later, and my parents ended up with a pretty sweet lifestyle."

"And they opted for boarding school?" I wondered aloud.

She paused contemplatively and pulled a chunk of bread from the roll in her hand. "It's not that they don't love me. I just think they weren't entirely sure what to *do* with me. They grew up in boarding schools, too—when my grandparents got their money, they made some pretty rich friends. They thought boarding school was the best thing you could do for your kids, so they sent my parents, and my parents sent me. Anyway, they have their schedules—Monte Carlo this time of year, Palm Beach that time of year, et cetera, et cetera. Boarding school made it easier for them to travel, to meet their social commitments, such as they were."

I couldn't imagine a life so separate from my family—at least, not before the sabbatical. "Isn't that . . . hard?" I asked her.

Scout blinked at the question. "I've been on my own for a long time. At this point, it just *is*, you know?" I didn't, actually, but I nodded to be supportive.

"I mean, before St. Sophia's, there was a private elementary school and a nanny I talked to more often than my parents. I was kind of a trust fund latchkey kid, I guess. Are you and your parents close?"

I nodded, and I had to fight back an unexpected wash of tears at the sudden sensation of aloneness. Of abandonment. My eyes ached with it, that threshold between crying and not, just before the dam breaks. "Yeah," I said, willing the tears not to fall.

"I'm sorry," Scout said. Her voice was soft, quiet, compassionate.

I shrugged a shoulder. "I've known for a while that they were leaving. Some of those days I was fine, some days I was wicked pissed." I shrugged. "I'm probably not supposed to be mad about it. I mean, it's not like they went to Germany to get away from me or anything, but it still stings. It still feels like they left me here."

"Well then," Scout said, raising her cup of water, "I suppose you'd better thank your lucky stars that you found me. 'Cause I'm going to be on you like white on rice. I'm a hard friend to shake, Parker."

I grinned through the melancholy and raised my own cup. "To new friendships," I said, and we clinked our cups together.

When dinner was finished, we returned to our rooms to wash up and restock our bags with books and supplies before study hall. I also ditched the tights and switched out my fabulous—but surprisingly uncomfortable—boots for a pair of much more comfy flip-flops. My cell phone vibrated just as I'd slipped my left foot into the second, thick, emerald green flip-flop. I pulled it out of my bag, checked the caller ID, and smiled.

"What's cooking in Germany?" I asked after I opened the phone and pressed it to my ear.

"Nothing at the moment," my father answered, his voice tinny through four thousand miles of transmission wires. "It's late over here. How was school?"

"It was school," I confirmed, a tightness in my chest unclenching at the sound of my dad's voice. I sat down on the edge of the bed and crossed one leg over the other. "Turns out, high school is high school pretty much anywhere you go."

"Except for the uniforms?" he asked.

I smiled. "Except for the uniforms. How was your first day of sabbaticalizing, or whatever?"

"Pretty dull. Mom and I both had meetings with the folks who are funding our work. A lot of ground rules, research protocols, that kind of thing."

I could practically hear the boredom in his voice. My dad wasn't one for administrative details or planning. He was a big-picture guy, a thinker, a teacher. My mom was the organized one. She probably took notes at the meetings.

"I'm sure it'll get better, Pops. They probably wanna make sure they aren't handing gazillions of research dollars over to some crazy Americans."

"What?" he asked. "We are not so crazy," he said, a thick accent suddenly in his voice, probably an impersonation of some long-dead celebrity. My dad imagined himself to be quite the comedian.

He had quite an imagination.

"Sure, Dad." There was a knock at the door. I looked up as Scout walked in. "Listen, I need to run to study hall. Tell Mom I said hi, and good luck with the actual, you know, research stuff."

"Nighty night, Lils. You take care."

"I will, Dad. Love you."

"Love you, too." I closed the phone and slipped it back into my bag. Scout raised her eyebrows inquisitively.

"My parents are safe and sound in Germany," I told her.

"I'm glad to hear it. Let's go make good on their investment with a couple hours of homework."

The invitation wasn't exactly thrilling, but it's not like we had another choice. Study hall was mandatory, after all.

Study hall took place in the Great Hall, the big room with all the tables where I'd first gotten a glimpse of the plaid army. They were in full attendance tonight, nearly two hundred girls in navy plaid filling fifty-odd four-person tables. We headed through the rows toward a couple of empty seats near the main aisle, which would give us a view of the comings and goings of St. Sophia's finest. They also gave the plaid army a look at us, and look they did, the thwack-thwack of my flip-flops on the limestone floor drawing everyone's attention my way.

That attention included the pair of stern-looking women in thick-soled black shoes and horn-rimmed glasses. Their squarish figures tucked into black shirts and sweaters, they patrolled the perimeter of the room, clipboards in hand.

"Who are they?" I whispered, as we took seats opposite each other.

Scout glanced up as she pulled notebooks and books from her bag. "The dragon ladies. They monitor lights-out, watch us while we study, and generally make sure that nothing fun occurs on their watch."

"Awesome," I said, flipping open my trig book. "I'm a fun hater myself."

"I figured," Scout said without looking up, pen scurrying across a page of her notebook. "You had the look."

One of the roaming dragon ladies walked by our table, her gaze over her glasses and an eyebrow arched at our whispering as she passed. I mouthed, "Sorry," but she scribbled on her clipboard before walking away.

Scout bit back a smile. "Please quit disturbing the entire school, Parker, jeez."

I stuck out my tongue at her, but started my homework.

We worked for an hour before she stretched in her chair, then dropped her chin onto her hand. "I'm bored."

I rubbed my eyes, which were blurring over the tiny print in our European history book. "Do you want me to juggle?"

"You can juggle?"

"Well, not *yet*. But there're books everywhere in here," I pointed out. "There's gotta be a how-to guide somewhere on those shelves."

The girl who sat beside me at the table cleared her throat, her gaze still on the books in front of her. "Really trying to do some work here, ladies. Go play *Gilmore Girls* somewhere else."

The girl was pretty in a supermodel kind of way—in a French way, if that made sense. Long dark hair, big eyes, wide mouth—and she played irritated pretty well, one perfect eyebrow arched in irritation over brown eyes.

"Collette, Collette," Scout said, pointing her own pencil at the girl, then at me. "Don't be bossy. Our new friend Parker, here, will think you're one of the brat pack."

Collette snorted, then slid a glance my way. "As if, Green. I assume you're Parker?"

"Last time I checked," I agreed.

"Then don't make me give you more credit than you deserve, Parker. Some of us take our academic achievements very seriously. If I'm not valedictorian next year, I might not get into Yale. And if I don't get into Yale, I'm going to have a breakdown of monumental proportions. So you and your friend go play clever somewhere else, alrighty? Alrighty," she said with a bob of her head, then turned back to her books.

"She's really smart," Scout said apologetically. "Unfortunately, that hasn't done much for her personality."

Collette flipped a page of her book. "I'm still here."

"*Gilmore Girls*," Scout repeated, then made a sarcastic sound. Apparently done with studying, she glanced carefully around, then pulled a comic book from her bag. She paused to ensure the coast was clear, then sandwiched the comic between the pages of her trig book.

I arched an eyebrow at the move, but she shrugged happily, and went back to working trig problems, occasionally sneaking in a glazed-eyed perusal of a page or two of the comic.

"Weirdo," I muttered, but said it with a grin.

After we'd done our couple of mandatory hours in study hall—not all studying, of course, but at least we were in there—we went back to the suite to make use of our last free hour before the sun officially set on my first day as a St. Sophia's girl. The suite was empty of brat pack members, and Lesley's door was shut, a line of light beneath it. I nudged Scout as we walked toward her room. She followed the direction of my nod, then nodded back.

"Cello's gone," she noted, pointing at the corner of the common room, which was empty of the instrument parked there when I arrived yesterday.

Music suddenly echoed through the suite, the thick, thrumming notes of a Bach cello concerto pouring from Lesley's room. She played beautifully, and as she moved her bow across the strings, Scout and I stood quietly, reverently, in the common room, our gaze on the closed door before us.

After a couple of minutes, the music stopped, replaced by scuffling on the other side of the door. Without preface, the door opened. A blonde blinked at us from the threshold. She was dressed simply in a fitted T-shirt, cotton A-line skirt, and Mary Janes. Her hair was short and pale blond, a fringe of bangs across her forehead.

"Hi, Lesley," Scout said, hitching a thumb at me. "This is Lily. She's the new girl."

Lesley blinked big blue eyes at me. "Hi," she said, then turned on one heel, walked back into the room, and shut the door behind her.

"And that was Lesley," Scout said, unlocking her own door and flipping on her bedroom light.

I followed, then shut the door behind us again. "Lesley's not much of a talker."

Scout nodded and sat cross-legged on the bed. "That was actually pretty chatty for Barnaby. She's always been quiet. Has a kind of savant vibe? Wicked good on the cello."

"I got goose bumps," I agreed. "That song is really haunting."

Scout nodded again, and had just begun to pull a pillow into her lap when her cell phone rang. She reached up, grabbed it from its home on the shelf, and popped it open.

"When?" she asked after a moment of silence, turning away from me, the phone pressed to her ear. Apparently unhappy with the response she got, she muttered a curse, then sighed haggardly. "We should have known they had something planned when we saw her."

I assumed "her" meant the blonde we'd seen outside at lunch.

More silence ensued as Scout listened to the caller. In the quiet of the room, I could hear a voice, but I couldn't understand the words. The tone was low, so I guessed the caller was a boy. Michael Garcia, maybe?

"Okay," she said. "I will." She closed the phone with a snap and paused before glancing back at me.

"Time to run?"

Scout nodded. And this time, there was a tightness around her eyes. It didn't thrill me that the tightness looked like fear.

My heart clenched sympathetically. "Do you need backup? Someone else to help clean up the litter?"

Scout smiled, a little of the twinkle back in her eyes. "I'd love it, actually. But community improvement isn't ready for you, Parker." She grabbed a jacket and her skull-and-crossbones bag, and we both left her room. Scout headed for a secret rendezvous; I wasn't entirely sure where I was going.

"Don't wait up," she said with a wink, then opened the door and headed out into the hallway.

Don't count on it, I thought, having made the decision. This time, I wasn't going to let her get away with mumbled excuses and a secret nighttime trip—at least not solo.

This time, I was going, too.

She'd closed the door behind her. I cracked it open and watched her slip down the hallway.

"Time to play Nancy Drew," I murmured, then slipped off my noisy flip-flops, picked them up, and followed her.

5

She was disappearing around the corner as I closed the door to the common room. The hallway was empty and silent but for her footsteps, the limestone floor and walls glowing beneath the golden light of the sconces.

Scout headed toward the stairs, which she took at a trot. I hung back until I was sure she wouldn't see me as she rounded the second flight of stairs, then followed her down. When she reached the first floor, she headed through the Great Hall, which, even after the required study period, still held a handful of apparently ambitious teenagers. Unfortunately, the aisle between the tables was straight and empty, so if Scout turned around, my cover was blown.

I took a breath and started walking. I made it halfway without incident when, suddenly, Scout paused. I dumped into the closest chair and bent down, faking an adjustment to my flip-flop. When she turned around again and resumed her progression through the room, I stood up, then hustled to squeak through the double doors before they closed behind her.

I just made it through, then flattened myself against the wall of the hallway that led to the domed center of the main building. I peeked around the corner; Scout was hurrying across the tiled labyrinth. I gnawed my lip as I considered my options. This part of playing the new Nancy Drew was tricky—the room was gigantic and empty, at least in the middle, so there weren't many places to hide.

Without cover, I decided I'd have to wait her out. I watched her cross the labyrinth and move into the hallway opposite mine, then pause before a door. She looked around, probably to see whether she was alone (we're all wrong sometimes), then slipped the ribboned key from her neck and slid the key into the lock.

The click of tumblers echoed across the room. She winced at the sound, but placed a hand on the door, took a final look around, and disappeared. When she was gone, I jogged across the labyrinth to the other side, then pressed my ear to the door she'd closed behind her. After the sound of her footsteps receded, I twisted the doorknob, found that it was still unlocked and—heart beating like a bass drum in my chest—edged it open.

It was another hallway.

I blew out the breath I'd been holding.

A hallway wasn't much to get stressed out about. Frankly, the chasing was getting a little repetitive. Hallway. Room. Hallway. Room. I reminded myself that there was a greater purpose here—spying on the girl who'd adopted me as a best friend.

Okay, put that way, it didn't sound so noble.

Morally questionable or not, I still had a job to do. I walked inside and closed the door behind me. I didn't see Scout, but I watched her elongated shadow shrink around the corner as she moved. I followed her through the hallway, and then down another set of stairs into what I guessed was the basement, although it didn't look much different from the first floor, all limestone and golden light and iron sconces. The ceiling was different, though. Instead of the vaults and domes on the first floor, the ceiling here was lower, flatter, and covered in patterned plaster. It looked like a lot of work for a basement.

The stairs led to another hall. I followed the sound of footsteps, but only made it five or six feet before I heard another sound—the clank and grate of metal on metal. I froze and swallowed down the lump of fear that suddenly tightened my throat. I wanted to call her name, to scream it out, but I couldn't seem to draw breath to make a sound. I forced myself to take another step forward, then another, nearly jumping out of my skin when that bone-chilling gnash of metal echoed through the hallway again.

Oh, screw this, I thought, and forced my lungs to work. "Scout?" I called out. "Are you okay?"

When I got no response, I rounded the corner. The hallway dead-ended in a giant metal door . . . and she was nowhere to be seen.

"Frick," I muttered. I glanced around, saw nothing else that would help, and moved closer so I could give the door a good look-see.

It was ginormous. At least eight feet high, with an arch in the top, it was outlined in brass rivets and joints. In the middle was a giant flywheel, and beneath the flywheel was a security bar that must have been four or five inches of solid steel. It was in its unlocked position. That explained the metal sounds I'd heard earlier.

I wasn't sure I wanted to know what that door was keeping out of St. Sophia's, but Scout was in there. Sure, we hadn't known each other long, and I wasn't up on all the comings and goings of her community improvement group, but this seemed like trouble . . . and help was the least I could offer my new suitemate.

After all, what were they going to do—kick me out?

"Sagamore, here I come," I whispered, and put my hands on the flywheel. I tugged, but the door wouldn't open. I turned the flywheel, clockwise first, then counterclockwise, but the movement had no effect—at least, not on this side of the door.

Frowning, I scanned the door from top to bottom, looking for another way in—a keyhole, a numeric pad, anything that would have gotten it open and gotten me inside.

But there was nothing. So much for my rescue mission.

I considered my options.

One: I could head back upstairs, tuck into bed, and forget about the fact that my new best friend was somewhere behind a giant locked door in an old convent in downtown Chicago.

Two: I could wait for her to come back, then offer whatever help I could.

I nibbled the edge of my lip for a moment and glanced back at the hallway from which I'd come, my passage back to safety. But I was here, *now*, and she was in there, getting into God only knew what kind of trouble.

So I sat down on the floor, pulled up my knees, and prepared to wait.

I don't know when I fell asleep, but I jolted awake at the sound of footsteps on the other side of the door. I jumped up from my spot, the flip-flops I'd pulled off earlier still in my hand, my only weapon. As I faced down the door with only a few inches of green foam as protection, it occurred to me that there might be a stranger—and not Scout—on the other side of the door.

My heart raced hammerlike in my chest, my fingers clenched into the foam of my flip-flops. Suddenly the flywheel began to turn, the spokes rotating clockwise with a metallic scrape as someone sought entrance to the convent basement. Seconds later, oh so slowly, the door began to open, hundreds of pounds of metal rotating toward me.

"Don't come any closer!" I called out. "I have a weapon."

Scout's voice echoed from the other side of the door. "Don't use it! And get out of the way!"

It wasn't hard to obey, since I'd been bluffing. I stepped aside, and as soon as the crack in the door was big enough to squeeze through, she slipped through it, chest heaving as she sucked in air.

She muttered a curse and pressed her hands to the door. "I'm going to rail on you in a minute for following me, but in the meantime, *help me close this thing!*"

Although my head was spinning with ideas about what, exactly, she'd left on the other side of the door, I stepped beside her. With both pairs of hands on the door, arms and legs outstretched, we pushed it closed. The door was as heavy as it was high, and I wondered how she'd gotten it open in the first place.

When the door was shut, Scout spun the flywheel, then reached down to slide the steel bar back into its home. We both jumped back when a crash echoed from the other side, the door shaking on its giant brass hinges in response.

Eyes wide, I stared over at her. "What the hell was *that?*"

"Litter," Scout said, staring at the closed door, as if making sure that whatever had been chasing her wasn't going to breach it.

When the door was still and the hallway was silent, Scout turned and looked at me, her bob of blond hair in shambles around her face, jacket hanging from one shoulder . . . and fury in her expression.

"What in the hell do you think you're doing down here?" She pushed at the hair from her face, then pulled up the loose shoulder of her jacket.

"Exercising?"

Scout put her hands on her hips, obviously dubious.

"I was afraid you were in trouble."

"You were nosy," she countered. "I asked you to trust me on this."

"Trusting you about a secret liaison is one thing. Trusting you about your safety is something else." I bobbed my head toward the door. "Call it community improvement if you want, but it seems pretty apparent that you're involved in something nasty. I'm not going to just stand by and watch you get hurt."

"You're not my mother."

"Nope," I agreed. "But I'm your new BFF."

Her expression softened.

"I don't need all the details," I said, holding up my hands, "but I am going to need to know what the hell was on the other side of that door."

As if on cue, a crash sounded again, and the door jumped on its hinges.

"We get it already!" she yelled. "Crawl back into your hole." She grabbed my arm and began to pull me down the hall and away from the ominous door. "Let's go."

I tugged back, and when she dropped my arm, slipped the flip-flops back onto my feet. She was trucking down the hall, and I had to skip to keep up with her. "Is it an axe murderer?"

"Yeah," she said dryly. "It's an axe murderer."

Most of the walk back was quiet. Scout and I didn't chat much, and both the main building and the Great Hall were dark and empty of students. The moonlight, tinted red and blue, that streamed through the stained glass windows was the only light along the way.

As we moved through the corridors, Scout managed not to look back to see whether the basement door had been breached or whether some nasty thing was on our trail. I, on the other hand, kept stealing glances over my shoulder, afraid to look, but more afraid that something would sneak up behind us if I didn't. That the corridors were peacefully quiet didn't stop my imagination, which made shapes in the shadows beneath the desks of the Great Hall when we passed through it.

Exactly what had been behind that door? I decided I couldn't hold in the question any longer. "Angry drug dealer?" I asked her. "Mental institution escapee? Robot overlord?"

"I'm not aware if robots have taken us over yet." Her tone was dry.

"Flesh-eating zombie monster?"

"Zombies are a myth."

"So you say," I muttered. "Just answer me this: Are you in cahoots with those Montclare guys?"

"What is a 'cahoot,' exactly?"

"Scout."

"I was exercising. Great workout. I got my heart rate up, and I got into the zone." Her elbow bent, she pumped one arm as if lifting a dumbbell.

When we opened the door to the building that held our dorm rooms, I pulled her to a stop. She didn't look happy about that.

"You were being chased," I told her. "Something behind that door was after you, and whatever it was hit the door after we closed it."

"Just be glad we got the door closed."

"Scout," I said. "*Seriously*. What's going on?"

"Look, Lily, there are things going on at this school—just because things seem normal doesn't mean they are. Things are rarely what they seem."

Things hardly seemed normal, from late-night disappearances, to the coincidental meeting of the boys next door, to this. And all of it within my first twenty-four hours in Chicago. "Exactly what does that mean, 'rarely what they seem'?"

She arched an eyebrow at me. "You said you had a weapon." She scanned me up and down. "Exactly what weapon was that? Flip-flops?"

I held up a foot and dangled my thick, emerald green flip-flop in front of her. "Hey, I could have beaned a pursuer on the head with this thing. It weighs like ten pounds, and I guarantee you he would have thought twice before invading St. Sophia's."

"Yeah, I'm sure that would hold them off." At my arch expression, she held up her hands. "Fine. Fine. Let's say, for the sake of argument, that I'm in a club for gifted kids. Of a sort."

"A club for gifted kids. Like, what kind of gifted?" Gifted at fibbing came immediately to mind.

"Generally gifted?"

The room was silent as I waited in vain for her to elaborate on that answer.

"That's all you're going to tell me?"

"That's as much as I *can* tell you," she said, "and I've already said too much. I wish I could fill you in, but I really, really can't. Not because I don't trust you," she said, holding up a defensive hand. "It's just not something I'm allowed to do."

"You aren't allowed to tell me, or anyone else, that something big and loud and powerful is hanging out beneath a big-ass metal door in the basement? And that you go down there willingly?"

She nodded matter-of-factly. "That's pretty much it."

I blew out a breath and shook my head. "You're insane. This whole place is insane."

"St. Sophia's has a lot to offer."

"Other than nighttime escapades and maniacs behind giant cellar doors?"

"Oh, those aren't even the highlights, Lil." Scout turned and resumed the trek back home.

When we reached the suite, Scout walked toward her room, but then paused to glance back at me.

"Whatever you're involved in," I told her, "I'm not afraid." (My fingers were totally crossed on that one.) "And if you need me, I'm here."

I could tell she was tired, but there was a happy glint in her eyes. "You rock pretty hard, Parker."

I grinned at her. "I know. It's one of my better qualities."

6

Whatever the St. Sophia's "highlights" were, they weren't revealed during the next couple days of school. I still wasn't entirely sure what Scout was doing at night, but I didn't see any strange bruises or scratches or broken bones. Since she wasn't limping, I kept my mouth shut about her disappearances . . . and whatever was going on in the corridors beneath the school.

On the other hand, the dark circles beneath her eyes showed that she was still going somewhere at night, that *something* was going on, regardless of how oblivious the rest of the school was. I didn't pester her, mostly because I'd weighed the benefit of pestering her (nil, given how stubborn she was) against the potential cost (hurting our new-found friendship). We were still getting to know each other, and I didn't want that kind of tension between us . . . even though her secret was still between us.

However, there was still one skill I knew I could bring to the Scout Green mystery game—I was patient, and I could wait her out. I could tell it bothered her to keep it bottled up, so I guessed it wouldn't take much longer before she spilled.

That mystery notwithstanding, things were moving along pretty much par for the course, or at least what I learned was par for the course by St. Sophia's standards. That meant studying, studying, and more studying. I managed to squeeze in some nerdly fun with Scout—a little sketching, checking out her comic book stash, walking the block over the lunch hour—and I'd had a few rushed conversations with my parents. (Everything seemed to be going fine in Deutschland.) But mostly, there was studying . . . at least until my first Thursday at St. Sophia's.

I'd been in European history when it happened. Without preface, in the middle of class, the door opened. Mary Katherine walked in, her hair in a long, thick braid that lay across one shoulder, a gray scarf of thick, felted wool knots wrapped around her neck.

She handed Peters, our surly history teacher, a note. Peters gave her a sour look—the fate of European peasants being the most important thing on his mind—but he took it anyway, read it over, and passed it back to M.K.

"Lily Parker," he said.

I sat up straight.

Peters tried to arch one eyebrow. But he couldn't quite manage it, so it just looked like an uncomfortable squint. "You're wanted in the headmistress's office."

I frowned, but bobbed my head in acknowledgment, grabbed the stuff on my desk with one hand and the strap of my bag with the other, and stood up. M.K., arms crossed, rolled her eyes as she waited for me. She was halfway to the door by the time I got to the front of the room.

"Nice shoes," she said when we'd closed the classroom door and had begun walking down the hall. She walked in front of me, the note between her fingers.

I glanced down at today's ensemble—button-up shirt, St. Sophia's hoodie, navy tights, and yellow boots in quilted patent leather—as I situated my messenger bag diagonally across my chest. The boots were loud and not everyone's style, but they were also vintage and made by a very chichi designer, so I wasn't sure if she was being sarcastic. I assumed, since they were pretty fabulous, that she was being sincere.

"Thanks," I said. "They're vintage." Unfortunately, the owner of the thrift shop in old, downtown Sagamore knew they'd been vintage, too. Three months of hard-saved allowance disappeared in a five-minute transaction.

"I know," she said. "They're Puccinis."

Her voice was mildly condescending, as if I couldn't possibly have been savvy enough to know that they were Puccinis when I bought them. Three months of allowance knew better.

That gem was the only thing Mary Katherine said as we walked through the Great Hall, crossed the labyrinth, and turned into the administrative wing. It was the same walk I'd taken when I'd met Foley at the door a few days ago, except in reverse . . . and presumably under different circumstances this time around.

When we reached the office, M.K. put her hand on the doorknob, but turned to face me before opening it. "You'll need a hall pass before you go back," she sniped. She opened the door and after I walked inside, closed it behind me. Friendly girl.

Foley's office looked the same as it had a few days ago, except that she wasn't in the room this time. Her heavy oak desk was empty of stuff—no pencil cups, no flowers, no lamp—but for the royal blue folder that lay in the exact middle, its edges parallel with the edges of the desk, as if placed just so.

I walked closer. Holding my bag back with a hand, I leaned forward to take a closer look. LILY PARKER was typed in neat letters across the folder's tab.

A folder bearing my name in an otherwise empty room. It practically begged to be opened.

I glanced behind me. When I was sure I was alone, I reached out a hand to open it, but snatched it back when a grinding scrape echoed through the room.

I stood straight again as the bookshelf on one side of Foley's office began to pivot forward. Foley, tall and trim, every hair in place, navy suit perfectly tailored, stepped through the opening, then pushed the bookshelf back into place.

"Can I ask what's behind the hidden door?"

"You could ask," she said, walking around the massive desk, "but that does not mean I'd provide an answer to you, Ms. Parker." Elegantly, she lowered herself into the chair, glanced at the folder for a moment, then lifted her gaze, regarding me with an arched brow.

I responded with what I hoped was a bland and completely innocent smile. Sure, I'd *wanted* to look, but it's not like I'd actually had time to *do* anything.

Apparently satisfied, she lowered her gaze again and, with a single finger, flipped open the folder. "Have a seat," she said without looking up.

I dropped into the chair in front of her desk and piled my stuff— books and bag—on my lap.

"You've been here three days," Foley said, linking her fingers together on top of her desk. "I have asked you here to inquire as to how you've settled in." She looked at me expectantly. I guessed that was my cue.

"Things are fine."

"Mmm-hmm. And your relationships with your classmates? Are you integrating well into the St. Sophia's community? Into Ms. Green's suite?

Interesting, I thought, that it was "Ms. Green's suite," and not Amie's or Lesley's suite. But my answer was the same regardless. "Yes. Scout and I get along pretty well."

"And Ms. Cherry? Ms. Barnaby?"

"Sure," I said, thinking a vague answer would at least save my having to answer questions about the brat pack's attitude toward newcomers.

Foley nodded. "I encourage you to expand your circle of classmates, to meet as many of the girls in your class as you can, and to make as many connections as possible. For better or worse, your success will be measured not only by what you can learn, by what you can be tested on, but on whom you know."

"Sure," I dutifully said again.

"And your classes? How are your academics progressing?"

I was only in the fourth day of my St. Sophia's education—three and a half pop-quiz- and final-exam-free days behind me—so there wasn't much to gauge "progressing" against. So I stuck to my plan of giving teenagerly vague answers; being a teenager, I figured I was entitled. "They're fine."

She made a sound of half interest, then glanced down at the folder again. "Once you've settled into your academic schedule, you'll have an opportunity to experience our extracurricular activities and, given your interest in the arts, our art studio." Foley flipped the folder closed, then crossed her hands upon it, sealing its secrets inside. "Lily, I'm going to speak frankly."

I lifted my eyebrows invitationally.

"Given the nature of your arrival here and of your previous tenure in public school, I was not entirely confident you would find the fit at St. Sophia's to be . . . comfortable."

I arched an eyebrow. "Comfortable," I repeated, in a tone as flat and dry as I could make it.

"Yes," Foley unapologetically repeated. "Comfortable. You arrived here not by choice, but because of the wishes of your parents, and despite your having no other connections to Chicago. I can only imagine how difficult it is for you to be here in light of your current separation from your parents. But I am acquainted with Mark and Susan, and we truly believe in their research."

That stopped me cold. "You know my parents?"

There was a hitch in her expression, a hitch that was quickly covered by the look of arrogant blandness she usually wore. "You were unaware that I was acquainted with your parents?"

All I could do was nod. The only thing my parents told me about St. Sophia's was that it was an excellent school with great academics, blah blah blah. The fact that my parents knew Foley—yeah. They'd kind of forgotten to mention that.

"I must admit," Foley said, "I'm surprised."

That made two of us, I thought.

"St. Sophia's is an excellent institution, without doubt. But you are far from home and your connections in Sagamore. I'd assumed, frankly, that your parents chose St. Sophia's on the basis of our relationship."

She wasn't just acquainted with my parents—they had a *relationship*? "How do you know my parents?"

"Well . . . ," she said, drawing out her one-word response while she traced her fingers along the edges of the folder. The move seemed odd for her—too coy. I figured she was stalling for time. After a long, quiet moment, she glanced up at me. "We had a professional connection," she finally said. "Similar research interests."

I frowned. "Research interests? In philosophy?"

"Philosophy," she flatly repeated.

I nodded, but something in her tone made my stomach drop. "Philosophy," I said again, as if repeating it would answer the question in her voice. "Are you sure you knew my parents?"

"I am well acquainted with your parents, Ms. Parker. We're professional colleagues of a sort." There was caution in her tone, as if she were treading around something, something she wasn't sure she wanted to tell me.

I dropped my gaze to the gleaming yellow of my boots. I needed a minute to process all this—the fact that Foley had known my parents, that they'd known her, and that maybe—just maybe—their decision to send me here hadn't just been an academic choice.

"My parents," I said, "are teachers. Professors, both of them. They teach philosophy at Hartnett College. It's in Sagamore."

Foley frowned. "And they never mentioned their genetic work?"

"Genetic work?" I asked, the confusion obvious in my voice. "What genetic work?"

"Their lab work. Their genetic studies. The longevity studies."

I was done, I decided—done with this meeting, done listening to this woman's lies about my parents. Or worse, I was done listening to things I hadn't known about the people I'd been closest to.

Things they hadn't told me?

I rose, lifting my books and shouldering my bag. "I need to get back to class."

Foley arched an eyebrow, but allowed me to rise and gather my things, then head for the door. "Ms. Parker," she said, and I glanced back. She pulled a small pad of paper from a desk drawer, scribbled something on the top page, and tore off the sheet.

"You'll need a hall pass to return to class," she said, handing the paper out to me.

I nodded, walked back, and took the paper from her fingers. But I didn't look at her again until I was back at the door, note in hand.

"I know my parents," I told her, as much for her benefit as mine. "I know them."

All my doubts notwithstanding, I let that stand as the last word, opened the door, and left.

I didn't remember much of the walk back through one stone corridor after another, through the Great Hall and the passageway to the classroom building. Even the architecture was a blur, my mind occupied with the meeting with Foley, the questions she'd raised.

Had she been confused? Had she read some other file, instead of mine? Had the board of trustees dramatized my background in order to accept me at St. Sophia's?

Or had my parents been lying to me? Had they kept the true nature of their jobs, their employment, from me? And if so, why hide something like that? Why tell your daughter that you taught philosophy if you had a completely different kind of research agenda?

What had Foley said? Something about longevity and genetics? That wasn't even in the same ballpark as philosophy. That was science, anatomy, lab work.

I'd been to Hartnett with my parents, had walked through the corridors of the religion and philosophy department, had waved at their colleagues. I'd colored on the floor of my mother's office on days when my babysitter was sick, and played hide-and-seek in the hallways at night while my parents worked late.

Of course there was one easy way to solve this mystery. When I was clear of the administrative wing, I stepped into an alcove in the main building, a semicircle of stone with a short bench in the middle, and pulled my cell phone from my pocket. It would be late in Germany, but this was an issue that needed resolving.

"HOW IS RESEARCH?" I texted. I sent the message and waited; the reply took only seconds.

"THE ARCHIVES R RAD!" was my father's time-warped answer. I hadn't even had time to begin a response when a second message popped onto my screen, this one from my mother. "IST PAGE IN GERMN JRNL OF PHILO!"

In dorky professor-speak, that meant my parents had secured the first article (a big deal) in some new German philosophy journal.

It *also* meant there would be a bound journal with my parents' names on it, the kind I'd seen in our house countless times before. You couldn't fake that kind of thing. Foley had to be wrong.

"Take that," I murmured with a slightly evil grin, then checked the time on my phone. European history class would be over in five minutes. I didn't think Peters would much care whether I came back for the final five minutes of class, so I walked back through the classroom building to the locker hall to switch out books for study hall later.

A note—a square of careful folds—was stuck to my locker door.

I dropped my books to the floor, pulled the note away, and opened it.

It read, in artsy letters:

I saw you and Scout, and I wasn't the only one. Watch your back.

A knot of fear rose in my throat. I turned around and pressed my back against my locker, trying to slow my heart. Someone had seen me and Scout—someone, maybe, who'd followed us from the library through the main building to the door behind which the monster lay sleeping.

The bells rang, signaling the end of class.

I crumpled the note in my hand.

One crisis at a time, I thought. One crisis at a time.

7

I waited until Scout had returned to the suite after classes, during our chunk of free time before dinner, to tell her about the note. We headed to my room to avoid the brat pack, who'd already taken over the common room. Why they'd opted to hang out in our suite mystified me, given their animosity toward Scout, but as Scout had said, they seemed to have a thing for drama. I guessed they were looking for opportunities.

When my bedroom door was shut and the lock was flipped, I pulled the note from the pocket of my hoodie and passed it over.

Scout paled, then held it up. "Where did this come from?"

"My locker. I found it after I left Foley's office. And that's actually part two of the story."

Scout sat down on the floor, then rolled over onto her stomach, booted feet crossed in the air. I sat down on my bed, crossing my legs beneath me, and filled her in on my time in Foley's office and the things she'd said about my parents. The genetic stuff aside, Scout was surprised that Foley seemed interested in me at all. Foley wasn't known for being interested in her students; she was more focused on numbers—Ivy League acceptance rates and SAT scores. Individual students, to Foley, were just bits of data within the larger—and much more important—statistics.

"Maybe she feels sorry for me?" I asked. "Being abandoned by my parents for a European vacation?"

Okay, I can admit that sounded pretty pitiful, but Scout didn't buy it, anyway. "No way," she said. "This is a boarding school. No one's parents are around. Now, she said what? That your parents are doing research in genetics?"

I nodded. "That's exactly what she said. But my parents teach philosophy. I mean—they do research, sure. They write articles—that's why they're traveling right now. But not on genetics. Not on biology. They were into Heidegger and existentialism and stuff."

"Huh," Scout said with a frown, chin propped on her hand. "That's really strange. And you went to their offices, and stuff? I mean, they weren't just dumbing down their job to help you understand what they did?"

I shook my head. "I've been there. Seen their diplomas. Seen their books. I've watched them grade papers." Scout pursed her lips, eyebrows drawn down as she concentrated. "That's really weird. On the other hand, maybe Foley was just confused. It's not that hard to imagine that she'd mistake one student for another."

"That's what I thought at first," I said, "but she seemed pretty sure."

"Hmm." Scout rolled over onto her back and laced her hands behind her head. "While we're contemplating your parents' possibly secret identities, what are we going to do about this note thing?"

"What do you mean 'we'? The note thing is your deal, not mine. Someone must have seen you."

"It was on your locker, Parker. They probably saw you following me. Probably heard you clomping through the hall in those flip-flops like a Clydesdale."

"First of all, I took off the flip-flops so they wouldn't make noise. And second, I do not *clomp*." I threw my pillow at her to emphasize the point. "I am a very slender, spritely young woman."

"Doesn't mean you can't clomp."

"I am not above hitting a girl."

Scout barked out a laugh. "I'd like to see you try it."

"Dare me, Pinhead. Dare me."

That time, I got a glare. She pointed at her nose ring. "Do you have any idea how much it hurt to get this thing? How much I endured to achieve this look?"

"That's a 'look'?"

"I am the epitome of high fashion."

"Yeah, *Vogue* will surely be calling you tomorrow for the fall spread."

Scout snorted out a laugh. "What did someone tell me once? That they're not above hitting a girl? Well, neither am I, Newbie."

"Whatever," I said. "Let's get back on track—the note."

"Right, the note." Scout crossed her legs, one booted foot swinging as she thought. "Well, clompy or not, someone saw us. Could have been one of our lovely suitemates; could have been someone else at St. Sophia's. The path to the basement door isn't exactly inconspicuous. I have to go through the Great Hall to get to the main building. That part's not so unusual—going into the main building, I mean. Girls sometimes study in the chapel, and there's a service in there on Wednesday nights." She sat up halfway and looked over at me. "Did you notice anyone noticing us?"

I shook my head. "I thought I was caught when you stopped in the Great Hall. I sat down at a table for a second, but I was up and out of there pretty fast afterward."

"Hmm," Scout said. "You're sure you didn't tell anyone?"

"Did I tell anyone I was running around St. Sophia's in the middle of the night, following my suitemate to figure out why she's sneaking around? No, I didn't tell anyone that, and I'm pretty sure that's the kind of thing I'd remember."

She grinned up at me. "Can you imagine what would have happened if one of the"—she bobbed her head toward the closed door—"you-know-what pack found us down there?" She shook her head. "They would have gone completely postal."

"I nearly went completely postal," I pointed out.

"That is true. Although you did have your flip-flop weaponry."

"Hey, would you want to meet me in a dark alley with a flip-flop?"

"Depends on how long you'd been awake. You're an ogre in the morning."

We broke into laughter that was stifled by a sudden knock on my bedroom door. Scout and I exchanged a glance. I unknotted my legs and walked to the door, then flipped the lock and opened it.

Lesley stood there, this time in uniform—plaid skirt, oxford shirt, tie—wide blue eyes blinking back at me. "I'd like to come in."

"Okay," I said, and moved aside, then shut the door again when she was in the room.

"Hi, Barnaby," Scout said from the floor. "What's kicking?"

"Those girls are incredibly irritating. I can hardly hear myself think."

As if on cue, a peal of laughter echoed from the common room. We rolled our eyes simultaneously.

"I get that," Scout said. "What brings you to our door?"

"I need to be more social. You know, talk to people." Still standing near the door, she looked at us expectantly. The room was silent for nearly a minute.

"Okaaaay," Scout finally said. "Good start on that, coming in here. How was your summer?"

Barnaby shrugged, then crossed her ankles and lowered herself to the floor. "Went to cello camp."

Scout and I exchanged a glance that showed exactly how dull we thought that sounded. Nevertheless, Scout asked, "And how was cello camp?"

"Not nearly as exciting as you'd think."

"Huh," Scout said. "Bummer."

After blinking wide eyes at the floor, Lesley lifted her gaze to Scout, then to me. "Last year was dull, too. I want this year to be more interesting. You seem interesting."

Scout beamed, her eyes twinkling devilishly. "I knew I liked you, Barnaby."

"Especially when you disappear at night."

Scout's expression flattened. With a jolt, she sat up, legs crossed in front of her. "What do you mean, when we disappear at night?"

"You know," Lesley said, pointing at Scout, "when you head into the basement"—she pointed at me—"and you follow her."

"Uh-huh," Scout said, picking at a thread in her skirt, feigned nonchalance in her expression. "Did you by any chance leave a note for Lily? A warning?"

"Oh, on her locker? Yeah, that was me."

Scout and I exchanged a glance, then looked at Lesley. "And why did you leave it?" she asked.

Lesley looked back and forth between us. "Because I want in."

"In?"

Lesley nodded. "I want in. Whatever you're doing, I want in. I want to help. I have skills"

"I'm not admitting that we're doing anything," Scout carefully said, "but if we are doing something, do you know what it is?"

"Well, no."

"Then how do you know you have skills that would help us?" Scout asked.

Lesley grinned, and the look was a little diabolical. "Well, did you see me following you? Did you know I was there?"

"No," Scout said for both of us, appreciation in her eyes. "No, we did not." She looked at me. "She makes a good argument about her skills."

"Yes, she does," I agreed. "But why leave an anonymous note on my locker? If you wanted in, why not just talk to us here? We do live together, after all."

Lesley shrugged nonchalantly. "Like I said, things are dull around here. I thought I'd spice things up."

"Spice things up," Scout repeated, her voice dry as toast. "Yeah, we could probably help you out with that. We'll keep you posted."

"Sweet," Lesley said, and that was the end of that.

Scout didn't, of course, fill Lesley in about exactly how interesting she was. I, of course, didn't contribute much to that interestingness. I hadn't been more than an amusing sidekick, if that. It was probably more accurate to call me a nosy sidekick.

I was relieved we'd solved the note mystery, but I was quiet at dinner, quiet in study hall, and quiet as Scout and I sat in the common room afterward—which was thankfully empty of brat packers. I couldn't get Foley's comments out of my mind. Sure, I'd seen the articles and the offices and met the colleagues, but I'd also seen *Alias*. People had created much more elaborate fronts than collegiate careers. Had my parents concocted some kind of elaborate fairy tale about their jobs to keep their real lives hidden? If so, I highly doubted they'd tell me if I asked. I'd walked into St. Sophia's thinking I was beginning day one of my two-year separation from the people who meant more to me than anyone else in the world—two people who'd been honest with me, even if we hadn't always gotten along. (I was a teenager, after all.) But now I had to wonder. I had to look back over my life and decide whether everything I knew, everything I believed to be true about my mother and father, was a lie.

Or maybe Foley was wrong. Maybe she'd confused my parents for someone else's parents. Parker wasn't such an unusual name. Or maybe she'd known my parents before I was born, at a time when they'd had different careers.

The biggest question of all, though, didn't have anything to do with my parents. It was about *me*. Why did Foley's questions bother me so much? *Scare* me so much? Why did I put so much stock in what she had to say? Foley's words had struck a nerve, but why? Did I have my own doubts?

I kept replaying the memories, going over the details of my visits to the college, conversations with my parents, the conversation with Foley, to milk them of every detail.

I didn't reach any conclusions, but the thought process kept me quiet as Scout lay on the floor of the common room with her iPod and the *Vogue* from the coffee table, and I lay on the couch with an arm behind my head, staring at the plaster ceiling.

When her cell phone buzzed, Scout reached up and grabbed it, then mumbled something about exercise. I waved off the excuse.

"I know," I told her. "Just do what you need to do."

Without explanation, she packed her gear—or whatever was in her skull-and-crossbones messenger bag—and left the suite. Since I was going to do us both a favor by not spying, I decided I was in for the night. I went back to my room, and grabbed a sketch pad and a couple of pencils. I hadn't done much drawing since I'd gotten to Chicago, and it was time to get to work, especially if I was going to start studio classes soon.

Studio was going to be a change, though. I usually drew from my imagination, even if Foley hadn't been impressed. No fruit bowls. No flowerpots. No portraits of fusty men in suits. And as far as drawing from the imagination went, the Scout Green mystery made for pretty good subject matter. My pencil flew across the nubby paper as I sketched out the ogre I'd imagined behind the door.

The hallway door opened so quickly, and with such a cacophony of chirping that I nearly ripped a hole in the paper with the tip of my pencil. The brat pack rushed into the suite, a girly storm of motion and noise. Thinking there was no need to make things worse for me or Scout, I flipped my sketchbook closed and stuffed it under my pillow.

Veronica followed Amie, Mary Katherine behind them, a glossy, white shoe box in her hands.

"Oh," M.K. said, her expression falling from devilishness to irritation as she met my gaze through my bedroom doorway. "What are you doing here?"

Amie rolled her eyes. "She lives here?"

"So she does," Veronica said with a sly smile, perching herself in the threshold. "M.K. tells us you met with Foley today."

M.K. was a talker, apparently. "Yep," I said. "I did."

Veronica crossed her arms over her untucked oxford and tie as Mary Katherine and Amie moved to stand behind her, knights guarding the queen. "The thing is, Foley never talks to students."

"Is that so?"

"That is very much so," she said. "So we were all interested to hear that you'd been invited into the inner sanctum."

"Did you learn anything interesting?" Mary Katherine asked with a snicker.

Out of some sarcastic instinct, I almost spilled, almost threw out a summary of how five minutes in Foley's office had made me doubt nearly sixteen years of personal experience and had made me question my parents, my family, a lifetime of memories. But I kept it in. I wasn't comfortable with these three having that kind of information about me or my fears. It was just the kind of weakness they'd exploit.

I was surprised, though, to learn that Mary Katherine hadn't simply listened at Foley's door. That also seemed like the kind of situation she'd exploit.

"Not really," I finally answered. "Foley was just checking in. Since I'm new, I mean," I added at M.K.'s raised brows. "She wanted to see if I was adjusting okay."

M.K.'s brows fell, her lips forming a pout. "Oh," she said. "Whatever, then." Her hunt for drama unsuccessful, she uncrossed her arms and headed toward Amie's room. Amie followed, but Veronica stayed behind.

"Well," she said, "are you coming, or what? We haven't got all day."

It took me nearly a minute to figure out that she was talking to me.

"Am I coming?"

She rolled her eyes, then turned on her heel. "Come on," she said, then beckoned me forward. I blinked, but ever curious, uncrossed my legs, hopped down off the bed, and followed. She walked to the open door of Amie's room and stood there for a moment, apparently inviting me inside.

I had no clue *why* she was asking me inside, and I was just nosy enough to wonder what she was up to. That was an opportunity I couldn't pass up.

"Sure," I said, then joined Veronica at the threshold. When she bobbed her head toward the interior of the room, I ventured inside and got my first look . . . at the room that pink threw up on.

Honestly—it looked like a Barbie factory exploded. There was pink everywhere, from the walls to the carpet to the bedspread and pillowcases. I practically had to squint against the glare.

On the other hand, the *stuff* in the room was choice: flat-screen TV; top-of-the-line laptop; fancy speaker system with an iPod port; thick, quilted duvet. I mean, sure it was all covered in kill-me-now pink, but I could appreciate quality.

"Nice room," I half lied, as Veronica shut the door behind me. Mary Katherine was already on Amie's bed, one leg crossed over the other and the glossy shoe box on her lap. Amie was in a sleek, clear plastic chair in front of a desk made of the same clear plastic. "Why, exactly, is she here?" Mary Katherine asked.

Veronica gave me an appraising look. "We're going to see how cool she is."

When Mary Katherine stroked the sides of the shoe box, I assumed my field trip into the Kingdom of Pink and the coolness test were related to whatever was in the shoe box in Mary Katherine's lap . . . or my reaction to it.

"How do we know she's not a Little Mary Tattletale?" Mary Katherine asked.

"Oh, come on, M.K. Lily's from New York. She's hip." Veronica arched a challenging eyebrow. "Aren't you?"

I was from Sagamore, *not* New York, but I was too busy contemplating the first-degree peer pressure to bother correcting her. But since the surprise invitation was a mystery that would be solved when M.K. flipped the lid off the shoe box, I figured I'd go for it. I wasn't getting a whole lot of closure on mysteries these days.

"I'm wicked hip," I agreed, my voice wicked dry.

"Are you ready?" Veronica asked, as Mary Katherine slipped her fingers beneath the lip of the shoe box.

"Sure," I said.

I'm not sure what I expected for all the buildup. Mind-altering substances? Diamonds? Stolen electronics? Weapons-grade plutonium? Or, if they'd been teenage boys, fireworks and nudie magazines?

It wasn't quite that dramatic.

With her girls—and me—around her, Mary Katherine lifted the lid. It was filled with candy, diet soda, back issues of *Cosmo*, energy drinks and clove cigarettes. It was like a supermodel's necessities kit.

"Well?" M.K. prompted. "Pretty sweet, huh?"

I opened my mouth, then closed it again with a snap. Surely they weren't so sheltered that issues of *Cosmo*—which were probably available at every drugstore, bodega, and grocery store in the United States—were contraband. Still, I was a guest in enemy territory. Now was not the time for insults. "There's definitely . . . all sorts of stuff in there."

Veronica reached in and grabbed a box of candy cigarettes, then pulled out a stick of white candy. "We have friends who bring it in," she said, nipping a bit off the end.

"And Mary Katherine's parents practically make shipments," Amie added, disapproval ringing in her voice.

M.K. rolled her eyes. "We *need* it," she said. "St. Sophia's is all about health and vigor, organic and free-range and vitamin-enhanced. Weaknesses like these don't figure into that. And if Foley ever found this stuff in our room, we'd be toast." She gave me an appraising glance. "So—can you keep your mouth shut?"

My gaze on a small bag of black licorice—my greatest weakness—I nodded. "That shouldn't be a problem."

Mary Katherine snorted and, seeing the direction of my gaze, reached over, grabbed the packet of licorice Scotties, and tossed it to me. I pulled it open—not even pausing to question why she was offering me candy—and began to nibble the head off a tiny, chewy dog.

Veronica looked at her BFFs, then slid a glance my way, her eyes bright with promise. "You know, Parker, we don't keep all of Mary Katherine's stash up here, just in case Foley decides to start doing room checks again. The rest of it is in our little hidey-hole. We call it our treasure chest. We were going there, you know, to replenish our stack." She glanced back at Mary Katherine. "M.K.'s almost out of Tab."

When Veronica looked at me again, her gaze was cool . . . and calculating. "You can go with us if you want. Share in the bounty."

I'd have been stupid not to be suspicious. The stash these trendy big-city girls played at being so excited about wasn't really that exciting. More important, they were being unusually nice. While I guessed it was possible they were still making some kind of misguided attempt to steer me toward "better" pals, it seemed more likely that something more nefarious was on their agenda.

But they weren't the only ones with secret plans. Foley had nearly ripped the rug out from under me earlier today; this was my chance to retake control, to take charge, to *act*.

"Where, exactly, is this stash?" I looked at Amie, thinking she offered the best chance to get an honest answer.

"Downstairs," she said. "Basement."

And we have a winner, I thought. A trip downstairs would get me one step closer to figuring out what Scout was involved in—and what else was going on at St. Sophia's School for Girls.

I nodded at the group. "I'm in. Let's go treasure hunting."

8

We were armed with pink flashlights, Amie having produced the set of them from a bottom-drawer stash. I also saw a set of pink tools, a pink first aid kit, and some pink batteries in there. Amie was apparently the prepared (and single-minded) type.

I was also armed with a pretty good dose of skepticism at their motives. I assumed the brat pack was leading me into trouble, that the "treasure" at the end of our hunt was a prank with my name on it. Given the strong possibility that I'd have to make a run for it, I was glad I'd worn boots. I figured they offered at least a little more traction than the flip-flops, and they'd probably pack a bigger wallop, if it came to that.

Scout was still gone when we left the suite, three brat packers and one hanger-on, Veronica in the lead. It was nearly ten p.m., and the hallways were silent and empty as we followed the same route I'd taken behind Scout two days ago—down the stairs to the first floor, back through the long, main corridor to the Great Hall, then through the Great Hall and into the main building. But instead of stopping at the door Scout had taken, we took a left into the administrative corridor I'd taken with M.K. earlier in the day.

We hadn't yet turned on our flashlights, so I'm not entirely sure why we had them. But when footsteps suddenly echoed through the hall, I was glad we hadn't turned them on. Veronica held out a hand, and we all stopped behind her. She turned, excitement in her eyes, and motioned us back with a hand. We tiptoed back a few steps, then crowded into one of the semicircular alcoves in the hallway. I gnawed my lip as I tried to control my breathing, sure that the thundering beat of my heart was echoing through the hallway for all to hear.

After what felt like an hour, the sound of footfalls faded as the person—probably one of the clipboard-bearing dragon ladies—moved off in the other direction.

Veronica peeked out of the nook, one hand behind her to hold us back while she surveyed the path.

"Okay," she finally whispered, and we set off again—Veronica, then Mary Katherine, Amie, and I. I couldn't help but glance behind us as we moved, but the hall was empty except for the cavernous silence we left in our wake, and the moonlight-dappled limestone floor.

We continued down the administrative hallway, but before we got as far as Foley's office, we turned down a side corridor that dead-ended in a set of limestone stairs. The air got colder as we descended to the basement, which didn't help the feeling that we were heading toward something unpleasant. We probably *were* headed toward the nasty that had been chasing Scout, but I couldn't imagine the brat pack had any clue what lurked in the corridors beneath their fancy school. If they had known, they surely would have tortured Scout about it. They seemed like the type.

"Almost there," Veronica whispered as we reached the bottom of the staircase. True to St. Sophia's form, we entered another limestone hallway. I'd heard about buildings that contained secret catacombs, but I wondered why the nuns had bothered building out the labyrinthine basement of the convent—a task they'd taken on without trucks, cranes, or forklifts.

"Here we are," Veronica finally said as we stopped before a simple, wooden door. The word CUSTODIAN was written in gold capitals across it, just like the letters on Foley's office.

I arched an eyebrow at the door. "We're going into the janitorial closet?"

Without bothering to answer, Mary Katherine and Veronica fiddled with the brass doorknob, then opened the door with a click.

"Check it," Veronica said, grinning as she held the door open.

I walked inside, and my jaw dropped at the scene before me.

The room was a giant limestone vault, completely empty but for one thing—it held an entire, little Chicago, a scale model of the city. From a two-foot-high Sears Tower and its two gleaming points (which even I could recognize), to the Chicago River, to the Ferris wheel at Navy Pier. All in miniature, all exactingly detailed, laid out across the floor of the giant room by someone who clearly loved Chicago—someone who *knew* Chicago.

"Who did this?" I asked.

"No clue," Veronica said. "It's been here as long as we've been here. Pretty sweet, huh?"

"Very," I muttered, eyes wide as I walked the empty perimeter of the limestone room, just taking it all in.

The model was almost totally devoid of color—the buildings and landscape rendered in various shades of thin, gray cardboard—but for symbols that were stamped on a few points across the city. In navy blue was a symbol that looked like four circles stuck together, or a really curvy plus sign. In apple green was a circle enclosing a capital Y.

Markers, I thought, pointing out the locations of two kinds of *something* across the city.

I moved into the middle of Lake Michigan—an empty space across the floor—and peered between the buildings, looking for St. Sophia's. When I found East Erie, I realized there were two symbols nearby: the four-circle thing on Michigan Avenue and, more interesting, the enclosed Y only a couple of blocks from St. Sophia's. "What do the symbols mean?" I asked.

I got only silence in response.

I glanced up and looked behind me just in time to watch them shut the door, and just in time to hear the lock tumblers click into place.

I hurdled Navy Pier, ran to the door, gripped the doorknob in both hands, and pulled.

Nothing.

I shook it, tried to turn it, pulled again.

Still nothing, not even a knob to unlock the door from the inside. Just a brass keyhole.

"Hello?" I yelled, then beat my fist against the door. "Veronica? Amie? Mary Katherine? I'm still in here!"

I added that last part in the off chance they were somehow unaware that they'd locked me into a room in the basement of the school; in case they'd forgotten that the four of us had traveled the halls of St. Sophia's to get to this underground room, but only three were headed back up.

But it wasn't an accident, of course, and the only answer I got back was giggling, which I could hear echoing down the hallway.

"Way mature!" I yelled out, then muttered a curse, mostly at my own stupidity.

Of course there was no candy, no Tab, no hidden cigarettes, or black-market energy drinks down here. There was a treasure—the brat pack had stumbled upon something, a hidden room that contained an intricate scale model of the city. But they'd probably missed the point, being only interested in how to use the room to prank me—how to punk me.

I kicked a foot against the door, which did nothing but vibrate pain up through my foot. Turned out, even my favorite boots didn't provide much more insulation than flip-flops. I braced one arm against the door and rubbed my foot with my free hand, berating myself for following them into the room.

Traipsing around the school was one thing; I'd done that already. But being locked in a custodial closet in the all-but-abandoned basement of a private school was something else. My love of exploration notwithstanding, I knew better.

When my foot finally stopped throbbing, I stood up again. For better or worse, I was stuck down here, in a hidden room that was probably a little too close to whatever lurked behind the metal door. It was time for action.

One hand around my pink flashlight, the other on my hip, I took a look around. Unfortunately, the obvious exit wasn't an option. The door was locked from the outside, and I didn't have a key.

"Hold that thought," I muttered, put my flashlight on the floor. This was an old building, and I had a skeleton key. I pulled the ribboned room key off my head.

"Come on, Irene," I said. Two fingers crossed for good luck, I slipped the key into the lock.

The tumblers didn't budge.

I muttered out another curse, then pulled back the key and slipped the ribbon over my head again. I slid my gaze to the flashlight on the floor and considered, for a minute, pummeling the lock with it, but God only knew how long I'd be down here. Sacrificing the flashlight probably wasn't the brightest idea (ha!).

I stepped back and surveyed the door. Like the doors in the main building, this one was an old-fashioned panel of thin wood, attached to the jamb by two brass hinges. The pins in the hinges were pretty big, so I figured I could try to pull them out, unhinge the door, and squeeze through the crack, but I really didn't like the thought of ending up in Foley's office again, this time for destruction of St. Sophia's property. There was no doubt the brat pack would tell her who was responsible, and I guessed that was the kind of thing she'd put in my permanent record.

All that in mind, I put "taking the door apart" at the bottom of my mental list and glanced back at the rest of the room, looking for another way. What about a secret door? Since Foley had one, it didn't seem far-fetched that I'd find one in a secret, locked basement room. I walked the perimeter of the room, pressing my palms against the limestone tiles as I walked, hoping to find some kind of trigger mechanism.

I made two passes.

I found nothing.

Just as I was about to give up on an escape route that didn't involve dismantling the door, something occurred to me. The model had obviously taken a lot of work, a lot of craftsmanship, with all those tiny buildings, all that architecture. And that meant someone spent a lot of time in here. A lot of *hours* in here.

But the door was locked from the outside, so what if the architects got locked in while they were whiling away the hours on their obsessively detailed project? Wouldn't they need another way out? Surely they—or he or she or whoever—had their own escape route. I must have missed something.

I was on the far side of the room when I saw it—when I noticed the glint of light, the reflection, on the eastern edge of the city. I cocked my head at it, realizing the glint was coming from the two spires on the Sears Tower.

I moved closer.

The spires were metal, which was weird because they were the only metal in the tiny city. Everything else was rendered in that same, gray paperboard.

"Interesting," I mumbled, and kneeled down in what I assumed was a branch of the Chicago River. I reached out and carefully, oh so carefully, tugged at a spire.

It didn't budge.

"Come on," I said, and reached for the second. I grasped the end, wiggled, and felt it begin to slide free of the cardboard. One tug, then another, just enough to pull the metal through, but not hard enough to tear the roof from the building.

It finally slid free. I held it up to the light.

It was a key.

"Oh, *rock on*," I said with a grin, then rose from the lake. It may not have been a huge victory—and I wasn't even sure the key would work in the lock—but it sure felt like one. A victory for the architect who'd been locked in, and a victory for me. And more important, a loss for the brat pack.

I walked along the river until I reached the lake, then turned for the door, where I slipped the key into the lock and turned.

The lock flipped open.

I'm not embarrassed to say that I did a little dance of happiness, yellow boots and all.

Thinking the next person who was locked into the room might need the key, I pulled it from the lock and returned it to its home in the Sears Tower. I glanced across the city, making a mental note to tell Scout about the model in case she hadn't already seen it. I had a suspicion the symbols on the buildings were related to whatever she was doing, and whatever "litter" she and her friends were battling against.

And speaking of battling, it was time to consider my next step.

Option one involved my returning to the suite to face down Veronica et al. They'd gloat about locking me in; I'd gloat about getting out. Not exactly my idea of a thrilling Thursday night.

Option two was a little riskier. I'd joined the brat pack in their trip to the basement on the off chance they might lead me somewhere interesting. Success on that one, I think.

Now that they'd returned to the Kingdom of Pink, I had the chance to do a little exploring of my own. So, for the second time in a single night, I opted for danger. I'd managed to finagle my way out of a locked room, so I figured luck was on my side.

I took a final look at the city and pulled the door closed behind me.

"Good night, Chicago," I whispered.

Maybe not surprising, the hallway was empty when I emerged from the custodian's closet, the brat pack nowhere to be seen. They were probably celebrating their victory somewhere. Little did they know. . . .

The corridor split into two branches—one that led back to the stairs and the first floor, and one that probably led deeper into the basement. My decision to play Nancy Drew already made, I took the road not yet traveled.

I moved slowly, one shoulder nearly against the wall, trying to make myself as invisible as possible. The hallway dead-ended in a T-shaped corridor; I headed for it. This part of the basement was well lit, so I kept the flashlight off, but gripped it with such force, my palm was actually sweating. I was still in the basement, still close to whatever nasties Scout had locked behind the big metal door. That meant I needed to be on my guard.

I made it to the dead end without incident, then glanced down the left- and right-hand corridors. Both were empty, and I had no clue where I was relative to the rest of the building. Worse, both hallways were long and dark. There were no overhead lights and no wall sconces—just darkness.

Not the best of choices. I didn't have a coin to flip or a Magic 8-Ball to ask, so I went with the only other respectable method of making a decision as important as this one.

Unfortunately, I'd only made it through "eeny meeny miney mo" when the ground began to rumble beneath my feet. I was thrown forward into the crux of the hallway, and had to brace myself against the limestone wall to stay upright as the floor vibrated beneath me.

But just as suddenly as it had begun, the rumbling stopped. My palms still flat against the limestone bricks, heart pounding in my chest, I looked up at the ceiling above me as I waited for screaming and footfalls and other telltale signs of the aftermath of the Earthquake That Ate Chicago.

There was only silence.

I snapped my gaze to the left as hurried footsteps echoed toward me from that end of the hallway and tried to swallow down the panic.

I flicked on my flashlight and swung the beam into the dark, the arc of light barely penetrating the blackness, even as I squinted to get a better look.

And then I saw them—Scout and Jason behind her, both in uniform, both running toward me as if they were running for their lives. I dropped the beam of the flashlight to the floor to keep from blinding them, afraid that's exactly what was happening.

"Scout?" I called out, but fear had frozen my throat. I tried again, and this time managed some sound. "Scout!"

They were still far away—the corridor was a deep one—but they were running at sprinter speed . . . and there was something behind them.

It almost didn't surprise me to see that they were being chased. After all, I'd already helped Scout try to escape from *something*. But I'm not sure what I expected to see chasing her.

As they drew closer, I realized that behind them was the blonde we'd seen outside the pillar garden on Monday—the girl with the hoodie who had watched us from the street. She ran full-bore behind Scout and Jason. But even as she sprinted through the corridor, her expression was somehow vacant, a strange gleam in her eyes the only real sign of life. Her hair was long and wavy, and it flew out behind her as she ran, arms pumping, toward us.

Suddenly she pulled back her hand, then shot it forward, as if to throw something at the two of them. The air and ground rumbled, and this time, the rumble was strong enough to knock me off my feet. I hit the ground on my knees, palms extended.

By the time I glanced up again, Scout and Jason were only feet in front of me. That meant the blond girl was only a few yards behind. I saw the look of horror on Scout's face. "Get up, Lily!" she implored. *"Run!"*

I muttered a curse that would have made a string of sailors blush, and ignoring the bruises blossoming on my knees, jumped to my feet and did as I was ordered. The three of us took off down the hallway, presumably for a safer place.

We ran through one corridor, then another, then another, heading in the opposite direction of the path I'd taken with the brat pack—probably a good thing, since there was no giant metal door in that part of the convent to keep them out.

To keep *her* out.

Whatever juju the blonde used before, she used again, the ground rumbling beneath our feet. I don't know how she managed it, how she managed to make the earth—and all the limestone above it—move, but she did it sure enough. We all stumbled, but Scout reached out a hand and grabbed at the wall to keep her balance, and Jason caught Scout's elbow. I caught limestone, the stones rushing toward my face as she knocked me off my feet again. I braced myself on my hands, the pads of my hands burning as I hit the floor.

They were on their feet again and yards ahead before they realized I wasn't with them.

"Lily!" Scout screamed, but I was already looking behind me, watching the blonde. The earthquake-maker just stood there, and I figured if I was already on the floor, there wasn't much else she could do to me.

Of course, that didn't mean the guy who stepped out from behind her couldn't do damage. He was older than she was—college, maybe. Curly dark hair, broad shoulders, and blue eyes that gleamed with a creepy intensity. With a hunger. And all that hunger and intensity was directed at me.

I swallowed down fear and panic and tried to make my brain work, tried to make my arms and legs push me up from the floor, but I was suddenly puppy-clumsy, unable to order my limbs to function.

The boy stepped beside the blonde, muttered something, and just as she had done, whipped his hand in my direction.

The air pressure in the room changed, and something flew my way, some *thing* he'd created with that flick of his hand. It looked like a contact lens of hazy, green smoke, but it wasn't really smoke. It wasn't really a *thing*. It was more like the very air in the room had warped.

Still on the floor—only a second or two having passed since I fell to the ground, time slowing in the midst of my panic—I stared, eyes wide, mouth open in shock as it moved toward me. Nothing in my life in Sagamore, or my week in Chicago, had prepared me for . . . whatever it was. And whatever it was, it was about to make contact.

They say there are moments in your life when time slows down, when you can see your fate rushing toward you. This was one of those times. I had a second to react, which wasn't enough time to move out of the way, so I turned my back on it. That warp of air slammed into me with the force of a freight train, pushing the air from my lungs. It arced across my body like alien fire, like a living thing that tunneled into my spine, through my torso, across my limbs.

"Lily!" Scout screamed.

The floor rumbled beneath me again, and I heard a growl, a roar, like the scream of an angry animal. I heard shuffling, the sounds of fighting, but I could do nothing but lie there, my body spasming as pain and fire and heat raced through my limbs. I blinked at the colors that danced before my eyes, the world—or the portions of the floor and room that I could see from my sprawled-out position on the floor—covered by a green haze.

I must have passed out, because when I lifted my eyelids again, I was in the air, cradled by strong arms. I looked up and found bright eyes, eyes the same blue as a spring prairie sky, staring back at me.

"Jason?" I asked, my voice sounding hollow and distant.

"Hold on, Lily," he said. "We're going to get you out of here."

The world went black.

9

I woke blinking, my eyes squinted against the sunlight that streamed through the wall of windows on my left, and bounced off white walls on the other three sides of the room I was in. I looked down. I was on a high bed, my legs covered by a white sheet and thin blanket, the rest of me wrapped in one of those nubby, printed hospital gowns.

"You're awake."

I lifted my gaze. Scout sat in a plastic chair across from my bed, a thick leather book in her hands. She was in uniform, but she'd covered her button-up oxford shirt with a cardigan.

"Where am I?" I asked her, shading my eyes with a hand.

"LaSalle Street Clinic," she said. "A few blocks from the school. You've been sleeping for twelve hours. The doctor was in a few minutes ago. She said you didn't have a concussion or anything; they just brought you in since you passed out."

I nodded and motioned toward the windows. "Can you do something about the light?"

"Sure." She put aside the book and stood up, then walked to the wall of windows and fidgeted with the cord until the blinds came together, and the room darkened. When she was done, she turned and looked at me, arms crossed over her chest. "How are you feeling?"

I did a quick assessment. Nothing felt broken, but I had a killer headache and I was pretty sore—as if I'd taken a couple of good falls onto unforgiving limestone. "Groggy, mostly. My head hurts. And my back."

Scout nodded. "You were hit pretty hard." She walked to the bed and hitched one hip onto it. "I'd say that I'm sorry you got dragged into this but, first things first, why, exactly, were you in the basement?"

There was an unspoken question in her tone: *Were you following me again?*

"The brat pack went down there. I was invited along."

Scout went pale. "The brat pack? They were in the basement?"

I nodded. "They fed me a story about a stash of contraband stuff, but it was just a prank. They locked me in the model room."

"The model room?"

I drew a square with my fingers. "The secret custodian's closet that contains a perfect-scale model of the city? I'm guessing you know what I'm talking about here."

"Oh. That."

"Yeah. Look, I was patient about the midnight disappearances, the secret basement stuff, but"—I twirled a finger at the hospital room around us—"the time has come to start talking."

After a minute of consideration, she nodded. "You're right. You were hit with firespell."

For a few seconds, I just looked at her. It took me that long to realize that she'd actually given me a straight answer, even if I had no idea what she'd meant. "A what?"

"Firespell. The name, I know, totally medieval. Actually, so is firespell itself, we think. But that's really a magical archaeology issue, and we don't need to get into that now. Firespell," she repeated. "That's what hit you. That green contact-lens-looking deal. It was a spell, thrown by Sebastian Born. Pretty face, evil disposition."

I just stared blankly back at her. "Firespell."

"It's going to take time to explain everything."

I hitched a thumb at the monitor and IV rack that stood next to my bed. "I think my calendar is pretty free at the moment."

Scout's expression fell, her usual sarcasm replaced by something sadder and more fearful. There was worry in her eyes. "I'm so sorry, Lil. I was so scared—I thought you were gone for a minute."

I nodded, not quite ready to forgive her yet. "I'm okay," I said, although I wasn't sure I meant it.

Scout nodded, but blinked back tears, then bobbed her head toward the table beside my bed. "Your parents called. I guess Foley told them you were here? I told them you were okay—that you fell down the stairs. I couldn't—I wasn't sure what to tell them."

"Me, either," I muttered, and plucked the phone from the nightstand. They'd left me a voice mail, which I'd check later, and a couple of text messages. I opened the phone and dialed my mom's number. She answered almost immediately through a crackling, staticky connection.

"Lily? Lily?" she asked, her voice a little too loud. There was fear in her tone. Worry.

"Hi, Mom. I'm okay. I just wanted to call."

"Oh, my God," she said, relief in her voice. "She's okay, Mark," she said, her voice softer now as she reassured my father, who was apparently beside her. "She's fine. Lily, what happened? God, we were so worried—Marceline called and said you'd taken a fall?"

I opened and closed my mouth, completely at a loss about how I was supposed to deal with the fact that I now had proof my Mom was on a first name basis with Foley—not to mention Foley's perspective on my parents' careers—so I asked the most basic question I could think of. "You know Foley? Ms. Foley, I mean?"

There was a weird pause, just before a crackle of static rumbled through the phone. I pressed my palm against my other ear. "Mom? You're cutting out. I can't hear you."

"Sorry—we're on the road. Yes, we're—*yes*. We know Marceline." *Crackle.* "—you all right?"

"I'm fine," I said again. "I'm awake and I feel fine. I just—slipped. Why don't you call me later?"

That time, I only heard "traveling" and "hotel" before the connection went dead. I stared at the phone for a few seconds before flipping it shut again.

"I just lied to my parents," I snottily said when I'd returned the phone to the table. I heard the petulance in my voice, but given my surroundings, I thought I deserved it.

Scout opened her mouth to respond but before she could get words out, a knock sounded at the door. Scout met my gaze, but shrugged.

"Come in?" I said.

The door opened a crack, and Jason peeked through.

"My, my," Scout murmured, winging up eyebrows at me. I sent her a withering look before Jason opened the door fully and stepped inside. He was out of his Montclare Academy duds today, and was dressed casually in jeans and a navy zip-up sweater. I knew this was neither the time nor the place, but the navy did amazing things for his eyes. On one shoulder was the strap of a backpack, and in his hand was a slim vase that held a single, puffy flower—a peony, maybe.

The flower and backpack weren't Jason's only accessories. When Michael appeared behind him, I gave Scout the same winged-up eyebrows she'd given me. A blush began to fan across her cheeks.

"Just wanted to see how you were feeling," Jason said, closing the door once he and Michael were in the room. He dropped his backpack on a second plastic chair, then extended his arm, a smile on his face. "And we brought you a flower."

"Thanks," I said, self-consciously touching a hand to my hair. I couldn't imagine that anything up there looked pretty after twelve hours of unconsciousness. Scout reached out to take the vase, then placed it atop a bureau next to a glass container of white tulips.

I pointed at the arrangement. "Where'd those come from?"

"Huh?" Scout asked, then seemed to realize the tulips were there. "Oh. Right. Let's see." She pulled out the card, frowned, then glanced back at me. "It just says, 'Board of Trustees.'"

"That was surprisingly thoughtful," I mumbled, thinking Foley must have given them a call.

"Garcia didn't want to study," Jason said, "so we thought we'd amble over."

Scout arched a brow at Michael. "Does Garcia ever want to study?"

"I have my moments, Green," he said, then moved toward the bed. When he reached me, he picked up my hand and squeezed it. "How are you feeling?"

"Like I was hit by a freight train."

"Understandable," Jason said behind him, and Michael nodded in agreement.

"Scout was just about to explain to me exactly what's going on beneath Chicago." Jason and Michael both snapped their gaze to Scout. I guessed they had mixed feelings about her confession. She waved cheekily.

"But now that the full club has convened," I continued, linking my hands in my lap, "you can decide amongst yourselves who wants to do the explaining. Blue eyes? Brown eyes?" I glanced over at Scout. "Instigator?"

"I am so *not* an instigator," Scout said. "I was the one being chased, if you'll recall, not doing the chasing."

"Instigator," Michael said with a grin. "I like that."

When Scout stuck her tongue out at him, he winked back at her. Her blush flared up again. I bit back a smile.

"All right," Jason said. "You got dragged into the conflict, so you deserve some answers. What do you want to know?"

"Scout already said I was hit by firespell," I said, "and I've figured out some of the rest of it. You three are in cahoots and you roam around under the convent and battle bad guys who make earthquakes and shoot fire from their hands."

Silence.

"That's not bad, actually," Scout finally said.

Michael cocked his head at me. "How are you feeling about the earthquakes-and-shooting-fire part of that?"

I frowned down at the thin hospital sheet, then picked at a pill in the fabric. It was probably time for me to give some thought to whatever it was I'd been dragged into—or, maybe more accurately, that I'd *fallen* into.

"I'm not sure," I said after a minute. "I mean, I'm not really in a position to doubt the earthquakes-and-shooting-fire part. I've felt the earthquakes, felt the fire. It hurt," I emphasized. The memory of that burning heat made my shoulders tense, and I rolled them out to relieve the tension.

"I'm alive," I said, glancing up at them, "which I guess isn't something I can really take for granted right now. But beyond that, I haven't really had time to think much about it. To process it, if that makes sense."

I glanced up at Scout. Her expression had fallen, and she nibbled the edge of her lip. There was fear in her face, maybe apology, as well. It was the insecurity that comes from knowing that someone you'd brought into your life could disappear again, leaving you alone.

"It makes sense," she quietly said. Her words were a statement, but there was a question in her tone: *Is this it for us? For our friendship?*

Scout and I looked at each other for a few seconds, and in the time that elapsed during that glance, something happened—I realized I'd been given an opportunity to become part of a new kind of family; an opportunity to trust someone, to take a chance on someone. My parents may have been four thousand miles away, but I'd gained a new best friend. And that was something. That was the kind of thing you held on to.

"Well then," I said, my gaze on hers, "I suppose you'd better fill me in."

It took her a moment to react, to realize what I'd said, to realize that I was committing to being a part of whatever it was they were really, truly involved in. And when she realized it, her face lit up.

But before we could get too cozy, Jason spoke up.

"Before you tell her more than she already knows," he said, "you need to think about what you're doing. She was underground for only a little while. That means there's a chance they won't recognize her. We can all go about our business, and there's no need for them to know she exists."

He crossed his arms and frowned. "But if you bring her into it, she becomes part of the conflict. Not a JV member, sure, but part of the community. You'll put her on the radar, and they'll mark her as a supporter of the enclave. She may become a target. If you tell her more, she's in this. For better or worse, she's in it."

I was okay with "for better or worse." It was "till death do us part" that I wasn't really excited about.

"Look around," Scout quietly said, her gaze on me. "She's in the hospital wearing a paper nightgown. She has a tube in her arm." She shifted her gaze to Jason, and there was impatience there. "She's already in this."

As if she'd made the decision, Scout half jumped onto the bed and arranged herself to sit on the edge. As she moved around, Michael and Jason took a step backward to get out of her way, exchanging a quiet glance as they waited for her to begin.

"Unicorns," she said.

There was silence in the room for a few seconds. "Unicorns," I repeated.

She bobbed her head. "Unicorns."

I just blinked. "I have no idea what I'm supposed to do with that."

"Aha," she said, a finger in the air. "You didn't expect me to start with that, did you? But, seriously, unicorns. Imagine yourself in medieval Europe. You've got horses, oxen, assorted beasts of burden. Times are dark, dirty, generally impoverished."

Jason leaned toward Michael. "Is this going somewhere?"

"Not a clue," Michael said. "This is the first time I've heard this speech."

"Zip it, Garcia. Okay, so dark, dirty, lots of peasants, things are dreary. All of a sudden, a maiden walks into a field or some such thing, and she expects to see a horse there. But instead, there's a unicorn. Horn, white mane, magical glow, the whole bit."

She stopped talking, then looked at me expectantly.

"I'm sorry, Scout, but if that was supposed to be a metaphor or something, I got nothin'."

"Seconded," Michael added.

Scout leaned forward a little, and when she continued, her voice was quieter, more solemn. "Think about what I said. What if, all of a sudden, every once in a while, it wasn't just another horse in the field? What if it really was a unicorn?"

"*Ohhh,*" Jason said. "Got it."

"Yep," Michael agreed.

"There are people in the world," Scout said, "like those unicorns in the field. They're unique. They're rare." She paused and glanced up at me, her expression solemn. "And they're gifted. With magic."

Okay, I guess with all the unicorn talk, I probably should have seen that coming. Still, I had to blink a few times after she laid that little egg.

"Magic," I finally repeated.

"Magical powers of every shape and size," she said. "I can see the doubt in your eyes, but you've seen it. You've felt it." She bobbed her head toward my IV. "You have firsthand experience it exists, even if you don't know the what or the why."

I frowned. "Okay, earthquakes and fire and whatnot, but magic?"

Jason leaned forward a little. "You can have a little time to get used to the idea," he said. "But in the meantime, you might want to have her move along with the explanation. She's got quite a bit to get through yet." He smiled warmly, and my heart fluttered, circumstances notwithstanding.

"You must be a real hit with the ladies, Shepherd, with all that charm." Scout's tone was dry as toast. I bit back a grin, at least until she looked back at me again. She gave me a withering expression, the kind of raised-eyebrow look you might see on a teacher who'd caught you passing notes in class.

"Please," I said, waving an invitational hand. "Continue."

"Okay," she said, holding up her hands for emphasis, "so there's a wee percentage of the population that has magic."

"What kind of magic? Is it all earthquakes and air-pressure-contact-lenses and whatnot?"

"There's a little bit of everything. There are classes of powers, different kinds of skills. Elemental powers—that's fire and water and wind. Spells and incantations—"

One of the puzzle pieces fell into place.

"That's you," I exclaimed, thinking of the books in Scout's room. Recipe books. *Spell* books. "You can do spells?"

"Of a sort," she blandly said, as if I'd only asked if she had a nose ring. "They call me a spellbinder."

I glanced over at Jason and Michael, but they just shook their heads. "This is your field trip. You can get to us later," Michael said, then glanced at Scout. "Keep going."

"Anyway," Scout said, "the power usually appears around puberty. At the beginning of the transition to adulthood."

"Boobs *and* earthquakes?" I asked. "That's quite a change."

"Seriously," she agreed with a nod. "It's pretty freaky. You wake up one morning and *boom*—you're sporting B cups and the mystical ability to manipulate matter or cast spells or battle Reapers for dominion over Chicago. *Gossip Girl* has nothing on us."

I just stared at her for a minute, trying to imagine exactly what that life would have been like. Not just the part about waking up with B cups—although that would be a pretty big adjustment. I glanced down at my chest. Not a horrible adjustment, I guessed, but nonetheless . . .

"You still with us?" Scout asked.

I glanced up quickly, a flush rising on my cheeks. She grinned cheekily. "I've thought the same thing," she said with a wink.

"Before you two get too friendly," Michael said, "tell her the catch."

"There's a catch?" I asked.

"Isn't there always?" she asked dryly. "The thing is, the magic isn't eternal. It doesn't last forever, at least, not without a price. When we're young—teens, twenties—the magic makes us stronger. It works in conjunction with our bodies, our minds, our souls. When we're young, it's like an extra sense or an extra way to understand the world, an extra way to manipulate it. We have access to something humans forgot about after the witch trials scared it out of everyone, after fear made everyone forget about the gift."

"And when you get older?"

"The power comes at a cost," Jason said. "And our position is, the cost is pretty nasty."

"Too high," Michael added with a nod.

I arched an eyebrow. "A cost? Like mentally? Does it make you crazy or something?"

"It could," Scout said. "It rots the body, the soul, from the inside out."

I raised my eyebrows. "What do you mean, it rots the body? Like, it kills people?"

She nodded. "The older you get, the more the magic begins to feed from you. It drains you, transforms you. The magic shifts, from something symbiotic to a parasite. And in order to stay alive, to keep up with the power's constant craving, you have to feed it."

"With what?" My voice was quiet. So was Scout's when she answered.

"With the energy of others. Those who keep their power must learn to drink the essence of others—like vampires of the soul. We call them Reapers."

"Takers of life," I thought aloud.

"Bringers of death," she said. "You want a shorter life span, they're the folks you call."

"You said they take the energy of others," I repeated. "What does that mean?"

Jason took a step forward. "Have you ever seen people who you thought seemed drained of energy? Depressed? Like, kids who are sleeping in class all the time, dragging around, that kind of thing?"

"I'm a teenager," I flatly said. "That's pretty much how we live."

"Puberty takes its toll," Scout agreed, "but hormones aren't the only problem. Reapers target people with self-confidence issues—people who don't fit in. And slowly, so they don't gain too much attention, the Reapers consume their energy. Call it their aura, their soul, their will to live. That spark that makes us who we are, that makes us more than walking robots."

"The earthquake and fire kids," I said, "The ones chasing you—chasing *us*—under the convent. Those were the Reapers?"

Scout nodded. "It's a belated introduction, but meet Alex and Sebastian. She's a senior in the publics; he's a sophomore at Northwestern. They don't actually need to do any reaping right now—they're too young—but they help find victims for the older ones. That's the Reaper way. Do whatever you have to do to keep your grip on the magic, regardless of how many people you hurt—or kill—to do it."

"Okay," I said. "So these bad guys, these Reapers, suck the souls out of people so they won't become walking zombies. But what about the rest of you?" I looked at each of them in turn. "I assume you don't plan on doing any soul sucking in the future?"

Before they could answer, there was another knock on the door. Before I could answer, a scrubs-clad nurse walked in, tray in hand.

"Good afternoon," she said. "How are you feeling?" She shooed Scout off the bed, then set down the tray—which held a small plastic tumbler of water, a small plastic pitcher, and a chocolate pudding cup.

"Okay. Considering."

"Mmm-hmm," she said, then came to my bedside and measured my pulse. She pulled the end of a tube from a machine connected to the wall, then held it toward me.

"Stick out your tongue," she said. When I did, she stuck the chunk of cold plastic beneath my tongue, then watched a readout behind me. "Shouldn't you all be in school right now?" she asked without glancing up.

"We have passes," Scout said.

"Mmm-hmm," she said again. When the machine beeped, she pulled out the thermometer, put it away, and then moved to the end of my bed, where she scribbled something on my chart. When she'd returned it to its slot, she looked at me. "Visiting hours are over in an hour."

"Sure," I said. After a final warning glance at Scout, Michael, and Jason, she disappeared out the door again.

Suddenly starving, I pointed at the tray at the end of the bed. "Hand me the pudding cup and get on with the story," I told Scout. She peeled off the foil top, then handed me the cup and spoon as she licked the remnant of chocolate pudding from the foil. I dug in.

"No soul sucking," Michael continued. "From our perspective, keeping the power isn't worth it—not to feed off others. We aren't willing to pay that cost, to take lives so we can wax poetic about how great it is to be an Adept."

I swallowed a giant spoonful of chocolate pudding—magical near misses really built up the appetite—then lifted my brows at him. "Adept?"

"Those of us with magic," he said, "but who are willing to give it up. It's what we call ourselves. Our philosophy is, we hit twenty-five, and we return our power to the universe. We stop using it. We make a promise, take a vow."

"It's an even trade," Scout said, with a small smile. "No more power, but no more upsetting the balance of the universe."

"No more being Adepts," Jason said, his voice quieter and, I thought, a little wistful, as if he'd considered the blow that giving up his magic would be, and he wasn't thrilled about it.

"Okay," I said. "So, to review, you've got kids with magical powers running around Chicago. Some of them are willing to give it up when the magic gets predatory—that would be you guys."

Scout bobbed her head.

"And some of them aren't willing to give it up, so they have a future of soul sucking to look forward to."

"That's a fair summary," Michael said with a nod.

"But that doesn't explain why you guys are running around under the convent throwing, what, firespell, at one another."

Scout looked up at Michael, who nodded, as if giving her permission to answer the question. "We found a list," she said. "A list of, well, I guess you'd call them leads. Kids who've been scoped out by Reapers. Kids they're targeting for a power lunch, no pun intended."

I nodded my understanding.

"I've been working out a spell of protection, a little half charm, half curse, to keep the Reapers from being able to zero in on their targets."

"How do you do that?"

"Have you ever tried to look at a faraway star," Scout asked, "but the closer you look at it, the fuzzier it gets?"

"Sure. Why?"

"That's what Scout's trying to do here," Michael said, crossing his arms and bobbing his head in her direction. "Making the targets invisible to the Reapers. She's been working on a kid who lives in a condo on Michigan, goes to a high school in South Loop. They haven't been real thrilled with that."

"And that's why they've been chasing you?" I asked, sliding my gaze to Scout.

"As you might imagine," she said, "we aren't exactly popular. Our ideas about giving up our power don't exactly put us in the majority."

"The gifted are proud to have magic," Jason said, "as well they should be. But most of them don't want to give it up."

"That puts us in the minority," Michael added. "Rebels, of a sort."

"A magic splinter cell?"

"Kinda," Scout said with a rueful smile. "So the Reapers identify targets—folks who make a good psychic lunch—and kids who are coming into their own, coming into their own gifts. Spotters," she added, anticipating my question. "Their particular gift is the ability to find magic. To detect it."

"Once a kid is identified," Michael said, "the Reapers circle like lions around prey. They'll talk to the kid, sometimes their parents, about the gift, figure out the parameters, exactly what the kid can do. And they'll teach the kid that the gift is nothing to be embarrassed about, and that any souls they take are worth it."

"The Reapers try to teach the kids that the idea of giving up your power willingly is a conspiracy," Jason said, "that feeding on someone else's energy, their essence, is a kind of magical natural selection—the strong feeding on the weak or something. We disagree. We work our protective spells on the targets, or we try to intercede more directly with the gifted, to get the kids to think for themselves, to think about the consequences of their magic."

"For better or worse," Scout added.

"So you try to steal their pledges," I concluded.

"You got it," Scout said. "We try to teach kids with powers that giving up their powers is the best thing for humanity. You know, because of the soul sucking."

I smiled lightly. "Right."

"That makes us pretty unpopular with them, and it makes the Reapers none too popular with us," she added. "We didn't need the original Reapers. And we certainly don't need Reapers spawning out there."

"Seriously," Jason muttered. "There're already enough Cubs fans in Chicago."

Michael coughed, but the cough sounded a lot like, "Northside."

I arched an eyebrow, and returned my glance to Scout. "Northside?"

"Where the Cubs are," she said. "They're territorial."

"I see. So, what do you do about the evangelizing? About the Reaper spawn, I mean?"

"Well, we *are* the good guys," Michael said. "They're bullies, and we're a nuisance. We make it harder for them to do their jobs—to recruit, to brainwash, to convince kids with magic that they can keep their powers and live long, fulfilling lives as soul-sucking zombies."

"We thwart with extreme prejudice," Scout said with a grin. "Right now, we're doing a lot of protecting targets, and a lot of befriending the gifted who haven't yet been turned toward the dark side."

"A lot of things that get you chased," I pointed out, giving Scout a pointed look.

"That is true," she said with a nod. "Reapers are tenacious little suckers. We spend a lot of time keeping ourselves alive."

I crossed my legs beneath the thin blanket. "Then maybe you shouldn't have let them into St. Sophia's."

Scout snorted. "We didn't *let* them in. The tunnels beneath the convent connect it to half the buildings in the Loop. Welcome to the Pedway."

"How many of them are there?" I asked.

"We think about two hundred," Scout said. "Sounds like a lot, but Chicago is the third-biggest city in the country. Two hundred out of nearly three million isn't a lot. And we don't really have an 'in' with them, obviously, so two hundred's only a best guess."

"And you guys?"

"This month, we're holding steady at twenty-seven identified Adepts in and around Chicago," Michael said. "That includes Junior Varsity—high schoolers—and Varsity. V-squad is for the college Adepts, their last chance to play wizard and warlock before it's time to return to a life of mundane living. We're organized into enclaves in and around the city. Headquarters, kind of."

Another puzzle piece fell into place. "That's what the symbols on the buildings in the model room mean." My voice rose a little in excitement. "There was a *Y* in a circle, and these kind of combined circles, sort of like a cross. Those are enclave locations?"

"Those circle things are called 'quatrefoils,'" Michael said. "The *Y* symbol indicates enclave and sanctuary locations—that's where the Reapers plan their minion baiting—around the city. There are six enclaves in Chicago. St. Sophia's is Enclave Three."

"Or ET, as the idiots like to call it," Scout added with a grin, bobbing her head toward the boys.

Jason lifted his gaze to mine, and there was concern there. "Did you say you've been to the city room?" He looked over at Scout, and this time his gaze was accusatory. "You let her into the city room?"

"I didn't let her in," Scout defended. "I wasn't even there. The preps found the room and led her down there, locked her in."

Jason put his hands on his hips. He was definitely not happy. "Regulars know about the city room?"

"I told you people would get through," Scout said. "Not all the tunnels are blocked off. I told you this was going to happen eventually."

"Not now," Michael interjected. "We don't need to talk about this right now."

A little tension there, I guessed. "Why the tunnels in the first place?" I wondered. "If Reapers are out to suck the souls from humans and keep you guys from getting in their way, why don't they just bust through the front door of St. Sophia's and take out the school?"

"We may be a splinter cell," Jason said, "but we've got one thing in common with the Reapers—no one wants to be outed to the public. We don't want to deal with the chaos, and Reapers like being able to steal a soul here and there without a lot of public attention."

"People probably wouldn't take that very well," I said.

"Exactly," Scout agreed with a nod. "Reapers don't want to be locked up in the crazy house—or experimented on—any more than we do. So we keep our fights out of the public eye. We keep them underground, or at least off the streets. We usually make it out and back without problems, but they've been aggressive lately. More aggressive than usual," she muttered.

I remembered what Scout had told me about their long, exhausting summer. I guessed ornery, magic-wielding teenagers could do that to a girl.

"They have given chase a lot lately," Jason said. "We're all thinking they must be up to something."

The room got quiet, the three of them, maybe contemplating just what the Reapers might be up to. Then they looked at me expectantly, maybe waiting for a reaction—tears or disbelief or enthusiasm. But I still had questions.

"Do you look forward to it?" I asked.

Scout tilted her head. "To what?"

"To giving up your powers?" I uncrossed my legs and buried my toes in the blanket—this place was as frosty as St. Sophia's. "I mean, you've got costs and benefits either way, right? Right now, you all have some kind of power. You hit puberty, and you get used to being all magically inclined, but then you have to give it up. Doesn't that bother you?"

They exchanged glances. "It's the way it is," Scout quietly said. "Magic is part of who we are now, but it won't be part of us forever."

"But neither will midnight meetings and obnoxious Reapers and power-happy Varsity Adepts."

Scout lifted her eyebrows at Jason's mini-tirade.

"I know," Jason said. "Not the time."

I guessed things weren't entirely hunky-dory in Enclave Three. "So the guy that blasted me, or whatever. You said his name was Sebastian. And he's a Reaper."

Scout nodded. "That's him."

"He said something before he blasted me. What was that?"

"*Ad meloria*," Michael said. "It's Latin. Means 'toward better things.'"

I raised my eyebrows. "I'm guessing that's their motto."

"You'd be right," Scout said. "They think the world would be a better place if they kept their magic. They think they're the elite, and everyone should give them their due. A survival of the fittest kind of thing."

"Survival of the craziest, more like," Jason muttered. He glanced down at his watch, then looked up at Michael. "We probably need to head," he said, then glanced at me. "Sorry to leave you in here. We've got some stuff at MA this afternoon."

"No problem. Thanks for coming by. And thanks for the flower."

He stuck his hands into his pockets and grinned back at me. "No problem, Parker. Glad you've rejoined the land of the living."

I grinned back at him, at least until Scout's throat clearing pulled my attention away.

"I should also head back," she said, pulling a massive, baffled down jacket off the back of her chair. She squeezed into it, then fastened the clips that held it together. The white jacket went past her knees, which made it look like she had on nothing but tights and thick-soled Dr. Martens Mary Janes beneath it.

"You look like the Pillsbury Snow Boy."

She rolled her eyes. "It's breezy out there today. Not all of us have these warm, lush accommodations to look forward to."

I snuggled into the bed, thinking I'd better gather what warmth I could, given the possibility that I'd be returning to my meat locker of a room tomorrow.

"Take care," Michael said, rapping his knuckles on the tray at the end of the bed. I assumed that was the macho-guy equivalent of giving me a hug. Either way, I appreciated the gesture.

I smiled back at him. "I'm sure I'll see you soon."

"And hopefully under better circumstances." He cast Scout a sideways glance. "Green."

She rolled her eyes. "Garcia." When she looked at me again, she was smiling. "I'll give you a call later."

I nodded.

The trio gathered up their things, and I clenched my fingers, itching to ask one final question. Well, scared to ask it, anyway. My palms were actually sweating, but I made myself get it out.

"Jason."

They all turned back at the sound of his name.

He arched his eyebrows. "Yeah?"

"Could I talk to you for a sec?"

"Um, sure." He shouldered his backpack, then exchanged a glance with Scout and Michael. She winged up her brows, but let Garcia push her toward and out the door.

When the door shut behind them, Jason glanced back at me. "Everything okay?"

"Oh, yeah." I frowned down at the blanket for a minute before finally raising my gaze to his crystal blue eyes. "Listen, I just wanted to say thanks. For getting me out of the basement, I mean. If it hadn't been for you and Scout—"

"You wouldn't have gotten hit in the first place," he finished.

I opened my mouth, then closed it again, not really able to argue that point.

"I'm glad you're okay," he softly said. "And for what it's worth, you're welcome, Lily."

I liked the way he said my name, as if it weren't just a series of letters, but a word thick with meaning. *Lily.*

"I mean, I'm not glad you got wrapped up in this—especially since you don't have magic to defend yourself with." He tipped his head to the side. "Although, I think I heard something about a flip-flop?"

"I guess Scout's been giving up all my offensive moves?"

He crossed his arms over his chest. "And impressive moves they are. I mean, who'd have thought that a few square inches of foam were really a technologically advanced—"

"All right, Shepherd. You've made your point."

"Have I?" he asked, with a half smile.

Turned out, Jason's half smile was even more deadly than the full, dimpled grin. The half smile was drowsier—almost ridiculously handsome.

"You did," I finally said.

We stared silently at each other for a moment before he bobbed his head toward the door. "I guess I should join Scout and Michael?"

He made it a question, as if he didn't want to leave, but could sense my nerves. Heart pounding fiercely in my chest, I stopped him. "Actually, one more thing."

He raised questioning brows.

"When we were down there in the basement. When I got hit. I thought—I thought I heard a growl. Like an animal."

His eyes widened, lips parting in surprise. He hadn't expected me to bring it up, but I couldn't get the sound out of my mind.

Jason hadn't yet given me an answer, so I pressed on. I knew the growling hadn't come from Scout—she'd admitted to being a spellbinder. And I didn't think it had come from earthquake girl or firespell boy. Jason was the only other person there.

"That sound," I said. "Was it you?"

He gazed at me, a chill in his blue eyes, shards of icy sapphire.

"Scout gave you the simple answer about Adepts," he finally said. "She told you that we each have magic, a gift of our own. That's a short answer, but it's not entirely accurate." He paused, then wet his lips. "I'm not like the others."

My heart thudded so fiercely, I wouldn't have been surprised if he could hear it. It took me a moment to ask him. "How much not like them?"

When Jason looked up at me again, the color of his eyes had shifted to green and then to a silvered yellow, like those of a cat caught in the light. And there was something wolfish in his expression.

"Enough," he said, and I'd swear his voice was thicker, deeper. "Different enough."

He turned to go.

My heart didn't stop pounding until the door closed behind him.

10

The room was quiet after the triplets left, at least for a few minutes. The doctor finally visited and looked me over, and reached the same conclusion that had been passed along earlier—I was fine. Notably, he didn't ask me what threat sent me from an all-girls' private school to a hospital.

Whatever he knew, I had hours yet to kill in the hospital. For the first ten minutes, I flipped my cell phone over and over in my hand, trying to gather up the nerve to call Ashley. But she was probably still in class and, besides, what was I going to tell her? That I'd met some magical weirdos who'd managed to rope me into their shenanigans? I wasn't crazy about the idea of that conversation, or how I was going to explain it without sounding completely loopy—so I put the phone down again and glanced around the room. Since no one had brought me homework—and I wasn't about to ask for any—I turned on the television bolted to the wall, settled back into the bed, and had just started watching a reality show about bored, rich housewives when there was a knock at the door.

I had no idea who else would visit—other than brat packers hoping to gloat about their victory—but I pointed the remote at the television and turned it off.

"Come in," I said.

The door opened and closed, followed by the sound of heels clacking on the tile floor. Foley appeared from around the corner, hands clasped before her, a tidy, pale suit on her slender frame, ash-blond hair tidy at her shoulders. Her expression was all business.

"Ms. Parker." Foley walked to the window, pushed aside a couple of the slats in the blinds, and glanced out at the city. "How are you feeling?"

"Good, considering."

"You lost consciousness," she said. Said, not asked.

"That's what I hear."

"Yes, well. I trust, Ms. Parker, that you understand the importance of our institution's reputation, and of the value of discretion. We, of course, do not wish to elicit untoward attention regarding the hijinks of our students. It would not serve St. Sophia's, nor its students or alumnae, for the community or the press to believe that our institution is not a safe place for its students."

I don't know what she knew about what went on—or what she thought went on—but she was certainly keen on keeping it quiet.

"I also trust that you understand well enough the importance of caring for your physical well-being, and that you will take sufficient care to ensure that you do not lose consciousness again."

That made me sit up a little straighter. What did she think—that I was starving myself and I'd passed out for lack of food? If only she'd seen the private moment I shared with the pudding cup earlier.

"I take care of myself," I assured her.

"All evidence to the contrary."

Okay, honestly, there was a tiny part of me that wanted to rat on Scout, Jason, Michael, and the rest of the Adepts, or at least on the brat packers who threw me into harm's way. It would have been satisfying to wipe that smug expression from Foley's face, and replace it with something a bit more sympathetic.

There were two problems with that theory.

First, I wasn't entirely sure Foley was capable of sympathy.

Second, I had to be honest. I hadn't gone downstairs because Veronica and the rest of her cronies had forced me. And I'd made my way down the other hallway—and into the Reapers' path—because I'd decided to play junior explorer. I'd been curious, and I'd walked that plank willingly.

Besides, I could have walked away from all of it earlier. I could have stepped aside, told Jason, Michael, and Scout that I didn't want to be included in their magical mystery tour, and let them handle their Reaper problems on their own. But I'd invited their trust by asking them to fill me in, and I wasn't about to betray it.

So this time, I'd take one for the team. But Scout *so* owed me.

"You're right," I told her. Her eyes instantaneously widened, as if she were surprised a teenager would agree with her orders. "It's been a stressful week." Total truth. "I should take better care of myself."

She lifted her eyebrows. "That's a surprisingly mature attitude."

"I'm surprisingly mature." It wasn't that I wanted to snark back to the principal of my high school, the head honcho (honchess?) of the place I lived, slept, ate, and learned. But her attitude, her assumption that I was here because I lacked some fundamental ability to keep myself safe, practically begged for snark.

On the other hand, since I'd made the decision to move deeper into the convent instead of heading back to my room, maybe I did.

Foley lifted her brows, and her expression made her thoughts on my snark pretty clear. "Ms. Parker, we take the well-being of our students and the reputation of our institution very seriously."

Given what was going on beneath her institution, I wondered about that. But I managed to keep my mouth shut.

"I expect you'll return to St. Sophia's tomorrow?"

"That's what they say."

Foley nodded. "Very well. I've asked Ms. Green to gather your assignments. Given that tomorrow's Saturday, you'll have some time to complete them before classes resume. I'll arrange for a car to transport you back to St. Sophia's. If you require anything before your return, you may contact our staff."

I nodded. Her work apparently done, she walked toward the door. But then she glanced back.

"About our conversation," she said, "perhaps I was . . . ill informed about your parents' professions."

I stared at her for a few seconds, trying to make sense of the about-face. "Ill informed?"

"I recognize that you, of course, would know better than I the nature of your parents' work." She glanced down at her watch. "I need to return to the school. Enjoy your evening."

My mind began to race, but I managed to bob my head as she disappeared around the corner, then opened and closed the door again.

I stared down at the remote control in my hand for a minute after she'd left, flipping it through my fingers as I ruminated.

It was weird enough that she'd dropped by in the first place—I mean, how many high school principals visited their students in the hospital? She clearly had her own theories about what had happened to me—namely, that it was my fault. I guess she wanted to cover her bases, make sure I wasn't going to spill to the media or call a lawyer about my "accident."

But then, out of the blue, she brought up my parents and changed her story? And even weirder, she actually seemed sincere. Contrite, even, and Foley didn't exactly seem like the nurturing type, much less the type to admit when she was wrong.

I gnawed the edge of my lip and gave the remote a final flip. Call it what you want—Reapers, Adepts, magic, firespell, whatever. Things were seriously weird at St. Sophia's.

True to the doc's word, I was released the next morning. True to Foley's word, one of the glasses-clad matrons who usually patrolled the study hall brought casual clothes for me to change into—jeans and a T-shirt, probably selected by Scout—and signed me out. A nurse wheeled me, invalid style, to the front door of the clinic and the St. Sophia's-branded minivan that sat at the curb. The matron was silent on the way back to the convent, but it was a pretty short ride—only a few blocks back to my new home on Erie. They dropped me off at the front door without a word, and I headed up the stairs and into the building. Although I'd been gone only a couple of days, the convent seemed almost . . . foreign. It hadn't yet begun to feel like home, but now, it felt farther from Sagamore than ever.

It was a Saturday afternoon, and the main building was all but empty. A handful of students peppered the study hall, maybe catching up on weekend homework or trying to get ahead to pad their academic resumes. The halls that held the suites were louder, music and television spilling into the hallway as St. Sophia's girls relaxed and enjoyed the weekend.

I unlocked the door to our suite. Scout jumped up from the couch, decked out in jeans and layered T-shirts, her hair pulled into a short ponytail, and practically knocked me over to get in a hug.

"Thank God," she said. "The brat packers were getting almost unbearable." She let me go, then gave me an up-and-down appraisal. "Is everything where I left it?"

"Last time I checked," I said with a smile, then waved at Barnaby, who sat on the couch behind us. She wore a fitted pale blue T-shirt with a rainbow across the front, and her hair was up in some kind of complicated knot. It was very *Sound of Music*.

"Hello, Lily," she said.

"Hi, Lesley."

The door to Amie's suite opened. Amie, M.K., and Veronica piled out of the room, their smiles fading as they realized I'd come home. They were all dressed in athletic shorts, snug tank tops, and sneakers. I assumed it was workout time.

Amie's smile faded to an expression that was a lot heavier on the contrition and apology. M.K.'s smile was haughty. Veronica was using both hands to pull her hair into a ponytail. I wasn't even on her radar.

"You were in the hospital," M.K. said. There was no apology behind her words, no indication that she thought they might have been responsible for anything that happened to me. They weren't, of course, responsible, but they didn't know that. I'd hoped for something a little more contrite, honestly—maybe something in a nice "sheepish embarrassment."

"Yep," I said.

"What happened to you?" M.K. had apparently skipped embarrassment and gone right to being accusatory.

"I'm not at liberty to say," I told them.

"Why? Is it catching?" M.K. snickered at her joke. "Something contagious?"

"There are certain . . . liability issues," I said, then looked over at Amie. She was the worrywart of the group, so I figured she was my most effective target. "Insurance issues. Parental liability issues. Probably best not to talk about it. We don't want to have to get the lawyers involved. Not yet, anyway."

Scout, half turning so that only I could see her, winked at me.

Veronica and Amie exchanged a nervous glance.

"But thanks for the tour," I added as I headed for my bedroom. I unlocked the door, then stood there as Scout and Barnaby skipped inside.

"It was very educational," I said, then winked at the brat pack, walked inside, and closed the door behind us.

As dramatic exits went, it wasn't bad.

I gave Scout and Lesley a mini-update, at least the parts I could talk about in Lesley's company. Lesley wasn't an Adept, at least as far as I was aware, so I kept my replay of Foley's visit and my chat with Jason purely PG. But I shooed them out of my room pretty quickly.

I needed a shower.

A superhot, superlong, environmentally irresponsible shower. As soon as they were out the door, I changed into my reversible robe (stripes for perky days, deep blue for serious ones), grabbed my bucket o' toiletries, and headed for the bathroom.

I spent the first few minutes with my hands against the wall, my head dunked under the spray. The heat probably didn't do much good for my hair, but I needed it. I had basement and hospital grime to wash off, not to mention the emotional grime of (1) more of Foley's questioning of my parents' honesty; (2) having been unconscious and apparently near death for twelve hours; (3) having been the victim of a prank that led to point number two; and (4) having been carried out of a dangerous situation by a ridiculously pretty boy and having almost *no* memory of it whatsoever. That last one was just a crime against nature.

And, of course, there was the other thing.

The magic thing.

Varsity, Junior Varsity, Adepts, firespell, Reapers, enclaves. These people had their own vocabulary and apparently a pretty strong belief that they had magical powers.

Sure, I'd seen *something*. And whatever was going on beneath St. Sophia's, beneath the city, I wasn't about to rat them out. But still— what had I seen? Was it really magic? I mean—*magic*, as in unicorns and spells and wizards and witchcraft magic?

That, I wasn't so sure about.

I gave it some thought as I repacked my gear and padded back to the room in my shower shoes, then waved at Scout and Lesley, who were playing cards in the common room. I gave it some thought as I scrubbed my hair dry, pulled flannel pajama bottoms from the drawer of my bureau, and got dressed again.

There was a single, quick rap at the door. I turned around to face it, but the knocking stopped, replaced by a pink packet that appeared beneath my door. I hung the damp towel on the closet doorknob, then plucked the packet from the floor. Out of an abundance of caution—I couldn't be too sure these days—I held it up to my ear. When I was pretty sure it wasn't ticking, I slipped a finger beneath the tab of tape that held the sides together.

And smiled.

Wrapped in the pink paper—that could only have come from Amie's room—was the rest of the bag of licorice Scotties I'd started on before my trip to the basement. I wasn't sure if the gift was supposed to be an apology or a bribe.

Either way, I thought, as I nipped the head from another unfortunate Scottie, I liked it.

Unfortunately, as I had realized on my way to pick up the Scotties, my knees still ached from the double falls on the limestone floor. I put my prize on the bureau, rolled up my pants legs, and moved in front of the mirror to check them out. Purple bruises bloomed on my kneecaps, evidence of my run-in with . . . well, whatever they were.

My back had cramped as I rolled the hems of my pants down. I twisted halfway around in the mirror, then tugged up the back of the Ramones T-shirt I'd paired with my flannel pajama bottoms to check out the place where the firespell had hit me. I expected to see another bruise, some indication of the force that had pushed me to the floor and knocked the breath from my lungs.

There was no bruise, at least that I could see from my position— half-turned as I was to face the mirror, one hip cocked out, neck twisted. I almost dropped the bottom of my shirt and went on my merry way—straight into bed with the coffee table's *Vogue*.

But then I saw it.

My heart skipped a beat, something tightening in my chest.

At the small of my back was a mark. It wasn't a bruise—the color wasn't right. It wasn't the purple or blue or even that funny yellow that bruises take on.

It was green. Candy apple green—the same color as the firespell that had bitten into my skin.

More important, there was a defined shape. It was a symbol—a glyph on the small of my back, like a tattoo I hadn't asked for.

It was a circle with some complicated set of symbols inside it.

I'd been marked.

11

I stood in front of the mirror for fifteen minutes, worrying about the mark on my back. I turned this way and that, my hem rolled up in my hands, neck aching as I stretched until I thought to grab a compact from my makeup bag. I flipped it open, turned around, and aimed it at the mirror.

It wasn't just a mark, or a freckle, or a weird wrinkle caused by lounging in a hospital bed for twenty-four hours.

It was a circle—a perfect circle. A circle too perfect to be an accident. Too perfect to be anything but purposeful. And inside the circle were symbols—squiggles and lines, all distinct, but not organized in any pattern that looked familiar to me.

But still, even though I didn't know what they meant, I could tell what they *weren't*. The lines were clear, the shapes distinct. They were much too perfect to be a biological accident.

I frowned and dropped my arm, staring in confusion at the floor. Where had it come from? Had something happened to me when I was unconscious? Had I been tattooed by an overeager ER doctor?

Or was the answer even simpler . . . and more complex?

The mark was in the same place I'd been hit with the firespell, where that rush of heat and fire (and magic) thrown by Sebastian had roared up my spine.

I had no idea *how* firespell could have had anything to do with the symbol, but what else could it have been? What else would have put it there?

Without warning, there was a knock at the door. Instinctively, I flipped the compact shut and pulled down my T-shirt. "Yeah?"

"Hey," Scout said from the other side of the closed door. "We're going to grab a Rainbow Cone at a place down the street. You wanna come with? It's only three or four blocks. Might be nice to get some fresh air?"

Something in my stomach turned over, maybe at the realization that, at some point, I'd have to tell Scout about the mark and enlist her help to figure out what it was. That didn't sit well. Her telling me about her adventures was one thing. My being part of those adventures and part of this whole magic thing—being permanently marked by it— was something else.

"No, thanks," I said, giving the closed door the guilty look I couldn't stand to give Scout. "I'm not feeling so great, so I think I'm just going to rest for a little while."

"Oh, okay. Do you want us to bring some back?"

"Uh, no, thanks. I'm not really hungry." That was the absolute truth.

She was quiet for a minute. "Are you okay in there?" she finally asked.

"Yeah. Just, you know, tired. I didn't get much sleep in the hospital." Also the truth, but I felt bad enough that I crossed my fingers, anyway.

"Okay. Well, take a nap, maybe," she suggested. "We'll check in later."

"Thanks, Scout," I said. When footsteps echoed across the suite, I turned and pressed my back against the door and blew out a breath.

What had I gotten myself into?

True to my word, I climbed into bed, pulling the twin-spired symbols of St. Sophia's over my head as I tried, unsuccessfully, to nap. I'd been supportive of Scout and the Adept story in the hospital. I'd made a commitment to believe them, to believe in them, even when Foley showed up. I'd also made a commitment not to let the basement drama—whatever it was about—affect my friendship with Scout.

And now I was in my room, head buried in cotton and flannel, hiding out.

Some friend I was.

Every five minutes, I'd touch the tips of my fingers gingerly to the bottom of my spine, thinking I'd be able to feel some change when, and if, the mark disappeared. Every fifteen minutes, I'd climb out of bed and twist around in front of the mirror, making sure the mark hadn't decided to fade.

There was no change.

At least, not physically. Emotionally, I was freaking out. And not the kind of freaking out that lent itself to finding a friend and venting. This was the kind of freaking out that was almost . . . *paralyzing*. The kind of fear that made you hunker down, avoid others, avoid the issue.

And so I lay in bed, sunlight shifting across the room as the day slipped away. The suite being relatively small, I heard Scout and Lesley return, mill about in the common room, and then head into their respective bedrooms. They eventually left for dinner, after a prospective knock on the door to see if I wanted anything. For the second time, I declined. I could hear Scout's disappointment—and fear—when she double-checked, but I wasn't up for company. I wasn't up for providing consolation.

I needed to be consoled.

Eventually, I fell asleep. Scout didn't bother knocking for breakfast on Sunday morning. Not that I could blame her, I supposed, since I'd ignored her for the last twenty-four hours, but her absence was still noticeable. She'd become a fixture during my first week at St. Sophia's.

I snuck down to breakfast in jeans and my Ramones T-shirt, my hair in a messy knot, the ribboned key around my neck. I wasn't dressed for brunch or socializing, so I grabbed a carrot-raisin muffin and a box of orange juice before heading back to my room, bounty in hand.

What a difference a day makes.

It was around noon when they knocked on the door.

When I didn't answer, Amie's voice rang out. "Lily? Are you in there? Are you . . . okay?"

I closed the art history book I'd been perusing in bed, went to the door, opened it, and found Amie and Veronica, both in jeans, brown leather boots, snug tops, and dangly earrings, standing there. Not bad outfits, actually, if you ignored the prissiness.

The last time they'd sought me out, they offered a chance to go treasure hunting. The offer this time wasn't much different.

"We're really sorry about what happened," Amie said. "We're heading to Michigan Avenue for a little shopping. Are you up for a field trip?"

I was an intelligent person, so my first instinct was, of course, to slam the door in their faces. But as they stood there in my doorway, hair perfect, makeup just so, they offered me something else.

Oblivion.

The opportunity to pretend to be an It Girl for a little while, in a world with much simpler rules, where what you wore meant more than how many Reapers you'd thwarted, how much firespell had taken you down.

Call it a weak moment, a moment of denial. Either way, I said yes.

Twenty minutes later, I was in boots and leggings, black skirt, black fitted shirt, jacket and drapey scarf, and I was following Amie and Veronica out the door and toward Michigan Avenue. We strode side by side down the sidewalk—Amie, then me, then Veronica—as though we were acting out the opening credits of a new teen drama.

Even on a Sunday, Michigan Avenue was full of tourists and locals, young and old, shoppers and picture-snappers, all out to enjoy the weather before the cold began to roll in. It was understandable that they were out—the sky was ridiculously blue, the temperature perfect. Windy City or not, there was just enough breeze to keep the sun from being oppressive.

This was my first time on Michigan Avenue, my first opportunity to explore Chicago beyond the walls of St. Sophia's (apart from my quick jaunt around the block with Scout). I was surprised at how open Chicago felt—less constricting, less overwhelming, than walking through the Village or midtown Manhattan. There was more glass, less concrete; more steel, less brick. With the shine of new condos and the reflection of Lake Michigan off mirrored glass, the Second City looked like Manhattan's younger, prettier sister.

We passed boutique after boutique, the chichi stores nestled between architectural masterpieces—the ribbon-wrapped Hancock Building, the castlelike form of the Water Tower and, of course, lots of construction.

"So," Amie said, "are you going to tell us exactly what went on in the basement?"

"What basement?" I asked, my gaze on the high-rises above us.

"Coyness is not becoming," Veronica said. "You were in the basement, and then you were in the hospital. We know those things happened." She slid me a sideways glance. "Now we want to know how they connect."

Sure, I was taking a breather from Scout and the rest of the Adepts, but I wasn't about to rat them out, especially to brat packers. Trying to be normal for a few minutes was one thing; becoming a fink was something else entirely.

"I fell," I told her, stating the absolute truth. "I was on my way back upstairs, and I slipped. The edges of those limestone stairs to the first floor, you know how they're warped?"

"You'd think they could fix those," Amie said.

"You'd think," I agreed.

"Uh-huh," Veronica said, doubt in her voice. "They sent you to the hospital because you fell down the stairs?"

"Because I was knocked unconscious," I reminded them with a bright smile. "And had I not been down in the basement in the first place . . ."

I didn't finish the sentence, letting the blame remain unspoken. Apparently, that was a good strategy. When I glanced over at Veronica, she was smiling appreciatively, as if my reminder of their culpability was just the kind of strategy she'd have used.

Suddenly, as if we were the best of friends, Veronica linked her arm in mine, then steered me in and through the pedestrian traffic.

"In here," she said, bobbing her head toward a shopping center on the west side of the street. It was three stories high, the front wall a giant window of mannequins and clothing displays. A coffee bar filled most of the first floor, while giant hanging sculptures—brightly colored teardrops of glass—rained down from the three-story atrium.

"Nice place," I said, my gaze rising as I surveyed the glass.

"It's not bad," Veronica said. "And the shopping's pretty good, too."

"Pretty good" might have been an understatement. The stores that spanned the corridors weren't the kind of places where you dropped in to pick up socks. These were *investment* stores. Once-in-a-lifetime stores. Stores with clothes and bags that most shoppers saved months or years for.

Amie and Veronica were not your average shoppers. We spent three hours working our way down from the third floor to the first, checking out stores, trying on clothes, posing in front of mirrors in clunky shoes, tiny jeans, and Ikat prints. I bought nothing; I had the emergency credit card, but buying off the rack didn't have much appeal. There was no *hunt* in buying off the rack, no thrill of finding a kick-ass bag or pair of shoes for an incredible discount. With occasional exceptions, I was a vintage and thrift store kind of girl—a handbag huntress.

Amie and Veronica, on the other hand, bought *everything.* They found must-haves in almost every store we stopped in: monogram-print leather bags, wedge-heeled boots with elflike slits in the top, leggings galore, stilettos with heels so skinny they'd have made excellent weaponry . . . or better weaponry than flip-flops, anyway. The amount of money they spent was breathtaking, and neither of them so much as looked at the receipts. Cost was not a factor. They picked out what they wanted and, without hesitation, handed it over to eager store clerks.

Although I put a little more thought into the financial part of shopping, I couldn't fault their design sensibilities. They may have been dressed like traditional brat packers for their excursion to Magnificent Mile, but these girls knew fashion—what was hot, and what was on its way up.

Even better, maybe because they were missing out on Mary Katherine's obnoxiously sarcastic influence, Amie and Veronica were actually pleasant. Sure, we didn't have a discussion in our three-hour, floor-to-floor mall survey that didn't involve clothes or money or who's-seeing-whom gossip, but I had wanted oblivion. Turned out, trying to keep straight the intermingled dating lives of St. Sophia's girls and the Montclare boys they hooked up with was a fast road to oblivion. I barely thought about the little green circle on my back, but even self-induced oblivion couldn't last forever.

We were on the stairs, heading toward the first floor with glossy, tissue-stuffed shopping bags in hand, when I saw him.

Jason Shepherd.

My heart nearly stopped.

Not just because it was Jason, but because it was Jason in jeans that pooled over chunky boots, and a snug, faded denim work shirt. Do you have any idea what wearing blue did for a boy with already ridiculously blue eyes? It was like his irises glowed, like they were lit by blue fire from within. Add that to a face already too pretty for anyone's good, and you had a dangerous combination. The boy was completely *en fuego*.

Jason was accompanied by a guy who was cute in a totally different kind of way. This one had thick, dark hair, heavy eyebrows, deep-set brown eyes, a very intense look. He wore glasses with thick, black frames and hipster-chic clothes: jacket over T-shirt; dark jeans; black Chuck Taylors.

I blew out a breath, remembered the symbol on the small of my back, and decided I wasn't up for handsome Adepts or their buddies any more than I had been for funky, nose-ringed spellbinders. Mild panic setting in, I planned my exit.

"Hey," I told Amie, as we reached the first floor, "I'm going to run in there." I hitched a thumb over my shoulder.

Amie glanced behind me, then lifted her eyebrows. "You're going to the orthopedic shoe store?"

Okay, so I really should have looked before I pointed. "I like to be prepared."

"For your future orthopedic shoe needs?"

"Podiatric health is very important."

"Veronica!"

Frick. Too late. I muttered a curse and looked over. Jason's friend saluted.

I risked a glance Jason's way and found blue eyes on me, but I couldn't stand the intimacy of his gaze. It seemed wrong to share a secret in front of people who knew nothing about it, nothing about the world that existed beneath our feet. And then there was the guilt about having abandoned Scout for Louis Vuitton and BCBG that was beginning to weigh on my shoulders. I looked away.

"That's John Creed," Veronica whispered as they walked over. "He's president of the junior class at Montclare. But I don't know the other guy."

I didn't tell her that I knew him well enough, that he'd carried me from danger, and that he was maybe, *possibly*, a werewolf.

"Veronica Lively," said the hipster. His voice was slow, deep, methodical. "I haven't seen you in forever. Where have you been hiding?"

"St. Sophia's," she said. "It's where I live and play."

"John Creed," said the boy, giving me a nod in greeting, "and this is Jason Shepherd. But I don't know you." He gave me a smile that was a little too coy, a little too self-assured.

"How unfortunate for you," I responded with a flat smile, and watched his eyebrows lift in appreciation.

"Lily Parker," Veronica said, bobbing her head toward me, then whipping away the cup John held in his hand. She took a sip.

"John Creed, who is currently down one smoothie," he said, crossing his arms over his chest. "Lively, I believe you owe me a drink."

A sly grin on her face, Veronica took another sip before handing it back to him. "Don't worry," she said. "There's plenty left."

John made a sarcastic sound, then began quizzing her about friends they had in common. I took the opportunity to steal a glance at Jason, and found him staring back at me, head tilted. He was clearly wondering why I was acting as if I didn't know him, and where I'd left Scout.

I looked away, guilt flooding my chest.

"So, new girl," John suddenly said, and I looked his way. "What brings you to St. Sophia's?"

"My parents are in Germany."

"Intriguing. Vacation? Second home?"

"Sabbatical."

John raised his eyebrows. "Sabbatical," he repeated. "As in, a little plastic surgery?"

"As in, a little academic research."

His expression suggested he wasn't convinced my parents were studying, as opposed to a more lurid, rich-folks activity, but he let it go. "I see. Where'd you go to school? Before you became a St. Sophia's girl, I mean."

"Upstate New York."

"New York," he repeated. "How exotic."

"Not all that exotic," I said, twirling a finger to point out the architecture around us. "And you Midwesterners seem to do things pretty well."

A smile blossomed on John Creed's face, but there was still something dark in his eyes—something melancholy. Melancholy or not, the words that came out of his mouth were still very teenage boy.

"Even Midwesterners appreciate . . . pretty things," he said, his gaze traveling from my boots to my knot of dark hair. When he reached my gaze again, he gave me a knowing smile. It was a compliment, I guessed, that he thought I looked good, but coming from him, that compliment was a little creepy.

"Cool your jets, Creed," Veronica interrupted. "And before this conversation crosses a line, we should get back to campus. Curfew," she added, then offered Jason a coy smile. "Nice to meet you, Jason."

"Same here," he said, bobbing his head at her, then glancing at me. "Lily."

I bobbed my head at him, a flush rising on my cheeks, and wished I'd stayed in my room.

12

'd spared myself a confrontation with Scout earlier in the day. Since she and Lesley were playing cards at the coffee table when I returned to the suite, two brat packers in line behind me, my time for avoidance was up.

I stopped short in the doorway when I saw them, Amie and Veronica nearly ramming me in the back.

"Down in front," Veronica muttered, squeezing through the door around me, bringing a tornado of shopping bags into the common room.

Scout glanced up when I opened the door. At first, she seemed excited to see me. But when she realized who'd followed me in, her expression morphed into something significantly nastier.

I probably deserved that.

"Shopping?" she asked, an eyebrow arched as Amie and Veronica skirted the couch on their way to Amie's room.

"Fresh air," I said.

Scout made a disdainful sound, shook her head, and dropped her gaze to the fan of cards in her hand. "I think it's your turn," she told Lesley, her voice flat.

Lesley looked up at me. "You were out—with them?"

Barnaby wasn't much for subtlety.

"Fresh air," Scout repeated, then put a card onto the table with a *snap* of sound. "Lily needed *fresh air*."

Amie unlocked her bedroom door and moved inside. But before Veronica went in, she stopped and gazed back at me. "Are you coming?"

"Yes," Scout bit out, flipping one card, then a second and third, onto the table. "You should go. You have shoes to try on, Carrie, or Miranda, or whoever you're pretending to be today."

Veronica snorted, her features screwing into that ratlike pinch. "Better than hanging out here with geeks 'r' us."

"Geeks 'r' us?" I repeated.

"She uses a bag with a pirate symbol on it," Veronica said. "What kind of Disney fantasy is she living?"

Oh, right, I thought. *That's* why I hated these girls. "And yet," I pointed out, "you hung out with me today. And you know Scout and I are friends."

"All evidence to the contrary," Scout muttered.

"We were giving you the benefit of the doubt," Veronica said.

Scout made a sarcastic sound. "No, Lively, you felt *guilty*."

"Ladies," Barnaby said, standing up to reveal the unicorn-print T-shirt she'd matched with a pleated skirt. "I don't think Lily wants to be fought over. This is beneath all of you."

I forced a nod in agreement—although it wasn't *that* horrible to be fought over.

"Uh-huh," Veronica said, then looked at me. "We did the nice thing, Parker. You're new to St. Sophia's, so we offered to help you out. We gave you a warning, and because you handled our little game in the basement, we gave you a chance."

"So very thoughtful," Scout bit out, "to make her a charity case."

Veronica ignored her. "Fine. You want to be honest? Let's be honest. Friends matter, Parker. And if you're not friends with the right people, the fact that you went to St. Sophia's won't make a damn bit of difference. Even St. Sophia's has its misfits, after all." As if to punctuate her remark, she glanced over at Scout and Lesley, then glanced back at me, one eyebrow raised, willing me to get her point.

I'm not sure if she was better or worse for it, but the bitchiness of her comment aside, there was earnestness in her expression. Veronica believed what she was saying—really, truly believed it. Had Veronica been a misfit once?

Not that the answer was all that important right now. "If you're saying that I have to dump one set of friends in order to keep another," I told her, "I think you know what the answer's going to be."

"There are only two kinds of people in this world," Veronica said. "Friends—and enemies."

Was this girl for real? "I'm willing to take my chances."

She snorted indignantly, then walked into Amie's room. "Your loss," she said, the door shutting with a decided *click* behind her.

The room was quiet for a moment.

I blew out a breath, then glanced over at Scout. Ever so calmly, without saying a word or making eye contact, she laid the rest of her cards flat on the table, stood up, marched into her room, and slammed the door.

The coffee table rattled.

I undraped the scarf from around my neck and dropped onto the couch.

Lesley crossed her legs and sat down on the floor, then began to order the deck of cards into a tidy pile. "Granted," she said, "I've only known you for a couple of days, but that was not the smartest thing you've ever done."

"Yeah, I know."

She bobbed her head toward Scout's closed door, which had begun to rattle with the bass of Veruca Salt's "Seether."

"How ballistic do you think she's gonna be?" I asked, my gaze on the vibrating door.

"Intercontinental missile ballistic."

"Yeah, that's what I figured."

Lesley placed her stack of cards gingerly on the tabletop, then looked over at me. "But you're still going in there, right?"

I nodded. "As soon as I'm ready."

"Anything you want in your eulogy?"

Lesley smiled tightly. I gathered up my scarf, rose from the couch, and headed for Scout's door.

"Just tell my parents I loved them," I said, and reached out my hand to knock.

13

Four minutes later, when Scout finally said, "Come in," I opened the door. Scout was on her bed, legs crossed, a spread of books before her.

She lifted her gaze and arched an eyebrow at me. "Well. Look who we have here."

I managed a half smile.

She closed a book, then uncrossed her legs and rose from the bed. After turning down the stereo to a lowish roar, she moved to her shelves and began straightening the items in her tiny museum. "You want to tell me why you've been avoiding me?"

Because I'm afraid, I silently thought. "I'm not avoiding you."

She glanced over with skeptical eyes. "You ignored me all weekend. You've either been holed up in your room or hanging with the brat pack. And since I know there's no love lost there . . ." She shrugged.

"It's nothing."

"You're freaked out about the magic, aren't you? I knew it. I knew it was going to freak you out." She plucked one of the tiny, glittered houses from a shelf, raised it to eye level, and peered through the tiny window. "I shouldn't have told you. Shouldn't have gotten you wrapped up in it." Shaking her head again, she put the house back onto the shelf and picked up the one beside it.

"You'd think I'd be used to this by now," she said, suddenly turning around, the second house in her hand. "I mean, it's not like this is the first time someone has walked away because I'm, you know, weird. You think my parents didn't notice that I could do stuff?"

As if proving her point, she adjusted the house so that it sat in the palm of her outstretched hand, then whispered a series of staccato words.

The interior of the house began to glow.

"Look inside," she quietly said.

"Inside?"

Carefully, she placed the illuminated house back on the shelf, then moved to the side so I could stand beside her. I stepped into the space she'd made, then leaned down and peeked into one of the tiny windows.

The house—this tiny, glittered, paper house on Scout's bookshelf— now bustled with activity. Like a dollhouse come to life, holograms of tiny figures moved inside amongst tiny pieces of furniture, like a living snow globe. Furniture lined the walls; lamps glowed with the spark of whatever life she'd managed to breathe into it with the mere sound of her voice.

I stood up again and glanced at her, eyes wide. "You did that?"

Her gaze on the house, she nodded. "That's my talent—I make magic from words. Like you said, from lists. Letters." She paused. "I did it the first time when I was twelve. I mean, not that particular spell; that's just an animation thing, hardly a page of text, and I condensed it a long time ago. That means I made it shorter," she said at my raised brows. "Like zipping a computer file."

"That's . . . amazing," I said, lifting my gaze to the house again. Shadows passed before the tiny glassine windows, lives being lived in miniature.

"Amazing or not, my mother freaked out. My parents made calls, and I was sent right into private school. I was put in a place away from average kids. Put into a home." She lifted her gaze and glanced around the room. "A prison, of sorts."

That explained Scout's tiny museum—the room she'd made her

own, the four walls she'd filled with the detritus of her life, from junior high to St. Sophia's. It was her magical respite.

Her cell.

"So, yeah," she said after a moment, waving a hand in front of the paper house, the lights in the windows dimming and fading, a tiny world extinguished. "I'm used to rejection because of my magic."

"It's not you," I quietly said.

Scout barked out a laugh. "Yeah, that's the first time I've heard that one." She straightened the house, adjusting it so that it sat neatly beside its neighbors. "If we're going to break up, let's just get it over with, okay?"

I figured out something about Scout in that moment, something that made my heart clench with protectiveness. However brave she might have been in fighting Reapers, in protecting humans, in running through underground tunnels in the middle of the night, fighting back against fire- and earthquake-bearing baddies, she was very afraid of one thing: that I'd abandon her. She was afraid she'd made a friend who was going to walk away like her parents had done, walk out and leave her alone in her room. That's what finally snapped me out of nearly forty-eight hours of freaking out about something that I knew, without a doubt, was going to change my life forever.

"It's probably nothing," I finally said.

I watched the change in her expression—from preparing for defeat, to relief, to crisis management.

"Tell me," she said.

When I frowned back at her, she glared back at me, daring me to argue.

Recognizing the inevitability of my defeat, I sighed, but turned around and lifted up the back of my shirt.

The room went silent.

"You have a darkening," she said.

"A what? I think it's just a funky bruise or something?" It wasn't, of course, just a funky bruise, but I was willing to cling to those last few seconds of normalcy.

"When did you get it?"

I stepped away from her, pulling down my T-shirt and wrapping my arms around my waist self-consciously. "I don't know. A couple of . . . days ago."

Silence.

"Like, a couple of firespell days ago?"

I nodded.

"You've been marked." Her voice was soft, tremulous.

My fingers still knotted in the hem of the shirt, I glanced behind me. Scout stood there, eyes wide, lips parted in shock. "Scout?"

She shook her head, then looked up at me. "This isn't supposed to happen."

The emotion in her voice—awe—raised the hair on my arms and made my stomach sink. "What isn't supposed to happen?"

She stood up, then frowned and nibbled the edge of her lip; then she walked to one end of the room and back again. She was pacing, apparently trying to puzzle out something. "Right after you got hit by the firespell. But you've never had powers before, and you don't have powers now—" She paused and glanced over at me. "Do you?"

"Are you kidding? Of course I don't."

She resumed talking so quickly, I wasn't sure she'd even heard my answer. "I mean, I guess it's possible." She hit the end of the room and, neatly sidewiping a footlocker, turned around again. "I'd have to check the *Grimoire* to be sure. If you don't have power, then you weren't really triggered, but maybe it's some kind of tattoo from the firespell? I can't imagine how you could have gotten a darkening without the power—"

"Scout."

"But maybe it's happened before."

"*Scout.*" My voice was loud enough that she finally stopped and looked at me.

"Hmm?"

I pointed behind me. "Hello? My back?"

"Right, right." She walked back to me and began to pull up the hem of her shirt.

"Um, I'm not sure stripping down is the solution here, Scout."

"Prude," she said dryly, but when she reached me again, she turned around.

At the small of her back, in pale green, was a mark like mine—well, not exactly like mine. The symbols inside her circle were different, but the general idea was the same.

"Oh, my God," I said.

Scout dropped the back of her T-shirt and turned, nodding her head. "Yep. So I guess it's settled now."

"Settled?"

"You're one of us."

14

Forty minutes—and Scout's rifling through a two-foot-high stack of books—later, we were headed downstairs. If she'd found anything in the giant leather volumes she pulled out of a plastic tub beneath her bed, she didn't say. The only conclusion she'd reached was that she needed to talk to the rest of the Adepts in Enclave Three, so she'd pulled out her phone, popped open the keyboard and, fingers flying, sent out a dispatch. And then we were on our way.

The route we took this time was different still from the last couple of trips I'd made. We used a new doorway to the basement level—this one a wooden panel in a side hallway in the main building—and descended a narrower, steeper staircase. Once we were in the basement, we walked a maze through limestone hallways. I was beginning to think the labyrinth on the floor was more than just decoration. It served as a pretty good symbol of what lay beneath the convent.

Despite how confusing it was, Scout clearly knew the route, barely pausing at the corners, her speed quick and movements efficient. She moved silently, striding through the hallways and tunnels like a woman on a mission. I stumbled at a half run, half walk behind her, just trying to keep up. My speed wasn't much helped by my stomach's rolling, both because we were actually going into the basement again—by choice—and for the reason we were going there.

Because I was her mission.

Or so I assumed.

"You could slow down a little, you know."

"Slowing down would make it harder for me to punish you by making you keep up," she said, but came to a stop as we reached the dead end of a limestone corridor that ended in a nondescript metal door.

"Why are you punishing me?"

Scout reached up, pulled a key from above the threshold, and slipped it into the lock. When the door popped open, she put back the key, then glanced at me. "Um, you abandoned me for the brat pack?"

"Abandoned is a harsh word."

"So are they," she pointed out, holding the door open so I could move inside. "The last time you hung out with them, they put you in the hospital."

"That was actually your fault."

"Details," she said.

My feet still on the limestone, hand on the threshold of the door, I peeked inside. She was leading me into an old tunnel. It was narrow, with an arched ceiling, the entire tunnel paved in concrete, narrow tracks along the concrete floor. Lights in round, industrial fittings were suspended from the ceiling every dozen yards or so. The half illumination didn't do much for the ambience. A couple of inches of rusty water covered the tracks on the floor, and the concrete walls were covered with graffiti—words of every shape and size, big and small, monotone and multicolored.

"What is this?"

"Chicago Tunnel Company Railroad," she said, nudging me forward. I took a step into dirty water, glad I'd worn boots for my shopping excursion, and glad I still had on a jacket. It was chilly, probably because we were underground.

"It's an old railroad line," Scout said, then stepped beside me. Cold, musty air stirred as she closed the door behind us. Somewhere down the line, water dripped. "The cars used to move between downtown buildings to deliver coal and dump ash and stuff. Parts of the tunnel run under the river, and some of those parts were accidentally breached by the city, so if you see a tsunami, find a bulkhead and make a run for it."

"I'll make a point of it."

Scout reached into her messenger bag and pulled out two flash-lights. She took one, then handed me the second. While the tunnels were lit, it made me feel better to have the weight in my hand.

Flashlights in hand, we walked. We took one branch, then an-other, then another, making so many turns that I had no clue which direction we were actually moving in.

"So this mark thing," I began, as we stepped gingerly through murky water. "What is it, exactly?"

"They're called darkenings. We all have them," Scout answered, the beam of light swinging as she moved. "All the members of the 'Dark Elite,'" she flatly added, using her hands, flashlight and all, to gesture some air quotes. "That's what some of the Reapers call us—all of us—who have magic. Elite, I guess, because we're gifted. They think we're special, *better,* because we have magic. And dark because the darkenings are supposed to appear when the magic appears. Well, except in your case." She stopped and looked at me. "Still no powers, right?"

"Not that I'm aware of, no. Is that why we're down here? Are you going to prod me or poke me or something, to figure out if I have secret powers? Like a chick on an alien spacecraft?"

"And you think I'm the odd one," she muttered. "No, Scully, we aren't going to probe you. We're just going to talk to the Adepts and see what they have to say about your new tat. No bigs." She shrugged non-chalantly, then started walking again.

Ten or fifteen minutes later, Scout stopped before a door made up of giant wooden beams, two golden hinges running across it, an arch in the top. A large numeral "3" was elegantly carved into the lintel above the door. And on the door was the same symbol I'd seen in the model room—a circle with a *Y* inside it.

This was Enclave Three, I assumed.

Scout flipped off her flashlight, then held out her hand; I pressed my flashlight into her palm. She flicked it off and deposited them both back in her messenger bag.

"Okay," she said, looking over at me. "I suppose I should prep you for this. The other seven Adepts in ET should be here. Katie and Smith are our Varsity Adepts. You remember what that means?"

"They're the college kids," I answered. "And Junior Varsity is high school. You just told me on Friday."

"You've brat-packed since then," she muttered. "Your IQ has probably dropped."

I gave her a snarky look.

"Anywho," she said, ignoring the look, "Katie's a manipulator. Literally and figuratively. You know, in history, when they talk about the Salem witch trials, about how innocent girls and boys were convinced to do all these horrible things because some witch made them?"

I'd read *The Crucible* in English last year (probably just like every other sophomore), so I nodded.

"Yeah, well, they probably *were* convinced. That stuff wasn't a myth. Katie's not a wicked witch or anything, but she's got the same skills."

"Well, that's just downright disturbing," I said.

"Yeah." She nodded, then patted my arm. "Sleep well tonight. Anyway, Katie manipulates, and Smith—and, yes, that's his first name—levitates. He lifts heavy stuff, raises things in the air. As for JV, you know me, Michael and Jason, obvs, and there are three more. Jamie and Jill, those are the twins. Paul's the one with the curls."

"You said you were a spellcaster?"

"Binder. Spellbinder."

"Okay. So what are these guys? Michael and the rest of them. What can they do?"

"Oh, sure, um"—she shifted her feet, her gaze on the ceiling as she itemized—"um, Jamie and Jill have elemental powers. Fire and ice."

"They have firespell?" I wondered aloud.

"Oh, sorry, no. Jamie can manipulate fire, literally—like a fire-starter. Set stuff ablaze, create smoke, general pyromania. She can work with the element without getting burned. Firespell is different—it's not about fire, really, but about power, at least we think. There aren't any Adepts with firespell, so we kind of go off what we've seen in action. Anywho, you put Jamie, Jill, and me together, and we're one medieval witch," she said, with what sounded like a fake laugh. "Paul is a warrior. A man of battle. Ridiculous moves, like something out of a kung fu movie. Michael is a reader."

"What's a reader?"

"Well, I bind spells, right? I take words of power, charms and I translate them into action, like the house I showed you."

I nodded.

"Michael reads objects. He can feel them out, determine their history, hear what they're saying about things that happened, conditions."

"Well that's . . . weird. I mean cool, but weird."

She shrugged. "Unusual, but handy. Architecture speaks to him. Literally."

"And for all that, you two still aren't dating."

She narrowed her gaze. "I'm not sure I should let you two talk to each other anymore. Now, are you done procrastinating? Can we get on with this?"

"I'm not procrastinating," I said, procrastinating. "What about Jason?" I already suspected, of course, what Jason's magic was. But he hadn't exactly confirmed it, and my own suspicions—that he had some kind of animal-related power—were strange enough that I wasn't ready to put them out there. On the other hand, how many teenage boys growled when they were attacked?

Okay, when you put it that way, it actually didn't sound that rare.

Scout dropped her gaze and fiddled with her messenger bag. "Jason's power isn't for me to tell. If he's ready for that, he'll tell you."

"I—I have an idea."

She went quiet and slowly lifted her gaze to mine. "An idea?"

We looked at each other for a minute, silently, each assessing the other: *Do you know what I know? How can I confirm it without giving it away?*

"I'll let you talk to him about that," she finally said, raising her hand to the door. "Are you ready *now*?"

"Are they gonna wig out that you're bringing me?"

"It's a good possibility," she said, then rapped her fist in a rhythmic pattern. Knock. Knock, knock. *Bang*. Knock.

"Secret code?" I asked.

"Warning," she said. "Jamie and Paul are dating. In case we're early, I don't want to walk in on that."

The joke helped ease my nerves, but only a little. As soon as she touched the door handle, my stomach began rolling again.

"Welcome to the jungle," she said, and opened the door.

The jungle was a big, vaulted room, of a quality I wouldn't have expected to see in an abandoned railway tunnel far beneath Chicago. It looked like a meeting hall, the walls covered in paintings made up of tiny, mosaic tiles, the ceilings girded with thick, wooden beams. It had the same kind of look as the convent—big scale, careful work, earthy materials. The room was empty of furniture—completely empty except for the seven kids who'd turned to stare at the door when it opened. There were three girls and four guys, including Michael and Jason.

Jason of the deadly blue eyes and currently frigid stare.

The room went completely silent, all fourteen of those eyes on us as we stepped into the room. Scout squeezed my hand supportively.

Silently, they moved around and formed a semicircle facing us, as if containing a threat. I shuffled a little closer to Scout and surveyed the judges.

Jamie and Jill were the obvious twins, both tallish and lanky, with long auburn hair and blue eyes. Paul was tall, lean, coffee-skinned and very cute, his hair a short mop of tiny, spiral curls.

The guy and girl in the middle, who looked older than the rest of them—early college, maybe—stepped forward, fury on their faces. I guessed these were Katie and Smith. Katie was cheerleader cute, with a bob of shoulder-length brown hair, green eyes, a long T-shirt, and ballet flats paired with jeans. Smith—shaggy brown hair pasted to his forehead emo-style—wore a dingy, plaid shirt. He was the rebel type, I assumed.

"Green," he bit out, "you'd better have a damn good reason for calling us in and, more important, for bringing a *regular* in here."

Okay, so pasty hair was clearly not impressed with me.

Scout crossed her arms, preparing for battle. "A," she said, "this is Lily Parker, the girl who took a hit of firespell to save us and wound up in a paper nightgown in the LaSalle Street Clinic because of it. Ring any bells?"

I actually took a hit because I'd tripped, but since the Adepts' expressions softened after she passed along that little factoid, I kept the truth to myself.

"B," Scout continued, "I have a damn good reason. We need to show you something."

Katie spoke up. "You could have showed us something without her being here."

"I can't show you what I need to show you without her being here." Her explanation was met with silence, but she kept going. "You have to know that I wouldn't have brought her here if it wasn't absolutely necessary. Trust me—it's necessary. The Reapers have already seen her, and they already think she's associated with us. They get ambitious and come knocking on our door tonight, and she's in even more trouble. She's here as a favor to us."

Katie and Smith glanced at each other, and then she whispered something to him.

"Five minutes," Smith finally said. "You have five minutes."

Scout didn't need it; it took two seconds for her to drop the bomb. "I think she might be one of us."

Silence, until Katie made a snorty, skeptical sound. "One of us?

Why in God's name would you think she's one of us? She's a regular, and getting hit with a blast isn't going to change that."

"Really?" Scout asked. "You don't think getting hit with a dose of firespell is going to have an effect? Given that we're all bouncing around Chicago with magical gifts, that's kind of a narrow-minded perspective, isn't it, Katie?"

Katie arched an arrogant brow at Scout. "You need to watch your step, Green."

Michael stepped forward, hands raised in peace. "Hey, if there's something we need to figure out here, the fewer preconceptions, the better. Scout, if you have something you need us to see, you'd better show it now."

Scout glanced over at me, nodded her head decidedly, then spun her finger in the air.

"Turn around," she said. I glanced around the room, not entirely eager to pull up my shirt before an assemblage of people I didn't know—and a boy I potentially wanted to know better. But it needed to be done, so I twisted around, pulled my shirt from the waist of my skirt, and lifted it just enough to show the mark across my lower back.

Their faces pinched in concentration and thought, the group of them moved around me to stare at my back.

"It's a darkening," Jason said, then lifted his killer blue eyes to mine. "Is it okay if I touch it?"

I swallowed, then nodded and gripped the hem of the shirt, still between my fingers, a little tighter. He stretched out his hand. His fingers just grazed my back, my skin tingling beneath his fingers. I stifled a shudder, but goose bumps arose on my arms. This wasn't the time or the place for me to get giggly about Jason's attentions, but that didn't make the effect any less powerful. It felt like a tingle of electricity moving across my skin, like that first dip into a hot bath on a cold night—spine tingling.

"It's definitely like ours," Jason agreed, standing again. "Have you developed any powers?" he quietly asked me.

I shook my head.

"I have no idea how she got it," Jason finally concluded, his brow furrowed. "But it's like ours. Or close enough, anyway."

"Yeah," Scout said, "but you nailed it—there's something different about hers, isn't there? The edges are fuzzier. Like a tattoo, but the ink bled."

"What could that mean, Green?" Katie asked.

She shrugged. "I have no clue."

"Research is your field," Smith reminded her. "There's nothing in the *Grimoire?*"

"Not that I could find, and I checked the index for every entry I could think of." I assumed the *Grimoire* was the giant leather-bound book she'd skimmed through before deciding to notify the elders.

Smith raised his gaze to me. "I understand that you've been provided with the basics about our enclave, our struggle, our gifts."

I nodded.

"And you're sure you haven't . . . become aware of any powers since you were hit?"

"I'd remember," I assured him.

"Maybe this is just a symbol of the fact that she was hit?" Jason suggested, frowning, head tilted as he gazed at my back. "Like, I don't know, a stamp of the shot she took?"

"I really don't know," Scout said quietly.

Their conversations got quieter, like scientists mumbling as they considered a prime specimen. I stared at the wall at the other end of the room while they whispered behind me and tried to figure out who—or what—I'd become.

Eventually, Smith straightened and, like obedient pups, the rest of the group followed suit and spread out again. I pulled my shirt back down and turned to face them.

Smith shook his head. "All we know is that she's marked. It might not be a darkening. Anything else is just speculation."

"Speculation?" Paul asked. "She's got a darkening, just like ours."

"Not exactly like ours," Katie reminded him.

I watched Michael struggle to keep his expression neutral. "Enough like ours," he countered, "to make it evident that she's like us. That she's one of us."

Katie shook her head. "You're missing the point. She's already told us she doesn't have skills, magic, power. Nothing but a fancy bruise." As if to confirm that suspicion, she turned her green-eyed gaze on me. "She's not one of us."

"A fancy bruise?" Scout repeated. "You're kidding, right?"

Katie shrugged, the movement and her expression condescending. "I'm just saying."

"Hey," Smith said, apparently deciding to intervene. "Let it go. It's better for her, anyway. Hanging out down here isn't fun and games. This job is dangerous, it's hard, and it's exhausting. This might feel like rejection. It's actually luck."

The room went quiet. When Scout spoke again, her voice was soft, but earnest.

"I know my place," she said, "and we all know this isn't the easiest job in the world. But if she's one of us, if she's part of us, she needs to know. *We* need to know."

"There's no evidence that she's one of us, Scout," Smith said. "A mark isn't enough. A mark won't stop Reapers, and it won't save regulars, and it won't help us. This isn't up for debate. You bring me some evidence—real evidence—that it's a darkening, and we'll talk about it again."

I could feel Scout's frustration, could see it in the stiffness in her shoulders. She looked at her colleagues.

"Paul? Jamie? Jill? Jason?" When she met Michael's gaze, her expression softened. "Michael?"

He looked down for a moment, considering, then up at her again. "I'm sorry, Scout, but I'm with Smith on this one. She's not like us. She wasn't made the way we were. She wasn't born with power, and the only reason she has a mark is because she got hit. If we let her in anyway, if we play devil's advocate, she takes our attention away from everything else we have to deal with. We can't afford that right now."

"Her being damaged isn't reason enough," Katie put in.

I arched an eyebrow. Scout may have had to play nice for hierarchy reasons, but I (obviously) wasn't part of this group.

"I am not *damaged*," I said. "I'm a bystander who got wrapped up in something I didn't want to be wrapped up in because you couldn't keep the bad guys in hand."

"The point is," Smith said, "you weren't born like us. The only thing you've got right now is a symbol of nothing."

"There's no need to be harsh," Michael said. "It's not like she got branded on purpose."

"Are you sure about that?"

The room went silent, all eyes on Katie.

"Are you suggesting," Scout bit out, "that she faked the darkening?"

Katie gazed at her with unapologetic snarkiness. This girl had college brat pack written all over her.

"So much for 'all for one and one for all,'" Scout muttered. "I can't believe you'd suspect that a person who'd never seen a darkening before faked having one forty-eight hours after she was put in the hospital because she took a full-on dose of firespell and managed to survive it. And you know what's worse? I can't believe you'd doubt me." She pressed a finger into her chest. *"Me."*

The JV Adepts shared heavy looks.

"Regulars put us all at risk. They raise our profile, they get in the way, they serve as distractions." Jason lifted his chin, and eyes of sea blue stared out. He gazed at me, anger in his eyes. My slight at the mall must have hurt more than I'd thought.

"Until we know more, she's a regular, and that's all she is. No offense," he added, his gaze on me.

"None taken," I lied back to him.

"We have other business to discuss," Smith said. "Escort her home."

"That's it?" Scout's voice contained equal parts desperation and frustration.

"Bring us something we can use," Smith said. "Some*one* we can use, and we'll talk."

Scout offered a sarcastic salute. "Let's go," she said to me, her hand on my arm, leading me away as the group turned inward to begin their next plan.

We were fifty yards away from the room before she spoke. "I'm sorry."

"It's not a problem," I said, not entirely sure if I believed that. I hadn't wanted to be the victim of the firespell attack, hadn't wanted to find the mark on my back, hadn't been thrilled about being dragged to a meeting of Adepts, or becoming one. I knew what Scout went through. Late-night meetings. Fear. Worry. Bearing the responsibility of protecting the public from soul-sucking adults and hell-bent teenagers—and not just your run-of-the-mill soul-sucking adults and hell-bent teenagers. I'd seen the exhaustion on her face, even as I appreciated her sense of right and wrong, the fact that she put herself out there to protect people who didn't know she was burning the candle at both ends.

So even though it wasn't something I'd asked for, or something I thought I wanted, it was hard not to feel rejected by Smith and Katie and the rest of Enclave Three. I was already the new girl—a Sagamore fish out of water in a school where everyone else had years of history together and lots of money to play with. Being treated like an outcast wasn't something I'd signed up for.

"I'll have to keep an eye on you," she said as we reentered the main building and headed across the labyrinth, "in case anything happens."

"In case I get attacked by a Reaper, or in case I suddenly develop the ability to summon unicorns?" My voice was toast-dry.

"Oh, please," Scout said. "Don't take that tone with me. You know you'd love to have a minion. Someone at your beck and call. Someone to do your bidding. How many times have you said to yourself, 'Self, I need a unicorn to run errands and such'?"

"Not that often till lately, to be real honest," I said, but managed a small smile.

"Yeah, well, welcome to the jungle," she said again, but this time, darkly.

It was nearly midnight by the time I was tucked into bed in a tank top and shorts, the St. Sophia's blanket pulled up to my chin. One hand behind my head, I stared at the stars on the ceiling, sleep elusive, probably because I was already too well-rested. After all, I'd spent half the weekend either hunkered beneath the sheets, an ostrich with its head in cotton, or ignoring my best friend by lollygagging on Michigan Avenue. I'd self-medicated with luxury goods. Well, by watching other girls buy luxury goods, anyway.

I wasn't thrilled with what I'd done, with my abandonment. But, whether I was the perfect best friend or not, the sounds of traffic softened, and I finally, oh so slowly, fell asleep.

15

I woke to pounding on the door. Suddenly vaulted from sleep, I sat up and pushed tangled hair from my face. "Who's there?"

"We're running late!" came Scout's frantic voice from the other side. I glanced over at the alarm clock. Class started in fifteen minutes.

"Frick," I said, adrenaline jolting me to full consciousness. I threw off the blankets and jumped for the door. Unlocking and opening it, I found Scout in the doorway in long-sleeved pajamas and thick blue socks.

I arched an eyebrow at the ensemble. "It's still September, right?"

Scout rolled her eyes. "I'm cold a lot. Sue me."

"How about I just take a shower?"

She nodded and held up two energy bars. "Get in, get out, and when you're done, art history, here we come."

Have you ever had one of those days where you give up on being really clean, and settle for being *largely* clean? Where you don't have time for the entire scrubbing and exfoliating regime, so you settle for the basics? Where brushing your teeth becomes the most vigorous part of your cleaning ritual?

Yeah, welcome to Monday morning at St. Sophia's School for (Slightly Grimy) Girls.

When I was (mostly) clean, I met Scout in the common room. She was sporting the preppy look today—Mary Janes, knee-high socks, oxford shirt and tie.

"You look very—"

"Nerdy?" she suggested. "I'm trying a new philosophy today."

"A new philosophy?" I asked, as we shut the common room door and headed down the hall. She handed over the energy bar she'd shown off earlier. I ripped down the plastic and bit off a chunk.

"Look the nerd, *be* the nerd," she said, with emphasis. "I figure this look could boost my grades by fifteen to twenty percent."

"Fifteen to twenty percent? That's impressive. You think it'll work?"

"I'm sure it won't," she said. "But I'm giving it a shot. I'm taking positive steps."

"Studying would be another positive step," I pointed out.

"Studying interferes with my world saving."

"It's unfortunate you can't get excused absences for that."

"I know, right?"

"And speaking of saving the world," I said, "did you have a call after we got back last night? Or did you just sleep late?"

"I sleep with earplugs," she said, half-answering the question. "The radio alarm came on, but it wasn't loud enough, so I dreamed about REO Speedwagon and Phil Collins for forty-five minutes. Suffice it to say, I can feel it coming in the air tonight."

"*Dum-dum, dum-dum, dum-dum, dum-dum, dum, dum,*" I said, repeating the drum lead-in, although without my usual air drumming. My reputation was off to a rocky-enough start as it was.

We took the stairs to the first floor, then headed through the corridor to the classroom building. The lockers were our next stop. I took the last bite of the energy bar—some kind of chewy fruit, nut, and granola combination—then folded up the wrapper and slipped it into my bag.

At our lockers, I opened my messenger bag and peeked inside. I already had my art history book, so I kneeled to my lower-level locker, opened it, and grabbed my trig book, my second class of the day. I'd just closed the door, my palm still pressed against slick wood, when I felt a tap on my shoulder.

I turned and found M.K. beside me—grinning.

"Fell down the stairs, did you?"

Scout slipped books into her locker, then slammed the door shut before giving M.K. a narrow-eyed glare. "Hey, Betty, go find Veronica and leave us in peace."

M.K. looked confused by the reference, but she shook it off with a toss of her long dark hair. "How lame are you when you can't even walk up a flight of stairs without falling down?" Her voice was just a shade too loud, obviously intended to get the other girls' attention, to make them stare and whisper and, presumably, embarrass me.

Fortunately, I didn't embarrass that easily. On the other hand, I couldn't exactly correct her. If I threw "secret basement room" at these girls, there'd be a mad rush to find out what lurked downstairs. That wasn't going to help the Adepts, so I opted to deflect.

"How lame do you have to be to push a girl down the stairs?"

"I didn't push anyone down the stairs," she clipped out.

"So you had nothing to do with my hospital visit?"

Crimson rose on her cheeks.

It was mean, I know, but I had Adepts to protect. Well, one nose-ringed Adept to protect, anyway. Besides, I didn't actually make an accusation. I just asked the right question.

As school bells began to peal, she nailed us both with a glare, then turned on a heel and stalked away, a monogrammed leather backpack between her shoulder blades.

I'm not sure what, or how much, the brat pack had spilled around school about my "fall" and my clinic visit, but I felt the looks and heard the whispers. They lasted through the morning's art history, trig, and civics classes, girls in identical plaid lowering their heads together—or passing tiny, folded notes—to share what they'd heard about my weekend.

Luckily, the rumors were pretty tame. I hadn't heard anything about bizarre rooms beneath the building, evil teenagers roaming the hallways, or Scout's involvement—other than the fact that people "wouldn't be surprised" if she'd had something to do with it.

Apparently, I wasn't the only one at St. Sophia's who thought she was a little odd.

I glanced over at her during civics—punky blond and brown hair in tiny ponytails, fingernails painted glossy black, a tiny hoop in her nose. I was kind of surprised Foley let her get away with all that, but I thanked God Scout stood out in this bastion of über-normalcy.

After civics, we headed back to our lockers.

"Let's go run an errand," she said, opening her locker and transferring her books.

I arched a skeptical eyebrow.

"Perfectly mundane mission," she said, closing the door again. She adjusted her skull-and-crossbones messenger bag and gave me a wink.

I followed as she weaved through girls in the locker hall, then through the Great Hall and main building to the school's front door. This one was an off-campus mission, apparently.

Outside, we found the sky a muted steel gray, the city all but windless. The weather was moody—as if we were on the cusp of something nasty. As if the sky was preparing to open on us all.

"Let's go," Scout said, and we took the steps and headed down the sidewalk. We made a left, walking down Erie and away from Michigan Avenue and the garden of stone thorns.

"Here's the thing about Chicago," she began.

"Speak it, sister."

"The brat pack gave you the Sex and the Windy City tour. The shopping on Michigan is nice, but it's not all there is. There's an entire city out there—folks who've lived here all their lives, folks who've *worked* here all their lives, blue-collar jobs, dirt under their fingernails, without shopping for thousand-dollar handbags." She looked up at a high-rise as we passed. "Nearly three million people in a city that's been here for a hundred and seventy years. The architecture, the art, the history, the politics. I know you're not from here, and you've only been here a week, and your heart is probably back in Sagamore, but this is an amazing place, Lil."

I watched as she gazed at the buildings and architecture around her, love in her eyes.

"I want to run for city council," she suddenly said, as we crossed the street and passed facing Italian restaurants. Tourists formed a line outside each, menus in hand, excitement in their eyes as they prepared to sample Chicago's finest.

"City council?" I asked her. "Like, Chicago's city council? You want to run for office?"

She nodded her head decisively. "I love this city. I want to serve it someday. I mean, it depends on where I live and who's in the ward and whether the seat is open or not, but I want to give something back, you know?"

I had no idea Scout had political ambitions, much less that she'd given the logistics that much thought. She was only sixteen, and I was impressed. I also wasn't sure if I should feel pity for her parents, who were missing out on her general awesomeness, or if I should thank them—was Scout who she was because her parents had freaked about her magic, and deposited her in a boarding school?

She bobbed her head at a bodega that sat kitty-corner on the next block. "In there," she said, and we crossed the street. She opened the door, a bell on the handle jingling as we moved inside.

"Yo," she said, a hand in the air to wave at the clerk as she walked straight to the fountain drink machine.

"Scout," said the guy at the counter, whom I pegged at nineteenish or twenty, and whose dark eyes were on the comic book spread on the counter in front of him, a spill of short dreadlocks around his face. "Refill time?"

"Refill time," Scout agreed. I stayed at the counter while she attacked the fountain machine, yanking a gigantic plastic cup from a dispenser. With mechanical precision, she pushed the cup under the ice dispenser, peeked over the rim as ice spilled into it, then released the cup, emptied out a few, and repeated the whole process again until she was satisfied she'd gotten exactly the right amount. When she was done with the ice, she went straight for the strawberry soda, and the process started again.

"She's particular, isn't she?" I wondered aloud.

The clerk snorted, then glanced up at me, chocolate brown eyes alight with amusement. "Particular hardly covers it. She's an addict when it comes to the sugar water." His brow furrowed. "I don't know you."

"Lily Parker," I said. "First year at St. Sophia's."

"You one of the brat pack?"

"She is mos' def' not one of the brat pack," Scout said, joining us at the counter, as she poked a straw into the top of her soda. She took a sip, eyes closed in ecstasy. I had to bite back a laugh.

Lips still wrapped around the straw, Scout opened one eye and squinted evilly at me. "Don't mock the berry," she said when she paused to take a breath, then turned back to the kid behind the counter. "She tried, unsuccessfully, to join the brat pack, at least until she realized how completely lame they are. Oh, and Derek, this is Lily. You two are buds now."

I grinned at Derek. "Glad to meet you."

"Ditto."

"Derek is a Montclare grad who's moved into the wonderful world of temping at his dad's store while working on his degree in underwater basketweaving at U of C." She batted catty eyes at Derek. "I got that right, didn't I, D?"

"Nuclear physics," he corrected.

"Close enough," Scout said with a wink, then stepped back to trail the tips of her fingers across the boxes of candy in front of the counter. "Are we thinking Choco-Loco or Caramel Buddy? Am I in the mood for crunchy or chewy today?" She held up two red and orange candy bars, then waggled them at us. "Thoughts? I'm polling, checking the pulse of the nation. Well, of our little corner of River North, anyway."

"Choco-Loco."

"Caramel Buddy."

We said the names simultaneously, which resulted in our grinning at each other while Scout continued the not-so-silent debate over her candy choices. Crispy rice was apparently a crucial component. Nuts were a downgrade.

"So," Derek asked, "are you from Chicago?"

"Sagamore," I said. "New York state."

"You're a long way from home, Sagamore."

I glanced through the windows toward St. Sophia's towers, the prickly spires visible even though we were a couple of blocks away. "Tell me about it," I said, then looked back at Derek. "You did your time at MA?"

"I was MA born and bred. My dad owns a chain of bodegas"—he bobbed his head toward the shelves in the store—"and he wanted more for me. I got four years of ties and uniforms and one hell of an SAT score to show for it."

"Derek's kind of a genius," Scout said, placing the Choco-Loco on the counter. "Biggest decision I'll make all day, probably."

Derek chuckled. "Now, I know that's a lie." He held up the front of the comic book, which featured a busty, curvy superheroine in a skintight latex uniform. "Your decision making is a little more akin to this, wouldn't you say?"

My eyes wide, I glanced from the comic book to Scout, who snorted gleefully at Derek's comparison, then leaned in toward her. "He knows?" I whispered.

She didn't answer, which I took as an indication that she didn't want to have that conversation now, at least not in front of company. She pulled a patent leather wallet from her bag, then pulled a crisp twenty-dollar bill from the wallet.

I arched an eyebrow at the gleaming patent leather—and the designer logo that was stamped across it.

"What?" she asked, sliding the wallet back into her bag. "It's not real; just a good fake I picked up in Wicker Park. There's no need to look like a peasant."

"Even the humblest of girls can have a thing for the good stuff,"

Derek said, a grin quirking one corner of his mouth, then lowered his gaze to the comic book again. I sensed that we'd lost his attention.

"Later, D," Scout said, and headed for the quick shop's door.

Without lifting his gaze, Derek gave us a wave. We walked outside, the sky still gray and moody, the city eerily quiet, and toward St. Sophia's.

"Okay," I said. "Let me get this straight. You wouldn't tell me—your roommate—about what you were involved in, but the guy who runs the quick shop down the street gets to know?"

Scout nibbled on the end of one of the sticks of chocolate in her Choco-Loco wrapper, and slid me a sideways glance as she munched. "He's cute, right?"

"Oh, my God, totally. But not the point."

"He has a girlfriend, Sam. They've been together for years."

"Bummer, but let's keep our eyes on the ball." We separated as we walked around a clutch of tourists, then came back together when we'd passed the knot of them. "Why does he get to know?"

"You're assuming I told him," Scout said as we paused at the corner, waiting for a crossing signal in heavy lunchtime traffic. "And while I'm glad he's supportive—seriously, he's *so* pretty."

"It's the hair," I suggested.

"And the eyes. Totally chocolatey."

"Agreed. You were saying?"

"I didn't tell him," Scout said, leading us across the street when the light changed. "Remember what I told you about kids who seemed off? Depressed?"

"Humans targeted by Reapers?"

"Exactly," she said with a nod. "Derek was a near victim. He and his mom were superclose, but she died a couple of years ago—when he was a freshman. Unfortunately, he rushed the wrong house at U of C; two of his fraternity brothers were Reapers. They took advantage of the grief, made friends with him, dragged him down even further."

"They"—how was I supposed to phrase this?—"took his energy, or whatever?"

Scout nodded gravely as we moved through lunch-minded Chicagoans. "There wasn't much left of him. A shell, nearly, by the time we got there. He was barely going to class, barely getting out of bed. Depressed."

"Jeez," I quietly said.

"I know. Luckily, he wasn't too far gone, but it was close. We identified him and had to clear away some nasty siphoning spells—that's what the younger Reapers used to drain him, to send the energy to the elders who needed it. We got him out and away from the Reapers. We gave him space, got him rested and fed, put him back in touch with his family and real friends. The rest—the healing—was all him." She scowled, and her voice went tight. "Then we gave his Reaper 'friends' a good talking-to about self-sacrifice."

"Did it work?"

"Well, we managed to bring one of them back. The other's still a frat boy in the worst connotation of the phrase. Anyway, Derek's one of a handful of people who know about us, about Adepts. We call them the community." I remembered the term from the conversation with Smith and Katie. "People without magic who know about our existence, usually because they were caught in the crossfire. Sometimes, they're grateful and they provide a service later. Information. Or maybe just a few minutes of normalcy."

"Strawberry soda," I added.

"That is the most important thing," she agreed. She pulled me from the flow of pedestrian traffic to the curb at the edge of the street. "Look around you, Lil. Most people are oblivious to the currents around them, to the hum and flow of the city. We're part of that hum and flow. The magic is part of that hum and flow. Sometimes people say they love living in Chicago—the energy, the earthiness, the sense of being part of something bigger than you are."

Glancing around the neighborhood, across glass and steel and concrete, the city buzzing around us, I could see their point.

"There have always been a handful of people who know about us. Who know what we do, know what we fight for," Scout said as we rounded the corner and walked toward St. Sophia's.

And there he was.

Jason stood in front of the stone wall, hands in his pockets, in khaki pants and a navy blue sweater with an embroidered gold crest on the pocket. His dark blond hair was tidy, and his eyes had turned a muted, steel blue beneath the cloudy sky, beneath those dark eyebrows and long lashes.

Those eyes were aimed, laserlike, in my direction.

Scout, who'd taken a heartening sip of strawberry-flavored sugar water after relaying Derek's history, released the straw just long enough to snark. "It appears you have a visitor."

"He could be here for you," I absently said.

"Uh, no. Jason Shepherd does not make trips to St. Sophia's to see me. If he needed me, he could text me."

I made a vague sound, neither agreeing nor disagreeing with her assessment, but my nerves apparently agreed. My throat was tight; my stomach fluttered. Had this boy—this boy with those ridiculous blue eyes—come here to see me?

Right before I melted into a ridiculous puddle of girl, I remembered that I was still irritated with Jason and wiped the dopey smile off my face. I'd show him "distraction."

"Shepherd," Scout said when we reached him, "what brings you to our fine institution of higher learning?" She managed those ten words before her lips found the straw again. I realized I'd found Scout's pacifier, should it ever prove necessary—strawberry soda.

Jason bobbed his head at Scout, then looked at me again. "Can I talk to you?"

I glanced at Scout, who checked her watch. "You've got seven minutes before class," she said, then motioned with a hand. "Give me your bag, and I'll stick it in your chair."

"Thanks," I said, and made the transfer.

Jason and I watched Scout trot down the sidewalk and disappear into the building. It wasn't until she was gone that he looked at me again.

"About yesterday." He paused, eyes on the sidewalk, as if deciding what to say. "It's not personal."

I arched my eyebrows. I wasn't letting him off the hook that easily.

He looked away, wet his lips, then found my gaze again. "When you were in the hospital, we talked about the Reapers. About the fact that we're in the minority?"

"A splinter cell, you said."

He bobbed his head. "In a way. We're like a resistance movement. A rebellion. We aren't equally matched. The Reapers—*we* call them Reapers—they're not just a handful of misfits. They're *all* the gifted— all the Dark Elite—except for us."

"All except for you?"

"Unfortunately. That means the odds are stacked against us, Lily." He took a step forward, a step toward me. "Our position is dangerous. And if you don't have magic, I don't want you wrapped up in it. Not if you don't have a way to defend yourself. Scout can't always be there . . . and I don't want you to get hurt."

An orchestra could have been playing on the St. Sophia's grounds and I wouldn't have heard it. I heard nothing but the pounding of my heartbeat in my ears, saw nothing but the blue of his lash-fringed eyes.

"Thank you," I quietly said.

"That's not to say I wasn't bitter that you ignored me Sunday."

I nibbled the edge of my lip. "Look, I'm sorry about that—"

Jason shook his head. "You saw the mark, and you needed time to process. We've all been there. I mean, you could have chosen better company, but I understand the urge to get away. To escape." Jason looked down at the sidewalk, eyebrows pulled together in concentration. "When I found out who I was, *what* I was, I ran away. Hopped a Greyhound bus and headed to my grandmother's house in Alabama. I camped out there for three weeks that summer. I was thirteen," he said, raising his gaze again. His eyes had switched color from turquoise to chartreuse, and something animal appeared in his expression— something intense.

"You're a . . . wolf?" I said it like a question, but I suddenly had no doubt, and no fear, about the possibility that he was something far scarier than Scout and the rest of the Adepts.

"I am," he said, his voice a little deeper than it had been a moment ago. Goose bumps rose on my arms, and a chill slunk down my spine. I wondered whether that was a common reaction—Little Red Riding Hood syndrome, maybe.

I stared at him and he stared back at me, my focus so complete that I actually shook in surprise when the tower bells began to ring, signaling the end of the lunch period.

"You should go," he said. When I nodded, he reached out and squeezed my hand. Electricity sparked up my spine. "Goodbye, Lily Parker."

"Goodbye, Jason Shepherd," I said, but he was already walking away.

He'd walked to St. Sophia's to see me—to talk to me. To explain why he hadn't wanted me to sit in on the Adepts' meetings, mark or not.

Because he was *worried* about me.

Because he hadn't wanted me to get hurt.

The moment I'd shared with Jason had been so incredibly phenomenal, the universe had to equalize. And what was the chosen brand of karmic balance for a high school junior?

Two words: pop quiz.

Magic in the world or not, I was still in high school, and a high school that prided itself on Ivy League admissions. Peters, our European history teacher, decided he needed to ensure that we'd read our chapters on the Picts and Vikings by using fifteen multiple-choice questions. I'd read the chapters—I was paranoid enough to make sure I finished my homework, magical hysterics notwithstanding. But that didn't mean my stomach didn't turn as Peters walked the rows, dropping stapled copies of the test on our desks.

"You have twenty minutes," he said, "which means you have a little more than one minute per question. Quizzes will account for twenty percent of your grade, so I strongly recommend you consider your answers carefully."

When the tests were distributed, he returned to his desk and took a seat without glancing up.

"Begin," he said, and pencils began to scribble.

I stared down at the paper, my nerves making the letters spin— well, nerves and the thought of a blue-eyed boy who'd worried for me, and who'd held my hand.

Twenty minutes later, I put my pencil down. I'd filled in the answers, and I hoped at least a few of them were correct. But I didn't stress over it.

Infatuation apparently made me intellectually lazy.

16

Scout waited until dinner to interrogate me about Jason's visit to campus. It being Monday, we'd been blessed with brand-new food. Since I didn't eat chicken, it was rice and mixed vegetables for me, but even simple food was better than dirty rice or stew. Or so I assumed.

"So, what did Mr. Shepherd have to say?" Scout asked, spearing a chunk of grilled chicken with her fork. "Are you engaged or promised, or what? Did you get his lavaliere? Did he pin you?"

"What's a lavaliere?"

"I don't know. I think it's a fraternity thing?"

"Well, whatever it is, there wasn't one. We just talked about the meeting. About the attitude he copped. He apologized."

Scout lifted appreciative brows. "Shepherd apologized? Jeez, Parker. You must have worked faster than I thought. He's as stubborn as they come."

"He said he was worried about me. About the possibility that I'd get wrapped up in a Reapers versus Adepts cage match and wouldn't have a way to defend myself, especially if you weren't there to work your mojo."

"And what spectacular mojo it is, too," she muttered. She opened her mouth as if to speak, then closed it again. "Listen," she finally said. "I don't want to warn you off some kind of budding romance, but you should be careful around Jason. I'm not sure I'd recommend getting involved with him."

"I'm not getting involved with him," I protested. "Wait, why can't I get involved with him?"

"He's just—I don't know. He's different."

"Yeah, being a werewolf does make him kinda unique."

She raised her eyebrows, surprise in her expression. "You know."

"I do now."

"How did you find out?"

"I heard him growl after I got hit with the firespell. I confirmed it."

"He admitted he was a wolf? To you?"

"He let me see his eyes do that flashy, color-changey thing. He did the same thing again when we talked in the hospital."

"After you made us leave?"

I bobbed my head. Scout made a low whistle. "In one week, you've gone from new kid in school to being wooed by a werewolf. You move fast, Parker."

"I doubt he's wooing me, and I didn't do anything but be my usually charming self."

"I'm sure you were plenty charming, but I just want you to be careful."

"Is that a little were-ism I'm hearing?"

"It's a little reminder that he's not like the rest of us. He's a whole different brand of Adept. And you don't have to buy my opinion. I'm just telling you what I think. On the other hand, in our short but explosive friendship, have I ever steered you wrong?"

"Did you want me to start with the getting hit by firespell or becoming an enemy to soul-sucking teenagers?"

"Did you mean the Reapers or the brat pack?"

I grinned appreciatively. "Ooh, well played."

"I have my moments. Besides, who'd you borrow those kick-ass flats from?"

I glanced down at the screaming yellow and navy patent leather ballet flats she'd let me borrow on our hurried way out the door this morning.

"Fine," I finally said. "Fashion trumps evil and prissy teenagers. You win."

Scout grinned at me. "I always win. Let's chow."

We noshed, said our hellos to Collette and Lesley, and when dinner was done, returned to the suite for our hour-long break before study hall. The brat pack had made camp in the living room, blond hair and expensive accessories flung about as we entered.

Veronica sat cross-legged on the couch, an open folder in her lap and M.K. and Amie at her feet like adoring handmaids.

"It also says," Veronica said, gazing at the folder, "that her parents dumped her here so they could head off to Munich." She lifted her head, a lock of blond hair falling across her shoulders, and gave me a pointed look.

Was that my folder she was reading? Had M.K. taken it from Foley's office while she was on hall-monitoring duty?

"Interesting, isn't it, that her parents left her? That they didn't take her with them? I mean, it's not like there aren't English-speaking private schools in Germany. She's not even *from* Chicago."

"How did you get that?" I bit out. All eyes turned to me. "How did you get my file?"

Veronica closed the navy blue folder, the St. Sophia's crest across the front, then held it up between two fingers. "What, this? We got it from Foley's office, of course. We have our ways."

I took a step forward, anger dimming my vision at the edges. "You have no right to go through my file. Who do you think you are?"

Outside, thunder rolled across the city, the steel gray sky finally preparing to give way. Inside, the room lights flickered.

"You need to back off," Scout said.

Veronica arched an eyebrow and uncrossed her legs. M.K. and Veronica shifted to give her room. She stood up, folder in her hand, and walked toward us, a haughty look aimed at Scout.

"You think you're queen of the school just because you've been here since you were twelve? Being abandoned by your parents isn't exactly a coup, Green."

Scout, amazingly, stayed calm after that outburst, an expression of boredom on her face. "Is that supposed to hurt me, Veronica? 'Cause, if I recall, you've been here as long as I have."

"Irrelevant," Veronica declared. "We're talking about you"—she shifted her gaze to me—"and your new friend. You both need to remember who's in charge here."

Scout made a sarcastic sound. "And you think that's you?"

Veronica flipped up the folder. "The ones with information, with access, always win. You should write that down in one of your little books."

M.K. snickered. Amie had the decency to blush, but her eyes were on the ground, apparently not brave enough to intercede.

"Give it back," I said, hand extended, fingers shaking with fury.

"What, this?" she asked, batting her eyelashes, waving the folder in her hand.

"That," Scout confirmed, reaching out her own hand, and taking a menacing step forward. When she spoke again, her voice was low and threatening. "Keep in mind, Lively, that in all the years you've been here, some interesting little facts have crossed my path, too. I assume you'd like to keep those facts between us, and not have them sprinkled around the sophomore and senior classes?"

There was silence as they faced off, the weirdo and the homecoming queen, a battle for rumor mill supremacy.

"Whatever," Veronica finally said, handing over the folder between the tips of her fingers, lips pursed as if the paper were dirty or infected. "Have it. It's not like I care. We've gotten everything we need."

Scout pulled the file from Veronica's manicured hands. "I'm glad we've concluded our business. And in the future, you might be a little more careful about where you get your information from and whom you share it with, capiche? Because sharing that information with the wrong people could be . . . costly."

Thunder rolled and rippled again, this burst louder than the last. The storm was moving closer.

"Whatever," Veronica said, rolling her eyes. She turned and, like a spinning dervish of plaid, took her seat on the couch again, attendants at her feet, the queen returned to her throne.

"Come on," Scout said, taking my wrist in her free hand and moving me toward her bedroom. It took a moment to make my feet move, to drag my gaze away from the incredibly smug smile on Veronica's face.

"Lily," Scout said, and I glanced over at her.

"Come on," she repeated, tugging my wrist. "Let's go."

We moved into her room, where she shut the door behind us. Folder in hand, she pointed at the bed. "Sit down."

"I'm fine—"

"Sit *down*."

I sat.

Thunder rolled again, lightning flashing through the room almost instantaneously. The rain started, a sudden downpour that echoed through the room like radio static.

The folder beneath her crossed arms, she walked to one end of the room, eyes on the floor, and then walked back again. "We're going to have to put it back." She lifted her head. "This came from Foley's office. We needed to get it out of their hands, which we did—yay, us—but now we're going to have to put it back. And that's going to be tricky."

"Great," I muttered. "That's great. Just one more thing I don't need to worry about right now. But before we figure out how to sneak into Foley's office and drop off a student file without her knowing it was gone, can I see it, please?"

"No."

That silenced me for a moment. "Excuse me?"

"No." Scout stopped her pacing and glanced over at me. "I really don't think looking through this is going to help you. If there's anything weird in here—about your parents, for example, since Foley likes to discuss them—it's just going to give you things to obsess over. Things to worry about."

"And it's better if only Veronica and M.K. have that information?"

Silence.

"Good point," Scout finally said, then handed it over. "You read. I'll plot."

My hands shaking, I flipped it open. My picture was stapled on the inside left, a shot of me from my sophomore year at Sagamore North, my hair a punky bob of black. On the inside right was an information sheet, which I skimmed—all basic stuff. A handful of documents was stapled behind the information sheet. Health and immunization records. A letter from the board of trustees about my admission.

The final document was different—a letter on cream-colored stock, addressed to Foley.

"Oh, my God," I said as I reviewed it, my vision dimming at the edges again as the world seemed to contract around me.

"Lily? What is it?"

"There's a letter. 'Marceline,'" I read aloud, "'as you know, the members of the board of trustees have agreed to admit Lily to St. Sophia's. We believe your school is the best choice for the remainder of Lily's high school education. As such, we trust that you will see to her education with the same vigor that you show to your other students.'"

"So far so good," Scout said.

"There's more. 'We hope,'" I continued, "'that you'll be circumspect in regard to any information you provide to Lily regarding our work, regardless of your opinion of it.' It's signed, 'Yours very truly, Mark and Susan Parker.'"

"Your parents?" Scout quietly asked.

I nodded.

"That's not so bad, Lil—she's just asking Foley not to worry you or whatever about their trip—"

"Scout, my parents told me they were philosophy professors at Hartnett College. In Sagamore. In New York. But in this letter, they tell Foley not to talk to me about their *work*? And that's not all." I flipped the folder outward so that she could see the letter, the paper, the logo. "They wrote the letter on Sterling Research Foundation letterhead."

Scout's eyes widened. She took the folder from my hand and ran a finger over the raised SRF logo. "SRF? That's the building down the street. The place that does the medical research. What are the odds?"

"Medical research," I repeated. "How close is that to genetic research?"

"That's what Foley said your parents did, right?"

I nodded, the edge of my lip worried between my teeth. "And not what they told me they did. They lied to me, Scout."

Scout sat down on the bed beside me and put a hand on my knee. "Maybe they didn't really lie, Lil. Maybe they just didn't tell you the entire truth."

The entire truth.

Sixteen years of life, of what I'd believed my life to be, and I didn't even know the basic facts of my parents' careers. "If they didn't tell me the entire truth about their jobs," I quietly said, "what else didn't they tell me?" For a moment, I considered whipping out my cell phone, dialing their number, and yelling out my frustration, demanding to know what was going on and why they'd lied. And if they hadn't lied exactly, if they'd only omitted parts of their lives, why they hadn't told me everything.

But that conversation was going to be a big one. I had to calm down, get myself together, before that phone call. And that's when it dawned on me—for the first time—that there might be huge reasons, *scary* reasons, why they hadn't come clean.

Maybe this wasn't about keeping information from me. Maybe they hadn't told me because the truth, somehow, was dangerous. Since I'd now seen an entirely new side to the world, that idea didn't seem as far-fetched as it might have a year ago.

No, I decided, this wasn't something I could rush. I had to know more before I confronted them.

"I'm sorry, Lil," Scout finally said into the silence. "What can I do?"

I gave the question two seconds of deliberation. "You can get me into Foley's office."

Fourteen minutes later—after the brat pack had left the common suite for parts unknown—we were on our way to the administrative wing. The folder was tucked into Scout's messenger bag, my heart pounding as we tried to look nonchalant on our way through the study hall and back into the main building. We had two missions—first and foremost, we had to put the folder back. If Foley found it missing, she'd only consider one likely source—me. I really wanted to avoid that conversation.

Second, since my parents' letter assumed Foley already knew about their research—and apparently didn't like it—I was guessing there was more information on the Sterling Research Foundation, or on my parents, in her office. We'd see what we could find.

Of course, it was just after dinner—and only a few minutes before the beginning of study hall—so there was a chance Foley was still around. If she was, we were going to make a run for it. But if she was gone, we were going to sneak inside and figure out what more we could learn about the life of Lily Parker.

17

Choir practice gave us an excuse to walk through the Great Hall and toward the main building, even as other girls deposited books and laptops on study tables and set about their required two hours of studying. Of course, when we got to the main building, the story had to change.

"Just taking an architectural tour," Scout explained with a smile as we passed two would-be choir girls. She blew out a breath that puffed out her cheeks after they passed, then pulled me toward the hallway to the administrative wing.

I wasn't sure if I was happy or not to discover that the administrative wing was quiet and mostly dark. That meant we had a clear path to Foley's office, and no excuse to avoid the breaking and entering—other than the getting-caught-and-being-severely-punished problem, of course.

"If you don't take the folder back," Scout said, as if sensing my fear, "we have to give it back to the brat pack. Or we have to come clean to Foley, and that means making even more of an enemy of the brat packers. And frankly, Lil, I'm full up on enemies right now."

It was the exhaustion in her voice that solidified my bravery. "Let's do it before I lose my nerve."

She nodded, and we skulked down the wing, bodies pressed as closely against the wall as we could manage. In retrospect, it was probably not the least conspicuous way to get down the hall, but what did we know?

We made it to Foley's office, found no light beneath the wooden door. Scout knocked, the sound muffled by timely thunder. After a few seconds, when no one answered, she rolled her shoulders, put a hand on the doorknob, and turned.

The door clicked, and opened.

We both stood in the hallway for a minute.

"Way easier than I thought that was going to be," she whispered, then snuck a peak inside. "Empty," she said, then pushed open the door.

After a last glance behind me to ensure the hallway was empty, I followed her in, then pulled the door carefully shut behind us.

Foley's office was dark. Scout rustled around in her messenger bag, then pulled out a flashlight, which she flipped on. She cast the light around the room.

The top of Foley's desk was empty. There weren't any file cabinets in the room, just a bookshelf and a couple of leather chairs with those big brass tacks in the upholstery. Scout moved to the other side of Foley's desk and began pulling open drawers.

"Rubber bands," she announced, then pushed the drawer closed and opened another. "Paper clips and staples." She closed that one, then moved to the left-hand side of the desk and opened a drawer. "Pens and pencils. Jeez, this lady has a lot of office supplies." She closed, then opened, another. "Envelopes and stationery." She closed the last one and stood straight again. "That's it for the desk, and there're no other drawers in here."

That wasn't entirely accurate. "I bet there are drawers behind the secret panel."

"What secret panel?" she asked.

I moved to the bookshelf I'd seen Foley walk out of, pushed aside a few books, and knocked. The resulting sound was hollow. Echoey. "It's a pivoting bookshelf, just like in a B-rated horror flick. The panel was open when Foley called me out of class. She closed it again after she came out, but I'm not sure how."

Scout trained her flashlight on the bookshelves. "In the movies, you pull a book and the sliding door opens."

"Surely it's not that easy."

"I said the same thing about the door. Let's see if our luck holds." Scout tugged on a leather-bound copy of *The Picture of Dorian Gray* . . . and jumped backward and out of the way as one side of the bookshelf began to pivot toward us. When the panel was open halfway, it stopped, giving us a space wide enough to walk through.

"Well-done, Parker."

"I have my moments," I told her. "Light it up."

My heart was thudding as Scout directed the beam of the flashlight into the space the sliding panel had revealed.

It was a storage room.

"Wow," Scout muttered. "That was anticlimactic."

It was a small, limestone space, just big enough to fit two rows of facing metal file cabinets. I took the flashlight from Scout's hand and moved inside. The cabinets bore alphabetical index labels.

First things first, I thought. "Come hold this," I told her, extending the flashlight. As she directed it at the cabinets, I skimmed the first row, then the second, until I got to the *P*s. I pulled open the cabinet drawer—no lock, thankfully—and slid my folder in between PARK and PATTERSON.

Some of the tightness in my chest eased when I closed the drawer again, part of our mission accomplished. But then I glanced around the room. There was a little too much in here not to explore.

"Keep an eye on the door," I said.

"Go for it, Sherlock," Scout said, then turned her back on me, and let me get to work.

I put my hands on my hips and surveyed the room. There hadn't been any other PARKER folders in the file drawer, which meant that my parents didn't have files of their own—at least not under their own names.

"Maybe our luck will hold one more time," I thought, and tucked the flashlight beneath my chin. I checked the *S* drawer, then thumbed through STACK, STANHOPE, and STEBBINS.

STERLING, R. F., read the next file.

"Clever," I muttered, "but not clever enough." I pulled out the file and opened it. A single envelope was inside.

I wet my lips, my hands suddenly shaking, lay the file on the top of the folders in the open drawer, and lifted the envelope.

"What did you find?"

"There's a Sterling file," I said. "And there's an envelope in it." It was cream-colored, the flap unsealed, but tucked in. The outside of the envelope bore a St. Sophia's RECEIVED BY stamp with a date on it: SEPTEMBER 21.

"Feet, don't fail me now," I whispered for bravery, then lifted the flap and pulled out a trifolded piece of white paper. I unfolded it, the SRF seal at the top of the page, but not embossed. This was a copy of a letter.

And attached to the copy was a sticky note with my father's handwriting on it.

Marceline,
I know we don't see eye to eye, but this will help you
understand.
—M.P.

M.P. My father's initials.

My hands suddenly shaking, I lifted the note to reveal the text of the letter beneath. It was short, and it was addressed to my father:

Mark,
Per our discussions regarding your daughter, we agree that it
would be unwise for her to accompany you to Germany or for
you to inform her about the precise nature of your work. Doing
so would put you all in danger. That you are taking a sabbatical,
hardly a lie, should be the extent of her understanding of your

current situation. We also agree that St. Sophia's is the best place
for Lily to reside in your absence. She will be properly cared for
there. We will inform Marceline accordingly.

The signature was just a first name—*William*.

That was it.

The proof of my parents' lies.

About their jobs.

About their trip.

About whatever they'd gotten involved in, whatever had given the
Sterling Research Foundation the ability to pass down dictates about
my parents' relationship with me.

"They lied, Scout," I finally said, hands shaking—with fear and
anger—as I stared down at the letter. "They lied about all of it. The
school. The jobs. They probably aren't even in Germany. God only
knows where they are now."

And what else had they lied about? Each visit I made to the college? To their offices? Each time I met their colleagues? Every department cocktail party I'd spied on from the second-floor staircase at our
house in Sagamore, professors—or so I'd assumed—milling about below with drinks in hand?

It was all fake—all a show, a production, to fool someone.

But who? Me? Someone else?

I picked up the envelope again and glanced at the RECEIVED BY
mark.

The puzzle pieces fell into place.

"When was the twenty-first?" I asked Scout.

"What?"

"The twenty-first. September twenty-first. When was that?"

"Um, today's the twenty-fifth, so last Friday?"

"That's the day Foley received the envelope," I said, holding it up.
"Foley got a copy of this letter the day I got hit by the firespell. The day
before I went into the hospital, the day before she came to the hospital

room to tell me she was wrong about my parents. That I was right about their research. There's probably a letter in here to her, too," I quietly added, as I glanced around the room.

"Foley told you about the genetic research when you came to her office," Scout concluded. "Then she got the letter and realized she really wasn't supposed to tell you. That's why she dropped by the hospital. That's why she changed her tune."

I dropped my gaze back down to the letter and swore out a series of curses that should have blistered Scout's ears. "Can anyone around here tell me the truth? Can anyone *not* have, like, sixty-five secret motives?"

"Oh, my God, Lily."

It took me a moment to realize she'd called my name, and to snap my gaze her way. Her eyes were wide, her lips parted in shock. I thought we'd been caught, or that someone—something—was behind us, and my heart stuttered in response.

"What?" I asked, so carefully, so quietly.

Her eyes widened even farther, if that was possible. "You don't see that?" She flailed her hands in the air and struggled to get out words. "This!" she finally exclaimed. "Look around you, Lily. The lights are on."

I looked down at the flashlight in her hands. "I'm having a crisis here, Scout, and you're talking to me about turning on a light?"

I could see the frustration in her face, in the clench of her hands. "I didn't turn on the light, Lily."

"So what?"

She put her hands on her hips. "The light is on, but I didn't turn on the light, and there's only one other person in the room."

I lifted my head, raising my gaze to the milk-glass light shade that hung above our heads. It glowed a brilliant white, but the light seemed to brighten and fade as I stared at it—*da dum, da dum, da dum*—as if the bulb had a heartbeat.

The pulse was hypnotic, and the light seemed to brighten the longer I stared at it, but the rhythm didn't change. *Da dum. Da dum. Da dum.*

"Think about your parents," Scout said, and I tore my gaze away from the light to stare at her.

"What?"

"I need you to do this for me. Without questions. Just do it."

I swallowed, but nodded.

"Think about your parents," she said. "How they lied to you. How they showed you a completely false life, false careers. How they have some relationship with Sterling that's going on around us, above our heads, that gives the SRF some kind of control over your parents' actions, what they say, how they act toward you."

The anger, the betrayal, burned, my throat aching with emotion as I tried to stifle tears.

"Now look," Scout said softly, then slowly raised her gaze to the light above us.

It glowed brighter, and the pulse had quickened. *Da dum. Da dum. Da dum.*

It was faster now, like a heart under stress.

My heart.

"Oh, my God," I said, and the light pulsed brighter, faster, as my fear grew.

"Yeah," Scout said. "It's strong emotion, I think. You get freaked out, and the light goes on. You get more freaked out, and the light gets brighter. You saw it kind of dims and brightens?"

"It's my heartbeat," I said.

"Well," she said, turning for the door, "I guess you have a little magic, after all."

She glanced back and grinned. "Twist!"

In no mood for study hall, we found a quiet corner of the main building—far from the administrative wing and its treasonous folders—and camped out until it was over. We didn't talk much. I sat cross-legged on the floor, my back against cold limestone, eyes on the mosaic-tiled ceiling above me. Thinking. Contemplating. Repeating one word, over and over and over again. One word—maybe the only word—momentous enough to push thoughts of my parents' secret life out of my head.

Magic.

I had *magic.*

The ability to turn on lights, which maybe wasn't such a huge deal, but it was magic, just the same.

Magic that must have been triggered somehow by the shot of fire-spell I'd taken a few days ago. I didn't know how else to explain it, and that mark on my back seemed proof enough. I'd somehow become one of them—not because I'd been born into it, like Scout said, but because I'd been running in the wrong direction in the basement of St. Sophia's one night.

Because I (apparently) had magic, and we were out and about instead of hunkered down in the file vault behind Foley's office, I was focusing on staying calm, controlling my breathing, and trying not to flip whatever emotional switch had turned me into Thomas Edison.

When study hall was over, we merged into the crowd leaving the Great Hall and returned to the room, but the brat pack beat us back. I guessed they'd decided that torturing us was more fun than spending time in their own rooms. Regardless, we ignored them—bigger issues on our plates—and headed straight for Scout's room.

"Okay," she said, gesturing with her hands when the door was closed and locked behind us, and a towel stuffed beneath it. "I need to check the *Grimoire* and see what I can find, but so I know what I'm looking for, let's see what you can do."

We sat there in silence for a minute.

"What am I supposed to be doing?" I asked.

Scout frowned. "I don't know. You're the one with the light magic. Don't you know?"

I gave her a flat stare.

"Right," she said. "You didn't even know you'd done it."

There was a knock at Scout's closed bedroom door. She glanced at the closed door, then at me. "Yes?"

There was a snicker on the other side. "Did you find anything interesting in that little folder?"

I nearly growled at the question. As if on cue, the room was suddenly flooded with light—bright light, brighter than the overhead fluorescents had any right to be.

"Jeez, dial it back, will ya?"

I pursed my lips and blew out rhythmic breaths, trying to calm myself down enough to dim the lights back below supernova.

"What?" M.K. asked from the other side of the door. "No response?"

Okay, I'd had enough of M.K. for the day. "Hey, Scary Katherine," I said, "don't make us tell Foley that you invaded her vault and stole confidential files from her office."

As if my telling her off had been cathartic, the lights immediately dimmed.

Scout glanced over appreciatively. "Why does it not surprise me that you have magic driven by sarcasm?"

There was more knocking on the door. "Scout?" Lesley tentatively asked. "Are you guys okay in there? Did you set the room on fire?"

"We're fine, Barnaby," Scout said. "No fires. Just, um, testing some new flashlights. In case the power goes out."

"However unlikely that appears to be now," I muttered.

"Oh," Lesley said. "Well, is there anything I can, you know, help with?"

Scout and I exchanged a glance. "Not just right now, Lesley, but thanks."

"Okay," she said, disappointment in her voice. Footsteps echoed through the common room as she walked away.

Scout moved to a bookshelf, fingers trailing across the spines as she searched for the book she wanted. "Okay, so it was triggered by the firespell somehow. We can conclude that whatever magic you've got is driven by emotion, or that strong emotions bump up the power a few notches. It's centered in light, obviously, but it's possible the power could branch out into other areas. But as for the rest of it—"

She stopped as her fingers settled on an ancient book of well-worn brown leather, which she slid from the shelf after pushing aside knick-knacks and collectibles.

"It's going to take me some time to research the particulars," she said, glancing back at me. "You want to grab some books, camp out here?"

I thought for a second, then nodded. There was no need to add academic failure to my current list of drama, which was lengthening as the day wore on. "I'll go grab my stuff."

She nodded and gave me a soft smile. "We'll figure this out, you know. We'll figure it out, go back to the enclave, get you inducted, and all will be well."

"When you say well, you mean I can start spending my evenings torturing soul-sucking bad guys and trying not to get shot in the back by firespell again?"

"Pretty much," she agreed with a nod. "But think about how much quality time you and Jason can spend together." This time, when she grinned, she grinned broadly, and winged up her eyebrows, to boot.

The girl had a point.

Later that night, when I was back in my room in pajamas, and calm enough to dial their number, I broke out my cell phone and tried again to reach my parents. It was late in Munich, assuming that's where they were, so they didn't answer. I faked cheerful and left a voice mail, still avoiding the confrontation and because of that, almost glad they hadn't answered. There were too many puzzle pieces—Foley, my parents, and now the SRF—that I still had to figure out. And if they thought keeping me in the dark was safer for all of us, maybe letting them think they'd kept their secret was the best thing to do. At least for now.

That didn't stop the hurt, though. And it didn't stop me from wanting to know the truth.

At lights-out, I turned out the overhead lights, but snapped on a flashlight I'd borrowed from Scout, and broke out my sketch pad and a soft-lead pencil. I turned off the left side of my brain and scribbled, shapes forming as if the pencil were driven by my unconscious. Half an hour later, I blinked, and found a pretty good sketch of Jason staring back at me.

Boy on the brain.

"And just when I needed more drama," I muttered, then flipped off the light.

18

Tuesday went by in a haze. My parents had left a voice mail while I'd slept, a hurried message about how busy they were in Munich, and how much they loved me. And again, I wasn't sure if those words made me feel better . . . or worse.

Mostly, I felt numb. I'd pulled a navy blue hoodie, the zipper zipped, over my oxford shirt and plaid skirt, my hands tucked into pockets as I moved from class to class, the same two questions echoing through my head, over and over and over again.

First, what was I?

Let's review the facts: An entourage of kids with magical powers was running around Chicago, battling other kids with magical powers. A battle of good versus evil, but played out by teenagers who'd only just become old enough to drive. One night I was hit by a burst of magic from one of those kids. Skip forward a couple of days, and I had a "darkening" on my back and the ability to turn on lights when I got upset. So I had that going for me.

Second, what were my parents *really* doing in Germany? They'd told me they'd been granted permission to review some famous German philosopher's papers, journals, and notes—stuff that had never before been revealed to the public. It was a once-in-a-lifetime opportunity, they'd told me, a chance to be the first scholars to see and touch a genius's work. He'd been a Michelangelo of the world of philosophy, and they'd been invited to study *David* firsthand.

But based on what I knew now, that story had been at least partly concocted to satisfy me, because they'd been directed to tell me that they were on a sabbatical. But if that's what they were "supposed" to tell me, what were they actually doing? I'd seen the plane tickets, the passports, the visas, the hotel confirmation. I knew they were in Germany. But why?

Those questions notwithstanding, the day was pretty dull. Classes proceeded as usual, although Scout and I were both a little quieter at lunch. It was a junk food day in the cafeteria—corn chip and chili pies (vegetarian chili for weirdos like me)—so Scout and I picked over our chili and chips with forks, neither saying too much. She'd brought a stack of notes she'd copied out of the *Grimoire* the day before, and was staring at them as she ate. That tended to limit the conversation.

As she read, I looked around the room, watching the girls eating, gossiping, and moving around from group to group. All that plaid. All those headbands. All those incredibly expensive accessories.

All those normal girls.

Suddenly, the theme from *Flash Gordon* began to echo from Scout's bag. Putting down her forkful of chips and chili, she half turned to pull the messenger bag from the back of her chair, then reached for her phone.

I arched an eyebrow at the choice of songs, as lyrics about saving the universe rumbled through our part of the cafeteria.

"I love Queen," Scout covered, her voice a little louder than the phone, the explanation for the folks around us. The song apparently signaling a text message, she slid open the keyboard and began tapping.

"*Flash Gordon?*" I whispered, when the girls had returned to their lunches. "A little obvious, isn't it?"

Pink rose on her cheeks. "I'm allowed," she said, still thumbing keys. She frowned, her lips pursed at the corner. "Weird," she finally said.

"Everything okay?"

"Yeah," Scout said. "We're supposed to meet tonight at five

o'clock—we're doing some kind of administrative meeting—but they want me to come down now. Something's gone down with one of our targets. A kid from one of the publics. That means I need to . . . run an *errand*." She winged up her eyebrows so I'd understand her not-so-tricky secret code.

Around us, girls began to put up their trays in preparation for afternoon classes. Scout had never been interrupted during classes, as far as I was aware. "Right now?"

"Yeah." There was more frowning as she closed the phone and slipped it back into her bag. She turned around again, hands in her lap, shoulders slumped forward, face pinched as she stared down at the table.

"Are you sure you're okay?" I asked her.

She started to speak, then shook her head as if she'd changed her mind, then tried again. "It's just weird," she said, lifting her gaze to mine. "It's way early for them to page me. They never page me during school hours. It's part of the whole, 'You need an education to be the best'"—she looked around, then lowered her voice—"'Adept you can be.'"

I frowned. "That is weird."

"Well, regardless, I need to go back to the room." She pushed back her chair, pulled off her bag, and settled it diagonally over her shoulder, the skull and crossbones grinning back at me. "Are you going to be okay?"

I nodded. "I'll be fine. Go."

She frowned, but stuffed her phone and books into her bag, stood up, and slung it over her shoulder. Then she was off, plaid skirt bobbing as she hustled through the cafeteria.

She didn't come back during fourth period. Or fifth. Or sixth. Not that I blamed her—European history wasn't my favorite subject, either—but I was beginning to get worried.

When I got back to the suite, I dumped my bag on the couch and headed for her door.

The door was cracked partially open.

"Scout?" I called out. I rapped knuckles against the wood, but got no answer. Maybe she was in the shower, or maybe she'd run an errand and didn't want to bother with the lock. But given her collections and the stash of magic books, she wasn't the kind to leave the door unlocked, much less open.

I put a hand on the door and pushed it open the rest of the way.

My breath left me.

The room was in shambles.

Drawers had been upended, the bed stripped, her collections tossed on the floor.

"Oh, my God," I whispered. I stepped inside, carefully stepping around piles of clothes and books. Had this been waiting for her when she'd come back to the room?

Or had *they* been waiting?

"What happened in here?"

I glanced back and found Lesley in the doorway, her cheeks even paler than usual. She was actually in uniform today. "I don't know," I said. "I just got here."

She stepped into the room, and beside me. "This has something to do with where she goes at night, doesn't it?"

"Yeah. I think so."

My gaze fell upon the bed, the sheets and comforter in disarray. And peeking from one edge, was the black strap of Scout's messenger bag.

I picked over detritus, then reached out an arm and pulled the bag from the tangle of blankets, the white skull on the front grinning evilly back at me.

My stomach fell. Scout wouldn't have gone anywhere without that bag. She carried it everywhere, even on missions, the strap across her shoulder every time she left the room. That the room was a disaster area, her bag was still here, and she was gone, did not bode well.

"Oh, Scout," I whispered, fear blossoming at the thought of my best friend in trouble.

The overhead light flickered.

I stood up again, decided now was as good a time as any to learn control, and closed my eyes. I breathed in through my nose, out through my mouth, and after a few moments of that, felt my chest loosen, as though the fear—the magic—was loosing its grip.

"Ms. Parker. Ms. Barnaby."

Jumping at the sound of my name, I opened my eyes and looked behind me. Foley stood in the doorway, one hand on the door, her wide-eyed gaze on Scout's room. She wore a suit of bone-colored fabric and a string of oversized pearls around her neck.

"What happened here?"

"I found it like this," I told her, working to keep some of my new-found animosity toward Foley—who knew more about my parents than I did—at bay.

"She left at the end of lunch—said she had to come back to the room for something." I skipped the part about why she'd come back, but added, in case it was important, "She was worried, but I'm not sure what about. The door was open when I got here a few minutes ago." I looked back at the tattered remains of Scout's collection. "It looked like this."

"And where is Ms. Green now?" Foley finally glanced at me.

I shook my head. "I haven't seen her since lunch."

Foley frowned and surveyed the room, arms crossed, fingers of her left hand tapping her right bicep. "Call the security office. Do a room-to-room search," she said. I thought she was talking to me, at least until she glanced behind us. A youngish man—maybe twenty-five, twenty-six—stood in the doorway. He was tall, thin, sharp-nosed, and wore a crisp button-down shirt and blue bow tie. I guessed he was an executive assistant type.

"If you don't find her," Foley continued, "contact me immediately. And Christopher, we need to be sensitive to her parents' being, shall we say, particular about the involvement of outsiders. I believe they're in Monaco at present. That means we contact them before we contact the police department, should it come to that. Understood?"

He nodded, then walked back toward the hallway door. Foley returned her gaze to the remains of Scout's room, then fixed her stare on Lesley. "Ms. Barnaby, could you excuse us, please?"

Lesley looked at me, eyebrows raised as if making sure I'd be okay alone with Foley. When I nodded, she said, "Sure," then left the room. A second later, her bedroom door opened and closed.

When we were alone, Foley crossed her arms over her chest and gazed at me. "Has Ms. Green been involved in anything unusual of late?"

I wanted to ask her if secret meetings of magically enhanced teenagers constituted "unusual," but given the circumstances, I held back on the sarcasm.

"Not that I'm aware of," I finally said, which was mostly the truth. I think what Foley would consider "unusual" was probably pretty average for Scout.

Then Foley blew that notion out of the water.

"I'm aware," she said, "of Ms. Green's aptitude as, let's say, a Junior Varsity athlete."

I stared at her in complete silence . . . and utter shock.

"You *know*?" I finally squeaked out.

"I am the headmistress of this school, Ms. Parker. I am aware of most everything that occurs within my jurisdiction."

The ire I'd been suppressing bubbled back to the surface. "So you know what goes on, and you let it happen? You let Scout run around in the middle of the night, put herself in danger, and you ignore it?"

Foleys's gaze was flat and emotionless. She walked back to Scout's door, closed it, then turned to me again, hands clasped in front of her—all business. "You presume that I let these things happen without an understanding of their severity, or of the risk that Ms. Green faces?" She'd spoken it like a question, but I assumed it was rhetorical.

"I will assume, Ms. Parker, that you are concerned about the well-being of your friend. I will assume that you are speaking from that concern, and that you have not actually considered the consequences of speaking to me in that tone."

My cheeks bloomed with heat.

"Moreover," she continued, moving to one of Scout's bookshelves and righting a toppled paper house, "regardless of what you think of my motivations or my compassion, rest assured that I understand all too well what Ms. Green and her colleagues are facing, and likely better than you do, your incident in the basement notwithstanding."

The house straightened, she turned and looked at me again. "Do we understand each other?"

I couldn't hold it back any longer, couldn't keep the words from bubbling out. "Where are my parents?"

Her eyes widened. "Your parents?"

I couldn't help it, potential danger or not. "I got . . . some information. I want to know where my parents are."

I expected more vitriol, more words to remind me of my position: Me—student; Her—authority figure. But instead, there was compassion in her eyes.

"Your parents are in Munich, Ms. Parker, just as they informed you. Now, however, is not the time to be distracted by the nature of their work. And more important, you should put some faith in the possibility that your parents informed you of the things they believed you should know. The things they believed it was safest for you to know. Do you understand?"

I decided that whatever they were involved in was unlikely to change in the next few hours; I could push Foley for information later. Scout's situation, on the other hand, needed to be dealt with now, so I nodded.

"Very well." And just like that, she was back to headmistress. "I cannot forgo calling Ms. Green's parents forever, nor can I forgo contacting the Chicago Police Department if she is, in reality, missing. But the CPD is not aware of her unique talents. Those unique talents—

and the talents of her friends—provide her with certain resources. If the state of her room indicates that she is in the hands of those who would bring harm to people across the city, then those friends are the best to seek her out and bring her back." She raised her eyebrows, as if willing me to understand the rest of what she was getting at.

"I can tell them," I said. "Scout said they're meeting at five o'clock."

Foley smiled, and there seemed to be appreciation in her eyes. "Very good," she said.

"The only problem is," I said, "I don't know exactly where they are. I've only been to the, um, *meeting room* once, and I don't think I could find it again. And even if I did," I added, before she could interrupt, "they don't think I'm one of them." That might change once they discovered my fledgling power, but I doubt Scout had had time to update them. "So even if I can get there, they may not listen to me."

"Ms. Parker, while I understand the nature of their work, I, like most Chicagoans, am not privy to the finer details of their existence. I am aware, however, that there are markers—coded markers—that guide the way to the enclave. Just follow the tags. And once you arrive, *make* them listen." She turned around and disappeared into the common room. A second later, I heard the door to the hallway open and close again.

It was three forty-five, which gave me time to get to the enclave, except for one big problem.

"Just follow the tags?" I quietly repeated. I had no clue what that was supposed to mean.

But, incomprehensible instructions or not, I apparently had a mission to perform . . . and I needed supplies.

I grabbed Scout's messenger bag—proof that she was missing— then left the room and shut the door behind me. When I was back in my room, I grabbed the flashlight I'd borrowed from Scout, dumped the books out of her messenger bag and stuffed the flashlight inside. In a moment of Boy Scout–worthy brilliance, I grabbed some yellow chalk from my stash of art supplies and stuffed it, and my cell phone, into her bag, as well.

Hands on my hips, I glanced around my room. I wasn't entirely sure what else to take with me, and I didn't really have a lot of friend-rescuing supplies to choose from.

"First aid kit," said a voice in the doorway.

I glanced back, found Lesley there, already having ditched the uniform for a pleated cotton skirt and tiny T-shirt. In her hands was a pile of supplies.

"First aid kit," she repeated, moving toward me and laying the pile on my bed. "Water. Granola bars. Flashlight. Swiss Army knife." She must have seen the quizzical expression on my face, as her own softened. "I said I wanted to help," she said, then returned her gaze to the bed. "I'm helping."

The room was quiet for a minute as I took it all in.

"Thank you, Lesley. I appreciate it. Scout appreciates it."

She shrugged her shoulders and smiled absently, then moved toward the door. "Just make sure you tell her I helped."

"As soon as I can," I murmured, just hoping I'd have the opportunity to *talk* to Scout again. I stuffed the supplies into the bag, and had just closed the skull-and-crossbones flap when visitor number two darkened my doorway.

"So your weirdo friend's gone AWOL?"

I glanced behind me. M.K. stood in the doorway, arms folded across a snug, white button-up shirt and the key on a silver chain that lay across it. She must have upgraded from ribbon.

"I don't know what you're talking about."

I turned around again, picked up Scout's bag, and slid the strap over one shoulder.

M.K. huffed. "Everyone is talking about it. Her room is trashed, and she's gone. We all thought she was a flake. Now we have proof. She obviously went postal. She's probably tearing around downtown Chicago in that gigantic coat, raving about vampires or something. I mean, have you seen her room? It was practically a fire hazard in there. About time someone cleaned it out."

I had to press my fingernails into my palms to keep the overhead light from bursting into flame.

"I see," I blandly responded, turning and heading for my bedroom door. "Excuse me," I said, when she didn't move. After rolling her eyes, she uncrossed her arms and ankles and stepped aside.

"Freak," she muttered under her breath.

That was the last straw.

With no fear and no thought of the consequences, I turned on M.K., stepping so close that she pressed herself back into the wall.

"I'm not entirely sure how you finagled your way into St. Sophia's," I said, "and I'm not entirely sure that you'll be able to finagle your way out again. But you might want to think about this—threatening the girls you think are freaks isn't really a good idea, 'cause we're the kind of girls who will threaten you right back."

"You can't—," she began, but I held a finger to her lips.

"I wasn't done," I informed her. "Before I was interrupted, I was making a point: Don't mess with the weirdos, unless you want to lie awake at night, wondering if one of those weirdos is going to sneak a black widow into your bed. Understood?"

She made a huffy sound of disbelief, but wouldn't meet my eyes.

I'd actually scared the bully.

"And M.K.," I said, stepping away and heading for the hallway door, "sleep well."

She didn't look like she would.

19

I took the route to the basement that Scout and I had taken a couple of days before. I wasn't sure how many paths led to the enclave, but I figured I had the best chance to get there if I stuck to the one I (almost) remembered.

I found the side hallway and the basement door, then took the steep stairs to the lower level. This part was more of a challenge. I hadn't been smart enough the last time to play Gretel or Girl Scout, to lay down a trail of crumbs or blaze a path back to the railcar line and the Roman numeral three.

But that didn't mean I couldn't learn from my mistakes. And there were plenty of mistakes, my luck having apparently exhausted itself. Fortunately, I'd left early, giving myself plenty of time to get to the enclave, because it took me half an hour to find the metal door that led to the railcar tunnels, and I had to backtrack two or three times. Each time I found the right route (read: eliminated another dead end from my list of routes to try), I made a little mark on the corridor wall with the yellow chalk from my bag. That way, if I made it through the evening without being beaten down by Adepts, I'd be able to find my way upstairs again.

The possibility that I wouldn't be coming back—that I was about to dive into something nasty in order to save my new BFF—was a thought I kept pretty well repressed. The risk didn't matter, I decided, because Scout would have come after me. She'd have come for me.

I'd heard someone say that bravery was doing the thing you were afraid to do, despite your fear. If that was true, I was the bravest person I knew; the lights that flickered above me as I walked through the hallway—an EKG of my emotions—were proof enough of that.

At the metal door, I reached up on tiptoes and felt for the key Scout had pulled down on our first trip to the enclave. I had a moment of heart-fluttering panic when I couldn't feel anything but dust above the threshold, but I calmed down a little when my fingertips brushed cold metal. I grabbed the key, slipped it into the lock, and unlocked the door.

It popped open with a *whoosh* of cold, stale air. My stomach rolled nervously, but I battled through it. I pulled out the flashlight, flicked the button, and took the step.

But I left the door open behind me, just in case.

"All right," I muttered, swinging the beam of the flashlight from one side of the tunnel to the other, trying to figure out the message Foley had given me.

Look for the tags, she'd said.

While I was willing to do a little backtracking in the tidy limestone basement, backtracking through musty, dirty, damp, and dark tunnels wasn't going to happen. I needed the right route the first time through. And that meant I needed an answer.

"Tags, tags, tags," I whispered, my gaze tracking from railcar tracks to concrete walls to arched ceiling. "Gift tags?" I wondered aloud, even at a whisper, my voice echoing through the hall. "Clothing tags?"

The circle of light swung across the curvaceous graffiti that swirled across one of the walls. I froze, my lips tipping up into a smile.

Turned out, Foley hadn't meant the gift kind or the clothing kind or the HTML kind.

She'd meant the spray paint kind.

Graffiti tags.

The walls were covered in them—a mishmash of pictures and

words. Portraits. Political messages. Simple tags: "Louie" had been here a lot. Complicated tags: Thick, curvalicious letters that wrapped around one another into amoebas of words I couldn't even read. However abandoned these tunnels seemed now, they'd been the site of a lot of spray painting, a lot of artistry.

I walked slowly down the first section of the tunnel, moving the circle of light from one wall to the other, trying to find the key that would decipher the code. It was hard enough to read them, much less to decipher them, the letters intertwined, the tags overlapping.

My eye caught a short tag in tidy, white letters, which was centered over an arch-shaped opening that led to the left.

MILLIE 23, it read.

I stilled the flashlight and stared at the tag.

St. Sophia's was located at 23 East Erie, and I'd bet money that Millie was short for Millicent—Scout's first name.

I peeked inside the tunnel and aimed the flashlight beam at the arches at the end of that part of the tunnel. One was blank.

The other, the one on the right, was tagged MILLIE 23.

"Very clever, Scout," I said, and stepped inside.

Thirteen tags, thirteen tunnels, and twelve minutes later, I emerged into the final corridor, stopping before the arched, wooden door of Enclave Three.

I wet my lips, tightened my fingers into a hand, and opened the door.

Heads turned immediately, their expressions none too friendly.

Smith stared at me, eyes wide, fury in his face, hair matted to his forehead. "What the hell are you doing here? And where's Scout?"

"She's gone," I said. "And I need your help."

"Gone?" asked a skeptical voice. Katie stepped beside him, her slim figure tucked into capri-cut jeans and layered V-neck T-shirts beneath a leather letterman jacket. "What do you mean, she's gone?"

"She's been taken." I ignored their gazes and looked to the folks more likely to actually believe me.

"She got a page at noon," I told Michael and Jason, both in uniform, both moving closer to me as I began to explain. "She thought it was strange, but she went anyway. Said she had to go back to her room. She didn't come back to class, and when I got back to the suite after school, her room was trashed."

"Trashed?" Michael asked, a pale cast to his face. "What do you mean, 'trashed'?"

"She has all sorts of collections—books and sculptures and these little houses. All of it was on the floor. Her pillows were slashed. Someone tore the sheets off the bed, emptied her drawers. And then there's this."

I rearranged her messenger bag on my shoulder, revealing the skull and crossbones. "It was still in her room. She never goes anywhere without this bag."

Michael slowly closed his eyes, grief in his expression. "They lured her out."

"Wait," Jason said, "Just wait. Let's not jump to conclusions." He looked at me. "She didn't say anything about meeting someone somewhere? About where she was supposed to be going? About what the emergency was?"

I shook my head.

"What about her cell phone?" asked one of the twins—Jamie or Jill, I wasn't sure—stepping forward. She brushed a waterfall of auburn hair over her shoulder, as if preparing to get down to business. "Do you have it?"

I glanced down at Scout's messenger bag. It had seemed empty after I'd taken her books out, but there was no harm in checking. I slipped a hand into the side pockets, then the interior pocket. Nothing, until I heard something clank against the snap that kept the front flap closed. I looked closer, found a small slit in the flap, and when I reached in a hand, touched cold, hard plastic. My heart sinking, I pulled out Scout's cell phone. Too bad I hadn't found it before, but at least I had it now.

"See who called her," Jamie quietly said. "See what the message said."

I slid the phone open and scanned her recent calls, recent texts, but there was nothing there. "Nothing," I announced. "She must have deleted it."

"We usually do," Michael said softly. "Delete them, I mean. To protect the identities of the Adepts, to keep the locations to ourselves. Simpler that way."

Unfortunately, that meant we wouldn't be able to figure out who'd sent Scout the text. But if she'd erased it as part of her standard Adept protocol, then she'd assumed the message was from another Adept.

Had the person who'd sent it, who'd lured her out, been in this room?

"They'll use her," Michael said. "They've taken her, and they'll use her." He walked to the other end of the room, picked up a backpack, and slung it over one shoulder. "I'm going after her."

Smith stepped in front of him. "You will not go after her."

The room got very quiet, and very tense.

"She's *missing*," I interjected into the silence. "Like Michael said, she was lured out of her room, she's been taken by one of the evil Reaper guys, and we need to find her before this messed-up situation gets any worse!"

Smith nailed me with a contentious glare. "*We*? You are not one of us."

"Really not the point," Michael said, stepping forward. "We can debate her membership later."

"She doesn't have *power*," Katie put in. "She's not one of us, and she shouldn't even be down here, much less giving us orders."

Michael rolled his eyes. "Whether she has power or not is irrelevant."

Smith made a disdainful sound. "You aren't in charge here, Garcia."

"If one of our own is in danger—"

"*Hey,*" I said, interrupting the fight. "Internal squabbling can wait. Scout's gone, and we need to get her back now. *Now,* and not after you guys have gone a couple of rounds about the enclave hierarchy."

Smith shook his head. "We can't worry about that right now."

Michael made a sound of disbelief, as if words of shock and awe had caught in this throat. I took the lead on his behalf.

"We can't worry about that?" I repeated. "She's one of you! You can't just leave her . . . wherever she is."

When no one spoke up, I glanced around the room, from Paul, to Katie, to the twins, to Jason. Guilty heads dropped around the room. No one would look me in the eye.

I put my hands on my hips, the fingers of my right hand tight around Scout's phone, my link to her. "Seriously? This is how you treat your teammates? Like they're disposable?"

"Getting dramatic isn't going to solve anything," Katie said, crossing her arms over her chest. For a cheerleader type, she managed a bossy, condescending stare pretty well. "We appreciate that you care about Scout, but it's not that simple."

I arched my eyebrows. "The hell it's not."

"Katie's right." Those words from the boy I'd almost decided to have a crush on. As Jason stepped forward, I was glad I'd stuck to "almost."

"If we go after her," he said, earnestness in his blue eyes, "we put ourselves, the city, the community around us, at risk. Being a member of the team means accepting the possibility that you'll become the sacrifice. Scout knew that. Understood it. Accepted that risk."

My heart tumbled, broken a little that this boy was so willing to give up our friend for the sake of people I wasn't sure were worth the sacrifice. And that included him.

"Wow," I said, honestly surprised. "Way to play well with others. Your whole existence is about saving people from Reapers, but you're willing to let her be a 'sacrifice'? I thought being Varsity, being Junior Varsity, being an Adept, was about being part of something bigger? Working together? What about all that talk?"

Smith shook his head. "It's just talk—only talk—if we dump our current agenda—the kids who need protecting—to find her. Think about it, Lily—they've managed to lure Scout into their clutches. They're probably using her as a lure for the rest of us. To pull us in." Smith shook his head. "If we're lucky, they'd just try to indoctrinate us. If not"—he glanced over, green eyes slitted shut—"the Reapers would be setting us up for a nasty night. In which we play the role of toast."

I couldn't argue with the logic—it probably *was* a trap.

But still. It was *Scout*.

I shook my head. "I can't believe you. I can't believe this. All that talk, and you bail when someone needs you. Trap or not, you make an effort. You make a plan. You *try*."

Smith looked away. There might have been a hint of guilt in his eyes, but not enough to force him to act. "I'll call the higher-ups and alert them," he said. "But that's all we can do. We aren't authorized to send out a rescue team. It's not done."

"It can't be," Katie put in, this time quietly. "We just can't do it."

Guilt—and maybe grief—hung in the silence of Enclave Three.

"You should probably go," Jason said. He wouldn't meet my eyes. "You know your way back?"

It took me a minute of staring daggers at all of them, a minute to overcome the disappointment that tightened my throat, before I could speak. "Yeah." I nodded. "Yeah. I can find my way back." My way back to the school and straight into Foley's office. If the Adepts wouldn't act, I'd go back to the principal. She'd know something—a source, a contact, a meaty guy with an attitude who could push through surly teenagers to rescue my BFF.

"It was nice knowing all of you," I said, slipping Scout's phone back into her bag, and putting the bag on my shoulder, then heading for the door. "No," I said, glancing back and arching an eyebrow at the blue-eyed werewolf in front of me. "I take that back. It actually wasn't."

I walked out and slammed the door shut behind me, its hinges rattling with the effort.

Time for Plan B.

I was roasting—not because of the heat (the tunnels were rocking a pretty steady fifty degrees or so), but because emotionally, I was livid.

Seven people had the power to help Scout—better yet, the *magical* power to help Scout. What had she called them? Elemental witches? A reader? A warrior?

So far, I wasn't impressed. Granted, I didn't know them very well, and their reticence to help her could have been the impact of poor, emo-inspired leadership, but still.

I stopped in the middle of the corridor, water splashing beneath my feet. These guys—these guys who wouldn't put their butts on the line to save her—they were the best we could do for good and justice? For rebels, they were pretty picky about obeying the rules. Even Smith's first reaction had been to tell me that I wasn't one of them—a rule that meant I didn't have the right to talk to them, much less make demands.

I stopped.

No way was I going out like this.

I turned around.

I went back.

After I pushed open the door, I opened with a biggie. "I can turn on lights."

Silence.

"You can what?"

"I can"—I had to stop and clear my throat, my voice squeaking nervously, and start over—"I can turn on lights. Dim them, turn them on, turn them off. I'm not sure if that's it, or if there's more, but that's what I know now."

Smith, standing before his troops, crossed his hands behind his head. "You can turn on lights." His voice could hardly have been drier—or more skeptical.

"I can turn on lights," I confirmed. "So you can pretend I'm an outsider, look at me like I'm crazy, but I'm not just someone off the

street. I am"—I had to pause for a minute to gather up my courage—
"an Adept like you. So you might want to pack away the attitude."

"Whatever," he muttered, as if I'd lied about the power thing just
to win points with him. Seriously—if I'd been faking it, wouldn't I
have faked something a little more interesting?

The rest of these repressed Adepts might have been intimidated by
the floppy hair and attitude, but as they'd so recently reminded me, I
wasn't one of them. And he wasn't the boss of me.

I held up an index finger. "Yeah, I may be an Adept, but I'm not a
member of your enclave, so I'm not really here to talk to you." I turned
my gaze to Paul, then to Jamie and Jill, then to Michael, then Jason.
"My best friend—your fellow Adept—is missing. Although I'm not
entirely full up on the details, I'm betting you all know what could happen to her out there if she's with *them*. She said something about siphoning spells, right? So even if she's only with the teenage Reapers,
the ones that still have power, they could be stealing her energy—her
soul—for the rest of them to use." I shook my head. "Unacceptable."

They looked at one another, shared glances.

"This is your chance to step forward," I said, my voice low, earnest.
"The chance to do the *right* thing, even if it's the *hard* thing."

"The rules—," Katie began, but Jason (finally!) shook his head.

"It's too late for that," he said. "For rules. We're losing this battle.
Today, we risk losing a spellbinder. We can't afford that." More softly,
he added, "Not as Adepts, not as friends."

He walked to me, then reached out his hand and slipped his fingers into mine. A spark slid up my arm at the contact, and I squeezed
his hand. He squeezed back.

"He's right," Michael said, then glanced around from Adept to
Adept. "They're both right, and you know it. All of you know it. It's
time to do things differently. To do the hard thing. Who's with me?"

Soft sounds filled the room as Adepts looked around, shuffled feet,
made their decisions.

"I'm in," Paul said, then smiled cheekily at me. "And, for the sake of having said it, it's nice to meet you."

I smiled back.

Jamie and Jill exchanged a glance, then stepped forward. "We're in," Jamie said.

Hands on my hips, a satisfied grin on my face, I glanced back at Katie and Smith, who now stood together, eyes narrowed, fury in their expressions.

"This is not how we operate," she said. "These are not the rules of the game."

"Then the rules need to change," Jason said, then looked over at me. "Let's go get your girl."

20

"I was going to find you," Jason whispered, his fingers still laced through mine as we left the enclave, two angry Varsity Adepts in our wake. But instead of walking toward St. Sophia's along the Millie 23 path, we moved deeper into the tunnels.

"As soon as I could get away, I was going to find you so we could get Scout together. But I couldn't say that in front of everyone else."

"Mmm-hmm," I vaguely said, not entirely sure I was ready to forgive him for not taking my side the first time around. Of course, I wasn't so unsure that I let go of his hand.

"Okay," he said, "then how about this—if you don't believe me, then consider this my one screw-up." He looked down at me. "I should have—we all should have—stuck up for her like you did in there. So let me make it up to you now. To both of you."

I squeezed his hand.

When we reached a crossroads—a union of four tunnels, the ceiling arched above us—we stopped.

"All right," Jason said, "we're here, and we've got a goal. Now we need a plan."

Paul snorted. "You mean now that we've thoroughly pissed off Varsity?"

"He's right," said the slightly taller of the twins. "We'll get a lecture supreme when we get back."

"If we get back," Michael muttered, then lifted worried eyes to Jason. "How are we going to manage this?"

"I'm still trying to figure that out."

I held up a hand. "First things first. Where are we going?"

"There's a sanctuary," Michael said, hitching a thumb toward one of the tunnels. "It's near here—the Reaper lodge for this part of Chicago. It's also where they store their vessels."

"Vessels?" I asked.

"The people—humans or Adepts—the older ones feed from. The ones the younger Reapers siphon energy from." So a sanctuary was a room of would-be zombies, their lives dripping away because members of the Dark Elite were too self-centered to let go of their magical gifts.

"My God," I muttered, my skin suddenly crawling. I glanced behind me in the direction of the tunnel we'd come from, suddenly unsure if walking into a trap was a good idea, rescue mission or not.

But then I looked down, my fingers skimming the fabric of Scout's messenger bag, and got an idea.

"The Reapers probably think we'll come for her," I said, looking up at Jason, spring blue eyes staring back. "That we'll storm the castle, this sanctuary, to get her back."

"Probably," Jason agreed, then tilted his head, curiosity in his expression.

"Well, if that's what they expect, then we should do the thing they aren't expecting. We flank them—create a distraction. Pull them out and away from Scout. And when they're distracted, we send in a team to sneak her out again."

There was silence for a moment, and I had to work not to shuffle my feet.

"That's actually not bad, Parker," Jason said. "I'm impressed."

"I ate a good lunch today."

"So who does what?" Paul asked.

"I can read the building," Michael said. "I can read it, figure out where she is." I guessed that meant Michael was preparing to use his powers.

"In that case, how about Jamie, Michael, and Parker go in, find Scout, get out." Jason looked at Paul. "You, me and Jill will play the distraction game. Are you guys up for a little snow and ice?"

The twins looked at each other and broke into precocious grins. "Absolutely," said the taller one, her aqua eyes shining. "Snow and ice are right up my alley."

Jason nodded managerially. "Then let's talk details."

Like the enclave, the Reaper sanctuary was housed underground in the cavelike innards of a former power substation, still connected to the tunnels beneath the city. We'd use two entrances—the main door, where Jill, Paul, and Jason would create their distraction—and the back door, where Jamie, Michael, and I would sneak in, hopefully un-detected, find Scout, and get out again. I was solely support staff—Michael and Jamie would handle any Reapers, while I'd help take care of Scout and get her safely from the building. We'd all rendezvous in the crossroads again, hopefully with one additional—and healthy—nose-ringed Adept in tow.

The plans and our cues established, we prepared to split up.

"Are you all right with this?"

I looked over at Jason, my heart quickening at the concern in his eyes, and nodded. "Turning on lights isn't much, but it's something. Maybe I can figure out a way to contribute." Assuming I could learn to control it in the next ten or fifteen minutes, I silently added.

He tilted his head at me. "You were serious about that—the lights?"

I smiled ruefully. "Turns out, the darkening wasn't a fake." I raised my hands and shook them in faux excitement. "*Yay.*"

"All right," Michael said. "Everybody ready?"

"Ready," Jason said, then leaned down and whispered, his lips at my cheek, "You take care, Lily Parker. And I'll see you in a little while."

Goose bumps pebbled my skin. "You, too," I whispered.

"All right," he said, his voice echoing through the tunnels. "Let's do this." He nodded at Paul and Jill, and they started on their way, moving through the tunnel to the left.

Michael, Jamie, and I shared a glance, nodded our readiness, and headed to the left.

The walk wasn't short, but the tunnels allowed us to move swiftly beneath the hustle and bustle of downtown Chicago to find the place where Reapers conducted some of their soul sucking. A few turns and corridors, and then the tunnel opened onto a platform, a set of stairs of corrugated iron leading up to a rusty metal door.

We stopped just inside the edge of the tunnel—Michael signaling quiet with a raised fist—and stared at the platform. No movement. No sound. No indication of surly, magic-bearing teenagers.

"Let's go," Michael whispered after a moment, and we crept toward the stairs—Michael in front, me in the middle, Jamie behind. Since Jill was going to be making ice for Jason's distraction, I assumed Jamie was the twin with fire powers. I still wasn't sure what a reader or fire witch could do, but I hoped that whatever it was could help us find Scout.

We took the steps to the door, but Michael, in the lead, didn't open it. Instead, he pressed his palm to it, then closed his eyes. After a moment of silence, he shook his head.

"Pain and loss," he said. "All through the building, through the steel, the brick, the city above. The pain leaks, fills the city. All because they won't make the sacrifice."

Another few seconds of silence passed. I stared at him, rapt, as he communed with the architecture. Suddenly, he yanked his hand back as if the door had gone white-hot. He rubbed the center of his palm with his other hand, then glanced back at us. "She's in there."

Jamie smiled softly at Michael "We'll find her."

At Michael's nod that he was ready to move, we tried the door, found it unlocked. It opened into a hallway that led deeper into the building. The hallway was empty. We stood in the threshold for a moment, gazes scanning for Reapers.

"It's too quiet," Jamie softly said, her tone unconvinced that it was going to stay that way.

"That's the point of distraction," Michael pointed out, "to keep things as quiet as possible for us."

A frigid breeze suddenly moved through the hallway.

"Jill is working," Jamie whispered, the breeze apparently evidence of the ice witch's work. "That's our cue to move."

We walked inside, Jamie lagging behind just long enough to ensure that the door closed silently behind us. "All right, Mikey," she said, "where do we go?"

Michael nodded, then pressed his hand to the hallway wall. "Down the hall. There's a room. Empty—no, not empty. A girl. A soul. Damaged. But she's there."

He opened his eyes again and looked at me, his expression tortured. It wasn't hard to guess how he felt about her, even if she didn't reciprocate those feelings. "She's there."

Jamie looked at me, her aqua irises suddenly swirling with fire. Goose bumps rose on my arms. "Then let's go," she said.

Without warning, a crash echoed through the building, the floor rumbling beneath us. "Alex," I murmured. The bringer of earthquakes.

"And probably her crew," Jamie agreed, taking the lead. "We need to move."

We hustled down the hallway, pausing at each open door to peek inside, look for Scout, make sure we weren't walking into a bevy of Reapers. But there was no one, nothing. No signs of people—Reaper or otherwise. Nothing but old industrial equipment and rusty pipes.

"It's too quiet," Jamie said as we neared a set of double doors at the end of the hall. "Distraction or not, this is too quiet."

"Here," Michael said, suddenly pushing through the double doors without thought of what might await him on the other side. "She's . . . here."

I followed him in, lights flickering above us, the rhythm of the lights as quick as my heartbeat. The room was big and concrete, giant tubs and shelving along the sides. It looked like a storage facility they'd tried to turn into some kind of ceremonial hall, a long red carpet running down the middle aisle, a gold quatrefoil on a purple banner hanging from one end. The Reaper symbol, I realized, there for all to see.

And below the banner lay Scout on a long table, her body buckled down with wide leather straps around each ankle and wrist, her arms pinned to her side.

"Oh, my God," I whispered.

She looked pale—even more so than usual. Her cheeks seemed sunken, and dark circles lay beneath her eyes. Her collarbone was visible. Her usually vibrant blond and brown hair lay in a pale corona around her head. But for the rise and fall of her chest, I'd have wondered if we'd arrived too late.

I had to bite my lip to keep tears from slipping over my lashes. "What happened to her?" I whispered.

Michael moved around her and began to work one of the buckles around her ankles. "Reapers," he said. "This is what they do, Lily. They steal things that don't belong to them."

Where there had been sadness, fear, trepidation, in his voice . . . now there was fury. Michael tugged at one leather buckle, freed the pin, then pulled loose the strap. "These kids, these adults, these people, think they have the right to take the lives of others, and for what? For *what*?"

Michael mumbled a string of words in Spanish, and while I didn't understand exactly what he'd said, I got the gist. The boy was *pissed*.

He bobbed his head toward her wrists, which were pinned near her head. "Jamie, keep an eye on the door. Get ready to raise flame if we need it. Lily, get her wrist restraints."

I jumped to the other end of the table and started fumbling with Scout's restraints. She lifted her head as I reached her, blinking with the one eye that wasn't bruised and swollen, but she didn't speak. They must have hit her while she was being restrained. I hoped she fought back. I hoped she gave as good as she got.

"I think you've managed to get yourself into some kind of mess here," I said with a small grin, trying to make her laugh, trying to keep my heart from thumping out of my chest. "I thought you were going to keep yourself safe?"

She tried a smile, but winced in pain. "I'll try harder next time, Mom," she said, her voice cracking.

"You'd better," I said, fumbling with the latch on the first buckle. "We're gonna get you out of here, okay?"

She nodded, then put her head back on the table. "I'm tired, Lil. I just—I think I'll just go home and sleep."

"Stay awake, Scout. We're going to get you out, but I need you to stay awake."

"Hurry, Lily," Michael implored, and I heard the clank as her first ankle restraint was loosed. "I don't know how much time we'll have." He moved around the table to get a better angle on her other ankle.

"I'm going as fast as I can," I assured him.

We'd just managed to untie her, to loosen all her restraints, and help her sit up and swing her feet over the bed when, without warning, the door at the other end of the room crashed open, falling in on its hinges.

Dark-haired Sebastian, the boy with firespell, walked inside. My breath quickened at the sight of him, and my back tightened at the memory of the pain he'd inflicted. Alex walked in behind him.

"Stay with Scout," Michael murmured. I nodded, and braced my body to help support her as he stepped away and in front of us, a human shield.

"Oh, look," Alex said. "It's an entire band of Buffy wannabes."

"Better Buffy wannabes than would-be zombies," Jamie said. "You guys are rotting corpses waiting to happen. That's gonna put a hitch in those Abercrombie catalog plans, don't you think?"

Alex growled and tried to take a step toward us, but Sebastian put a hand on her arm.

"I assume the vitriol means you're all acquainted," a third person said. Sebastian and Alex stepped aside, and he stepped into the gap between them.

He was tall, thin, silver haired, distinguished looking. He wore a crisp black suit, with a white, button-up shirt beneath. Every hair was in place, every bit of fabric perfectly creased. His eyes were pale blue, watery, red at the edges. But there was something about his eyes—something wrong. They were empty—dangerously empty.

"Mr. Garcia," he said, his voice flat, bored, as he bobbed his head toward Michael. Jamie moved to stand beside Michael, a supernatural barrier between us and the bad guys. "Ms. Riley," he said. I guessed that was Jamie.

And then the man leveled his watery gaze at me, and I shuddered reflexively.

"I don't believe we're acquainted," he said, just before Sebastian leaned in and whispered something to him.

The man's eyebrows lifted in interest.

My stomach fell, and I hunched a little closer to the table behind me. I was confident I did not want this guy interested in me.

"Aha," he said, sliding his hands into his pockets. "The girl who, shall we say, became closely acquainted with Mr. Born's magic?"

I took a moment to glare at Sebastian, who I assumed had mentioned that he'd hit me with firespell during my fateful trip into the basement.

But more interesting was the look I got back from him. I expected disdain or irritation—the emotions on Alex's face. But Sebastian looked almost . . . apologetic.

"I'm Jeremiah," the older man said, drawing my attention away from Sebastian. "And I can't tell you how interested I am to make your acquaintance. I hope you weren't harmed?"

"I'm fine," I gritted out, doubtful that he cared whether I'd been harmed or not. The lights above us flickered once, then twice. When Jeremiah's eyes flicked with interest to the fixtures, I knew I had to tamp it down. I didn't want him knowing that I was now an Adept, thanks to "Mr. Born's magic," and that I was now one of his enemies.

As if she understood the struggle, Scout squeezed my hand. I squeezed back and forced myself to stay calm.

Since Jeremiah was older than the Reapers around him, I assumed he was a leader, one of the self-centered asses who'd decided that taking the lifeblood of others was a cost worth paying to keep his own magic.

He looked from me to Michael and Jamie. "Your distraction was just that," he said. "Merely a distraction. Next time, you might do a little more planning. But, since you're here, what brings you to our little sanctuary?"

As if he didn't know. "You kidnapped my friend," I reminded him.

Jeremiah rolled his eyes as if bored by the accusation. "Kidnapping is a harsh word, Ms. Parker, although given the fact that you've undoubtedly been brainwashed by these agitators, these troublemakers, I'll forgive the transgression. These children don't understand the gifts they've been given. They reject their power. They turn away from it, and they blame us for accepting it. For abiding by the natural order. They cast us as demons."

"The power corrupts," Michael said. "We don't reject it. We give it back."

"And what do you have to show for that decision?" Alex asked. "A few years of magic until you're normal again. Ordinary."

"*Healthy*," Michael said. "Helpers. Not parasites on the world."

Jeremiah barked out a mirthless laugh. "How naïve, all of you." He aimed his gaze at me. "I would hope, Ms. Parker, that you might spend some time thinking critically about your friends and whatever lies they told you. They are a boil on the face of magic. They imagine themselves to be saviors, rebels, a mutiny against tyranny. They are wrong. They create strife, division, amongst us when we need solidarity."

"Solidarity to take lives?" I wondered aloud. "To take the strength of others?"

Jeremiah clucked his tongue. "It's a pity that you've succumbed to their backward belief that the magic they've been given is inherently evil. That it is inherently bad. Those are ideas for the small-minded, for the ignorant, who do not understand or appreciate the gifts."

"Those gifts degrade," Jamie pointed out. "They rot you from the inside."

"So you've been taught," Jeremiah said, taking a step toward us. "But what if you're wrong?"

"Wrong?" Scout asked hoarsely. "How could they be wrong?"

"You steal other peoples' essences," Michael said, pointing at Scout, "from people like her, in order to survive. Does that sound right to you?"

"What is right, Mr. Garcia? Is it right that you would be given powers of such magnitude—or in your case, knowledge of such magnitude—for such a short period of time? Between the ages of, what, fifteen and twenty-five? Does it seem natural to you that such power is intended to be temporary, or does that seem like a construct of shortsighted minds?"

I glanced over at Scout, who frowned as if working through the logic and wondering the same thing.

"We *agree* to give up their powers," Jamie pointed out, "before they become a risk. A liability. Before we have to take from others."

"A very interesting conclusion, Ms. Riley, but with a flawed center. Why should you protect humans who are not strong enough to take care of themselves? What advantage is there in stepping forward to protect those who are so obviously weak? Whose egos vastly outpace their abilities? Those who are gifted with magic are elite amongst humans."

As if bored with the conversation, he waved a hand in the air. "Enough of this prattle. Are you willing to see the error of your ways? To come back to the fold? To leave behind those who would rip you from your true family?"

Reaper or cult leader? I wondered. It was hard to tell the difference with this one.

"Are you high?" Michael asked.

Jeremiah's nostrils flared. "I'll take that as a juvenile 'no,'" he said, then turned on his heel. "*Ad meloria*. Finish them."

21

"Aw, this is my favorite part," said Alex, then outstretched her hands.

But before she could shake the earth, Jamie wound up her left hand as if bracing for a pitch. "Keep your issues," she said, then slung her arm forward, "to yourself." A wave of heat blew past us as pellets of white fire shot from Jamie's hand like sparks from a sparkler.

"Holy frick," I muttered, instinctively covering my head even though the fire wasn't meant for me. But it was enough to temporarily subdue Alex, who drew back her hand and hit the ground, wrapping her arms around her head to avoid the burn.

"Help me off this thing," Scout muttered, grasping my arm. I pulled her to her feet as Michael glanced around at the movement.

"Green," he yelled over the crackle of falling sparks, "get behind the table!"

"Garcia," Scout said, fingers biting into my hand as she kept herself upright, "I'm the spellbinder here. You get *your* ass behind the table."

"They're reloading," Jamie said, turning to grab my arm. She pulled me behind the table, and I dragged Scout with me. "Let's all get behind the table."

We'd just managed to hit the deck when the pressure in the room changed. I knew what was coming, deep in my bones. I clapped my hands to my ears against the sudden ache, as if my blood and bones remembered it, *feared* it.

The air in the room vibrated, contracted, and expanded, and the light seemed to shift to apple green, the table suddenly flying above our heads with Sebastian's burst of firespell. I covered Scout's body with mine and we were both saved the impact, but the move stripped us of our cover. We were all but naked, nothing but air between us and two Reapers who appeared to be better equipped for the battle than we were.

"I'm on it," Jamie yelled, turning from her crouch, fingers outstretched in front of her, her irises shifting to waves of flame again. There was another crackle of sound and energy as a wall of white fire began to rise between us and the Reapers. I kneeled up to sneak a glance and saw Sebastian on the other side, black brows arched over hooded blue eyes. He stared at me, his gaze intense, one arm outstretched, his chest heaving with the exertion of the firespell he'd thrown, lips just parted.

I don't know why—maybe because of the intensity in his eyes, in his expression—but I got goose bumps again, at least until the growing barrier of flame blocked my view. I guessed it was a foot thick, nearly six feet tall, and it crossed the room from one side to the other, a blockade between us and the Reapers.

For a moment, as if entranced, I stared at the wall of white fire, the heat of the dancing flames warming my cheeks. "Amazing," I murmured, turning to gaze in awe at Jamie.

"More amazing if it could withstand that earthquake business," she said as the ground rumbled beneath us. "I braided the strands of flame together. It's hard to penetrate, at least at first, but it won't hold forever. Flame acts like a fluid. It flows, sinks. The strands will separate."

"Scout," Michael called, "can you do anything? Reinforce the wall?"

She squeezed my hand, closed her eyes, and was quiet for a moment. And then she began to chant.

"Fire and flame/in union bound/from parts, a whole/from top to ground." Her body suddenly spasmed; then she went limp. I glanced behind us at the wall. It shivered, seemed to ripple with magic, then stilled again.

She'd tried, but whatever she'd done hadn't quite taken.

Scout tightened her grip on my hand, then opened her eyes and glanced over at Michael. "I can't," she whispered, tears pooling in her eyes. "I'm sorry. I can't. I don't have any mojo left. They took it, Michael."

"It's okay," Michael said, pressing his lips to her forehead. "You'll heal. It's okay."

"I can spark them again," Jamie said, "but I need to recharge for a minute, and the wall isn't going to keep them away for long."

I inched up to peek over the fire, assessed, and quickly sat down again. "There're two more of them. Are we toast?"

"Reaper toast," Scout agreed, then leaned into a fit of coughing.

"Scout?" Michael asked.

When she looked up at him, there were tears in her eyes. "It was a nightmare, a black hole. They trapped me, and they'd have kept going until there was nothing left. No energy, no magic—just a shell."

"They must have doubled their efforts," Michael said, his eyes scanning her face, like a doctor checking her injuries. "Siphoned more greedily than their usual one-day-at-a-time protocol. Probably weren't sure how long they'd be able to keep her." He glanced at me. "Energy taken from Adepts is more potent, more powerful, than energy from folks without gifts, so they'd have taken what they could get while they could get it, passed it on to elders like Jeremiah. You said they trashed her room, right? Maybe they were looking for her *Grimoire*, her spell book, something to try and capture some of her gifts, as well as her energy."

"They'll keep coming," Scout said quietly. "They won't kill us. They'll just suck us dry until there's nothing left. Until we leave everyone and everything else behind and do exactly what they want."

"Like magical brat packers," I muttered, sarcasm the only way I knew to deal with a future that terrifying.

"What can you do?" Jamie suddenly asked me. "You said something about lights? If we could distract them, maybe we could make a run for the door? Scatter through the tunnels?"

I nodded, my heart pounding, and looked up at the fluorescent lights overhead. I stared at them, concentrating, trying to speed my heart into whatever state was going to trigger the magic. Into whatever state was going to turn off all the lights.

"You can do it, Lil," Scout whispered, leaning her head against my shoulder. "I know you can."

I nodded, squeezing my fingers into fists until my nails cut crescents into my palms.

Nothing.

Not even a flicker, even as my heart raced with the effort.

"Scout, I don't know how," I said, staring up at the lights again, which burned steadily—not even a hiccup—in their fixtures. "I don't know how to make it happen."

"'S okay, Lil," she said softly. "You'll learn."

But not fast enough, I thought.

The ground rumbled again, the flames shaking on their foundations. It was another of Alex's earthquakes, and that wasn't all—the wall vibrated, wavered, at three or four other points along the line. They were hammering at it, trying to break through.

And despite my chest being full of fear, there wasn't so much as a flicker in the lights above us.

Maybe it had been a fluke before, a power surge in the building at the same time I'd been afraid or excited, and not magic after all. Maybe I had been a fluke.

But there was no time to worry about it . . . because the wall began to unravel.

I watched as the strands unbraided, listened as Reapers began to yell around us.

"It's going," Jamie warned over the motion and noise.

She was right, but it had help.

The air pressure changed again, the light turning a sickly green.

"Firespell!" I yelled, both Michael and I hunkering down to cover Scout with our bodies, my arms wrapped around her head.

The very walls seemed to contract, then expand with a tremendous force. The shot of firespell Sebastian threw across the room turned Jamie's fluid fire into a brittle wall that shuddered, then exploded, shards flying out in all directions before crashing to the ground like shattered glass.

When the air was still again, a haze of white smoke filling the room, I glanced over at Jamie. Her eyes were closed, and there was blood rushing from a gash in her forehead.

"Michael?" I asked, shaking white powder from my hair.

He muttered a curse in Spanish. "I'm okay." He sat up again, chunks of white . . . *stuff* . . . falling around his body. "Scout?"

I moved my arms and she lifted her head. "I'm okay, too."

"I think Jamie's hurt," I said.

Michael looked at her, then glanced around. The room was in chaos, Reapers yelling at one another, smoke wafting through the room.

"We've got to make a run for it," he said, "use the chaos to our advantage. It's our best chance."

I nodded, then put a hand on Jamie's shoulder and shook gently. "Hey, are you okay?"

Her eyelids fluttered, then opened. She raised a hand to her face and wiped at the blood streaming from the gash at her temple.

"Here," I said, pulling off my plaid tie and wrapping it around her head tight enough to put pressure on the wound and keep the blood out of her eyes.

"Can you get up?" I whispered. "We're going to try to make a run for it."

She nodded uncertainly, but it was a nod just the same. I helped her to her feet as Michael helped Scout behind me. As stealthily as we could, we began to move through the smoke and back toward the door, picking our way through the remains of the transfigured wall, me trying to hold Jamie upright, Michael all but carrying Scout.

We made progress, the haze aiding our escape, and managed to get halfway closer to the door . . . at least until a voice rang through it.

"*Stop.*"

We looked over. Alex emerged from a swirl of white, Sebastian beside her.

She stretched out a hand. "You can come willingly, or I can knock you all on your asses."

Reapers—the ones we hadn't been introduced to—began closing in from the left and right.

"Michael?" I asked.

"Um," was all he said, his own gaze shifting from side to side as he tried to figure a way out.

I'm not sure what made me do it, but I chose that moment to glance at Sebastian, who stood just behind Alex, his hooded gaze on me again. And while I looked at him and he looked back at me, he mouthed something.

Let go.

I frowned, wondering if I'd seen that correctly.

As if in confirmation, he nodded again. "Let go," he mouthed again. No sound, just the movement of his lips around the words.

I stood quietly for a moment as the Reapers gathered around us. Somehow, I knew he was right. And although he was supposed to be kicking our collective butt right now, I knew he was trying to help.

I didn't know why, but I knew it as surely as I knew that I was standing in the midst of people I wanted to protect.

People I *could* protect.

I took a chance.

"Get down," I told Jamie, Michael, and Scout.

"Lily?" Scout asked, confusion in her voice.

"We know what you've got in store," Alex said. "We know what you can dish out, and I think we've demonstrated that it ain't real much, so it's our turn to teach you all a lesson. To teach you about who matters in this world, and who doesn't."

"Trust me, Scout," I repeated, suddenly as sure about this as I'd ever been about anything else. I was where I should be, doing what I should be doing, and Sebastian had been right.

After a half second of deliberation, Scout nodded to Jamie and Michael. I waited until they'd all crouched down beside me, and then I did as he'd directed.

I stopped *trying* to make magic.

And I let the magic make itself.

I outstretched my arms and trained my gaze on Sebastian, and felt warmth begin to flow through my legs, my torso, my arms.

Firespell.

Not Sebastian's.

Mine.

My magic to wield, triggered by the shot of firespell I'd received a few days ago, but mine all the same.

I held my arms open wide. He nodded at me, then put a hand on his head and crouched down behind Alex.

I pulled the power, the energy, into my body, the room contracting around us as it filled me. My eyes on Alex, one eyebrow arched, I pushed it back.

"Bet you didn't know about *this*," I said.

The room turned green, a wash of power vibrating through it with a bass roar, knocking down everyone who wasn't already crouched behind me.

It took a second to overcome the shock at what I'd done, at what had seemed natural to do. I shivered at the power's sudden absence, wobbling a little until the pressure in my head equalized again.

The ground rumbled a little, an aftershock; then the room went silent, a spread of unconscious Reapers around us.

Michael stood again and helped Scout and Jamie to their feet. "Well-done, Parker. Now let's get out of here."

I offered an arm to Jamie, then glanced back at the dark-haired boy who lay sprawled on the floor a few feet away. "Let's go," I agreed, positive that I'd see him again.

22

We regrouped in the catacombs, Jason, Jill, and Paul emerging from their tunnel at a run. Jill and Paul both went to Jamie—sisterly concern in her eyes, something altogether different from brotherly concern in his.

Jason's eyes had shifted again from blue to the green of flower stems, a color that seemed unnaturally bright for a human . . . but better for a wolf. His hair was in disarray, sticking up at odd angles, a bruise across his left cheekbone. His gaze searched the crossroads, then settled on me, ferocity in his eyes.

His lips pulled into a wolfish grin, dimples at the corners of his mouth. I swallowed, the hairs on my neck standing on end at the primal nature of his gaze. I wasn't sure if I was supposed to run and hide, or stand and fight, but the instinct had certainly been triggered.

He looked me over, and once assured that I was fine, checked out Michael and Scout. She was on the ground, sitting cross-legged. Michael sat beside her, holding her hand.

When the two groups had reunited, everyone had made sure that everyone else was okay, and everyone had been debriefed about the rescue, Scout spoke up.

"Thanks, everyone," she said quietly. "If you hadn't come—"

"Thank Lily," Michael said, smiling up at me with appreciation in his dark eyes. "She's the one who led the charge. She did good."

"Parker showed some hustle," Jason agreed, offering me a sly smile, his eyes now back to sky blue. "She'll make a good addition to the team."

Scout humphed. "She'll make a good addition if Varsity lets her join, but that would require Varsity pulling their heads out of their butts. Katie and Smith are being total jerks."

"They'll unjerkify," Jason said confidently. "Have faith."

"I always have faith in us," she said. "It's them I'm not too sure about."

"Have some water," Michael said, passing her the bottle I'd pulled from my messenger bag. "You'll feel better. And when we get back to the enclave, you can tell us what happened to you."

Scout snorted defiantly, but did as she was told.

I stood up and stepped away to a quiet corner and looked down at my hands, still in awe at what I'd managed to do.

And I was still unsure how I'd managed to do it.

Okay, that was a lie. I knew exactly what I'd done, the sensation of doing it somehow as natural—as expected—as breathing. It wasn't that I'd suddenly *learned* how to do it, but more that my body had *remembered* how to do it.

I just had no idea how that was possible.

Jason walked over, pulled a candy bar from his pocket, ripped off the wrapper, snapped off an end, and handed it to me.

I took it with a smile, then nibbled a square of chocolate-covered toffee. I didn't have much of a sweet tooth, but the sugar hit the spot. "Thanks."

"Thank you," he said. "You saved our butts today. We appreciate that, especially since your last visit to the enclave wasn't very pleasant."

"Yeah, I don't think Smith and Katie liked me very much. And they definitely aren't going to like me now. Not after this."

"Like it or not, you're one of us, so I guess they'll get used to you."

"I guess," I said with a shrug. "The bigger question is, can *I* get used to it? Can my parents"—wherever, whoever they were—"get used to it?"

"My parents did," he said. "Get used to it, I mean."

I glanced over. "They got used to the idea that you're a werewolf?"

He gave me a sly, sideways glance. "Yes," he admitted. "They got used to that. But it's hereditary, so it wasn't much of a surprise when I started howling at the moon."

"They knew, and they sent you to Montclare anyway?"

He nodded. "Montclare was better for everyone."

"Why?"

"The principal knows what I am," he said. "He's a friend of my parents'—grew up with my mother. They shared my secret with him so that someone would understand how to deal with me if something happened."

"If you went all *Teen Wolf*, you mean?"

He grinned at me, his ridiculously blue eyes tripping my heart. "You say what's on your mind, don't you, Parker? I like that."

I rolled my eyes. "You have to stop flirting with me, Shepherd, or we're never going to get anything done."

"Flirting? You're the one who's getting me all riled up."

"Oh, please. You're all, 'Here, Lily, have some candy.' It's obvious who's flirting here."

"Then maybe I should kiss you."

I blinked, my cheeks suddenly on fire. "Oh. Well. If you think that's best."

He smiled softly, then leaned in toward me, smoke over sapphires as his lashes fell. I closed my eyes, blocking out the world around us, my heart pounding as he *almost* pressed his lips to mine.

"Well, well."

Did I mention the "almost"? I mentally cursed my best friend before we jerked apart and sat up straight. Scout stood in front of us, one hand on Michael's shoulder, looking a little better than she had a few minutes ago. The water and few minutes of rest in Michael's company must have helped. And if anyone could summon up a little spirit and energy after a round of soul sucking, it was Scout.

"I assume I'm not interrupting anything?"

"I wouldn't go that far," Jason mumbled.

I snickered and gave him a gentle elbow to the ribs. "You're fine," I told Scout. "We were just taking a break."

"I can see that," she said. "We're ready to hike back, if you want to join us."

Jason turned back and offered me a hand.

"I think I can manage," I said.

"Whatever you need, Parker," he said, offering me a dimple-laced smile.

I had an unfortunate inkling that I knew what that was.

The air in the enclave was thick with tension when we arrived. Katie and Smith weren't thrilled that we'd walked out on them, but they were happy to see Scout. They seemed considerably less happy to see me, and gave me dirty looks as we sat around the table and Michael, Jason, and Scout detailed our adventure.

As it turned out, the message Scout received said that an Adept had been hurt. Scout didn't say which Adept, but given her glances in Michael's direction, I reached my own conclusion. She'd gone back to her room to put up her books and prepare for a trip into the tunnels; that's when they grabbed her. There had been two Reapers, probably college age, but not people she recognized. She had no idea how they'd gotten into the school, but they'd been dressed, she said, like maintenance men—complete with badges and name tags. They'd already tossed her room when she arrived.

"Why you?" Michael asked, eyebrows furrowed. "If they were looking for a double shot of power, they could have chosen any of us."

Scout dropped her hand, outstretched both of them, and stared at her fingertips. "I think it has something to do with my power," she said, then clenched her hands into fists and raised her gaze to us again. "They kept talking about spellbinders and spellcasters, about the differences between them." She shook her head. "I don't know. I didn't understand most of it. I mean, 'spellcaster' is a made-for-television word as far as I'm aware, not an actual description of power. I'll have to check the *Grimoire*, see what I can find."

"Are you sure you still have it?" I asked. "What if they took it when they went through your stuff?"

Scout grinned widely. "What kind of spellbinder would I be if my *Grimoire* looked like a giant book o' magic? Remember that comic book I showed you the other day?"

"Ah," I said, understanding dawning. "That's sneaky and impressive." She winked back.

"What happened after they grabbed you?" Smith asked, with more concern in his voice than I would have given him credit for.

Scout's voice got softer as she retold that part of her tale, and she gripped my hand as tightly as she had in the sanctuary itself. The Reapers had used siphoning spells to begin the process of ripping away her energy, her will. They'd dispersed to deal with Jason's distraction, and that's when we'd found her.

Jason and Michael replayed their respective parts of the story, the room quieting again when Michael told them I'd used firespell to subdue the Adepts.

But Smith and Katie still looked unconvinced. They apparently didn't buy that I had magic, much less that particular kind of magic.

"It's not possible," Smith said, shaking his head. "A shot of magic, firespell or otherwise, can't transfer magic to someone else. That's not the way it works."

"You're right," Scout said, "but that's not what happened." She pulled a folded sheet of paper from the pocket of her skirt, then spread it flat on the table. "I've done some research. It turns out, there have been a handful of gifted folks whose magic wasn't obvious until something happened, until some act triggered their power."

"So it doesn't just develop on its own," Jill put in, "like you'd normally expect?"

Scout nodded. "Right. Lily didn't get the magic at puberty, unlike the rest of us. It's more like the magic is latent, in hiding, until something comes along and kicks it into gear. And once it's kicked, it's usually pretty big."

"What do you mean 'usually'?" Smith asked, brows furrowed together.

"Lily's not the first," Scout said. "There's an entire line of Contingency Adepts. Twelve of them. Half of them have power magic—the ability to wield electricity."

"Power," I quietly repeated. "That's why I can dim the lights?"

Scout nodded. "Exactly. And like I told you, that's what firespell's made of."

"Well, that sounds okay," I said. I wasn't sure I was thrilled to be an Adept, but there was something comforting about knowing what had happened. I mean, the whole thing was only barely believable, but in the context in which I was currently working—and having shot magic from my fingertips—it was comforting.

But as I scanned the faces around me, which suddenly looked a little peaked, I guessed they weren't as comforted. "Except everybody looks weird. Why does everybody look weird?"

"There aren't any firespell Adepts," Jason said, "at least not that we're aware of. They have an uncanny willingness to stay with the herd."

"To stay evil," I clarified dryly, and he nodded.

"And there is the other catch," Scout said.

"Wait," I said, holding up a hand. "Let me guess. Using this newfound power will slowly make me more and more evil, until there's nothing left of me but a cold, crusty shell of emptiness and despair. Lovely!"

"But we've all got to deal with *that*," Paul said with a grin.

"I mean, there is a benefit," Scout said. "You have a pretty kick-ass power, and you're obvs the only Adept with firespell, so that's awesome for *us*. You're a solid addition to the team."

I lifted my brows. "A solid weapon, you mean?"

"A solid *shield*," Michael said, his voice quiet and serious. "And we can use you."

"Whoa," Smith said, slicking the hair down over his forehead. "Let's not get too excited. So-called contingency magic or not, she's still not one of us. She's not an enclave member until we run things past the supervisors."

I leaned in toward Scout. "Supervisors?"

"The folks with authority," Scout said. "They keep to themselves, and we get their dictates through charming members of the Varsity squad. Lucky us."

"And because of that," Smith said, "there's nothing more we can do tonight. I'm going to make a call to see if another enclave is willing to babysit our targets tonight. Head back home. We'll be in touch."

Not taking no for an answer, he went for the door, six Adepts and one not-quite Adept behind him, heading off to bed before another routine day of classes, and another routine night of battling evil across the city.

Scout yawned hugely, her eyes blinking sleepily when the spasm passed. "I'm about done," she said, then slid an arm through mine after I'd returned her messenger bag and she'd situated it. "Let's go home."

"We should get back, too," Jason said, then glanced warmly at me. "You take care, Parker."

"I always do, Shepherd."

He winked; then he and Michael set off down the tunnels. Jamie and Jill and Paul said their goodbyes, but Scout and I stood in front of the door for a moment. She looked over at me, then enveloped me in a gigantic hug.

"You came after me."

"You're my new best friend," I said, hugging her back.

"Yeah, I know, but still. Weren't you scared witless?"

"Completely. But you're Scout. I told you I'd be there for you, and I was."

Scout released me, then wiped tears from beneath her eyes. Catharsis, I guessed. "I've said it before and I'll say it again—you seriously rock, Parker."

"Tell me again, Green," I said as we switched on flashlights and headed through the tunnel.

"Seriously, you rock."

"One more time."

"Don't press your luck."

It was late when Scout and I returned to St. Sophia's, but while she showered and headed to her room for some much-needed sleep (under Lesley's watchful eye), I plucked my cell phone from her bag and headed out on one last journey I wasn't entirely excited about taking.

Have you ever been in a car or on a walk, and all of a sudden you look up, and trees and blocks have passed you by? When you end up in a spot, but you don't remember much of how you got there? I found myself, a few minutes later, staring at the tidy gold letters on Foley's door. Light seeped beneath it despite the late hour.

I lifted a hand, knocked, and when Foley called my name, walked inside. She stood at the window, still in her suit, a porcelain teacup cradled in her hands. She glanced back at me, one eyebrow arched. "Ms. Green?"

"She's fine. She's back in her room."

Foley closed her eyes and let out a breath of obvious relief. "Thank God for small favors." After a moment, she opened her eyes, then moved to her desk and placed the teacup on the desktop. "I assume you're now interested in discussing your parents?"

I rubbed my arms and nodded.

"I see," she said, then pulled out her chair and lowered herself into it. She motioned toward the chairs in front of her desk. I shook my head and stayed where I was. It wasn't stubbornness; my knees were shaking, and I wasn't sure I'd be able to make it over there without tripping.

"As you know," she said, "your parents are very intelligent people.

They are currently working to resolve a somewhat, shall we say, awkward problem. That work has taken them to Europe. I have a personal interest in that work, which is why we're acquainted."

When she suddenly stopped talking, I stared at her for a few seconds, waiting for elaboration. But I got nothing more. "That's all? That's all you're going to tell me?"

"That's more than your parents told you," she pointed out. "Are you asking me to trump a decision made by your parents? Or, more important, have you decided that your need to know trumps their decision not to tell you?"

That made me snap my lips closed again. "I don't know."

This time, I really did take a seat, slinking down into a chair and staring at the desktop. I finally raised my eyes to Foley's. "They're okay, right? Because they're really hard to get in touch with, and their phone keeps cutting out."

"Your parents are safe and sound," she said, her voice softer now. "*For now*. You might consider, Ms. Parker, the possibility that they are safe, in part, because of the current status quo. Because you are safe and sound in this institution, and suspicions are not being raised. Because uncomfortable questions aren't being asked. Because," she added after a moment, lifting her eyes to mine, "the members of a certain dark elite are not aware of where they are, what they're doing, or where you've been placed in their absence."

My heart filled my throat. "They know about the dark elite? About the magic?"

Foley shook her head. "Unfortunately, that is a question I can't directly answer."

My head was spinning and my patience had finally worn thin. "Whatever," I threw out, then stood up and pushed back my chair. "I'll just ask them myself."

My hand was on the office doorknob before she spoke again.

"Is it worth the risk?"

I wet my lips.

"Your trust has been shaken, Lily. I realize that." I glanced back at her. "But if you search your soul, your memories, and you decide that your parents love you, perhaps you'll be willing to give them the benefit of the doubt on this one. You might realize that if they didn't give you all the details of their work, of their lives together, they had a very good reason for it. That the consequences of your knowing might not be worth the risks you'd be creating. The risk to you. The risk to your parents."

I lifted an eyebrow. "And when do I get the benefit of the doubt?"

She smiled, slowly. "You're here, aren't you?"

When I was back in the suite, I checked in on Scout. She was snoring peacefully in Lesley's room, and Lesley was curled up on a sleeping bag at the foot of the bed. I quietly closed the door and slipped into my room, then closed and locked it behind me. I grabbed my cell phone from the top of my bookshelf, sat down on my bed, and dialed.

It took two tries for my phone to actually make a connection to my parents. The third time, my mom answered.

"Lily?" There was a pause, maybe while my mom scanned a clock. "Are you okay?"

I opened my mouth, then closed it again, tears suddenly welling in my eyes. I wanted to yell at her, scream at her . . . and tell her that I loved her. I wanted to rail against her and my dad for not telling me the truth, whatever it was, for holding back so much from me. I wanted to tell her about my classes, about Scout, about the brat pack, about Jason, about firespell. About the fact that I had *magic*, power that flowed from my hands.

But maybe Foley was right. Maybe it was dangerous. Maybe their safety—*our* safety—was somehow dependent on my pretending to be an average high school kid.

Maybe there were more important considerations than Lily Parker getting a chance to throw a tantrum.

"I'm fine," I finally said. "I just wanted to hear your voice."

Smith kept his promise to keep in touch, but it was still two days before Scout got paged again. We walked together into the tunnels, headed for the enclave, the mood very different than the last time we'd taken that walk. Nevertheless, Enclave Three was still quiet when we entered.

Everyone was there. Michael, Jason, Paul, and the twins chatted together. Katie and Smith stood at the edge of the room, unhappy expressions on their faces.

"What's going on?" Scout asked when we reached the knot of JV Adepts.

Jamie and Jill shrugged simultaneously. "No clue."

Smith, a supersnug long-sleeved plaid shirt and skinny jeans all but pasted to his thin frame, opened his mouth, but before he could speak, the door creaked open. Our gazes snapped to the doorway.

A guy stepped inside. Tall, blondish, and well built, he had blue eyes, a dimpled chin, and strong features. He wore a snug U of C T-shirt and dark jeans over brown boots.

"Yowsers," Jill muttered.

"Good evening, Adepts."

"Yo," Scout said, her head tilted to the side, curiosity in her expression.

He shut the door behind him, then pressed his hand to the door. For a second, it pulsed with light, then faded again.

"I think he just warded the door," Scout whispered, awe in her voice. "I've never seen that before. He has got to teach me how to do that. It *rocked.*"

"I thought I rocked?" I whispered.

"Oh, you do," she assured me, patting me on the arm. "This is a totally different kind of rockage."

The blond walked to Katie and Smith and shook their hands. They looked none too excited to meet him; Smith's lip was actually curled in disgust. When they'd said their hellos, Katie and Smith stepped aside. The blond stepped toward us.

"I'm Daniel Sterling," he said. "And I'm your new team captain."

That must have meant something to the rest of the Adepts, who exchanged knowing glances.

"New team captain?" Paul asked.

Daniel looked at Paul, hands on his hips. "Your handlers and mine have become aware of a certain lack of . . . cohesiveness within this enclave. I am here to remedy that lack of cohesiveness." He slid a narrowed glance to Katie and Smith, who looked down, rebuked.

Scout and I exchanged a grin.

Daniel glanced at each of us in turn. "We're a team," he said after a minute. "High school or college, human or"—he paused, glancing at Jason—"*other*. All of us, together. Indivisibly."

The Adepts smiled. I appreciated their enthusiasm.

"It has also come to my attention that there's a new Adept amongst you." Daniel moved until he stood directly in front of me, then stared down, one eyebrow arched. "Lily Parker?"

"All day long," I answered.

He managed to stifle a grin, then slid his hands into his jeans pockets. "I understand that you were hit by firespell a few days ago, that a darkening subsequently appeared, and that you then discovered you had some power magic?"

I nodded.

"I further understand that you encouraged these Adepts to enter the sanctuary and retrieve Scout, and that you discovered, while you were there, that you had firespell abilities. I understand that all of you were able to escape largely unharmed?"

My cheeks warmed, and I nodded. Scout gave me a pat on the back. "Go, you," she whispered.

"That was a completely inappropriate course of action."

That wiped the smile off my face, and put a big grin on Smith's and Katie's.

"This organization works because we have a hierarchy, a chain of authority responsible both for the assignments given to Junior Varsity members and for taking responsibility when those assignments are unsuccessful. You had no right to encourage these Adepts into danger against the express wishes of their Varsity squad. Do you understand that?"

I nodded sheepishly, eyes on the floor, humiliation bubbling in my chest. Nobody liked a dressing-down.

"On the other hand," he said, turning back to Katie and Smith, "you were willing to sacrifice one of the most powerful members of your squad because you were unwilling to take a chance on her extraction. That reeks of cowardice. And cowardice is not why we're here.

"From now on," Daniel said, walking to the end of the room, then turning around again so that he faced all of us, "we work together, as a team, with one goal, and one set of leaders. Is that understood, Varsity?" he asked Katie and Smith. When they nodded, Daniel looked back at us. "Is that understood, Junior Varsity?"

We all nodded. I wasn't entirely sure if I was supposed to nod, but I wasn't going to risk this guy's wrath again.

"Now that we've settled that, we have some business to attend to."

Despite my attempt to blend in, he looked over at me. "Ms. Parker, you have demonstrated abilities that indicate that you're an Adept. Are you on our side or theirs?"

There was no need to ask which "theirs" he meant. "Yours," I answered.

"Then welcome to the squad." With that, he turned on his heel and walked back to the table, where he, Katie, and Smith began to chat.

I looked over at Scout. "That's it? I'm in?"

"What'd you think—you'd take an oath or something?"

"Something," I said with a nod. "You know, something more symbolic for the fact that I'll be sleeping less and battling bad guys more."

"Two words," she said. "Strawberry sodas."

"Congratulations," whispered a voice behind me. When I glanced back, Jason stood there, a knowing smile on his face.

"I need to go . . . somewhere else," Scout said, bumping me with an elbow. "You two kids have fun."

I made a mental note to talk to Scout later about "subtlety," but smiled at Jason. "Thanks, I think."

"So you're now an official member of Enclave Three. You weirdo."

I snorted. "I'm a weirdo? You're a werewolf."

"I suggest you say that with respect, Parker."

"Or what?"

"Or I'll have to bite you." His lips widened into a grin of heart-stopping proportions. I guessed it would have been pretty effective on him in werewolf form, too.

"I don't think you'll bite me," I offered back, although I wasn't entirely sure about that.

"I guess we'll just have to see what happens, won't we?"

Jason gazed down at me, those ocean blue eyes swimming with promise, at least until a cell phone rang. After a moment of chatting, cell pressed to his ear, Daniel clapped his hands.

"Saddle up, kids," he said. "We've got an assignment."

"We'll finish this later," Jason whispered. "I promise."

I believed him, so I offered him a wink, and we rejoined the others. I took my place at their sides, Scout squeezing my hand when I stood beside her, ready to take on evil in the Second City.

HEXBOUND

"Diamonds are forever. Magic, not so much."

—Scout Green

1

I stayed absolutely still, my eyes closed, the sun warm on my face. As long as I didn't fidget too much, the noon sun was just strong enough to cancel out the chilly October breeze that blew through our part of downtown Chicago.

I guess there was a reason they called it the Windy City.

It was a Sunday afternoon at St. Sophia's School for Girls, and I was squeezed into a tiny square of sunshine on the lawn with my friend Scout. She sat beside me with her arms stretched out behind her, eyes closed and head tipped up to the sky. I sat cross-legged, art-history book open in my lap. Every few minutes we'd inch our legs a little farther to the left, trying to take in the last warm bit of fall.

"This totally beats sitting in class," Scout said. "And wearing uniforms."

Scout was dressed in a black skirt and shirt she'd sewn from two White Sox T-shirts. It was quite a change from the navy-and-yellow private school plaid we usually wore. And then there were the shoes (Converses she'd coated in gold glitter), the hair (a short blond bob with dark tips), and the silver nose ring. There was no mistaking Scout Green, even in the uniform, for the average "St. Sophia's girl."

"You are totally rocking those clothes today."

Scout opened an eye and glanced down at her jersey skirt. "I appreciate your appreciation of my obvious good taste. Besides, someone had to rock it out. This place is like a dismal swamp of *bleh*."

I put a hand over my heart. "Thank God you're here to save us, Saint Scout."

Scout snorted and crossed one ankle over the other, her shoes glinting in the sunlight.

"And now I know why I keep finding glitter on my bedroom floor."

"Whatever. My shoes do not shed."

I gave her a dubious look.

"Seriously. That's just . . . um . . . horn dust from the unicorns that braid your hair while you sleep."

Scout and I both looked at each other. Unfortunately, while I didn't remember waking up with any mysterious braids, we couldn't exactly rule out the unicorn part.

Oh, did I mention Scout could do magic?

Yeah, you heard me. And I know what you're thinking: "Lily Parker, there's no such thing as magic. The tofu is starting to go to your head."

You're going to have to trust me on this one. See, as it turns out, Chicago is home to an underground world of magicians battling it out while the rest of the city is asleep. And those magicians included the girl, who was now humming a song from *High School Musical 3*, beside me.

Scary, right?

Millicent Green, aka Scout, was actually an Adept and a member of Enclave Three.

And here's the second twist—so was I.

See, I was actually from upstate New York, but when my parents decided to head to Germany for a research sabbatical, they figured St. Sophia's, deep in the heart of Chicago, was the best place for me to spend my junior and senior years of high school.

They said parents knew best. To my mind, the jury was still out.

I didn't come to Chicago with any powers, at least not that I was aware. And my parents certainly weren't doing magic in their free time.

Again, at least not that I was aware. But with a secret trip to Germany? Who really knew? I'd been told by Marceline Foley, the headmistress of St. Sophia's, that their work had something to do with genetics. She'd changed her tune later on, but there was no unringing that bell—or the fact that their European vacation was related to a place called the Sterling Research Foundation. For their safety, I'd made a promise to let my parents' secrets, whatever they were, stay secret.

Anyway, it took a trip into the basement of St. Sophia's—and a shot of magic from one of the bad guys—to trigger my own magic.

Firespell.

To be honest, I'd been an Adept for only a few weeks, and I was still fuzzy on the details. But firespell had something to do with light and power—manipulating it and throwing it back at the bad guys.

And that was exactly how I'd ended up with firespell—a shot from Sebastian Born. He might have been tall, dark, and handsome, but he was also a Reaper. A teenager who refused to give up his magic when the time came—and it came for everyone—and who now spent his time recruiting kids the older Reapers could feed from.

As it turns out, magic's only a temporary gift. We have it for only a few years, from puberty to age twenty-five or so. After that, the magic begins to degrade you, to devour your soul like some kind of rangy tentacled monster.

As Adepts, we promise to give up our magic, to give it back to the universe before it turns us into soul-suckers. Reapers don't. And in order to keep their suddenly hungry power from devouring them from the inside out, they have to feed from the souls of Adepts or humans.

So, yeah. Reapers—or, as they called themselves, the Dark Elite—weren't going to win any congeniality awards.

That put us pretty squarely against each other, like a football rivalry but with much higher stakes. So by day, we were high school juniors—wearing our plaid uniforms, doing our homework, ignoring our brattier classmates, and wishing we were in a public high school without a two-hour mandatory study hall.

And by night, we were dueling Adepts.

Scout suddenly sighed, a long, haggard breath that made her entire body shudder. She still looked a little pale, and she still had blue circles under her eyes.

A wounded Adept.

These were the scars left over from her own experience with the Reapers. She'd been kidnapped, and her room had been ransacked. It had been me and the other Junior Varsity Adepts from Enclave Three—and very little help from the Varsity Adepts, the college-age kids—that had fought to get her back from the Reaper sanctuary where Jeremiah, the baddest of the baddies, had begun the process of stripping away her soul.

It was days before she could sleep without nightmares, nearly a week before she was mostly back to her old self. But I still saw shadows from her time in the sanctuary—those moments when she disappeared into herself, when her mind was pulled back into the empty spot the Reapers had created.

Regardless, she was here now. We'd gotten her back.

Not everyone was so lucky. Sometimes we discovered too late that a Reaper had been befriending someone, too late for Adepts, friends, family, coaches, or teachers to pull him or her back from the brink.

Sometimes, fighting the good fight meant losing a battle or two.

That was a hard lesson at almost-sixteen.

"Lils, any thoughts about running away and joining a circus?"

I smiled over at Scout. "Are we talking pink poodles and clowns stuffed into a car, or creepy freak show?"

Scout snorted. "Since it's us, probably freak show. We could travel around the country from city to city, putting up one of those giant red-and-white-striped tents and sleeping in a silver trailer shaped like a bullet." She slid me a knowing glance. "You could bring along your own personal freak show."

This time, it wasn't just the sun that heated my cheeks. "He's not *my* freak show."

"He'd like to be."

"Whatever. And he's not a freak show." I glanced around to make sure we were alone. "He's a *werewolf.*"

"Close enough. The point is, he'd be your werewolf if you let him."

It was the "letting him" that was the hard part. Jason Shepherd, the resident werewolf of Enclave Three, was definitely interested. He was sixteen years old and, like Michael Garcia, another Adept with a massive crush on Scout, was a student at Montclare Academy, St. Sophia's brother school. I'd learned Jason had been born in Naperville, a suburb west of Chicago, listened to whatever music happened to be on the radio at the time, and was a devoted White Sox fan. He didn't like football and loved pepperoni pizza. And, of course, there was the werewolf thing.

I guess I was interested back, but spending nights fighting evil didn't exactly make it easy to get to know a boy.

"It's too soon," I told her, trying to make my voice sound as casual as possible. "Besides, you're the one who warned me away from him."

"I did do that," she quietly said. "I just don't want you to get hurt." Problem was, she wouldn't tell me why she thought that might happen. She kept saying I needed to hear it from him, and that wasn't exactly the kind of thing that made a girl feel comfortable about a boy.

"There's always something," I whispered. As if on cue, a grim-looking cloud passed over the sun, a dark streak in the sky that sang of impending rain. The breeze blew colder, raising goose bumps on my arms.

Scout and I exchanged a glance. "Inside?" I asked.

She nodded, then pointed at her shoes. "The glue's not water-proof."

Decision made, we gathered up our books and walked back across the campus's side lawn and around to the main building. The school—a former convent—was dark and gothic-looking, a weird contrast to the rest of the glass-and-steel architecture in this part of downtown Chicago.

That was what I was thinking when I happened to glance across the street . . . and saw him.

Sebastian Born.

He stood on the sidewalk in jeans and a dark polo shirt, his hands tucked into his pockets. His blue eyes gleamed, but not like Jason's eyes gleamed. Jason's eyes were spring-bright. Sebastian's were darker. Deeper. *Colder.*

And those eyes were focused on me.

The Reapers obviously knew Scout attended St. Sophia's, since they'd kidnapped her from her room. And another Reaper, Alex, had seen all of us one day in the concrete thorn garden behind the school. But that didn't make me any less weirded out by the fact that Sebastian was standing across the street, perfectly still, gaze on yours truly.

"Lily?"

At the sound of my name, I looked back at Scout. Frowning, she moved toward me. "What is it?"

"I think I just saw Sebastian. He was right . . ." By the time I'd pointed to the spot on the sidewalk where he'd stood, he was gone. "There," I finished, wondering if I'd actually seen him, or if I'd just seen some tourist with the same dark hair and blue eyes and I'd imagined it was him.

I wasn't crazy about either idea.

"Sebastian? Out here? Are you sure?"

"I thought so. I mean, I thought he was right there—but maybe not."

Scout put her hands on her hips and frowned as she scanned the street. "There's no sign of him now. I can text Daniel"—he was the newish leader of Enclave Three—"and let him know something's up."

Gaze scanning the street, I shook my head. "That's okay. Maybe I imagined it. It was only for a second—maybe I just saw someone who looks like him."

"Simplest explanation is usually the truth," she said, then put an arm around my shoulders. "No more sunshine for you. You've been indoors so much, I think the sun actually makes you crazy."

"Maybe so," I absently said. But I had to wonder—was I losing it, or were the Reapers watching us?

I had a dark-haired, blue-eyed boy on my mind.

This was a bad idea for two reasons.

First, I was in European-history class, and said dark-haired boy wasn't a king or soldier or historical figure of any type.

Second, the boy I'd been talking to was definitely not dark-haired.

The boy, of course, was Sebastian. And the obsession? I don't know. I'm sure he was on my mind in part because I'd (maybe?) just seen him. But it also felt like we had unfinished business. In a couple of glances and whispered instructions, Sebastian had taught me how to use firespell—that it wasn't about controlling the power, but trusting the power enough to let it control me. It was about letting the power move, instead of trying to *move* the power.

But *why* had he helped me? He was a Reaper, and I was an Adept, and at the time we'd been trying to rescue Scout and escape the Reaper sanctuary. There was no reason for him to help me, which made the act that much stranger . . . and meaningful?

"Ms. Parker."

I mean, not only had he helped me, but he'd helped me in the middle of a battle against him and his Reaper friends. Was there a chance he was really . . . *good*?

"*Ms. Parker.*"

Finally hearing my name, I slammed my elbow on the top of my desk as I bolted upright and glanced up at Mr. Peters, our Euopean-history teacher. "Yes? Sorry?"

The classroom burst into snickers, most of it from the three members of St. Sophia's resident brat pack: Veronica, Mary Katherine, and Amie. Veronica was the queen bee, a blond Gossip Girl wannabe currently wearing a pair of thousand-dollar designer ballet flats and at least a couple of pounds of gold around her neck. Veronica and I had tried being friends one Sunday afternoon after I'd first seen my Darkening—a mark on my lower back that pegged me as an Adept. I had been in denial about my new magic, and in the middle of a misunderstanding with Scout, so I'd offered Veronica a shot as best friend.

She didn't make the grade.

M.K. was the haughtiest of the crew. Today she was dressed like a goth-prep mash-up—a navy shirt and cardigan over her plaid skirt; knee-high navy socks; and black platform heels with lots of straps. Her long hair was tied in long braids with navy ribbon, and her lips were outlined in dark lipstick.

Amie was the quiet one—the type who seemed to go along to get along. She was also a roommate, sharing a suite with Scout, me, and a cello-playing, mostly quiet girl named Lesley Barnaby.

"Is class a little too difficult for you today, Parker?" M.K. snickered.

"Since you were apparently absorbed in your own thoughts," Peters said, "anything you'd like to share with the class?"

"Um, I was just"—I glanced up at the scribbled text that filled the whiteboard at the front of the room and tried to make sense of it—"I was just . . . thinking about federalism."

More snickering, probably deserved. I swear I was smart, even if I was still adjusting to the run-all-night, study-all-day schedule.

"And did you reach any conclusions about federalism, Ms. Parker?"

Deer in headlights, much? "Well," I slowly said, trying to buy time to get my mental gears moving, "it was really important to the founding of the country and . . . whatnot."

There was silence until Peters huffed out a sound of intellectual irritation and looked around the room. "Does anyone have anything more enlightening to add to the conversation?"

Veronica popped a hand into the air.

"Ms. Lively. Can you contribute to our conversation?"

"Actually, I need to make an announcement to the class."

He looked suspicious. "About what?"

"Well," Veronica said, "regarding our upcoming girls-only health-education class, if you get my drift."

Peter's cheeks flushed pink. He nodded, then cleared his throat, and after tapping some papers together on the podium, headed for the door. "For tomorrow," he said on the way, "finish chapter two."

With Peters on his way out, Veronica rose and moved to the podium, Amie beside her. Veronica tucked her hair behind her ear, her gaze on the door until Peters was out of the room. As soon as it clicked closed, she turned her attention to us.

"It's time to begin planning our annual holiday festivities."

The girls began to hoot like boys at a frat party. I glanced back at Scout, who rolled her eyes and propped her hand on her chin. I have to admit, I was mostly relieved I wasn't going to have to listen to Veronica drone on about sex ed. I mean, surely St. Sophia's could afford an actual teacher for that kind of thing.

"And when I say holiday, I obviously mean this year's Halloween Sneak. As you know, it's up to the junior class to plan the Sneak. This year's theme will be Glam Graveyard."

"Gravestones and glitter," Amie added.

"Precisely," Veronica said. "Our first planning committee meeting will be tomorrow. You can sign up on the sheet outside the door. Weirdos need not apply," she snarkily added, haughty gaze pinpointed at Scout.

"She's just *so* high school," Scout muttered behind me. I bit back a smile.

"Anyone interested in the planning committee has to swear not to squeal about the location of the Sneak, because the final location won't be revealed to the rest of the class until it's time to go. Any questions?"

M.K. raised a hand. "Will there be boys there?"

Veronica smiled smugly. "We're playing sister school to Montclare Academy again."

That smug look on her face worried me. Jason went to Montclare, but I wasn't so much worried about him. Michael, however, was a different matter. While Michael had a pretty big crush on Scout, she was playing very hard to get. Veronica, on the other hand, seemed determined to take her place. Veronica had made a point of asking Scout about Michael one day, hinting around that she had a thing for him.

The interest was understandable. Michael was totally cute. Dark, curly hair. Big brown eyes. A huge smile that was impossible to ignore . . . unless you were Scout Green. She managed pretty well. Of course, if Scout didn't ask Michael, then technically he was fair game.

The bell rang. Veronica made a little curtsy before she and Amie were joined by M.K., and they headed out the door. I waited for Scout to gather up her books.

"So," I began, "exactly how uncool would it be if I wanted to be on the Sneak committee?"

Scout pulled her messenger bag over her shoulder and gave me a sideways glance. "Purposefully involve yourself in brat drama? Why would you want to do that?"

"Decorating and design and stuff is right up my alley," I reminded her. "My art studio hasn't started yet, and I really need a creative outlet, even if it does involve the brat pack."

"Don't you already have a creative outlet?"

I rolled my eyes. "I'm not sure I'd call what we do 'creative.'"

"Have you ever done it before?"

"Well, no."

Scout grinned at me. "Then it's creative."

Drama notwithstanding, I concluded I was going it alone on the planning committee front. But as we walked down the hall toward our lockers, I decided to try something else Scout might be interested in. "Do you think Veronica asked him?"

"Asked who?" She sounded completely unconcerned, but I knew her better than that.

"I know your real first name, Scout. Don't make me use it."

"Fine, fine. Don't have a conniption. Yeah, she probably asked Garcia. Or she will, if she hasn't already. It's just the kind of thing she'd do."

"Maybe he wants to ask you."

"Then it serves him right for waiting," she muttered.

I slid her a glance. "So if he asks you, you'll say yes?"

"Just because I don't trip over him every time he comes into the room doesn't mean I don't, you know, appreciate him."

"I knew it," I said, a grin breaking out. "I knew you had a thing for him. So, are you going to tell him? Are you two going to start dating? Officially, I mean? This is huge."

"Pump the brakes," she warned, heading into the bay where our fancy wooden lockers were located. "Pump the brakes, or I tell Amie you want decorating advice. You'll have to wear shades just to sleep in your room."

Virtually everything in Amie's room was an eye-scarring shade of Barbie pink. "Now, that's just rude."

"I'm not above rude, Parker. You keep that in mind."

I took her word for it, which is why I snuck back alone to sign up for the Sneak committee. An artist had to do what an artist had to do, right?

2

A dozen or so hours later, we'd ditched our plaid for jeans and boots, tonight's uniform of the Adepts of Enclave Three.

It would have been cool to say we dressed that way because we were out pummeling Reapers into oblivion. But for now, Enclave Three was acting more like an Adept advance unit. Daniel tended to give us two kinds of assignments—trying to bring back kids who we thought had been targeted by Reapers, and patrolling the cold, damp tunnels beneath Chicago to keep an eye out for Reapers and, if necessary, battle them back.

There weren't any Reaper targets at St. Sophia's right now, at least not that we'd identified. (Although the soul-sucking would have explained a lot about M.K.'s personality.) So really, the boots were mostly to protect our feet from dingy water while we were on patrol. On the other hand, Jamie and Jill, auburn-haired twin Adepts with elemental fire and ice power, had been gone a lot recently, spending their evenings befriending a sad-eyed boy from their high school and trying to keep him from completely disappearing into himself as the Reapers used him to sate their hunger.

Tonight we were walking the tunnels that connected Enclave Three to St. Sophia's to make sure they were Reaper free. Unfortunately, they often weren't. I'd had my first run-in with Sebastian in these tunnels, and the Reapers had used the tunnels to kidnap Scout and to snag her *Grimoire*. Since they hadn't managed to grab it, odds were they'd try again.

We walked two by two, Scout and Michael in the lead, me and Jason behind. It's not like the tunnels were superplush or anything—they used to hold the tracks for small railroad cars that ran between downtown buildings. They had carried stuff into the buildings, and carried out ash from the boilers. Now they looked pretty much exactly how you'd expect abandoned miniature railcar tunnels to look.

On top of that, of course, the threat of Reapers was always there. But even with all that, there was something a little romantic about walking along in flashlight-lit tunnels together.

Scout looked back at me, determination in her eyes. "Lights on," she ordered.

From what we knew so far—since I was the only local Adept with firespell—my magic was all about power, the raw force of the universe. That meant I could throw out shock waves of power that would knock people down and out, and I could manipulate electricity. But I still wasn't entirely sure about the "how" of it.

I stopped walking, clenched my eyes shut, and concentrated on filling the tunnel with light. It was a matter of allowing the energy to flow into me, letting it pool and fill my veins with warmth, and then sending it out again.

"Very nice, Lil," Scout said. But I knew it had worked before she'd spoken, the insides of my eyelids turning red from the sudden glare in the frosty corridor. I opened my eyes, squinting against the sudden gleam of the cage-wrapped lightbulbs that hung above us. I was getting a little better at controlling it, learning to spark the light and douse it again by concentrating, instead of only when my emotions became overwhelming.

Scout hopped across one of the rails in the concrete floor, flashlight in her hand, her signature messenger bag—with its grinning skull and crossbones—bouncing as she moved.

"All right," she said. "Off again."

I blew out a breath, and pulled the power back out again. It was like turning the lights on, but in reverse—letting the power release again, freeing it from the bulbs in which it was bound. For a moment, the lights wavered, then went dark.

Jason took my free hand and laced our fingers together. "Your control is seriously improving."

"Only because I've been working on it like two hours a day."

Scout glanced back, her features thrown into strange relief by the flashlight beneath her face. "Hobbies are fun, aren't they?"

"In this case, they would be more fun if I had any clue what I was doing."

Jason leaned toward me. "You're doing great, Lily," he said, squeezing my hand. I squeezed back.

"I'm doing better than I was," I agreed. "But I'd feel a whole lot better if I could do it on command every time. I'm still a little unpredictable."

"One of these days," Jason said. Since his eyes were on Scout and Michael, who were walking side by side in front of us, Michael's arm around her shoulders, I assumed Jason was no longer talking about me.

"One of these days," I agreed. "They'll be good for each other. They *are* good for each other."

"Yes, they are," he said, before his gaze shifted back to me again. "But enough about them. You know, we haven't had a lot of time to talk. To get to know each other."

The warmth on my cheeks was a weird contrast to the chilly tunnel air. "That's true," I said, my heart suddenly thudding in my chest. What was it about this guy that made me feel like a nervous kid? I hated feeling that way, so I took the lead. "So, say something."

"Something."

I bumped him with my shoulder. "I'm serious."

"So was I. Maybe you just don't appreciate my sense of humor." But when I gave him a flat stare, he laughed. "Okay, okay. So, um, what is Sagamore like compared to Chicago?"

"Oh. Well, it's beautiful," I told him. "It's a small town, kind of in the country. Trees everywhere, rolling hills. Our neighborhood was on a hill, so when you looked outside in the fall, you could see the fog over the valley. It was like living in a fairyland."

"Wasn't 'The Legend of Sleepy Hollow' supposed to take place in New York?"

I frowned. "I don't know. Was it?"

"I wanna say we learned that last year in English." He shrugged. "I don't know. Could be wrong. Anyway, if it was, probably says a lot about upstate New York, right?"

"Are you suggesting I was living in a fairyland?"

"Well, at least a land with headless horsemen." He dropped my hand and half turned around, fingers arched into claws. "Headless horsemen who cut the heads off fair maidens in the night!" He tweaked my waist, just enough to make me yelp. I batted his hands away.

Scout glanced back, eyebrow arched. "What's going on back there?"

"Nothing," I said. "Some dork is trying to scare me with tales of murderous creatures."

She snorted. "What, 'cause that's so different from an average Monday around here?"

"Seriously, right?"

"People," Jason said, "I'm busy trying to work my mojo."

Michael turned around and offered Jason his fist, and they did a manly knuckle-bump thing.

Scout and I simultaneously rolled our eyes. But before I could respond, Jason grabbed my hand again and pulled me to a stop. My stomach fluttering, I kept my eyes on Scout and Michael, who continued in front of us, flashlights bobbing until they realized that we weren't following behind.

Scout looked back. "What's up, peeps?"

"Could you, maybe, give us a minute?" Jason asked.

"You are *not* serious."

"Do you have any idea how difficult it is to find time to kiss an Adept?"

Scout blew out a dramatic breath that puffed out her cheeks, grabbed Michael's hand, and pulled him down the hall. "Fine. Have a hot make-out session. But we're going to be like twenty feet down the hallway. I hope they get eaten by one of those headless horsemen," she muttered. "Or the Chicago version, anyway."

As they walked down the hallway, I kept my gaze on them, still too nervous to look at Jason.

"What would that be exactly?" I heard Michael ask.

"What would what be?"

"The Chicago version of the headless horseman?"

"Oh, I don't know. Maybe a fangless vampire? Or—or a werewolf with mange?"

"We can still hear you!" Jason called out. "And werewolves don't get mange!"

That earned him a huff from Scout. I finally screwed up my courage and looked back at Jason.

He had the bluest eyes I'd ever seen. But they weren't royal blue or the blue you'd see in the middle of a rainbow. They were so blue they were nearly turquoise, the color so deep it seemed that he stared out with precious jewels instead of irises.

Currently, those crazy eyes were trained on me. His lips curled, the dimple at the corner of his mouth puckering as he smiled.

My nerves tumbling, I kept things light.

"So you're trying to kiss an Adept?"

"Very, very diligently," Jason said. Before I could get out a snarky answer, he was dipping his head. His lips found mine, his mouth soft and warm. He put his hands at my waist and kissed me until I felt a little light-headed, until my heart fluttered in my chest. I'd been kissed before, sure, but I hadn't been kissed like this. Not by him, since we'd been interrupted when he'd tried to kiss me before. And not like my feet were going to lift off the ground and I was going to float right up to the ceiling.

I almost opened my eyes to make sure that hadn't happened—I mean, we were Adepts, after all.

Jason sighed and wrapped his arms around my back, and we kissed in the darkness beneath Chicago.

At least until Scout let out a *"Holy crap!"* that poured through the tunnel.

We separated and ran full out, relieved when we saw Scout and Michael still standing at the edge of the next segment of tunnel.

"What happened?" Jason asked, his gaze scanning the two of them. "Are you okay?"

"There," Scout said, swinging her flashlight across the tunnel in front of us.

It took me a minute to process exactly what I was seeing. The floor of the tunnel and part of the walls were coated in some kind of clear slime, five or six trails of it from one end of the corridor to the next.

"Wait," Jason said. "Is that— Is that slime?"

"Appears to be," Michael said. "It looks like they filmed *Aliens* in there."

Jason kneeled down, found a piece of metal on the tunnel floor, and stuck it into the goo. When he raised it again, he pulled up a long, stringy strand of slime.

"Eww," Scout said. "That is heinous. That's even worse than the time we fought off that nematode."

"What's a nematode?" I asked.

"I'm not going to tell you," she said. "I think you should have the joy of looking it up on the Internet and seeing the kind of pictures I had to see."

"So what did this come from?" I asked. "Some kind of animal?"

"Maybe not," Michael put in. "Maybe there's a leak somewhere. Some kind of—I don't know—industrial fluid or something?"

We all looked up. The ceiling of the tunnel looked old and nasty, but not even a little slimy.

"Hmm," Jason said, then tossed the metal into a corner. "That's definitely new."

"What do we do now?"

Scout put her hands on her hips. "Since the exit is in that direction, I guess we should see how far it goes."

"Lily and I will take the lead," Jason said, stepping forward into the tunnel. When I snapped to face him, shocked that we'd be going first, his expression was apologetic.

"Firespell," he explained. "Just in case we need it."

It was definitely an adjustment to play the lead heroine, but I sucked it up, nodded, and stepped beside him.

With flashlights aimed before us and Michael and Scout behind us, we took one tentative step into the tunnel. And then another. And then another.

"I'm not seeing anything," Scout said, flashlight beam circling across the ceiling of the tunnel as she searched out whatever had slimed the corridor.

"One tunnel at a time," Jason said. My hand in his, we took the lead, walking to the end of the corridor.

I was scanning the walls, bouncing my flashlight beam along them, looking for a hint of slime. So when Jason came to a full stop, I almost tripped forward, but he pulled my hand—and me—back.

That was when I saw them—and screamed. There were five of them—half walking, half crawling toward us. They were human-shaped, but a little smaller than your average adult. They were bald, with pointed ears and milky eyes, and their fingers were thin and tipped by long, pointed white nails. They scowled and snorted as they moved toward us. Their naked skin glistened in the light, a trail of slime on the ground beneath and behind them.

"What—" I began, but Jason shook his head. "Scout, Michael. Stop walking, and move backward. Just a few feet."

Scout and Michael began to move behind us. With each step they took, we followed suit until the four of us stood in a cluster a dozen feet or so away from the creatures. Still, they lurched in our direction, their movements coordinated like a school of nasty, pasty fish.

I could feel my chest tightening as panic began to take over. Staring down a group of hell-bent teenagers was one thing. This was . . . completely out of my league.

"What the hell are those?" I whispered.

"No clue," Jason said. "But they don't exactly look friendly."

One of them hissed, revealing long fangs amid an entire row of sharp teeth. "Are they some kind of vampire?" Michael asked.

"I've never seen a vamp that looked like that," Scout said.

Maybe it was coincidence, or maybe they were offended by what she'd said. Either way, one of them decided it was time for action. It put its front hands on the ground, then pushed off and leaped toward us.

Okay, not just us—toward *me*.

But there was someone there to save me.

It started with fur—thick and silver—that sprouted across Jason's body, replacing his clothes like they were nothing more than an illusion. Then he went down on all fours and stepped in front of me. His nose elongated into a snout, and his hands and feet became long, narrow paws. His tail extended, and the rest of his fur grew in, and by then there was no mistaking what he was—a silvery wolf, bigger than any I'd seen at a zoo.

Every survival instinct I had kicked in, and I had to lock my knees to keep from running away. Jason lifted his head and looked at me for a moment, his head tilted to the side like a dog, his eyes now spring green.

I stood frozen in place, my gaze locked on his—on this wolf that suddenly stood before me.

That look only took a second, but that was long enough for hell to break loose.

The creature apparently wasn't intimidated by Jason's new form, and it didn't stop running toward me. It continued its galloping gait, taking air in the last couple of feet and landing with an attack on Jason's muzzle.

"Jason!" I screamed, but Michael pulled me back. I'm not sure what I would have done, but someone had to do *something*. Jason was taking an attack meant for me, and I didn't want him hurt on my behalf.

I looked back at Michael with panic in my eyes. "We have to help him."

Michael's answer was nearly instantaneous. "Firespell it."

I reached down, could feel the quiet hum of energy, and nodded at him. "I think I can knock them down. But you have to get Jason out of the way or I'll take him out, too."

Michael nodded. "We'll get him focused. You get ready to firespell. The timing on this one's gonna be close. When I give the word, you send it out."

I nodded, then looked back. Jason and the monster were rolling on the ground, but at least its friends were smart enough to stay back. Jason was getting in nips at the creature's arms and legs, so the thing's *yips* and *yelps* were probably warning enough to the rest of them. It opened its mouth and screamed, revealing rows of tiny sharp teeth and clawing at Jason's muzzle as Jason tried to get a grip with his own teeth.

"*Jason!*" Michael yelled out. "Get clear so Lily can take a shot."

Jason let out a yip as the thing bit down on one ear and raked its claws across Jason's back. Jason shook the creature off, but it kept coming, clawing and biting as it attemped to take him down.

"Use the tunnel walls!" Scout yelled out. "Ram him!"

I made myself close my eyes. It was hard to shut out Jason when he needed me, but if I kept watching, I wouldn't be able to prep the firespell. I blew out a breath, and then began to slowly breathe in again. And as I inhaled, I pulled in as much power as I could, letting it rise through my body from my feet to my hands.

The tunnel shook from impact—I assumed that was the sound of Jason ramming a monster into the wall. I heard a wolfish yip and squeezed my hands into fists to keep from launching myself forward.

I heard scuffling as the power rose. I waited as long as I thought we could risk it, until I held the power—which ached to be loosed into the tunnel—by a thin string of energy.

"Anyone who doesn't want to end up on the floor needs to be behind me right now!"

More scuffling. As soon as the sounds moved behind me, Michael yelled out, "Now, Lily!"

I opened my eyes—and with a final check to make sure there were no Adepts in front of me—I lifted my hands and pushed them forward, moving all that power toward the monsters that were now only a few inches away.

The firespell moved forward, warping the air as it traveled, a vertical plane of green light and haze that shot out from my hands. It hit the creatures like a shock wave, knocking them all backward, the rest of the energy vibrating the walls of the tunnel as it moved forward.

I probably should have given a little more thought to whether using firespell in a century-old underground tunnel was a good idea. But there was nothing to do about it now.

The five of them lay on the floor, definitely down, but still twitching a little. I hadn't knocked them out completely.

First things first, though.

My heart still pounding from the exertion, I glanced back. Michael and Scout were crouched together on the floor. Jason sat in front of them, back in human form, blood seeping from a wound at his ear. There were scratches on his face and hands, but he looked pretty good otherwise.

I crouched in front of him. "Are you okay?"

Jason glanced up at me, a twinkle in his turquoise eyes. "Are you kidding me? That's the most fun I've had all night. Well, except for kissing you, of course."

Not a bad answer from a werewolf, I guess.

3

Jason held out his hands. I stood up, then took his hands and pulled him to his feet.

"You know," he said, "if you're open to a little constructive criticism, you cut it a little close there."

"Maybe next time you should be a little more careful where you fight."

He rolled his eyes, but he was grinning when he did it.

"Thanks for taking the hit," I said, pulling off my hoodie and pressing the sleeve to his ear, wiping away some of the blood.

Jason shrugged. "The wolf wanted to fight. And maybe I like rescuing the damsel in distress."

"Just to clarify, I did rescue you back."

He slid me a sly glance. "Then that makes us even. For now."

I grinned back, then checked out Michael and Scout. "You two okay?"

They nodded, then helped each other up.

"Well done," Michael said, then looked at Jason. "You good?"

Jason nodded.

"You okay, Lils?"

I nodded at Scout, but the relief at putting them down—and keeping us all relatively safe—gave way to exhaustion. I suddenly felt like I was about to get the flu—body aching, drained of energy. I needed warm soup and an equally warm bed. Instead, I still had five twitching slimy things to deal with.

"That's all I've got," I quietly said. "I can walk out of here, but that's about the only thing I'm going to be able to do. And we still have a problem."

We looked back at the creatures.

Jason stepped beside me. "At least they stopped moving closer. That's something."

"Since we've taken them out, can we please get out of here?" Scout asked.

"We still have to get past them," Michael pointed out. "And we can't just leave them here to roam the tunnels. God only knows where they'd end up."

"Or who they'd attack," Jason said. "That means we need a plan for part two. We need to get these things out of here, and we need it really quicklike. Scout? Got anything in the hopper?"

"I don't—I don't know—"

"You don't have to kill 'em," Michael said. "Maybe you can just transport them or something? I mean, since we aren't sure what they are?"

"What?" Scout said, a thread of panic in her voice. "Because those claws and teeth are for eating carrots? These aren't happy, fuzzy bunnies we're talking about."

I knew that sound in her voice. I'd heard that panic before, when she'd been taken by the Reapers to their sanctuary. I turned around and looked her in the eyes, and saw the terror there. She was panicking again, and God only knew what kinds of things she was remembering.

"You can do this, Scout."

She shook her head. "I can't. I don't remember how."

"Michael, Jason, and I are here. And those creatures aren't Reapers. They aren't going to use magic against you."

She sniffed. "They might eat us."

I put my hands on my hips. "You honestly think a werewolf is going to let those things eat his girl and her best pal? You've already seen him in action. And that was just an appetizer."

She only blinked.

"Look," I said, bravado bubbling up from somewhere I hadn't known existed. "We only have to kick a little butt here. You *love* kicking butt. And if nothing else, Jason can shift and we can let his wolf have an early breakfast."

"Not that I don't appreciate that offer," Jason muttered, "but I have no interest in eating those things, wolf or not."

Scout's eyes were still frozen on the creatures on the floor.

I tried again. *"Scout."* I waited until she made eye contact, then leaned down and put my hands on the sides of her face to make sure she was looking at me.

"Scout, you and Jason saved me from Sebastian and Alex, and we came and got you out of the sanctuary. Whatever our weaknesses, we are a team. And we're here, now, together. You can do this. I believe in you."

"I'm not sure what to do."

Michael snapped his fingers. "I've totally got it. Scout, you could flutterby them."

She blinked at Michael. "What?"

"Flutterby them. Use a transmogrify spell like you did on that Frankenstein thing last year. Remember?"

Scout was quiet for a couple more seconds. "I can't use a flutterby down here. I don't have anything. I don't have an incantation prepared."

Michael grinned over at her. "Scout, you are an Adept extraordinaire. If anyone could do a transmog spell off the cuff, it would be you."

For a moment, there was silence. And then she reached out and grabbed his cheeks and planted a kiss right on his lips. "You are *brilliant*," she said.

When she let him loose again, his cheeks were flushed bright red, his eyes wide. Probably the best part of *his* day, I figured.

"You're right," she said. "I can totally do this. But it's going to take a few minutes, and I need space to work."

We all looked down at the creatures, which were beginning to stir again, heads lolling as they fought off the firespell.

"First off," Scout said, "let's all back up a little."

Carefully and quietly, we took a few more steps backward, putting space between us and them.

"And now for something a little more formal," Scout said. She looked around at the floor of the tunnel, which was relatively dry compared to some of the other areas we'd been in.

"Protection circle?" Jason asked.

"Protection circle," she confirmed with a nod.

"What's a protection circle?" I asked.

"It's like a safety bubble," Scout said, fumbling around in her messenger bag. "Like a little snow globe of happiness that will keep us safe from them." She pulled out a small zip-top case. She opened it, then pulled out a small plastic hourglass filled with bright orange sand.

"You keep an hourglass in your messenger bag?" I wondered.

"Found it at a thrift store. Kept it for just such an occasion. Keep an eye on the biters."

I made sure Jason and Michael were doing just that, then turned back to watch Scout work her juju. No way was I going to miss this.

She pulled a small screwdriver from the case and pried off the end of the hourglass. And then, starting behind us, she began to pour the sand in an arc around me. She completed most of a six-foot circle, but stopped when a gap of about a foot separated the two ends.

"Everyone inside," she said. Michael and Jason both stepped carefully over the sand circle. When we were all inside, she went to her knees, put her hands on the floor, and pressed her lips to the gap in the circle.

"What's she doing?" I whispered to Michael.

"She's starting the Triple I," he answered without looking back. "It stands for 'intent, incantation, incarnation.' The three parts of a major spell."

Okay, magic had officially become school.

"We ask a wish," Scout said, sitting back on her heels. "We ask for peace. We ask for space between us and those who would harm us."

She held the hourglass in her hands, then closed her eyes.

After a moment of silence, I leaned toward Michael again. "Is this part of it?"

"This is the part where I have to draft a spell on the fly since I haven't poured a circle in forever," Scout huffed. "It's also the part where it helps if Adepts don't ask questions while I do it."

I zipped up my lips, just in time for Jason and Michael to take a step backward, bumping into me a little.

"They're moving, Scout," Michael said. "Draft faster."

I glanced back. The *things* were starting to stumble their way to their feet.

Scout cleared her throat, then began her incantation. "Silence, serenity, solitude, space. We ask for protections inside of this place. Empower this circle with magical grace, and keep us all safe . . ."

She stopped. I looked over and saw the blank expression on her face.

". . . and keep us all safe," she repeated, desperation in her voice. She couldn't seem to find the right phrase to end the poem.

"Hurry *up*, Scout."

At Jason's harried tone, I looked up again. All five of the creatures were on their feet, and they looked pretty angry. There were only ten or fifteen feet between us, and they were lumbering forward, fangs bared, claws beginning to scrape the concrete like nails on a chalkboard.

"Don't listen to them," I told her, "and don't worry—you can do this."

"And keep us all safe . . ."

Michael glanced back. "Anytime now!"

She snapped her fingers. "—in this circle we trace!" She poured the rest of the sand in a line, just as claws struck out at Michael. He jumped back, but she'd finished the circle just in time—the creature was out of luck.

The bubblelike shield shimmered as the creature made contact with it, then disappeared again when it yanked back its claw with a fierce whine. The pain didn't deter it or the rest of them. They all began to attack. We stood there and watched them claw and scrape at the energy to get at us. The shield shimmered a little every time they made contact, but it held.

"Just in time," Scout finally said.

Jason nodded. "You did good. Now, are you actually going to transmogrify them?"

Scout nodded, then knelt on the floor and began to pull stuff from her messenger bag. "A woman's work never ceases."

Scout Greene was a taskmaster worthy of any St. Sophia's professor. She folded a piece of paper from a notebook into an origami cup in the shape of a bird, and started quizzing us to find stuff to put into it.

So far, I'd offered up a chunk of granola bar and three drops of water from my bottle. Jason and Michael didn't have man purses, so she took stuff from their pockets—sixty-two cents, a ball of stringy blue jeans lint, and a tube of lip balm. Together, all that stuff was supposed to represent our sacrifice of various bits of earth—water, metal, food, etc.

When everything was in the paper cup, she folded the top carefully again, then scribbled out what I assumed was an incantation on another piece of paper. While she drafted, the monsters poked around the bubble, looking for a weak spot. Although they weren't successful, from what I could tell, the shield wasn't going to last forever.

When Scout had the finished incantation in one hand and the closed paper cup in another, she glanced around at each of us. "Are we ready?"

"I've never been more ready to climb into bed," I told her. Michael and Jason nodded in agreement.

"Here's the plan." She held up the piece of paper. "I'm going to repeat the incantation, and as soon as I'm done, I'm gonna wipe out the circle and throw the charm. If I've done this right, the spell will trigger as soon as the charm hits."

Michael pulled the cell phone from his pocket.

"Really," Scout said flatly, "you're going to make a call right now?"

Michael aimed the phone toward the creatures and began snapping. "I'm going to take pictures of these things in the likely event Smith and Katie don't believe what we saw." Smith and Katie were Varsity Adepts and the former leaders of Enclave Three. They'd held the reins when Scout had been kidnapped. Good riddance, if you asked me.

"Oh. Well, good call," Scout allowed.

Michael smiled sweetly at her. "I'm entitled to a few good ideas, you know."

She blushed.

When Michael was done and the cell phone was tucked away again, Jason clapped his hands together. "Okay, let's get this show on the road. Everyone in the back of the bubble. Puts more space between us and them when the circle goes down," he explained.

When we'd stepped back, Scout glanced at each of us in turn. "Are we ready?" When we'd all nodded, she did the same. "Then here goes nothing."

Michael, Jason, and I each put up our fists, like we were heading into a schoolyard fight.

Scout closed her eyes and held the crane in her lifted hands. "Beauty comes in many sizes, but these guys just aren't prizes. Give them all a new disguise, and make them change before our eyes!"

She cocked back her arm to throw the bird. "And three . . . two . . . and one!" She used her toe to push some sand out the circle. As soon as it was breached, the shield gave one final shimmer and dropped away. They lunged forward, and Scout threw the paper bird into the middle of the group.

The tunnel exploded into noise and white light.

I dropped down, hands over my head, waiting for an attack—that didn't come.

I opened an eye. The air was filled with a thousand tiny white paper cranes, all of them flapping their little paper wings as they spun around us. The creatures were nowhere to be seen.

"What just happened?" I asked.

"She transmogrified them," Michael said, surprise in his voice.

I stood up, waving a hand in front of my face so that I could see through the cranes. After a moment, they formed a long *V* and flew past us down the tunnel, leaving us alone, the floor littered with bits of origami confetti.

Michael stared openmouthed at the birds as they disappeared into the next chunk of the tunnel. "This is just . . . fricking amazing! You did it! You actually did it!" He picked Scout up and spun her around in the air, just like in the movies.

I grinned at the look of total shock on her face. Considering the fact that she'd actually kissed him a few minutes ago, my math said Garcia, two. Scout, zero.

"It was teamwork," she said, adjusting her shirt when he finally put her down again. Her cheeks were pink, but I could tell she was trying really hard not to smile. Before I could say anything to her, Scout jumped at me and wrapped her arms around my neck.

"Can't breathe," I said, patting her back. "Dial it back."

When she finally loosened up, I rubbed my neck. "What was that for?"

"You believed in me," she said simply, and then put an arm around my shoulders.

"Of course I did. Now, shouldn't we tell somebody about those things?"

"On it," Michael said, tapping the keyboard on his phone. "Gave Daniel the heads-up," he said, then nodded when the phone beeped only a second later. "Enclave tomorrow night for the debriefing."

"Then I think that means our work here is done," Scout said. "Let's go home."

I couldn't have said it better myself.

Just in case there were any more nasties lumbering around, Jason and Michael escorted us to the door into St. Sophia's. And then, wolfless, Scout and I made our way back through the main part of the convent and the Great Hall, where we studied during our mandatory two-hour study hall (I know, right?), to the building that housed our suite. The common room was dark when we unlocked the door and tiptoed inside, as was Lesley's room.

But Amie's door was open. The bedroom light was off, but Veronica was standing in the doorway.

My stomach turned.

Veronica took a step forward, closing Amie's door behind her. She was dressed for bed in yoga pants and a tank top, her hair long and styled straight, circles beneath her eyes. She looked us over.

"Where have you two been?" she asked, crossing her arms and leaning back against the doorway.

I glanced between mine and Scout's rooms, which faced each other across the suite, the doors wide open. That was an obvious signal that we weren't tucked in like we were supposed to be—and hadn't been for a while.

But Scout stayed calm. "We couldn't sleep," she said, "so we walked around for a little while." She walked toward her room. When Veronica didn't budge, Scout stopped and looked back at her. "What are you doing in our suite anyway?"

Veronica took a step forward and closed Amie's door behind her. "We were studying. Unlike the two of you."

Her voice rose at the end, like she was asking a question—or daring us to prove her wrong.

"I mean, it's pretty weird," she said. "You two just heading out to walk around or whatever. It doesn't even look like you've been in bed at all."

Scout and I exchanged a glance. This was going to be tricky. If we stuck to our "we were just walking around" story, she might think we were lying and do some investigating that would only inconvenience both of us.

We obviously couldn't exactly tell her what we'd really been doing. But maybe if we told her something a *little bit* bad, we might answer her questions . . . and keep her from asking too many more.

"I went to meet my boyfriend," I threw out. Okay, so I was fudging about our status, but the rest was true enough. "And Scout went with me. To, you know, prop the door open so I wouldn't get locked out." That sounded legit to me, anyway.

"You haven't been here that long. You don't have a boyfriend."

I managed a bored eye roll. "That you *know of*."

"Who is it?"

I made a little mental apology to Jason for outing our almost-relationship, but figured he'd get over it. "Jason Shepherd."

Veronica's eyes widened, and she uncrossed her arms. "From Montclare?"

I nodded.

"Isn't he, like, John Creed's friend?"

I opened my mouth to answer yes—Creed was a friend of Jason's, a guy I'd met when Veronica and I had had our afternoon of friendship. He'd shared a flirty moment with Veronica at the store where we'd met them. Creed had dark hair and dark eyes, and just looked *wealthy*. It was obvious in the way he carried himself, in the way he talked. He was just comfortable in a way that said, "The world is at my feet." But most important, he had a unique look. Funky designer watch, square-toed shoes, that kind of thing. I'd known rich kids who were joiners—who dressed just like everyone else—and rich kids who were so rich they didn't have to be joiners. He was the nonjoiner type.

And Creed seemed friendly enough, but there was still something—I don't know—*odd* about him. Something shadowy. Not like Reaper shadowy—I didn't think he had magic, and he didn't strike me as the type to run around in dark and damp tunnels in the middle of the night.

But I closed my mouth again. Had we just jumped from being in trouble for sneaking out to Veronica asking about Creed? Scout and I weren't out of the woods yet, and we could probably use that.

Trying to play it cool, I just shrugged. "I guess they're friends, yeah. Why?"

"No reason," she said, but her cheeks blossomed pink. "Was he here?"

"Creed? No, just me and Jason and Scout." I saw no need to also drag Michael into this. Besides, maybe Veronica had actually decided to turn her attentions elsewhere. Creed seemed more her speed anyway.

Veronica's expression went flat again. "And where, exactly, did you meet Jason?"

"Admin wing," Scout offered. "The very same door M.K. uses when she sneaks out to meet her boyfriend."

Well, that was information I didn't need.

Veronica's eyes flashed, but since she didn't move from her spot in the doorway, I guess the threat against M.K. hadn't been all that effective. Scout tried again.

"They were in there, like, forever," she said, sliding me a look of disgust. I tried to look guilty, shuffling my feet a little for good measure.

"That's against the rules, you know."

"Yeah, whatever." I looked away, tucked some hair behind my ear and faked an attitude. "I'm almost sixteen. I do what I want."

"She is from the East Coast," Scout said. "They mature differently out there."

"Well, whatever. It's against the rules."

"So's spending the night in someone else's suite," Scout pointed out. "And I know you don't want to get in trouble for that. So why don't we all just go to bed and get in a good night's sleep?"

Veronica's lip curled, but she spun on her heel, walked into Amie's bedroom, and slammed the door shut behind her.

Almost immediately, the door beside Amie's opened. Lesley, our third roommate, glanced out. She was dressed in rainbow-striped pajama bottoms and a T-shirt with a pot of gold on it. Lesley knew about our midnight ramblings because—just as I'd done to Scout—she'd followed us into the basement one night. But she'd offered to help us, and she'd helped me out the night Scout disappeared. So as far as I could tell, she was one of the good guys. Or good girls. Whatever.

Lesley offered a thumbs-up.

Scout gave her back a thumbs-up. Apparently satisfied with that, Lesley popped back into her room and closed the door behind her.

Scout glanced over at me. "Next time you decide you want to make out with your boyfriend, call someone else." Her voice was just a shade too loud—it was another scene in our little play for Veronica.

She rolled her eyes and stuck out her tongue, then turned on her heel and walked to her bedroom door. "Good night, Parker."

"Good night, Green."

I went to my own room and shut and locked the door behind me. My messenger bag hit the floor, and I threw on pajamas that might have matched, but probably didn't. My room, with its stone walls and floor, was always cold, so I went for warmth over beauty.

Grateful that I'd made it safely back—slimy monsters notwithstanding—I grabbed my cell phone and checked for messages from my parents. My father and mother had each sent me a text. Both of them said they loved me. My mother's text message was straight and to the point: "HOW WAS YOUR MATH TEST? R U EATING PROTEIN?" I was a vegetarian; she usually just said I ate "weird."

My dad always tried to be funny. That was his thing. His message read: "R U BEING GOOD IN THE WINDY CITY? SANTA WILL KNOW."

Unfortunately, he wasn't nearly as funny as he liked to think he was. But he was my dad, you know? So I typed out a couple of quick texts back, hoping they were somewhere safe and could actually read them.

After I'd pulled on thick, fuzzy socks, I climbed into bed and pulled the St. Sophia's blanket over my head, blocking out the dull sounds of Chicago night traffic and the faint glow of plastic stars on the ceiling above my head.

I was asleep in minutes.

4

When my alarm clock blared to life, I woke up drenched in sweat, my St. Sophia's blanket pulled completely over my head.

I'd had a nightmare.

I sat up and pushed the damp hair from my face, my heart still racing from the dream. I was awake, sure, but I hadn't yet recovered. I still felt like I was there . . .

I'd dreamed that I'd been home in Sagamore. I'd been upstairs in my room reading a book. The house had been quiet; I think my parents had been downstairs watching television or something. I'd heard the front door open and close again, and out of curiosity, I'd put down my book and walked to the window, pushing the blinds aside.

Two men in black suits had gotten out of a boxy sedan. They'd looked at each other before walking toward our front door. They'd adjusted their suit coats as they'd moved, and I'd seen the glint of metal in one of their coat pockets.

I'd heard the doorbell ring, and the front door open and close, and the low murmurs of conversation that filtered upstairs.

And then the conversation had gotten louder. I'd heard my father demand the men leave.

I'd put my cell phone into my pocket—just in case—and I'd begun to walk toward my bedroom door. But with each step I'd taken, the door had gotten farther and farther away. My bedroom had expanded exponentially until the door was just a small rectangle in the distance. My heart had pounded in my chest, and my vision had narrowed until everything was fuzzy at the edges and the door was a tiny glint at the end of a tunnel.

That was when the yelling had begun.

I'd reached out for the door, but it was too far away. I'd begun to run, but each step felt like I was running through molasses. And even though I wasn't going anywhere, my chest tightened like I'd been running a marathon. With no means to get to the door, I'd turned around and stared at the window like it was my only means of oxygen.

I'd run to the window—which stayed in place—and thrown it open. The men had walked outside again. One man had gotten back into the car on the driver's side. The other had stopped and looked up at me. Our stares had locked, and there had been an evil glint in his narrowed eyes. He'd mouthed something I couldn't catch—but there'd been no mistaking the symbol on the side of his car.

It was a quatrefoil—four circles stacked together like a curvy cross.

The symbol of the Reapers—of the Dark Elite.

The entire scene played in my mind like a movie. Just as real—the sounds and sights and smells of home the same. And that was the scariest part. Something about the dream felt familiar—familiar enough that I wasn't sure if it had been a dream . . . or a memory. But I couldn't remember seeing two men in black suits in an old-fashioned car arriving at the house. I didn't remember yelling on the first floor or being unable to check on my parents. But still, something rang true. And I was afraid that something had something to do with the Reaper symbol on the car.

Shaking it off, I pulled on my robe, grabbed my shower kit, and headed down the hallway to the bathroom. I stood under the spray for a good, long while, but I couldn't erase the feeling that I was still *in* the dream. That I'd try to turn the shower handle but it would move out of reach, or I'd return to the suite and find the man in black outside my door.

When I was dressed—skirt and St. Sophia's polo under a hoodie—I walked across the suite to Scout's room and knocked on the door. She answered with a "Yo!"

I opened the door and found her standing beside her bed, stuffing books into her messenger bag. At the sight of me, her expression fell. "Geez, you look awful. What happened?"

"Nightmare."

Frowning, she glanced at the clock, then patted the bed beside her. "We've got a couple minutes. Bring her in for a landing."

We both sat down on the bed. I told her about the dream. She listened patiently while I rehashed the details, occasionally patting my knee supportively. When I was done, I let out a slow breath, trying to remind myself that it had been just a dream . . . except it didn't really feel that way.

"I think that's the thing that bothers me the most," I told her. "I mean, I know I didn't see any of that stuff. I don't think I've ever heard anyone yell at my parents. But it felt real."

"Dreams can do that, you know. This one time, I dreamed I was being booed off the stage at this outdoor concert where I was playing the French horn. I don't play the French horn, nor do I aspire to play the French horn. Couldn't even pick one out of a lineup, probably. But when I woke up, I still *felt* like I was up there. I'd been humiliated in that dream, and the whole rest of the day I felt like I'd just walked off that stage."

"French horn in hand?"

"Exactly." Scout stared blankly ahead for a few seconds, like she was reliving the memory. "I knew it was just a dream—I mean, logically I knew it. But that didn't make it feel any less real. It took a while to, like, shake off the psychic funk or whatever." She grinned a little and bumped me with an elbow. "You just need to shake off your psychic funk."

"You know, you are a pretty good friend. Those things they say about you are hardly true."

Scout snorted, stood up, and shouldered her messenger bag. "They say I'm fabulous. And it's crazy true. Now let's go chow."

. . .

It was just common sense that Adepts who spent their evenings fighting evil needed a good breakfast to start their day. Unfortunately, there was only one route to breakfast, and that was in the cafeteria through the horde of teenagers already in line for their own breakfasts.

Scout and I muscled into line.

Okay, that might be overstating it. Our evening adventures were one thing. Down there, we ruled the night with magic and firespell and flirted with werewolves. We had supernatural muscle.

But up here, we were the weirdish girl and her weirder friend—just two high school juniors trying to get enough credits for graduation while avoiding as much brat-pack drama as possible.

Not that that was easy.

Scout and I had just taken breakfast (hot tea and giant muffins) to a table when they walked in, Veronica in the lead, M.K. and Amie behind. They wore the same skirts that we did, but you could still tell they were different. They had *swagger*. They sauntered across the room like every eye was on them—and they usually were—and like there was no doubt in the world who they were, what they wanted, or what they were going to get.

The attitude aside, you kinda had to admire the confidence. Even Amie, who was a worrier, moved like the cafeteria was her personal catwalk.

"If you keep staring, your head's gonna get stuck that way."

I glanced back at Scout and stuck my tongue out at her, then nibbled on a giant blueberry from my muffin. "I can't help it. They're like a really rich, super-put-together train wreck."

Scout rolled her eyes. "I've totally taught you better than that. The brat pack is to be *ignored*. We rule the school around here."

"Mm-hmm. If that's true, why don't you head on over to the front of the room"—I pointed out a perfect spot—"and tell them that?"

"Oh, I totally could if I wanted to. But right now"—she bent over her muffin and began to cut it into tiny squares with a knife and fork—"I am totally focused on nourishment and noshing."

"You're totally focused on being a dork."

"You better respect me, Parker. I know where you sleep."

"I know where you snore."

After a few minutes of quiet munching, the bell rang, our signal that it was time to play goodly St. Sophia's girls for the next few hours. "You know what's crazy true?" I said, standing up and grabbing my messenger bag.

"That summer vacation can't come fast enough?"

"Bingo."

"I am a genius," Scout said. "Ooh—do you ever worry I'll become an evil genius?"

"The thought hadn't really crossed my mind. You're a pretty good kid. But if you start moving toward the dark side, I promise I'll pull you back over." We headed into the throng of teenagers heading for the cafeteria door.

"Do it," she said. "But pull me back onto Oak Street Beach in the summertime, when everyone else is at work."

"Consider it done," I said, and we disappeared into the plaid army.

This time, the interruption came during European-history class. Mr. Peters had his back to us, and was filling the whiteboard with a chronology of Renaissance achievements.

The intercom beeped in warning, and then the message began. "Instructors, please excuse the planning committee members for a meeting in classroom twelve. Thank you."

"Not much of a 'sneak' if they're making announcements, is it?" Scout whispered behind me.

"It gets me out of history class," I reminded her, giving her a wink as I grabbed my books and bag. I smiled apologetically at Peters as I followed M.K., Amie, Veronica, and a couple of girls I didn't know well—Dakota and Taylor, maybe?—to the front of the room. None looked happy that I was joining them, but we filed out of the room without argument. That was good enough for me.

The brat pack walked down the hall, and then into a small room at the end.

It was a conference room with an oval table surrounded by office chairs.

We filed down one side of the table. I took a chair a couple of seats from the end beside Dakota or Taylor (whichever they were) while M.K. flounced dramatically into her own chair and pasted a bored expression on her face. Amie took a seat beside Veronica near the head of the table, then arranged her pink pen and notebook just so.

And on the other side of the table, something much more pleasant—a contingent from Montclare. Michael, Jason, and John Creed—of the dark brows and moody dark eyes—sat in a line, all spiffy and perfect in their sweaters and button-up shirts. All three boys smiled when they saw me, but Michael's smile flattened pretty fast, probably when he realized Scout wasn't following me into the room.

"She's not much of a party planner," I quietly explained.

"Party pooper," he muttered.

I smiled at him, and then at Jason, my cheeks warming a little at the secret smile on his face and the glow in his sky blue eyes. I felt like a nervous little kid, my stomach full of butterflies. Here I was—only a few weeks out of Sagamore, and I was talking to a boy who turned into a wolf at will. A boy who'd jumped in front of me to keep me safe. Was it crazy cool? Yes. And unexpected and strange, and still a little bit nerve-racking. We hadn't really gotten to that point of comfort yet, where you just sink into the relationship, where you're actually just *dating*, instead of thinking about the possibility and constantly analyzing it.

Veronica cleared her throat, then gazed at us expectantly.

"Now that we're all here," she said, "let's get down to business. Our theme for this year's Halloween Sneak, already decided, is Graveyard Glam."

John gave three loud claps. "I like it already. Meeting dismissed."

Veronica gave him a half smile. "Keep your pants on, Mr. Creed. The theme is only the first item on the checklist."

Did Adepts even get Halloween off? It seemed like that would be a busy night for us.

"Last year's Sneak was held at Navy Pier."

There were *oooh*'s and *aaah*'s from the other girls. I knew what Navy Pier was—an amusement park–type complex deal a few blocks away—but I hadn't yet been there.

"This year, we want to do something a little more mysterious."

Dakota/Taylor popped up a hand. "How about the Art Institute? Plenty of secret corners in there."

"Already done," Veronica said. "Two years ago."

"Pritzker Pavilion?" Taylor asked. "We could have it outside?"

M.K. huffed. "Have you been outside in Chicago in October? Nobody's gonna want to wear a Marchesa mini in the 312 when it's rainy and fifty degrees."

"It was just an idea."

"And we've ixnayed it," Veronica matter-of-factly said. "Next?"

Creed raised a hand.

Veronica gave him a catty look. "Do you have something substantive to add?"

"Only that my father has a yacht."

Figured.

Veronica crossed her arms. "I've seen your father's yacht, John Creed. It's not enough boat for all of us."

"Are you insulting the size of my father's boat?"

"Only in reference to Sneak. Other ideas?" Veronica scanned the room, and her gaze stopped on me. "Parker?" she asked, with a challenging bob of her shoulders.

"Um, I really haven't been in Chicago very long." And more important, you don't want any part of the things I've seen.

"*Great*. You're all clearly going to be a huge asset to getting this thing off the—"

"Field Museum."

Veronica stopped midinsult, then tilted her head at Jason. "What do you mean, Field Museum?"

"The Chicago Field Museum." He leaned forward and linked his hands on the table. "I went to a bar mitzvah there once. You can rent out the main hall. I'm sure it's not cheap"—he shrugged—"but we can party with Sue. That might be sweet, especially for Halloween."

I wasn't sure if I was supposed to be jealous or not. "Who's Sue?"

"Sue," Jason said, "is Chicago's favorite *Tyrannosaurus rex*." He mimicked claws and bared his teeth. "Very scary."

"I'm not afraid of dinosaurs," I assured him. "Trust me, I've seen worse." Personally, I thought that was true, but I crossed my fingers just in case I was jinxing myself.

"Grizzly bears?" Jason asked.

"What about grizzly bears?"

"Have you seen worse things than, let's say, grizzly bears?"

I smiled slyly. "Yeppers."

"What about wolves?"

"Those aren't even a little scary."

"Hmm," he said, smiling slyly back. "Good to know."

Veronica tapped her fingers on the tabletop. "Excuse me? Can we ixnay the bizarre wild kingdom flirting—assuming that's what this is—and get back on topic?"

"Seriously," M.K. said, putting a hand to her stomach. "It's making me nauseous."

I bit back a smile. Sure, Jason and I weren't exactly being subtle, but this time *I'd* been the one to create drama for the brat pack, instead of the other way around. That made a nice change.

"I like the Field Museum idea," Veronica said. "I have to check with the boosters about the price, but it shouldn't be a problem. One or two of them might even be on the board of directors."

The "boosters," I assumed, were the St. Sophia's alumni who'd be donating a pretty penny so the juniors and seniors could have a luxe fall formal.

"Make the call," John said. "And let us know."

"Rest assured that I will," Veronica said, then glanced at the clock on the wall behind her. "That didn't take nearly as long as it should have. Anything else we should discuss right now, unless any of you are dorky enough to want to go back to history class?"

I guess I wasn't supposed to be flattered that M.K. turned and looked at me.

"Drinks. Food. Transportation. Dress code," Amie recited.

Veronica rattled off responses: "Drinks and food will depend on the location. The Field Museum probably has some kind of contract with a caterer. Limos for the transpo, and the dress code will be formal."

"Looks like you have things well in hand," John said.

"I always do. If there aren't any more questions, let's break into subcommittees and get into the details."

We all just looked at each other. Even M.K. looked confused. "V, you haven't assigned any subcommittees."

"They're DIY subcommittees," she said. "And if you don't DIY, we have to go back to class."

She stood there for a few seconds to let the implication sink in.

"Subcommittees it is," John said, pushing back his chair and standing up. "My subcommittee's meeting over here."

"And what's your subcommittee?" Amie asked, pen in hand.

"That would be the subcommittee on rocking. Rocking hard."

I bit back a snort.

The girls divvied up their committees—decorations, food, etc.—and then everyone began milling around. I walked over to the Montclare side of the table. After all, how often did we get a daytime visit from the boys in blue?

John Creed smiled in his way: a lazy half smile. "Hello, Saga-more."

"Hello, Chicago."

"You and Jason became fast friends." He slid a glance to Jason, who was talking to one of the other girls. Since I'd been in Adept-denial at the time, I'd pretended not to know Jason the day I met John Creed. (I know, I know. I'd apologized later.)

"We've gotten to know each other," I said vaguely. "I'm surprised you're into party planning."

"I'm into skipping class and spending time with private school girls."

Mm-hmm. "Well, good luck with that."

"Are you two going to Sneak together?"

I tried for a casual tone. "I don't know. We haven't really talked about it."

His thick eyebrows lifted. "Really? Weird."

"Have you invited someone?"

He scanned the girls in the room. "I'm keeping my options open. One never knows when opportunity is going to come knocking." When his gaze landed on M.K., I tried not to grimace. I also bet money that Veronica was not going to be happy with that.

With perfect timing, Jason interrupted further discussion of what-ever brat-pack "knocking" John was going to pretend to hear.

"So," Jason said, "if you're handing out rides on the yacht . . ."

"We can probably arrange something," John said, then glanced at me. "Have you been out on the lake yet?"

"There's a lake?"

It took him a second to realize I was joking. "Tell me they let you out more than that."

"They let me out plenty." Just not usually aboveground, and usu-ally after the sun went down. "And no, I haven't been on the lake yet. Or the river either, actually, now that I think about it."

"We definitely need to remedy that. It won't be long before winter's here and the boat's in dry dock. And then you'll get to experience your first Chicago winter."

"Winters in Sagamore were plenty wintry," I pointed out.

"I'm sure. Add thirty-miles-per-hour wind to that, and you'll get closer to Chicago." He watched M.K. brush her hair over her shoulder, and then he was off, heading right for St. Sophia's least saintly girl.

I glanced over at Veronica, and watched her face tighten with the realization that her crush had picked a different victim.

"Hello, *Sagamore*."

I glanced up at Jason, and his mocking of John Creed's apparent nickname for me, and smiled. "Hello, Naperville." I gestured toward Creed. "Are you two friends? I can't get a read on him."

Jason shrugged. "We're friends of a sort, I guess. We've known each other for a long time, but we're not close like Michael and I are. Creed's the kind of person who pretty much always has an agenda. That doesn't exactly make for a strong friendship."

"More like a business alliance," I said.

John lifted M.K.'s wrist to take a look at her watch. Since he had his own undoubtedly expensive version, I figured it was just an excuse to touch her.

"Looks like he's getting along with her pretty well," Jason said.

I nodded. "That's M.K. Problem is, I think her BFF has a thing for him." I gestured toward Veronica, who was talking to one of the other Montclare boys while sliding secretive glances at Creed. She definitely had it bad. On the other hand, Garcia definitely seemed to be off the hook.

"Bummer," Jason said. "Nobody likes to be the one left out."

"Unfortunately true," I said, anticipating what Scout liked to call "TBD"—Total Brat Drama. If there was anything likely to be worse than the brat pack left to their own devices, it was internal brat-pack squabbles.

Nothing good could come from that.

When the bell rang, everyone began to gather up their goods. Jason leaned down and pressed a kiss to my cheek. "See you tonight at the Enclave?"

"With bells on," I whispered back. "And firespell in hand."

"I look forward to seeing that," he said. And with a wink, the Montclare boys left St. Sophia's once again.

Scout was in her room, granola bar and magazine in hand, when I made it back to the suite. She looked up when I walked in.

"You look like the cat that ate the canary."

"As a vegetarian, I object to that metaphor."

Scout grinned teethily at me. "As a carnivore, I object to your pickiness. Now spill the goods."

"There were Montclare boys at our party-planning committee."

She rolled her eyes, but her cheeks were flushed. "Like I care."

"Oh, you care. Jason was there, and Michael, of course, and their friend John Creed."

She spun a finger in the air like she was twirling a party favor. "I know who John Creed is."

"Did you know Veronica has a thing for him? But that he has a thing for M.K.? I feel like that's information we can use to our advantage."

Slowly, she looked up and grinned. "I knew there was a reason I liked you, Parker."

5

What, you might ask, was the best thing about being forced to attend an all-girls' boarding school? Was it the lack of cute boys? The bratlets? The complete lack of a social life?

Maybe. But the mandatory study hall was right up there on the list.

Scout and I were seated beside each other in the Great Hall, a giant room of stained-glass windows and books. We sat across from Colette, another girl in our class, at one of the dozens of tables, the room around us full of plaid-wearing teenagers in varying levels of study comas.

Since I'd already filled Scout in about the party-planning meeting, I was actually doing my trig homework. Anyone who passed by the table might think Scout was reading up on European history . . . or the comic book that was stuck in between the pages of the textbook.

They'd be wrong.

The comic was actually a cover for Scout's *Grimoire*, her main book of magic. She'd worked a charm to make it look like a racy comic book featuring a big-busted heroine with long hair and longer legs. I thought that was a dangerous disguise, especially if one of the dragon ladies who roamed the room decided it needed to be pitched. But Scout was smart enough to think ahead—she had disguised the book in the first place—so I assumed she had a clever magical backup plan.

Personally, I was waiting for the day the comic book characters appeared in 3D at our suite door, ready to perform their magic at Scout's command. Geeky, sure, but that still would have been sweet.

Scout had her faux comics, and I had my sketchbook. I loved to draw, and I was supposed to start studio classes anytime now. I could do still lifes—drawings of real objects—but I preferred to lose myself in the lines and let my imagination take over. I kept a stash of favorite pencils in my messenger bag. And since my parents apparently felt guilty about sending me to Chicago while they did whatever they were doing in Germany, I also had a new stash of sweet German notebooks they'd mailed out last week. When I finished with the trig problems, I pulled one from my bag, grabbed my pencil case, and set to work.

I was in a roomful of characters—rich girls in plaid, weird girls in plaid, and the dragon ladies who patrolled the room and made sure we were doing homework instead of flipping through *Cosmo*. I was also in a room of cool architecture, from the dozens of stained-glass windows to the huge, brass chandeliers that hung above us. Each chandelier was made up of slender statues of women—ancient goddesses, maybe—holding up torches.

I opened the first notebook—a thin one with a pale blue cover—and touched the pencil lead to the slick paper. I picked a goddess from the nearest chandelier and started drawing. I started with a light line to get the general shape of her body, just to make sure I had the proportions correct. As I worked on the drawing, I'd darken a final line and fill in the details.

It wasn't magic. It wasn't trig. And best of all, the dragon ladies couldn't complain. I was studying, after all.

I'd just finished the sketch when the Great Hall went silent. It was usually pretty quiet, but there was always an undercurrent of sound—papers shuffling or low whispers as girls tried to entertain themselves.

But this was *quiet* quiet.

Scout and I glanced up simultaneously. My first thought had been that a spindly-legged monster had walked into the room. But it was just the headmistress.

Marceline Foley strode confidently down the aisle in a trim suit and the kind of heels an adult would call "sensible." Her eyes scanned the room as she moved, probably taking in every detail of the students around her.

Foley was still a mystery to me. She was the first person I'd met when I arrived at St. Sophia's a few weeks ago, and she'd given me a very cold welcome to Chicago. She'd also been the one who'd suggested my parents weren't who they seemed to be. She had changed her tune, but when I had tried to talk to her about what was really going on, she'd convinced me to let things lie. Foley knew my parents, and she seemed convinced that they'd had a reason for not telling me what was really going on.

A reason that put their safety at risk.

What else could I do but believe her?

Tonight, she held a stack of small cards—like index cards—in her hands. As she walked past the tables, she occasionally stopped and handed a card to one of the students at the table. And then she stepped forward, and she handed one to me.

"Instructions for your studio art class," she said.

I hadn't realized I'd been holding my breath until I let it out again. I'd been fighting tunnel-crawlers, but it was the principal who really tied my stomach in knots. I'm not sure what that said about me.

I took the card from her. It was a schedule for the studio classes, which were supposed to start tomorrow. I'd have class in the "surplus building." Didn't that sound glamorous?

I glanced up again. Foley stayed at the edge of the table for a moment, the rest of her cards in hand, looking down at me. I waited for her to speak, but she stayed silent. After a nod, she moved along to the next table.

"That was weird," Scout said. "What did she give you?"

I flipped the card her way so she could see it.

"Huh. Looks like you've found your creative outlet."

I'd only just stuffed the card into my notebook when noise erupted across the room. We all looked over to see Veronica standing at a table, her chair now on the floor, her face flushed and eyes pink. M.K., arms crossed over her chest, stared back, a single eyebrow arched at Veronica.

"Things just went nuclear," Collette muttered.

"You are a witch," Veronica hissed out, then stepped over the chair and ran to the door.

You could have heard a pin drop in the Great Hall.

M.K. rolled her eyes and leaned toward the girl beside her, gossiping together while one of her best friends ran away from her. A dragon lady moved to the table and picked up the chair Veronica had knocked over. A low rumble of whispering began to move across the room.

"At least that's over with," Colette said. "Can we all get back to studying now?"

Scout and I exchanged a glance, and I read the same thoughts in her face that I had in mine: Could it really be that easy?

A few hours later we were back in the tunnels, Scout and I making our way back to the arched wooden door to Enclave Three, its status as an Adept HQ marked by the "3" above the door and the symbol on the door—the letter Y inside a circle, a symbol Scout had told me could be seen across the city of Chicago. It was the mark of an Adept.

Sure, putting symbols on buildings and bridges across the city wasn't exactly in line with the Adepts' idea of keeping their work under the radar. On the other hand, I got the feeling the symbols were a kind of reminder that they were *here*. That they fought the good fight, even if no one else knew about the war.

Scout opened the door, and the Junior Varsity Adepts of Enclave Three looked toward us: Michael Garcia, Jason Shepherd, Jill and Jamie Riley, and Paul Truman. Each of them had their own unique magical talent. Michael was a reader, which meant he could "read" the history of a building just by touching it. Jamie and Jill were the elemental witches. Jamie could manipulate fire, and Jill could manipulate ice. Paul was a warrior. His magic gave him the ability to adapt his fighting style to whatever man or monster faced him. Paul was tall with skin like rich coffee. He was also cute and lanky enough that it was hard to imagine him in some kind of ferocious battle, but the determination in his eyes gave him away. As lanky as he was, he may not ultimately have the strength to beat that monster, but his magic always gave him a fighting chance.

We walked into the giant room—big, vaulted ceiling and tile-covered walls—toward Jill and Jamie, who stood apart from the guys. But that didn't stop Jason from winking at me, or Michael from making doe eyes at Scout. She rolled her eyes, but there was a hint of a smile on her face.

"What's up, Adepts?" Scout asked.

"Just waiting for the head honcho to get started," Jill said, nodding toward Daniel.

Daniel was our new leader, a guy sent down from the bigwigs to keep an eye on Katie and Smith. Daniel, let's say, was easy on the eyes. He was tall and blond, with strong shoulders, blue eyes, and one of those chin dimples. He was talking to Katie, who was cheerleader-cute and very petite, and Smith, an emo-wannabe with greasy hair and clothes that were always a couple of sizes too tight. Katie and Smith were the Varsity Adepts who'd refused to send someone to rescue Scout; that was why Daniel had replaced them. I'd been the one begging them to go after her, and I'd seen the stubborn looks on their faces when they'd said no. That was the kind of thing that made me question exactly who the "good guys" were. I was still wary of them.

Scout smiled at Daniel with big, wide eyes. "I'd be happy to help out Daniel with any special projects he has in mind."

I rolled mine. "I'm guessing he's not going to take you up on that offer since he's four years older than you. And in college."

"Don't rain on my parade. I know he's a little out of my league, but he's just kind of . . . dreamy, don't you think?"

"He's not bad," I allowed, "in a gorgeous, totally platonic, 'Let's get this magical show on the road' kind of way."

"You know those movies where the blond girl walks by—and time slows down? She swings her hair back and forth"—Scout gave me a demonstration, her short hair hardly moving as she shook her head—"and all the guys stare. I feel like Daniel could pull that off."

"He could pull off staring?"

"No—the time-slowing-down part. I mean, just watch him."

We were probably a pretty entertaining sight—four high school juniors, two of us in smokin'-hot plaid uniforms, staring down a college sophomore. But she really did have a point. Daniel walked across the room to talk to Smith, and there was something about the way he moved—like he wasn't just walking, but making a statement.

Daniel also had swagger.

"Okay, he's impressive," Jamie said.

"I so told you."

"What are you two whispering about?" Michael's head popped between us, gaze shifting left and right as he waited for details.

"None of your beeswax, Garcia."

I could see the sting of defeat in his eyes, but he kept a smile on his face. "You know what you need?"

Ever so slowly, Scout turned her head to look at him, one eyebrow arched. Her expression was fierce. "What?"

"You need a man who respects you. Who treats you like his equal."

Not bad, I thought. But Scout wasn't buying. Sure, there was a little surprise in her eyes, but that was all she gave back to him.

She put a hand on his arm. "The problem, Garcia, is that no one's my equal. I'm the most ass-kickingest spellbinder in Chicago."

I rolled my eyes, but really didn't have much reason to disagree.

Before Michael could retort, Daniel clapped his hands together. "All right, kids. Let's get this show on the road."

We all clustered together, the Junior Varsity members of Enclave Three. Katie and Smith—still Adepts but not quite like us—stood a little farther away. They both looked miffed to have been replaced. Katie's arms were crossed over her chest as she glared daggers at Daniel, while Smith whipped his head to the side to throw his bangs out of his eyes. Given how many times I'd seen him do that in the last couple of weeks or so, I almost volunteered to grab scissors from my room.

"First matter of business," Daniel said. "Tell me what you saw last night."

Scout popped a hand into the air. "Things. Big, nasty, naked, crawly things. They had pointy teeth, and they moved weird."

"Like a school of fish," I put in.

"Like barracudas," Jason put in. "We found this slime in one of the corridors near St. Sophia's, and next thing you know they were coming at us. It took a dose of firespell, a protection circle, and"—he glanced at Scout—"what did you call it?"

"A flutterby spell," Scout offered.

"A flutterby spell to take them out."

Katie rolled her eyes. "It was probably just Reapers."

"No," Scout said, her fierce expression not allowing argument. "First, they were naked. Second, they weren't Reapers or trolls or anything else we've seen before. They were something new. Something outside my *Grimoire*—I spent study hall today looking it up."

I held up my right hand. "She did. I totally saw her reading."

"They looked like something that walked straight off Dr. Moreau's island," Jason added.

Paul crossed his arms over his head. "And you're sure they weren't sewer rats? Those things can go nuclear after a while."

"Only if rats grow to five feet tall and began to walk upright. Well, mostly upright." She bumped Michael with an elbow. "Show 'em what you got."

Michael pulled the cell phone from his pocket, tapped around for a few seconds, and handed it to Daniel.

Smith peeked over Daniel's shoulder to look. It was very satisfying to watch that smug expression fall right off his face. "What is that?"

"I don't have a clue," Daniel said, frowning down at the phone, then rotating it to get a different perspective. "Where were you exactly?"

"One of the utility tunnels," Jason said. "Maybe ten or twelve corridors from St. Sophia's?" He looked at me for confirmation, and I nodded.

"And the slime?" Daniel asked.

"Mostly floor," Michael said, "but it wasn't contained there."

"There was a lot of it," Scout confirmed.

Frowning, Daniel ran his hands through his hair. Beside me, Scout actually sighed.

"This isn't the first time we've seen the slime," Daniel said.

The room went silent.

"Excuse me?" Scout said. "This isn't the first time? There've been others, and no one bothered to tell us?"

Even Katie and Smith looked surprised. All eyes turned to Daniel.

"It was only slime," he said, "and it was just last week. We had no idea what it was or where it came from. There were no signs of any new creatures—just the stuff. And we've seen slime before."

There were reluctant nods of agreement.

"Ectoplasmic slime," Michael began to rattle off, "auric slime, that half-fish thingy that slimed the tourist boat at Navy Pier, that time the Reaper used the allergy spell and Adepts were all dripping snot like water all over the city—"

"Point made," Daniel said, holding up a hand. "And now that we know what it is—and where it's coming from—it's time do something a little different."

Just like he'd scripted it, a knock sounded at the Enclave door.

Katie hustled over, turning the handle and using her small cheerleadery stature to pull open the door.

Two girls stood in the doorway. One was tall with whiskey brown eyes and cocoa-kissed skin, a cloud of dark hair exploding from a slick ponytail. There was something ethereal about her, and something slightly vacant in her expression.

The second girl was shorter, a petite blonde with a shaggy crop of pale, shoulder-length hair. She wore an outfit appropriate for a punk stuck in Victorian England: short poofy black skirt; knee-high black boots; a locket necklace; and a thin, ribbed gray T-shirt beneath a complicated black leather jacket that bore panels of thick black fur. In her black-gloved hands was an old-fashioned leather doctor's bag.

"Yowsers," Michael muttered, earning him an elbow in the ribs from Scout.

Daniel waved them in, and the girls stepped inside. Katie closed the door behind them.

"Enclave Three," Daniel said. "Meet Naya Fletcher—"

The taller girl offered a wave.

"—and Bailey Walker."

"I go by Detroit," the blonde corrected, offering a crisp salute.

"Oh, I'm going to like this one," Scout murmured with a grin. "She's got sass. Kind of like you, Parker."

"I am quite sassy," I agreed.

"Detroit," Daniel corrected, then gestured toward Naya. "Naya is a caller. For the newbies among us, that means she speaks to the recently deceased."

I raised my eyebrows. "Ghosts?"

Naya lifted a shoulder. "That's how they're generally known by the public, but they prefer 'recently deceased.' Calling them 'ghosts' makes it sound like they're a different species. Like vamps or werewolves or the fey. They're still human. They're just . . . well . . . less breathy than we are."

"And Detroit is a machinist."

There were mumbled sounds of awe around the room. Being a "machinist" didn't mean anything to me, but it clearly meant something to the rest of the Adepts.

"That means she gadgets," Scout whispered.

"Detroit and Naya have seen the slime in other tunnels," Daniel explained. "As you know, Enclave Two is an enclave of information, of technology. They aren't used to battling it out with Reapers."

When he paused, I knew exactly where this was heading. My stomach sank.

"Tonight," he continued, "you'll be escorting them out to determine if their slime is our slime—"

"And if there are more creatures out there," Katie added.

The Enclave went silent.

"Detroit has mapped out a passage from here to their slime spot," Daniel continued, "so she and Naya will play compass on this one. Jill, Jamie, and Paul—take point and travel in front of them. Once you get to the halfway point, you'll stop there to give everyone a green zone so they can get back. Michael will do what reading he can. Lily and Jason are on offense if necessary."

We waited for more, but Daniel didn't say anything else.

Scout and I exchanged a glance. He hadn't said her name.

"What about me?" she asked.

Daniel looked at her for a few seconds, then turned back to Detroit and Naya. "Ladies, if you'll give us just a minute, I'd like to talk to Enclave Three."

They nodded, then disappeared out the door. When it shut behind them, all eyes turned to Daniel.

"It's your decision," he told Scout, "but I'd like you to consider sitting out for this one."

The room went silent.

"Sitting out?" she asked.

"You've had a pretty rough go of it lately, and last night took a lot out of you—physically, magically, emotionally. Enclave Three's job will be to protect Enclave Two if the creatures pop up, not to—"

"Oh, *no,*" Scout said, holding up a hand. "You are not going to go there. Varsity or not, you are not going to suggest that I can't go on a mission because my teammates, my Adepts, don't have time to babysit me."

I grimaced on Daniel's behalf.

"Scout, let's be reasonable—"

"I *am* being reasonable," she said, picking up her messenger bag and slinging it over her shoulder. "These people rescued me. They risked getting sucked dry by Reapers and they went to the sanctuary and they rescued me. No mother-trucking way are they going out there without me at their back. Not going to happen."

Michael took a step forward to stand behind Scout. "She doesn't go, I don't go. And you know what I can do at the place."

There was silence for a moment as Daniel considered their position. Finally, he looked at Scout. "You're ready?"

"I'm ready," she confirmed.

"Okay," he said. "Then get to it."

Everyone gathered up their bags and supplies and headed for the door—and the Adepts waiting for us outside.

I glanced back at Daniel, saw a sneaky smile on his face. I realized he'd done it on purpose—baited her on purpose—in order to rile her up, to get her ready to face whatever we might find in the tunnels.

No wonder he was sent in to supervise Katie and Smith. He was *good*. Sneaky, sure, but good.

Daniel caught my glance and nodded at me, then pointed at the door. "Get to it, Lily."

I got.

6

There might have been sun outside, but the tunnels were still cold and damp.

"Do you ever wish you were an Adept in Miami or Tahiti?" I whispered to Scout, zipping up the hoodie I'd pulled over a St. Sophia's oxford shirt.

"You mean instead of this moist, cold Midwestern underbelly?"

I hopped over the other side of the rail to avoid a puddle of rusty liquid. "Something like that, yeah."

Since I'd given him an opening, Michael snuck between me and Scout, then slung an arm over my shoulder. "You know, if you'd been in Miami, you wouldn't have met us."

Scout rolled her eyes. "And what a crime that would have been."

"Whatever. You know you love me."

"I beg to differ, Garcia."

He faked a smile, but it was easy to tell he'd been hurt. Stung, he moved back to walk alongside Jason.

"You're being kind of growly with Michael," I whispered to Scout when he was out of hearing range.

"He's being kind of annoying."

"He's just being himself."

She rolled her shoulders. "I'm sorry. I'm just—I don't know. Maybe Daniel was right and I'm not ready for this, you know? I mean, I did freak out last time."

"Maybe you should tell Michael that. Let him comfort you instead of pushing him away."

"No more daytime television for you, missy."

"Oh, my God. Did I just give you relationship advice?"

"Yeppers."

"Sorry. Won't happen again."

"I knew you were teachable."

I rolled my eyes.

"Are you guys always this chatty?" asked Detroit. She walked with determination, her arms crossed against the chill.

"We try to keep it light," Scout said. "There's more than enough darkness in the world as it is."

"The dark isn't as dark as you'd think." We all glanced over at Naya, who was walking with arms extended, the tips of her fingers trailing against the wall.

"What do you mean?" Scout quietly asked.

She glanced back at us, her cloud of coffee-colored hair bobbing as she moved. "We aren't the only ones here, or there, or anywhere. *They're* all around us. They live in the gray land—the not-quite world—all around us."

I swallowed thickly, goose bumps lifting on my arms as I fought the urge to look around me, scanning the near darkness for shadowy figures.

"Can you see them?" Scout quietly asked, and Naya shrugged.

"Sometimes. Mostly, I call to them. Talk to them. It takes a lot of energy to become visible. Sound is easier. Temperature is lots easier." Suddenly, she stopped, eyes wide. "Have you ever been somewhere dark and quiet, and you felt a cold chill? Like the wind had blown right through your soul?"

I nodded, eyes wide, like a kid around a spooky campfire. I also wondered about that first time—the first time she'd seen them, or heard them, or called them. Can you imagine what it would have been like to learn about the *other* in the world by hearing, suddenly one day, the living dead?

I decided learning about a weird tattoo and a little electricity was a pretty good way to go.

Detroit glanced over at Scout. "So Daniel said you were a spellbinder?"

"Yeah," Scout said. "Why?"

"I heard you were a spellcaster. And I thought, wow, big whoop, spellcaster, dime a dozen."

"Dime a dozen?" Scout asked. "I thought spellcasters were a myth?"

"Do you know what a spellcaster is?"

I lifted a hand. "I actually don't."

Detroit held out her hand. "Okay, so there're the three I's, right?"

"Intent, incantation, incarnation," I offered up.

"Right. So it takes intent and incantation to get to the incarnation part. Writing the incantation is basically the spell*binding*. You're putting the right words together in the right order to create a spell. So when you're looking through your *Grimoire*—you're looking at a flip book of spells, which are the result of the spellbinding."

"Following you so far," I added (helpfully).

"Once you get to *saying* the incantation, using the intent of it to make an incarnation of some kind happen, you've got the spell*casting*. Making the magic take life. Spellcasters just work from *Grimoires* that have been passed on to them. Or the Internet."

Scout lifted her eyebrows. "They get spells from the Internet?"

"Well, not *all* of them."

Okay, apparently the Internet was a magical forest just waiting to be explored.

Detroit waved her hand. "But you've got something special, Scout. You can do more than just repeat some words and make magic happen. You can *bind* the spells in the first place. You can transmute them from letters and words into magic."

"*That's* why the Reapers were so interested in you," I said. "You said they mentioned that, right, when you were at the sanctuary? That they were after your *Grimoire*, and that they were talking about the difference between spellcasters and spellbinders?"

Scout nodded. "That would explain why they came after me, and why they wanted my book."

"That makes sense," Detroit agreed. "It's a rare power. And if the whole point of your organization is to support the use of magic, finding someone who can actually make new spells would be huge."

"Wicked huge," Scout agreed. "I had no idea. I mean, I just assumed I did what everyone else did, you know? Writing spells, then actually making the incantations work."

"Wow," I said. "For once, you were actually being too modest."

She stuck her tongue out at me. Probably I deserved that.

We eventually came to a fork in the tunnels and took the path to the left. This one sloped upward, and continued on for only a few dozen yards.

We stopped at a jagged hole that had been ripped into the brick.

"In there," Detroit said.

Scout gave the hole in the wall a suspicious look. "What do you mean, 'in there'? Where does that thing lead?"

"Into a janitor's closet, actually," Detroit said. "We have to switch over from the railway tunnels to the Pedway."

I leaned toward Scout. "What's the Pedway again?"

"Stands for pedestrian walkway," she said.

"The Pedway is a set of walkways through buildings in the Loop," Detroit said. "Some aboveground, some underground. It's supposed to give people a way to get around downtown when it's too cold to walk outside. It's also lit and a lot less damp."

Scout looked weirdly unhappy about the possibility of walking through what I assumed were aboveground, carpeted hallways. "We usually try to avoid the Pedway," she said.

Detroit nodded solemnly. "I know."

I made a mental list of the things we might be trying to avoid: security guards, security cameras, locked doors. Or maybe anyone who thought a band of teenagers running around Chicago in the middle of the night was a little off.

"Vamps patrol the Pedway at night," Scout complained.

Well, I obviously forgot to mention them. "What do you mean 'vamps'?"

"The usual," Scout said with a dismissive gesture. "Goth, fangs, death by crucifix, never see 'em eating garlic bread. Vampires aren't friendly with Adepts."

"They aren't friendly with anybody," Detroit said. "It's not personal. And we might not even see any. The covens stick to quiet parts of the Pedway. The odds we'd actually run across them are pretty low."

Scout didn't look impressed with the logic.

"Look," Detroit said. "The Pedway is a shortcut. It takes a lot longer if we stick to the tunnels. And we'll only be in the corridor for a few blocks before we drop back into the tunnels anyway."

We stood there for a few minutes, the Adepts of Enclave Three exchanging glances as they figured out what to do. Since I was still a newbie, I figured I'd leave the decision-making to the more experienced members.

Jason looked at Jill, Jamie, and Paul. "What do you think?"

"Well," Paul said, "I'm not crazy about having vamps between us and wherever we're going, but I like the idea of being in the tunnels for as short a time as possible. Besides, if we have trouble on the way in, we can always take the long way back."

"Good enough for me," Jason said.

And so it was decided. One by one, Jamie and Jill in the lead, we ducked into the hole in the wall. We emerged, just as Detroit had promised, into a janitor's closet. All nine of us stuffed into a tiny, dark room among push brooms, mops, and buckets on wheels.

"Would you like some light?" I whispered.

"Let's keep it dark," I heard Jill say. "At least until we figure out if anyone is out there. Michael—you wanna fill us in?"

"On it," Michael said. I heard shuffling, probably as he squeezed through to get to a wall.

"Echoes of business," he finally said. "Busy. Always walking, moving. Faster. Faster. The world spins, and the feet keep moving." He paused. "That's all I got.".

"Hmm. Doesn't tell us much about whether the vamps are out there," Detroit said.

"No, it doesn't," Jason agreed. "But we've got to get out there regardless."

I heard shuffling; then a glow lit the room from something in Detroit's hand. It was the locket she'd worn, now open in her palm. She swiveled it until it projected a complicated map onto one of the closet's walls.

We *oooohed* and *aaaahed* at the sight.

"Gadgets are my gig," Detroit matter-of-factly explained. "Now, when we open the door, we're going right. We stay straight until the corridor ends; then we take a left. Halfway down that corridor there's an emergency stairwell. I've got to pop the sensor on the door, and then we're in. We take the stairs all the way down, and we're back in the tunnels. Everyone got it?"

"We've got it," Paul said. "Let's do this." He cracked open the door and peeked through it, light slicing through the darkness.

"Clear," he said, and one by one we slipped into the Pedway.

It looked exactly like you'd expect a pedestrian walkway to look. This part of the corridor was wide and made of concrete, and the floor was made of chips of stone and tile stuck into concrete. Not much to look at, but it would certainly keep you out of the snow.

We all run-walked through the corridor toward our next turn until Paul, panicked expression on his face, motioned us back against the wall. My heart suddenly pounding, we flattened against it.

I blew out a nervous breath, my ears straining to hear whatever had triggered Paul's concern, but heard nothing. The hallway was silent except for the hum of the fluorescent lights above us.

And then the voice behind us.

"Well, well, well. What have we here?"

Slowly, I turned around. There were three of them—a tall and dark-haired boy stood in the front; two girls stood behind him. All three wore gray and black clothes in complicated layers over bodies that were supermodel—or maybe just anorexically—thin. By the look of them, I would have guessed they were about my age. But then I got a look at their eyes—dark, dilated, and definitely not young. Better yet, none of them looked happy to see us, and they were positioned between us and the janitor's closet. Our escape route.

"Vampires," Jason murmured. He glanced back at me. "Be ready," he said and then stepped forward. Paul stepped behind him. I reached out and grabbed Scout's hand. She squeezed back.

"You're out late, aren't you?" asked the vampire in front. He had a low, heavy accent, and when he talked I could see the tips of his fangs.

One of the girls behind him hissed like a cat, her fangs gleaming in the overhead lights. She took a half step forward. I pushed back against the wall a little more, my muscles suddenly straining to run. It was like my body *knew* they were bad—and wanted to get away from them as quickly as possible.

"We're on our way out of your territory," Jason said. "All we ask is safe passage for a few hundred yards." He hitched a thumb over his shoulder. "We only want to go as far as the next corridor. Just to the stairwell, then we're out of your way."

The vampires spread out, forming a line—and now a total barrier to the closet.

"Safe passage is expensive," said the one in front. "You want to dance with the devil, you have to be prepared to pay the price." The female who'd hissed stepped toward him, then draped herself along his side like a languid cat, one hand on his shoulder, the other across his stomach. She made a low growl. There was something very disturbing about watching these kids play at being monsters. . . . It didn't help that they actually *were* monsters.

The other girl pulled a wicked-looking knife from her knee-length gray vest. Its blade gleamed in the overhead lights. She licked her lips.

I guess blood was the price they wanted us to pay.

"We pay the price every day," Jason said darkly. "You know who we are?"

The boy in front scanned each of us in turn, his dark eyes judging and evaluating.

"I know," he agreed after a moment. "But your sacrifice doesn't pay the fee. This is my land. *My* territory." He slapped a hand to his chest. "If we let you move through our land, the thieves begin asking questions of us. And we don't like questions."

I couldn't help it. The words were out of my mouth before I could stop myself. "The thieves?" I asked. Scout called my name in warning, but it was too late. All their eyes—dark and dilated—were fixed on me. The boy in front tilted his head and let his gaze slip up and down my body.

Gooseflesh lifted on my arms. Scout squeezed my hand harder and moved incrementally closer, like she could protect me just by being nearer.

"Your magic is young," he said. "Untested." He sounded intrigued by the idea, maybe by the possibility that someday, someone would test it. That thought wasn't exactly comforting.

I may not have been thrilled to have his attention, but I wasn't going to cower. Vampire or not, he wasn't going to bully me. "It's been tested enough," I assured him. "Who are the thieves?"

He blinked slowly, like a drowsy tiger. "I believe you call them 'Reapers.' We refer to them as the thieves of life."

I almost pointed out that he and his crew were vampires. I wasn't sure how they could drink blood without a little thieving of their own.

"And our passage?" Jason asked, getting the vampire back on track.

"I believe I mentioned the expense?"

"Name your price." I could hear irritation rising in Jason's voice . . . and in the new one that chimed in.

"I don't think the price is yours to name, *iubitu.*"

We all turned to look behind us. At the other end of the corridor— the one we needed to get to—stood another group with the same dark hair and the same black eyes, the same young skin and very old eyes. But these vampires wore lighter colors, and their clothes were all old-fashioned. Pencil skirts, red lipstick, and short fur coats for the girls; greased-back hair and long trousers for the guys. They looked like they'd stepped right out of the 1940s.

At the front of the group was a girl with long blond hair that fell in tight curls across her shoulders. She was the one who'd spoken.

The boy in black spoke again. "This is not your concern, Marlena."

"Oh, but it is my concern," Marlena replied. "You're here, enter-taining guests, in my territory."

Oh, great. Not only were we standing in the middle of a mess of vampires, we'd walked into some kind of fangy landgrab.

The boy showed his fangs to Marlena, and my heart began to thud in my chest like a bass drum. I felt like I was standing in a room with a wild animal . . . or a pack of them.

"Your territory stops three blocks back, Nicu."

"My territory stops where I say it stops."

I leaned toward Scout. "Are they arguing about a couple of blocks of industrial carpeting?"

"Not just carpeting—entrances and exits to the tunnels. They con-trol getting in and getting out from the Pedway. That means Adepts, Reapers, and anyone else who uses them. *That's* why we avoid the Pedway."

"Guess they're a little fuzzy on the boundaries right now."

"Sounds like it," she agreed.

"Lily?" Jason asked, without turning around. "Can you do some-thing if we need it?"

"Yes," I told him, answering the unspoken question—could I use firespell to take them out? "But it's a lot easier if they're standing together."

"Perhaps now is not the time to have this discussion," Nicu said. "Not when there are Adepts in our midst."

Marlena barked out a laugh. "I don't care anything about Adepts, *iubitu*. Nor, I think, do they care for us." She put her hands on her hips, her short red nails tapping against her skirt. "Are you scared?"

This time, the bravado came from Paul. "Hardly. But we do have things to do tonight. So if you'll give us passage, we'll get out of your way."

Marlena and her crew took a step forward, their movements synchronized. "Vampires do not give. Vampires *take*."

Paul made a sarcastic noise. "You think no one will notice if you harm us here? You think no one will care if you spill Adept blood in your hallways?"

"I think I find it amusing you believe we would *spill* your blood." She ran the tip of her tongue across one of her inch-long canines. "Oh, to be young again."

Ironic, I thought, since she looked like she was barely older than me.

"Lily?" Jason prompted.

"I'm not sure I have enough juice to take two shots," I whispered. Even if I took out Nicu's crew, that left another set of vampires who clearly weren't conflicted about drinking from well-intentioned teenagers.

"No worries, Shepherd," Scout quietly said. "I got this one. Parker, rile them up. I'll keep them talking. And when I give the word, lose the lights."

Scout's lids fell, and she began to mouth words. I couldn't hear what she was saying, but it must have been a spell. I also had no idea what she was planning, but I trusted her. She'd been an Adept longer than I'd been in high school, so I ignored the panicked roll in my stomach, sucked in a breath, and took a step to the left—directly into their line of sight.

"Hi," I said, waving until all eyes were on me. "So, Nicu, what were you saying earlier about this being your land? I think you said this was your territory?"

Just as I'd predicted, Marlena wasn't thrilled by that. She let out a low, threatening growl. "Your kingdom? Such hubris from someone so undeserving of it."

The woman who'd wrapped herself around Nicu untwined her arms and pulled out her own set of weapons—some kind of sharp, round blades that fit over her knuckles. Nothing you wanted to run into in a dark alley—or even a well-lit pedestrian walkway.

"And what have you done to deserve it, you harpy?"

"Me? I honor our memories, our traditions. You, on the other hand, are an embarrassment to the *vampyr*," Marlena said. "You and yours are *pitiful*. And we know that you are *weak*."

The vampires around Nicu began to hiss and show their fangs. He glared across at Marlena, his eyes half-hooded. "Never forget, Marlena, who *made* me vampire."

"Mistakes," she growled out, "can be remedied."

Scout was still mouthing her spell. With each word she spoke, the vampires seemed to become more and more angry. Soon they were screaming at each other in a heavy language I didn't understand.

I stood at the ready, hands at my sides, wiggling my fingertips as I waited for Scout to give me the signal to douse the lights.

"Three," she finally said, "two, and *one*."

I tugged on the power, and the lights went out above us. The vampires began to yelp. I wasn't sure if they could see any better in the dark than we could, but they clearly weren't happy about being plunged into darkness while enemies were in their midst.

On the other hand, they seemed to think their fellow vampires were the only enemies that mattered. As the groups rushed each other to wage their battle, we became irrelevant.

I felt a hand at my elbow. *"Go,"* Jason said, and we moved in a tight knot, staying close to the wall as we ran for the next corridor. They ignored us, but the sounds of a fight—ripping flesh, bruising strikes—erupted behind us.

We ran full out in the darkness. When we made it to the next corridor, Detroit finagled a light to lead the way. It was a glowing ball that bounced through the hallway, leading us to the end of the corridor and then to the left until we reached the gunmetal gray fire door. The stairwell was lit from within, and it cast an orange glow into the hallway. The bouncing light disappeared into the puddle of light.

Paul pushed at the long bar across the door, but it wouldn't budge. "Locked," he said, glancing back at us.

"There's an access pad," Jill said, gesturing toward the small white box that sat beside the door. "You need a card to open the door."

Scout pointed at Detroit, before casting a nervous glance back at the hallway. "Can you do something, or do we need to have Paulie rip the thing off its hinges?"

"I'm on it," Detroit said. She moved to the wall and elbowed the panel. Just like in the movies, the plastic cover popped off. She whipped out a set of tiny tools from her leather jacket, and then she was working. A tiny screwdriver in each hand, she began to pick and pluck at the sensor's insides.

"You okay?"

I looked over and found Jason behind me, worry in his eyes. "I'm good."

He touched a fingertip to my thumb. "Good. Otherwise, I'd have to run back and take a bite out of crime, if you know what I mean."

"Show-off."

He winked.

"Got it," Detroit announced. She pressed the plastic cover back into place, then waved her giant black watch over the pad.

For a moment there was silence, and then the door clicked as the mechanism unlocked.

Detroit pushed through the door.

"Nice job," I said, passing by as she held the door open.

"It's not firespell," she said, "but it works for me."

No argument there.

7

Detroit and Paul stayed by the door until we were done, then pulled it closed until it clicked shut again behind us. We filed down the stairs. A steel bar stretched across the final landing, probably to keep folks out of the basement and the tunnels. We hopped over it to reach the tall, metal fire door that punctuated the dank bottom of the stairwell and waited while Detroit jimmied the lock on a chain on the door.

I'll admit it; I was impressed. Detroit had skills that made caper movies look low budget. But I wasn't the only one pleased with our trek so far.

"Nice job back there," Scout said, nudging me with her elbow. "I'm calling that Adepts, one. Vampires, zero."

"Agreed," I said, holding up a hand. "I'm gonna need some skin on that one." She reached out and high-fived me.

It took only a couple of seconds before Detroit tripped the tumblers and was pulling the chain away. "All right," she said. "Last part of the trip."

"And this was supposed to be a shortcut," I muttered.

"At least we got to spend some quality time together."

I gave Jason a dry look. "Be honest. You were hoping I'd use firespell. You wanted to see it."

"Well, if you want me to be honest, then yeah. I wanted to watch you work your mojo."

"*Jeeeez*, you two," Scout said. "Make out somewhere else."

"Spoilsport," I told her.

The fire door led back into the railway tunnels. Maybe the Pedway architect figured they'd be put back into use someday.

"We'll stay here and watch your back," Paul said, pointing between himself, Jamie, and Jill. "We can ice out the vamps if they make it in, make sure you have a clear path back to the Enclave."

"Especially since we're taking the long way home," Jason advised.

Detroit grumbled, but seemed to get his point.

From there, it was only a couple hundred yards before we reached a ramshackle wooden door.

"This is it," Detroit whispered, opening the door and giving us a peek of a walkway between our wooden door and a set of metal double doors at the other end of a long corridor. The walkway's ceiling was covered by grates, and we could hear the sounds of music and engines above us as cars passed by.

"This is what?" Jason asked, confusion in his expression as he surveyed the hallway. "What are we supposed to be seeing?"

Naya's face fell. "It's gone."

"The slime," Detroit said. "This is where we saw it."

"I definitely don't see any slime," Scout said, cramming beside me in the doorway. She was right. I mean, we were underground, so it wasn't like it was sparkling clean in there, but there was definitely no slime.

Detroit looked crestfallen. "I don't understand. This is really where we saw it. It couldn't have just disappeared."

Jason gestured toward the double doors at the other end of the corridor, which were marked with those pointy biohazard stickers. "No," he said. "But someone could have cleaned up the slime."

"Reapers?" I wondered. "You think the Reapers know something about the creatures?"

"Maybe, maybe not," he said. "After all, we didn't, not until we saw them last night." He looked at Michael. "What can you tell us?"

Michael nodded decisively, then rubbed his hands together like he was getting ready to roll some dice. He stepped forward into the corridor, put a palm flat against the wall, and closed his eyes.

"It's muddy," he said. "Unclear. So many coming and going. So much birth and death. Change . . ." But then he shook his head.

"I can't read anything else clearly." When he opened his eyes again, there was defeat there. "I can't see anything else."

"What does that tell you?" Scout asked, tilting her head at him. "What does it mean if you can't read anything?"

Michael shook his head, clearly flustered by whatever he'd seen—or hadn't seen. "Could be that too much went on—too much magic for any one message to filter through. Or could be some kind of blocking spell."

"We've seen those before," Detroit agreed. "Spells to erase the magic's fingerprints, scramble the magic's DNA. Reapers use obfus for things like that."

I lifted a hand. "Sorry. What's an 'obfu'?"

"Obfuscator," Detroit explained. "Something that obfuscates— makes it hard for Michael to get a read on the building."

"Any chance you've got a magic detector in your bag of tricks?" Scout asked.

"Oh!" Detroit said, fumbling through the pockets of her leather jacket until she pulled out something tiny and black that was shaped like a pill. She held it up between two fingers.

"Magic smoke," she said. After Scout pulled Michael back into the doorway, Detroit leaned forward and tossed the pill into the hallway.

It hit the concrete floor and rolled a little, finally settling against the double doors.

"Four, three, two, and—"

Before she could say "one," the pill emitted a puff of blue smoke. As it rose through the far end of the corridor, we could see pale green lines crisscrossing the air, like dust highlighting a laser beam.

"What is that?" I wondered.

"Trip wires," Scout said. "Magical trip wires. And I have *got* to get one of those spells."

"I've got a box at the Enclave," Detroit whispered. "I'll bring you a couple."

"We are now besties," she whispered.

"What do they do?" Michael asked.

Scout pointed toward the smoke. "They set wards," she said. "They're like trip wires. If we breach one as we try to cross the door, whoever set the spells them gets a signal. Like an alarm bell."

"And I bet Reapers would be on us in nothing flat," Jason predicted. "This has got to be their handiwork. I mean, it's got to be someone with magic, and if this was an Adept hidey-hole, we'd know about it."

"Well, we're definitely not going in there looking for slime," Michael said. "What's plan B?"

"I am," Naya said. "I will call someone."

"One of the recently deceased," Detroit clarified, gesturing toward Naya. She took a step out of the crowded doorway into the corridor, blew out a slow breath and moved her hands, palms down, in front of her as she exhaled like she was physically pushing the air from her body.

Jason bumped my arm. "Let's set up a protective area while she's getting ready," he said, then pointed to each of us in turn. Michael and Scout made a line between Naya and the wooden door into the tunnels, and Jason and I stepped around them all to create a barrier between Naya and the trip wires. Two lines of Adept defense in case something nasty popped through either way.

Once in position, we waited silently, gazes skimming nervously around the corridor, waiting for something to happen.

As if the air conditioner had suddenly kicked on, the temperature in the room dropped by ten or fifteen degrees. I stuffed my hands into my pockets. "It's superchilly down here today."

All eyes turned to me. Understanding struck, and the hair at the back of my neck lifted. The corridor felt like a field of power lines, abuzz with potential energy.

"That wasn't just a breeze, was it?" Michael whispered.

The sidewalk grates began to vibrate, then clank up and down in their moorings as something moved into the corridor. The air got hazy, and a cold, thick fog sank down among us.

"She's here," Naya whispered.

Jason muttered a startled curse, then reached out for my hand. I laced my fingers with his and squeezed. Michael and Scout were also holding hands. About time.

The mist swirled, but didn't take shape.

"She is having trouble heeding the call," Naya said. "The energy . . . is scattered."

"Is that why we can't see her?" I whispered to Detroit. The question seemed rude—like this poor girl could help that she didn't have a body—but important nonetheless.

"It takes a lot of power for the spirit to make contact, to penetrate the veil between the gray land and ours. Making herself visible would take more power than she's got. But that won't stop him or her from reaching out, or helping us."

Naya finally opened her eyes. "Her name is Temperance Bay. She was one of us, an Adept. Her skill was illusion. She could change the physical appearance of an object. She died—was taken—by a Reaper at nineteen. Ten years ago." Naya shook her head. "That's all she can tell me—and she had trouble getting that much across. The energy down here is bad. Noisy."

"That explains why I couldn't get a good read," Michael said.

"What would cause that?" I asked.

Jason pointed up. "Could be the trip wires. Could be because we're down here in a hole. Could be because of whatever went on in this place before we got here."

That didn't exactly bode well.

"Hey," Detroit said, looking at me curiously. "You've got firespell, right?"

"Um, yeah. Why?"

"Well, firespell is power magic. So maybe you could send her some firespell power, like an amplifier?"

Was she kidding? I barely knew how to turn the lights on and off. "I wouldn't know how to do that."

Undeterred, Detroit shook her head, then began tapping at the screen of her big black watch. "No, I think we can do this. It's just a matter of energy. Of plugging you in, I guess."

I looked at Scout, who shrugged, then Jason.

"This one's all you, kiddo. You're the only one who knows what it feels like. Do you think you could do it?"

I frowned, then looked at Naya. "Can you ask Temperance if she has any idea how to do it? How that might work? I don't want to hurt her. I mean, could I hurt her?"

"Of course you could," Naya said. "She's deceased, not nonexistent. Her energy remains. If you unbalance her energy, she's gonna feel it."

"So no pressure," Scout added from across the room.

No kidding, but I was an Adept, and I knew what needed to be done. "Okay," I said. "Ask her what I need to do."

Naya nodded, then rubbed the saint's medal around her neck. Her expression went a little vacant again. "Temperance, we await your direction. You have heard our plea for assistance. How can we help you make manifest?" Her eyelids fluttered. "Nourish her with the energy," she said, "to help her cross the veil. She says that I can bridge the gap to help you focus it. To help you direct it."

I nodded again. I didn't fully understand what Temperance was, but I had an idea of how it could work. Temperance was basically a spirit without a body. Naya was the link between us, the wire for the current I could provide. If I pretended Temperance was like a light-bulb in the tunnels, I might be able to give her some energy.

The only question was—could I do it without killing both of us?

"Give me your hand," I told Naya. She reached out and took my palm, and I squeezed our fingers together. "With your other hand, can you—not touch—but somehow reach Temperance? Like, have her center herself near you?"

Naya nodded, and Temperance must have moved, because I felt the spark of energy along the length of our arms.

"Here goes," I said, and closed my eyes. I imagined the three of us were a circuit, like the connected wires in a circuit board. I pulled up the well of energy, and instead of letting it flow into a bulb above me, tried to imagine it twisting, funneling from my extended arm into Naya's, slinking softly through her, and into the ghost at her side.

I felt my hair rise and lift around my head as energy swirled and Naya's fingers began to shake in my hands.

"Holy crap," I heard Scout say.

My eyes popped open, and I glanced at Naya. "Are you okay?"

Her eyes were clenched closed. "I'm fine. Just keep going."

"I saw her."

I looked back at Scout, her face pale, her eyes wide, and the key around her neck—something worn by every girl at St. Sophia's—lifting in the currents of magic. "I saw her. She wore a brown skirt. You were doing it. Keep going."

I nodded, then closed my eyes again and imagined a long cord of energy between the three of us—two current Adepts and an Adept from a former time. I pushed the energy along the current, not too much, just a little at a time, narrowing in as it spindled between us, like a fine thread being spun from a pile of frothy yarn.

I imagined the energy moving through Naya, slipping past her again, into the whirl of energy that was Temperance Bay. I tried to fill her with it, and with Naya acting as a conduit, I could *feel* her on the other side—her ache to be heard by the world around her, to be seen and remembered once again. It was a hunger, and as I offered her the energy, I felt her relief. When that hunger eased, I pulled back on the power again, slowing it to a trickle, and finally cutting it off.

Our hands still linked together, I opened my eyes. Everyone's gazes were focused to my right, past Naya, at the girl who stood beside her, gaze on me.

She wasn't quite solid—more like an old movie projection than an actual girl. But even still, there she was. She had wavy brown hair that fell nearly to her waist, and she wore a simple, straight brown skirt and long-sleeved sweater. Her eyes were big and brown, and although she wore no makeup, her cheeks were flushed pink, like she'd just come in from the cold.

Maybe she had. Maybe the gray land was cold.

She moved toward me, her image flickering at the edges as she moved, her body transparent. She held out her hands. I let go of Naya's hand and extended both of my shaking hands toward Temperance.

And then we touched.

I couldn't hold her hands—but I could *feel* them. Their outlines. Their edges. She was made of energy and light, coalesced into a form we could see, but still not quite real.

"Temperance Bay," she said, her voice soft and barely audible.

"Lily Parker."

She smiled back at me. I knew she was thanking me, so I returned her smile. "How long will it last?"

"Not long," she said, then turned to look at Naya, who nodded at both of us.

"Temperance," she said, "we think that building was used by the enemy, but we aren't sure why. We need to know what went on in there, and we need to know if anyone is still using it. Can you move through it? Take a look and see what kinds of things they were doing? We need to know if there are computers or papers—documents of any kind that might be useful."

Temperance nodded, then walked toward the doors, one slow step at a time. She moved right through the trip wires and then the doors—and then she was gone.

"And now we wait," Naya said.

"Waiting" meant sitting cross-legged on the ground, the others chatting while I waited to get a little of my own energy back. It hadn't occurred to me that filling Temperance up with power meant draining some of my own. My arms and legs felt heavy, like I'd run a marathon or was coming down with the flu. Jason sat beside me, eyes scanning the corridor as he offered me granola bars and water to boost my energy.

For Detroit, "waiting" meant working her mechanical magic. While we crouched in the entryway, she pushed the buttons on the sides of her giant black watch. After a second, a coin-shaped piece of black plastic popped out like a CD being ejected from a laptop.

"What's that?" Scout asked.

"Camera," Detroit whispered, then gestured toward the double doors. "I figure since we're here, we might as well be proactive. The pictures aren't fabulous, but it'll give us eyes on the doors without risking Adepts."

She glanced around, her gaze settling on the concrete eave at our end of the corridor. "That'll work. Should give us a clear view." She looked around. "Could anyone help me get a lift up?"

"I'll help," Jason said. He went down on one knee, the other propped up like a step, and held out a hand. Without hesitation, Detroit took his hand for balance, stepped up onto Jason's propped knee, and pressed the plastic coin into the concrete.

"Now I have a way to check in on whatever this is at the lab," Detroit said.

"You guys have a lab?" Scout asked.

Detroit looked up, surprise in her face. "Sure. Don't you?"

"You're joking, right?"

Detroit just blinked at Scout. "No."

"Uh, yeah, that room we met in earlier? That's our entire Enclave."

"No way. You guys are running a low-budg operation. We've got a lab, conference rooms, kitchenette, nap rooms. I mean, it's not lush or anything—it's a bomb shelter built in the nineteen sixties or something."

"Not lush, she says, but they have a nap room." Scout made a noise of disgust, then glanced at me. "You know what we need? A benefactor."

"Aren't your parents, like, superwealthy?" I wondered.

"We need a *generous* benefactor," she clarified. "My parents are pretty Green-focused. Ah! I made a pun."

Detroit offered Scout an arch look, like she didn't appreciate the use of humor in dire Adepty situations. I was beginning to wonder how they ran things over in Enclave Two. So far, it seemed like a pretty (up)-tight ship.

"You know, I hate that we've come this far—and through a gauntlet of fangs—and we aren't even going to take a look inside that building."

We all looked at Michael, who shrugged. "I'm just saying. I mean, I know there's bad juju there, but I hate to have come all that way for nothing."

"Not nothing," Naya pointed out. "You'll find out what's inside when Temperance returns."

"She's right," Jason said. "And we don't need to go looking for more trouble. We have to tell him about the vamps, and we've already got a black mark against the Enclave. We don't need another one."

"Yeah, we heard about that," Detroit said. She opened a pocket in her jacket, then pulled out a pack of gum. After pulling out a stick, she passed it around the room. I took one, unwrapped the foil, and popped it in my mouth. It was an odd flavor—something old-fashioned that tasted like spicy cloves—but it wasn't bad.

Scout frowned at Detroit. "What exactly did you hear?"

"Just that you guys had some internal issues. That you didn't follow Varsity's lead on some mission. You're kind of a cautionary tale now."

Scout's features tightened. "Varsity's lead was to leave me locked down in a Reaper sanctuary while Jeremiah and his minions ate me for lunch."

Detroit's lips parted. "I'm—oh, my God. I'm so sorry. That's not what they said and I hadn't heard—"

Scout held up a hand. "Let's just drop it."

"I'm really, truly sorry. I didn't know. They didn't tell us the whole story."

Scout nodded, but the hallway went silent, and the tension in the air wasn't just because of the secret building next door.

8

It was another fifteen or twenty minutes before our ghostly spy made her way back to the doors where we waited. By that point, she was mostly a cold mist, a fuzzy outline of the girl we'd seen a little while ago.

"She's fading," Naya said, standing up as Temperance came through the door—literally.

Temperance tried to speak, but the sound was a tinny whisper.

"She's communicating that the place is big," Naya said. "She saw only a little of it, but thinks there's more to see."

Temperance suddenly pulsed—her light completely fading before she popped back into the visible world again.

I looked around. "Should we try another dose of power?"

Jason stepped beside me, gaze on Temperance. "I'm not crazy about that idea," he said. "You're still pretty drained, and we still need to get back to the enclave. If you totally burn out now, that leaves us without even a chance of firespell on the way back. And we're taking the *long* way back." He gave Detroit a pointed look.

"I can fix this," she said. She opened her bag and pulled out a small black box. She put the box on the floor, then fiddled with it until it began to hum, and the top slid open. A lens emerged from the top and a cone of pale, white light shined upward toward the ceiling.

Detroit frowned at it, probably tuned in to some kind of mechanical details the rest of us couldn't even see, then sat down on her knees beside it and began to adjust dials and sliding bars on the side. "I wasn't really keen on using it this go-round—it's a new prototype. But since we can't use firespell, might as well try it out." She sat back on her heels and glanced up at Naya. "Okay, you're 'go' for launch."

Naya nodded, then closed her eyes and offered an incantation. "By the spirit of St. Michael, the warrior of angels and protector of spirits, I call forth Temperance Bay. Hear my plea, Temperance, and come forth to help us battle that which would tear us asunder."

The light flickered once, but nothing else happened.

I glanced sideways at Scout, who shrugged.

"Temperance Bay," Naya called again. "We beseech you to hear our request. There is power in this room. Power to make you visible. Come forth and find it and be seen once more."

A rush of cold air blew across our little alcove, the box vibrating with the force of it. My hair stood on end, and I clenched Jason's hand tight. However helpful Temperance might have been, she carried the feeling of something *wrong*. Maybe it wasn't because of who she was, but of what she was, of where she'd come from. Whatever the reason, you couldn't deny that creepy feeling of something *other* in the room.

"The power is here, among us," Naya said.

The air began to swirl, the cone of light flickering as Temperance moved among us trying to figure out how to use Detroit's machine. The light began to flicker wildly like a brilliant strobe before bursting from the box.

And it wasn't just light.

Temperance floated above us in the cone of light, again in her brown skirt and sweater. I wondered if those were the clothes she'd worn when she died—if she was doomed to wear the same thing forever.

She began to talk, and we could hear the staticky, faraway echo of her voice from Detroit's machine. "I am here—here—here," she said, her words stuttering through the machine.

"Temperance," Naya asked, "what did you see?"

"It is a sanctuary," she said.

I gnawed on the edge of my lip. That was so *not* the news we wanted.

"How do you know it's a sanctuary?" Scout asked. Her voice was soft.

"The mark—mark—mark of the Dark Elite is there, but dust has fallen. The building is quiet. Quiet."

"Keep going," Naya said, her voice all-business. Not a request, but a demand. Her own magic at work.

"It's like a clinic," Temperance said.

"What do you mean, a clinic?" Michael asked.

"Instruments. Machines. Syringes."

"That can't be right," Jason put in. "The Reapers don't need medical facilities. Their only medical issue is energy, and they've already got that covered."

A sudden breeze—icy cold and knife sharp—cut across the corridor. Temperance's image glowed a little brighter, her eyes sharpening. Without warning, her image blossomed and grew, and she was nine feet tall, her arms long and covered in grungy fabric, her hair streaming out, her eyes giant dark orbs. "The unliving do not make mistakes."

There were gasps. But I remembered what Naya had said—Temperance was an Adept of illusion. The image, however creepy, wasn't real. Naya's eyes were closed again, probably as she concentrated on keeping Temperance in the room, so I took action.

"Temperance," I said.

She turned those black eyes on me. I had to choke down my fear just to push out words again.

"He didn't mean to offend you. He's just surprised. Can you drop the illusion and tell us more about what you saw?"

The giant hag floated for another few seconds, before shrinking back to Temperance's slightly mousy appearance. "There are needles. Bandages. Monitors. It looks like a clinic to me."

I bobbed my head at her. "Thank you."

"You are welcome, Lily."

"Well, that's definitely new," Scout said, frowning. "What could Reapers need with medical facilities?"

"The Reapers get weaker over time," Jason pointed out. "Maybe they're trying to figure out some way to treat that?"

"Maybe so," I said. I liked the idea of Reapers turning to medicine—instead of innocent teenagers—to solve their magical maladies.

But I still had a pretty bad feeling about it.

We couldn't avoid a return to the Enclave. Not with that kind of information under our belts. We also couldn't risk another trip through the Pedway, so after meeting up with Jamie, Jill, and Paul, we took the long way back, Detroit checking her locket every few hundred feet to make sure we were on track. The route was definitely longer, but it was also vampire-, Reaper-, and slime-free. Thumbs-up in my book.

Daniel, Katie, and Smith jumped up from the floor when we walked in, their smiles falling away as they took in our expressions.

"It's all bad news," Scout said. "Might as well cop a squat again."

When we were all on the floor—the JV Adepts exhausted, the Varsity Adepts in preparation for the shock—we laid out the details. We told him the slime was gone, but the Reapers had been there. We told him about the new sanctuary—the medical facility—and the other things Temperance had seen.

Daniel rubbed his forehead as we talked, probably wishing he hadn't taken over the unluckiest of the Enclaves.

"We didn't see anyone the entire time we were there," Jason pointed out. "And Temperance said the building looked unused. So that means they're gone, right?"

"Not necessarily," Daniel said. "Sometimes they rotate sanctuaries, especially if humans get too close. They move around to decrease the odds they get discovered, so an empty sanctuary doesn't mean an abandoned sanctuary."

330 · CHLOE NEILL

"We planted a camera," Detroit said. "We'll have Sam call you if there's anything to report."

"Sam?" I asked.

"Sam Bayliss. Head of Enclave Two—and Daniel's girlfriend," Detroit helpfully threw in. All eyes went to Daniel; Scout let out a low swear. So much for her happily ever after with Daniel.

"Thank you," Daniel grumbled. "If that's all—"

Scout held up a hand. "Before you send Enclave Two off into the sunset, you'll probably want to hear the rest of it."

"The rest of it?"

"I'm gonna throw a word at you." She mimicked throwing something at him. *"Vampires."*

Daniel's expression turned stone cold. "Spill it."

"Well," Scout said, "as it turns out, we needed to use a little, tiny, eentsy bit of the Pedway, and ran into a couple of warring nests of vampires. Long story short, I used a charm to rile them up against each other; then Lily doused the lights so we could escape back into the tunnels. Oh—and Detroit's great with locks and such."

"Warring nests of vampires?"

"Turf war," Jason said. "Two covens. Nicu and Marlena. I think she said she made him."

Daniel frowned. "She must have made him a vampire. He was in her coven, then broke off to start his own. Covens don't split very often. That's probably not good news."

"Especially if we want to use the Pedway," Detroit mumbled. "Double your vamps, definitely not double your pleasure."

Daniel made a sound of agreement.

"You know," Scout said, "those things that attacked us had fangs. First we see them, and now we find out vampires are in some kind of turf war? That's a lot of fangs for a coincidence."

"That's a good point," Daniel said. "Not a happy one, but a good one." He looked at Smith. "Do some research. Figure out what you can about the vamps, about the coven split."

Smith flipped his hair out of his eyes, an emo "yes."

"And us?" Jason asked. "What are we going to do?"

"I'll be in touch," Daniel said. "In the meantime, stay away from fangs." He rose, then walked to the Enclave door and opened it.

"Go home," was all he said.

9

knew they were busy. I knew they had lessons to prepare and exams to write. But that was no excuse.

What made teachers think having students grade each other's trig homework was a good idea? My carefully written pages were now in the hands of the brattiest of the brats—Mary Katherine—who kept giving me nasty looks as our trig teacher explained the answers. By some freak accident of desk arranging, this was the third time she'd ended up with my paper. She took notes every day with a purple glitter pen, so my trig homework came back with huge X-marks on my wrong answers . . . and nasty little notes or drawings wherever she could find room. Seriously—she was such a witch.

And not the good kind.

When the time came to pass back everyone's answers, I noticed she'd added a special note this time: "Loser" in all caps across the top of my page, right next to the total of wrong answers. Since I'd gotten only one wrong—and I also knew how many M.K. usually got wrong—I held up my paper toward her, and batted my eyelashes.

She rolled her eyes and looked away, but the paper on her desk was dotted with X-marks. I guessed she was going to have to find a tutor soon, 'cause money or not, I couldn't imagine Foley would be happy about her failing trig.

Between classes I checked my phone and found a message from Ashley, my BFF from Sagamore. She was still in the public school back home since my attempt to move in with her and her parents—or have her parents ship her out here—failed pretty miserably. I felt a little guilty when I saw the message. Ashley and I hadn't talked as much since I'd started at St. Sophia's. There was the usual adjustment period, sure, but she had her own stuff in Sagamore, and I had a lot of paranormal (and brat-pack) drama. Add those to mandatory study hall, and I didn't have a lot of texting time.

But that didn't make it any less fun to hear from her, so I tapped out a quick response. I'd actually gotten halfway through asking her to come visit me until I realized what a truly horrible idea that was. I added "hard to have non-Adept friends" to my list of Adept downsides. You know, in addition to the Reapers and lack of sleep and near-death experiences.

I settled for "I MISS YOU, TOO!" and a quick description of Jason. Well, minus the werewolf bit. No sense in worrying her, right?

When the bell rang for lunch, Scout and I stuffed our books into our lockers and headed to the cafeteria.

"I've got a surprise for you today," she said, her arm through mine as we joined the buffet line.

"If it crawls or bites, I don't want to know about it."

"Hey, what you and Shepherd do on your own time is up to you."

That stopped me in my tracks. "What do you mean, me and Shepherd?"

She did a little dance. "We're going to have lunch in the park with Jason and Michael."

"You arranged a double date?"

"Not if you're calling it a double date. You can scratch it right off your list. But we are sharing in a communal meal, or whatever fancy East Coast terminology you folks like to use."

"I'm not sure upstate New York qualifies as 'East Coast.' But either way, we call it lunch."

"Lunch it is." She grabbed two paper bags from the buffet. Since our lunch hour was one of the only times the powers that be at St. Sophia's let us off campus (at least as far as they knew), they were pretty good about stocking brown-bag lunches. According to their decorator-perfect labels, one held a turkey sandwich, and the other held a Greek wrap with hummus. Being the resident vegetarian, I assumed the wrap was for me.

"Nothing for the boys?" I wondered, pulling two bottles of water from an ice-filled tub.

"The boys are bringing their own lunch. I told you it wasn't a date."

"Well, not a fancy date anyway." Unless, of course, you counted Scout's rainbow-esque ensemble. She'd paired her blue-and-gold plaid with red wool clogs, a lime green cardigan, and thin orange-and-purple headbands to hold back her hair. Whatever you might say about Scout, her wardrobe was definitely not boring. With my blue cardigan and yellow Chuck Taylors, I felt practically preppy.

Lunch in hand, we passed the brat pack and their snarky comments and thousand-dollar messenger bags and went through the school to the front door of the main building. The fresh air was a relief, especially after spending most of my days moving between the classroom building and the suite, and most of my evenings in damp tunnels.

It was a gorgeous fall day. The weather was crisp, and the sky was infinitely blue, the color reflected across the glass buildings that surrounded our gothic campus in downtown Chicago.

We walked up the street and past St. Sophia's next-door neighbor, Burnham National Bank. The bank was housed in a fancy glass skyscraper. It was a pretty building, but still a strange sight—it looked like a giant kid had stacked glass boxes on top of one another . . . but not very well.

My heart sped up as we reached the next building. It was a pretty, short brick thing—like the slightly mousier older sister of the bank building. It was also the home of the Sterling Research Foundation, the other link in the chain that connected my parents to Foley and St. Sophia's. While I'd basically promised Foley not to ask any questions that would hurt my parents, I didn't think checking into the SRF was going to hurt anyone. I just had to figure out how to do it on the sly.

For a moment, I thought about walking to the front door and peeking inside, maybe offering up some excuse about it being the wrong building. I chewed the edge of my lip, considering the possibilities.

"Lils?"

I glanced back, saw that Scout was waiting at the corner, and nodded my head. "I'm right behind you."

We slipped into the alley that separated the two buildings, and then to the left when the alley dead-ended. No—we weren't meeting Jason and Michael in a dirty alley among Dumpsters and scattered bits of trash.

The alley held a secret.

Well, actually, it was the grass just beyond the alley that held the secret—a secret garden of lush grass and concrete thorns. It was a hidden refuge that was technically just beyond the wall of St. Sophia's, but it carried the same sense of mystery as the convent itself.

We slithered in between the concrete columns and found Jason and Michael in the middle, sitting on a fleece blanket they'd stretched over the grass. Both of them wore their Montclare Academy uniforms. The plaid skirts were bad enough, but at least our school didn't make us dress like accountants.

They'd already spread their lunch—or what passed for lunch for sixteen-year-old boys—on the blanket: fast food burgers, fries, and foam cups of pop.

"Welcome to paradise!" Michael said, lifting a cup. It was a high school toast, I guess.

"Shepherd. Garcia," Scout said, kneeling down on the blanket. I joined her. Jason leaned over and kissed me lightly on the lips.

"Hello there," he whispered.

I got a full and complete set of goose bumps. "Hello back."

Michael munched on some fries. "How's life at St. Sophia's today?"

Scout unwrapped her sandwich. Little fringes of turkey peeked from between the layers of bread. "Pretty much the same as every day. Brat pack. Teachers. Lily getting her learnin' on."

Jason smiled and his dimple perked up. "Her learnin'?"

"Thomas Jefferson," I said, nibbling a black olive that had fallen out of my wrap. "I do a lot of thinking about federalism."

"It's true," Scout said. "She is all up in the federalist period."

"Mad props for checks and balances," I said, offering her knuckles. She knuckled back.

Jason snorted. "How did you two survive before knowing each other?"

"That is one of the great mysteries of the universe, amigo," Michael said. "But since we're all here together, maybe we should talk about the other mystery."

"Not a bad idea," Jason said. He half unwrapped his burger and arranged the paper so it made a sleeve, then took a bite. "At least Daniel believed us about the—what are we calling them? Rat things?"

"That's close enough," Scout said. "And Daniel is definitely an improvement. So far, I approve of him."

"I'm sure he'll be thrilled to hear it," I said.

"Don't tell me you're crushing on him, too?" Jason asked, mouth full and eyebrow arched. Scout's cheeks flushed.

She popped a corner of her sandwich in her mouth. "I don't crush. I appreciate."

"You should appreciate someone your own age," Michael muttered. Scout humphed.

Our phones chose that moment to simultaneously start ringing. If we were all getting a call, it must have been a message about Adept business.

Michael made it to his phone first. "Daniel's called off tonight's meeting. He's still figuring out what to do about the vampires."

"So we don't end up in the middle of a turf war?" Scout asked.

"That would be my guess."

Scout sighed, then pulled another chunk from her sandwich. "Sometimes I dream of lying in bed and spending my nights—and hold on to your hats, 'cause this is pretty crazy—sleeping."

"At least it's not every night," Michael said.

"Yeah, but it's more on the nights we do go out. More monsters, more Reapers, more 'operations,' " she added with air quotes.

Michael patted her shoulder. "Someday I'll take you on a trip, and we'll spend our days relaxing in luxury."

"Hawaii?"

"I'm on scholarship. How about Kenosha?"

Scout shrugged. "That works, too." She looked down and began plucking through the paper bag and empty sandwich wrapper. "What happened to the other half of my sandwich?"

"You just ate it," Michael said.

"Nah, I couldn't have. Not that fast." She put a hand to her stomach, then pressed a little. "I do feel full. But I seriously don't even remember eating it."

"Maybe you're also distracted." Michael winged up his eyebrows for effect.

"You ate it, didn't you? You ate my sandwich?"

Jason leaned toward me. "Whatever you might say about Scout, the girl's tenacious."

"That she is. Did you eat her sandwich?"

He made a huff. "A gentleman does not take a lady's sandwich."

"Are you a gentleman?"

"I am a gentlewolf. I did rescue a beautiful damsel in distress, after all."

"You did do that. And I appreciate it very, very much. Being alive rocks."

He lifted a hand and brushed a lock of hair from my face. His eyes were the same color as the wickedly blue sky. "Of course I did. I think you're pretty cool, you know."

My toes practically curled from the heat in his eyes.

Scout cleared her throat. Loudly. "Hey," she said, bumping Michael with her elbow. "Could I talk to you for a sec?"

"I didn't eat your sandwich."

Scout made a sound of frustration, then grabbed Michael by the hand and helped him to his feet. "I know you didn't eat my sandwich, but we need to talk," she said, then pulled him between the thorns until they disappeared from view.

"What's that about?"

"I am not entirely sure."

We sat quietly for a minute.

"You know, we haven't known each other very long, and we met under kind of strange circumstances."

I glanced over at him. This sounded like some kind of relationship talk. Was he going to ask me to Sneak? My heart sped up, but I went for a casual tone. "That is true."

"I just—I guess I think we should, you know, actually go out sometime."

I was a little disappointed I hadn't gotten an invite to the Sneak, but I guess an actual date of any kind would work for now. I managed a smile. "We could probably make that happen."

"I was thinking Saturday."

Okay, a definite date helped. "Saturday works."

"Cool."

Scout and Michael popped out from between the thorns. His curly hair was standing up; her cheeks were flushed. I had to bite my lip to keep from saying something snarky.

"All right, Parker. You ready for school?"

I nodded. "Let's do it."

I picked up the remains of our lunch, then stood up so Jason could fold up the blanket.

"We'll walk you," Michael said, extending his crooked elbow toward Scout. She rolled her eyes, but took it.

Jason glanced at me with amusement.

"Don't even think about it," I warned him, but didn't object when he entangled our fingers together.

We walked back through the alley and past the SRF and bank building, then hit the Erie Avenue sidewalk back toward the school.

That was where we found John Creed, standing beside the low stone fence that contained the St. Sophia's grounds, his heavy eyebrows pinched together as he gazed at the phone in his hands. He looked up when we approached, then slid his phone into his pocket.

"I didn't know we had plans," Jason said.

"We don't. I had to drop by Franklin's. That's my dad," he explained, gaze on me. "He's got an office up the street."

"How is Franklin?" Jason asked.

"Knee-deep in money." Creed looked at Scout. "And you are?"

"Scout Green," Michael said. "She's another St. Sophia's girl."

"Swell to meet you, Scout Green, St. Sophia's girl."

"Ditto," Scout said.

"I figured I'd wait so we could walk back together. But you weren't at the school." His gaze followed the sidewalk to the spot where we'd emerged onto the street. "What's over that way?"

"Just a shortcut," Jason said, squeezing my hand as if to keep me quiet. I guess he wanted to keep the thorn garden to himself.

Creed looked doubtful, but nodded anyway, at least until we lost his attention. M.K. and Veronica crossed the street toward us, steaming paper coffee cups in hand. Figured. They seemed like the expensive-coffee type.

"I guess they made up," Scout whispered to me.

"Guess so."

Creed stuck his hands into his pockets. "Afternoon, ladies."

"Hello, again," M.K. said, giving him a catty look.

Veronica smiled at Creed, but the smile drooped a little when she realized that he was slumming with us. "You're far from home," she said. "Paying a visit to the convent?"

Creed smiled. "Waiting for my brothers-in-arms."

"Cute," M.K. said, giving Scout and me a dirty look. "And they're just tagging along?"

"Sagamore and Scout are friends of Jason's," Creed said with a big smile. "And that makes them friends of mine."

Jason leaned toward me. "Just a warning, friendship with Creed comes with a lengthy disclaimer."

"Funny man," Creed said. "Very funny." He glanced over at Veronica. "How's the party planning coming?"

"Good," she said. "It's going to be pretty sweet when it's all said and done."

He nodded dutifully at Veronica, then slid M.K. an inviting glance that deflated Veronica's smile—but strengthened the resolve in her expression.

"Um, so how's the boat?" Veronica asked.

"My father's? Still pretty good, I imagine."

The church bells began to chime, signaling the end of lunch.

"We should go," Jason said, untangling our fingers. "We'll see you later."

"Later," I said with a smile.

"Oh, crap," Scout exclaimed. "I forgot to grab my chemistry book." She gave me an apologetic look. "I'm gonna run to my locker. I'll see you in class."

I'd barely nodded when she took off running down the sidewalk and toward the front door.

"I'll catch you ladies later," Creed said, taking a position next to Jason and Michael. They started down the street, their escape leaving me, M.K., and Veronica standing awkwardly on the sidewalk.

"Give us a minute, M.K.," Veronica said.

M.K. arched a questioning eyebrow.

"I'll meet you inside."

Apparently knowing when an order had been given, M.K. shrugged and started for the door.

When she was gone, Veronica looked back at me. "So you and Creed are friends?"

"We know each other. I wouldn't say friends." *At least not before I heard Jason's disclaimer.* "Why do you ask?"

"I thought you didn't know him." Her voice was snotty, like I'd been keeping John Creed locked away from her on purpose.

"I know who he is. That's it."

"Mm-hmm." There was obvious doubt in her voice. Why did she care if I knew him or not? She'd seen me holding hands with Jason. "He calls you 'Sagamore' like you two are close."

"You were with me the first time I met him. You heard him call me Sagamore."

That didn't seem to stop her. The thing she apparently had for Creed must have been shorting her logic circuits, as it didn't seem to compute.

"Yeah, well. I just think you need to stop playing coy."

I almost called her out, almost reminded her that it was her best friend—M.K.—who seemed to have an in with John Creed, not me.

But before I could speak, someone else jumped in.

"Is there a problem?"

We looked behind us to where he stood on the sidewalk in jeans and a long-sleeved T-shirt, stormy blue eyes trained on Veronica.

Sebastian. Reaper . . . and now stalker?

My heart began to pound in my chest, and my fingers began to tingle with anticipatory magic. The Darkening on my back warmed, maybe from my proximity to him, my heart suddenly thudding in my chest. I'm not going to lie—I was scared out of my mind. This guy was a Reaper. I mean, I didn't think he was going to blast me right here on the sidewalk, but I could still remember how much the firespell had hurt. I really didn't want to go through that again.

Of course, now I had firespell, too.

"What?" Veronica stuttered out, her gaze moving between me and Sebastian.

"I asked if there was a problem." His voice was cold and smooth like marble, his steely eyes on the brat in front of me. I wasn't sure if I should applaud him . . . or feel sorry for her.

"No."

"Great. Probably you should get to class, then."

She started to argue, but before she could get out word one, he'd dropped his head a quarter of an inch, leveling his gaze at her.

"We're done," she said, evil eyes on me, before turning and hurrying toward the gate. Since the first bell had already rung, I needed to do the same thing. But before I could bolt, he put a hand on my arm.

A shiver trickled down my spine.

"Get your hand off me."

"I'm not done with you."

I made myself look back at him, made myself look him in the eyes. "We're on the street. You can't do anything here."

"Sure I could," Sebastian said. "But I won't." He glanced back at Veronica's bobbing form. "Is she giving you trouble?"

"*You're* giving me trouble," I told him. "I knew I saw you on the street the other day. Why are you following me around?"

"Because we need to talk."

At least he wasn't going to deny it. "We have nothing to talk about."

"We have firespell to talk about."

"No," I corrected, "we have firespell, period. End of story. There's nothing that needs to be talked about."

"Really." His voice couldn't have been drier. "Because you're an expert in using it? In manipulating it? In creating the spark?"

"In creating the—"

"The spark," he interrupted. "You know nothing about your power. And that's ridiculously dangerous."

I crossed my arms and huffed out a breath. "And what—you should be the one to teach me?"

The look he gave back suggested that was *exactly* what he thought he should do. But then his eyes clouded. "The world isn't nearly as black and white as you believe, Lily."

I'd actually begun to ask him what he meant until I remembered who he was and whose side he was on. That made me turn my back and start down the sidewalk again. I wouldn't run away from him. Not again. But that didn't mean I was stupid enough to stand around with a sworn enemy.

"Quit following me," I called back, loud enough for him to hear. "We're done."

"No, we're not. Not by a long shot."

I shook my head, forcing my feet to the ground even as my knees wobbled. But that didn't stop me from glancing back when I was inside the gate.

This time, he was gone.

I kept my head down in class, my eyes on my books, glad that Scout sat behind me. I wasn't sure I should tell her about Sebastian—either that he had been following me, or that he'd tried to save me from Veronica.

He'd tried to intervene.

What was that about?

I mean, he was a *Reaper*. The sworn enemy of Adepts, the folks who thought it was okay to buy a few more years of magic with someone else's soul.

And yet he was also the guy who'd given me the clue to using firespell and who'd stepped into a near-fight with Veronica.

Something strange was going on. I wasn't sure what—I certainly didn't think he was some kind of Robin Hood of magic—but whatever it was, I wasn't ready to tell Scout.

No, this was going to need a little more time.

I hoped I had it.

10

Dinner was Tex-Mex food, which St. Sophia's managed pretty well for a snotty private boarding school in the middle of downtown Chicago. And as a vegetarian, it was usually a favorite of mine. Tex-Mex at St. Sophia's meant tortillas and beans and peppers and cheese, so it was usually easy to whip up something meat-free.

We had an hour after dinner before study hall for Scout and, according to Foley, art studio for me, so we headed back to our suite for some time off—and so I could get my materials together.

When we got in, Amie's door was open, the light off. Lesley's door was shut, cello music drifting from beneath the door. She played the cello and spent a lot of time practicing. Luckily, she was really good at it, so it was kind of like having a tiny orchestra in the room. Not a bad way to live, as it turned out.

When Scout and I walked in and shut the door behind us, the music came to a stop. A few seconds later, Lesley emerged from her room. She wore a pale green dress with a yellow cardigan over it, her blond hair tucked behind her ears, her feet tucked into canvas Mary Janes. She stood in her doorway for a moment, blinking blue eyes at us.

Lesley was definitely on our side, but she was still a little odd.

"What's up, Barnaby?" Scout asked, dropping onto the couch in the common room. "Sounds like the cello playing is going pretty well."

Lesley shrugged. "I'm having trouble with some of the passages. Not as vibrant as I want them to be. Practice, practice, practice."

I took a seat on the other end of the couch. "It sounds good to the plebeians."

"Ooh, nice use of today's Euro-history lesson," Scout complimented.

"I am all up in the vocab."

Lesley walked around the couch and sat down on the floor, her skirt fluttering as she moved. She wasn't an Adept, but she was pale and blond and had a very old-fashioned look about her. It wasn't hard to imagine that she'd stepped out of some fairy tale and into modern-day Chicago.

"How's it going with your secret midnight missions?"

Although she wasn't totally up to speed on the Adept drama, she knew Scout and I were involved in something extracurricular at night.

"The missions are going," Scout said. "Some nights are better than others." She bobbed her head toward Amie's door. "Amie's little minion saw us coming in on Monday night. Has she said anything about it to you?"

Lesley shook her head. "Not to me. But I heard Veronica tell M.K. and Amie about it. She said Lily was out with a boy." Lesley looked at me. "Do you have a boyfriend?"

"Kinda," I said, my cheeks heating up.

"They say anything else?" Scout asked. "Or did they believe us?"

Lesley shrugged. "Mostly they wondered who the boy was. They didn't think you'd been here long enough to meet a boy."

"Our Parker moves pretty fast."

I kicked Scout in the leg. "Stifle it," I said, then smiled at Lesley. "Thanks for the update."

"I could do some opp research if you want."

Scout and I exchanged a puzzled glance. "Opp research?" she asked. "What's that?"

"Opposition research. I could follow them around, eavesdrop, take notes. Maybe find something you could blackmail them with?"

"For a nice girl, Les, you've definitely got a dark side."

Lesley smiled grandly—and a little wickedly. "I know. People look at me and they don't really think I'm up to it. But I'm definitely up to it."

"We will mos' def' keep that in mind," Scout said. "But for now, since we've got an hour"—she paused to pick up the remote control for the small wall-mounted television—"how about a little oblivion?"

I gave her forty-five minutes before I headed back to my room to assemble my supplies.

I had no idea what we'd be doing in art studio—drawing, painting, ceramics, collage—so I put together a little of everything.

First step, of course, was to take stock of the supplies I'd brought with me from home. A couple of sketch pads. Charcoal. Conté crayons. My favorite pencils, a sharpener, and a couple of gummy erasers. A small watercolor box with six tiny trays of color and a little plastic cup for water. Three black microtip pens I'd nabbed at the Hartnett College bookstore, where my parents had been professors. (College bookstores always had the best supplies.)

I tried not to think about Sebastian or the things he wanted to talk to me about, and instead focused on the task at hand. I put the supplies into a black mesh bag, zipped it up, and threw the whole shebang into my messenger bag.

When I was ready to go, I headed out and locked my door behind me. The common room was empty again. Scout's door was shut, and when I tried the knob, it was locked.

Weird. Since when did Scout lock her door?

I knocked with a knuckle. "Hey, you okay in there? I'm heading out for studio."

It took a second before she answered, "I'm good. Just about to head to study hall. Have fun."

I stood there in front of her door for a few seconds, waiting for something more. But she didn't say anything else. What was she up to?

I shook my head and walked toward the hallway. I definitely did not need another mystery.

The surplus building was a steeply roofed box that sat behind the classroom building. The classroom building was pretty new, but the surplus building was definitely old—the same dark stone and black slate roof as the main building. Maybe it had been a stable or a storage building when the nuns still lived at St. Sophia's.

I had to walk around the building to find the door. And when I opened it, I stared. Small or not, the building definitely had pizzazz. It was one big room with an open ceiling all the way up to the pitched roof. Skylights had been cut into one side of the ceiling, so the room—at least earlier in the day—would have been flooded with light.

One wall was made of windows, the ceiling a high vault with huge crisscrossing wooden beams. A dozen or so standing wooden easels made a grid across the floor.

"You can take an easel, Parker." I turned and found Lesley behind me, a canvas tote bag brimming full of supplies in her hand. For anyone else, I would have thought it strange that she hadn't mentioned she was in art studio when we were in the common room. For Lesley—not so much.

She walked to an easel, then began pulling supplies and sketchbooks out of her tote and arranging them on a small shelf beneath her easel. I took the one beside hers.

"You'll keep your easel for the year," she said, arranging empty baby food jars and cups of pencils and brushes. "So you can unload your stuff and come back after study hall. The TAs usually keep a still life ready so you can practice drawing forms, or whatever." She inclined her head toward a table at one end of the room.

"What's a TA?" I asked, pulling out my own bag of pencils and sketch pads.

"Teaching assistant. They usually get an art major from Northwestern or Illinois Tech or whatever to teach the class."

With great care, she organized her supplies, creating a little nest of tools around her easel. I didn't have much to arrange, but I placed everything within arm's reach, put my bag on the floor, and took a seat on my stool.

The room filled after a couple of minutes, the rest of the small studio class taking their own easels. Just like in any other high school, the room was a mix of types. Some looked preppy, some looked average, and some looked like they were trying really hard not to look preppy or average. There were girls I didn't know, who I assumed were in the classes behind and ahead of me.

And when everyone had taken an easel and arranged their things, he walked in.

I kept blinking, thinking that my eyes were deceiving me, until he walked by—as if in slow motion—and gave me a tiny nod.

Daniel was my studio TA.

I bit back a grin as he walked to the front of the room, and began thinking of ways to break the news to a very jealous suitemate. And she wasn't the only ones with eyes for His Blondness. The other girls' gazes followed him as he moved, some with expressions that said they'd be happy to spend an hour drawing his form.

He turned to face us, then stuck his hands in his pockets. "So, welcome to studio art. I'm Daniel Sterling. I'll be your TA this year."

"There is a God," whispered the grateful girl beside me.

"We're going to spend the first few weeks on some basic representational exercises. Still lifes. Architecture. Even each other."

Lesley and I exchanged a flat glance. It looked like she was as thrilled at the idea as I was—namely, not at all. I was perfectly happy with my body, but that didn't mean I needed it to be the source of other people's art.

"Today we're going to start with some basic shapes." He began to pick through a plastic milk crate of random objects, then pulled out a small lamp and its round lamp shade, a couple of wooden blocks, and three red apples. He draped a piece of blue velvet over the table, setting the blocks beneath it to create areas of different heights. Then he put the lamp and apples on the table and organized them into a tidy arrangement.

When he was done, he turned back to us. "All right," he said. "Use whatever media you choose. You've got two hours. Let's see what you're made of."

Drawing was a strange thing. Probably like other hobbies—basketball or cello playing or baking or writing—there were times when it felt like you were going through the motions. When you put pencil to paper and were aware of every dot, every thin line, every thick shade.

At other times, you looked up from the page and two hours had passed. You lost yourself in the movement, in the quiet, in trying to represent on paper some object from real life. You created a little world where there'd only been emptiness before.

This was one of those times.

Daniel had come around a couple of times to offer advice—to remind me to draw what I actually *saw*, not just to rely on my memories of what the objects looked like, and to remind me to use the tip of my pencil instead of mashing the lead into the paper—but other than those trips back to the real world, I spent the rest of the time zoned out, my gaze darting between the stuff on the table and the sketchbook in front of me.

That was why I jumped when he finally clapped his hands. "Time," he said, then smiled at us. "Great job today." When everyone began to pack up their supplies, he held up a hand.

"You didn't think you were going to get out of here without homework, did you?"

There were groans across the room.

"Aw, it's not that bad. Before we meet again, I want you to do a little Second City appreciation. Find a building in the area and spend an hour getting it on paper. You can use whatever materials you want—paint, ink, pencil, charcoal—but I want to see something representational when you're done. I want you to think about line and shadow. Think about positive and negative space—what parts of space did the architect choose to fill? Which parts did he decide to leave empty?"

We waited for more, but he finally bobbed his head. "Now you're dismissed."

The girl beside me grumbled as she stuffed a small, plastic box of watercolors into her bag. "I liked him a lot better when he was just the pretty new TA."

"Ah," he said, suddenly appearing to walk past us. "But that's not going to make you a better artist, is it?"

She waited until he'd passed, then raised hopeless eyes to me. "Do you think that's going to hurt my grade?"

I glanced back at Daniel, who'd paused at the threshold of the door to talk to a student. He held her sketch pad in one hand and used the other one to point out various parts of her drawing.

"I think he's going to be pretty fair," I decided. What I hadn't yet decided was whether he was here by accident . . . or on purpose.

I practically ran back to the suite after class was over, then slammed into Scout's room.

I probably should have knocked.

She was on her bed and wearing gigantic headphones. She'd already changed into a bright green tank top and pajama bottoms, and in her hand was a hairbrush she was using as a microphone to belt out a Lady Gaga song at the top of her lungs.

I slapped my hands over my ears. Was Scout generally cool? Yes. Unfortunately, she was also pretty tone-deaf.

She yelped when she saw me, then fell to her knees on the bed. She dropped the brush and whipped off the headphones. "Seriously— knocking?"

I chewed my lips to keep from laughing.

"Parker, if you so much as snicker, I will bean you with this brush."

I turned my head into my shoulder to stifle the snort and winced when the brush hit my shoulder. "Ow," I said, rubbing it.

Scout sniffed and put the headphones on the floor. "I spend my days in class and most of my nights saving the world. I'm allowed to have a little Scout time."

"I know, I know. But maybe you could, you know, focus it in a more productive direction. Like drawing."

"I don't like to draw."

"I know." I shut the door behind us. "But you know who *does* like to draw?" Don't you love a good segue?

"You?"

I rolled my eyes. "Other than me, goofus."

"I give up."

"Our intrepid leader. Daniel's my studio teacher."

"No. Freaking. Way."

"Totally." I dropped my bag and sat down on the edge of her bed. "He walks in, and I was like, 'Holy frick, that's Daniel.'"

"You would say that. Is he good at drawing?"

"Well, I didn't see a portfolio or anything, but since Foley hired him, I'd assume so." And then I thought about what I'd just said. "Unless she hired him because he's an Adept. Would she do something like that?"

Scout frowned. "Well, she does know about us. I wouldn't put it past her to offer an Adept a job. On the other hand, the board of directors would have her head if she hired anyone less than worthy of her St. Sophia's girls."

"True. I can tell you this—he likes to give out homework in studio just like he does in the Enclave."

"What do you have to do?"

"Draw a building downtown." I pulled up my legs and crossed them. "I had an idea—I'm thinking about drawing the SRF building."

"Really?" I saw the instant she realized what I was up to. "Your parents," she said. "You think you might learn something?"

I shrugged. "I don't know. And Foley basically told me not to ask questions about my parents. But it seems like a way to get a good look at the building, maybe glance around inside, without causing trouble."

Scout bobbed her head left and right. "That is true. I don't know how they could connect you back with your parents, anyway." She gestured toward my skirt. "They might guess you go to St. Sophia's, but they're practically next door. They probably see the uniforms all the time, so they wouldn't think too much of it."

"That sounds reasonable. You can actually come up with pretty good ideas when you put your mind to it."

"Even though I'm not going to win a talent contest anytime soon?"

"Well, not at singing anyway."

She hit me with a pillow. I probably deserved that.

"So, at lunch today, Jason didn't ask me to Sneak."

"Lils, you've barely even *planned* Sneak yet. Give it time. He'll get there."

"He did ask me out on Saturday."

"OMG, you two are totally getting married and having a litter of babies. Ooh, what if that's literally true?"

I gave her a push on the arm, then changed the subject. "Did Michael ask you to Sneak?"

"Not exactly."

She sounded a little odd, so I glanced over at her. "What do you mean, 'not exactly'? Did it come up?"

"Yeah, I mean, we talked about it . . ."

It took me a minute to figure out what she was dancing around. "You asked him, didn't you?"

Her cheeks flushed. "Maybe that was discussed in a general sense."

I poked a finger in her shoulder. "Ha! I knew you had a thing for him!"

I'd expected a look of irritation; instead, she was blushing.

"Oh, my God," I said, realization hitting. "You guys *totally* made out behind the concrete things."

"Oh, my God, shut *up*," she said.

We spent the next couple of hours like true geeks. We studied trig, then rounded out the night with some European-history review, and I sent messages to my parents. I walked a weird line between missing them, worrying about them, and trying—like Foley had suggested—to keep them out of my mind. But I was surrounded by weirdness, and that just made me think of them even more. There was so much I wanted to tell them—about Scout and Jason, about being an Adept, about the underground world I'd discovered in Chicago.

Maybe they already knew some of it. Foley had hinted around that they might know about the Dark Elite. But they didn't know about Jason or firespell, and they certainly couldn't know how my life had changed over the last couple of weeks. I wasn't going to break it to them now—not over the phone or via text message and not when they were thousands of miles away. For now I'd trust Foley. But that didn't mean I wasn't going to check out the SRF building. After all, how much trouble could drawing a building get me into?

When it got late enough that my eyes were drifting shut, I packed up my stuff to head back to my room.

"You can sleep here if you want," Scout said.

I looked up at her from my spot on the floor, a little surprised. I'd slept over before, when Scout had had trouble sleeping after her rescue. But I hadn't done it in a few days, and I wondered if everything was okay. "You good?"

She rolled her eyes. "I'm fine. We're teenagers," she reminded me. She uncurled her legs, then bent over the side of her bed and pulled out a thick blanket in a boxy plastic wrapping. It was the same one she gave me every time I bunked over. "We're not setting a precedent here or anything."

"And they definitely don't do bed checks or anything."

"M.K. thanks her lucky stars for that," Scout muttered.

"Seriously—that is grade A disturbing. I don't want to think about the extracurricular field trips she's taking." I hitched a thumb toward the door. "I'm going to go throw on some pajamas."

"Go for it." Scout punched her pillow a couple of times, then snagged a sleeping blindfold from one of the bedposts. She slid it on, then climbed under the covers.

"Nice look."

She humphed. "If I'm asleep when you come back, let's keep it that way."

"Whatever. You snore."

"I am a very delicate sleeper. It complements my delicate beauty."

"You're a delicate dork."

"Night, Lils."

"Night, Scout."

I woke up suddenly, a shrill sound filling the air. "What the frick?"

"Whoozit?" Scout said, sitting up in bed, the sleeping mask across her eyes. She whipped it off, then blinked to orient herself.

I glanced around. The source of the noise was one of the tiny paper houses on her bookshelves. It was fully aglow from the inside, and it sounded like a fire alarm was going off inside it.

Scout let out a string of curses, then fumbled out of bed. And I do mean fumbled—she got caught in the mix of blankets and comforters, and ended up on the floor, half-trapped in quilts, before she managed to stand up and pluck the house from the bookshelf.

"Oh, crap," she intoned, lifting up the house to eye level so that she could peer into it. When she looked back at me, forehead pinched, I knew we were in trouble. "That's my alarm. My ward got tripped."

11

stood up and walked toward her. "What does that mean, 'My ward got tripped'?"

Scout closed her eyes, then pursed her lips and blew into the house's tiny window. By the time she opened her eyes, the house was silent and dark again, as if its tiny residents had gone back to sleep.

She put it carefully back on its shelf, then looked at me. "Daniel's been teaching me how to ward the basement doors—it's supposed to keep the nasties out or send out an alarm if they make it through. You know, since they kidnapped me and all."

"I do recall that," I agreed supportively—and wondered if that was what she'd been working on in her room.

"This house was keyed to the vault door in the basement—the big metal one with the locks and stuff?"

"So the house is, what, some kind of alarm?"

She nodded, then grabbed a pair of jeans from her closet. "Pretty much. Now, go get dressed. We're going to have to handle this."

My stomach knotted, nerves beginning to build. "What do you think it is?"

She blew out a breath. "I don't know. But I'm guessing it's not going to be pretty."

Unfortunately, I guessed she was right.

. . .

We'd both pulled on jeans, shirts, and sneakers to make our way downstairs. We'd decided we didn't want to be captured by Reapers or rescued by Adepts—or worse—in silly pajamas. The school was quiet as we moved through the hallways, probably not a surprise since it was nearly two o'clock in the morning. On the other hand, I half expected M.K. to jump out from behind a corner. I figured her being out on some secret rendezvous was only slightly less likely than the possibility that we'd soon be staring down half a dozen creeping monsters.

We made it through the Great Hall and labyrinth room, then through the door that led to the stairs. We stayed quiet until we'd made our way into the locked corridor that led down, after two staircases and a handful of hallways, into the basement. I'd taken this route before— the first time I'd followed Scout on one of her midnight rambles, actually. And we all knew how that had ultimately turned out.

"Do we have a plan of action here?" I quietly asked, tiptoeing behind Scout.

She adjusted the strap of her messenger bag. "If I'm as good as I think I am, we don't need one."

"Because your ward worked."

"Not exactly. This was only my first time warding, so I'm not expecting much. But I also worked a little magic of my own. And if that works—I am officially da bomb."

"Wow. You really went there."

"I totally did."

"What kind of magic did you work?"

"Well, turns out, Daniel's a protector."

"You are seriously stalking him, aren't you?"

"Ha. You'd be amazed what you can find on the Internet. Anyway, a protector is a guardian angel type. His magic's all about protecting breaches. But his magic works more like an alarm. I like to be a little more walk and a little less talk. A little less conversation and a little more action."

I guessed her endgame. "You booby-trapped it, didn't you?"

"Little bit," she said, then stopped short. She glanced back at me and put a finger to her lips as we neared the final corridor. "I'll go first," she whispered. "You follow and firespell me if my hex didn't work."

I nodded. "Good luck."

"Let's hope it doesn't come to that," she said, and we moved.

The door was nearly twice as tall as I was. The entire thing was edged in rivets, and a huge flywheel took up most of the middle of the door, as did a giant steel bar.

But the bar and the flywheel and the fact that the door itself weighed a ton hadn't stopped the two girls who lay on the floor in front of it, arms and legs pinned to their sides, rolling around on the floor.

I couldn't stop my mouth from dropping open. "What the—"

"Oh, *nice*," Scout smugly said. She walked into the corridor, hands on her hips, and surveyed the damage. One of the girls wore a green-and-gold cheerleading uniform, her wavy, dark blond hair spilling out on the floor as she rolled around, trying to unglue her arms and legs. The second girl was curvier and wore an oversized dark T-shirt and jeans over big, clunky shoes. She was pale, and there were dark circles under her eyes.

Realizing they weren't alone, the Reapers took the opportunity to blister our ears with insults. Scout rolled her eyes. "Hey, this is a convent, Reapers. Watch your language."

"Unmake this spell, *Millicent Green*," spat out the cheerleader, half sitting up to get a look at us. "*Right* now."

"You couldn't pay me enough to unmake it, *Lauren Fleming*." There was equal venom in Scout's voice. Obviously, she and Lauren were acquainted. "What are you doing in our territory?"

The second girl lifted her head from the floor. "What do you think we're doing here, genius?"

"Being completely and totally hexbound would be my first guess. Lily?"

Technically, I had no idea what "hexbound" was, but Scout had said she'd done a hex, and these two girls seemed like they were tied up with some kind of invisible magic, so I made an educated guess. "Certainly looks that way. How do you two know each other?"

"Millicent remembers the agony of defeat," the second girl put in.

Scout's lip curled. "There was no defeat. I forfeited the game because Lauren locked me in the green room."

"Like that mattered. You would have lost anyway. I'd been training for six weeks straight."

"Because your mom was your coach."

"At least my mom was in the state at the time."

The room went silent, and my gaze darted back and forth between the two of them. I was waiting for Scout to growl or hiss or reach out to rake her nails across Lauren's face.

"So, what game?" I asked. "Basketball or softball or . . . ?"

"Quiz Club," they simultaneously said.

I had to bite back a snicker, and got a nasty look from Scout.

She walked closer and prodded Lauren's cheer shoe with a toe. "How did you get through the door?"

"How do you think? Your wards are crap."

"It was locked the old-fashioned way."

"Hello?" said the second girl. "I'm a gatekeeper? I pick locks?"

Lauren made a sound of irritation. I got the sense she wasn't friends with her uncheerleadery teammate. On the other hand, Reapers probably didn't care much about friendship when teaming up for infiltrations. They were evil, after all. Being BFFs probably didn't figure into it.

"Frick," Scout muttered. "I didn't know they had a gatekeeper."

"Clearly," snarked out the apparent gatekeeper.

Scout rolled her eyes. "Let's recall who's spindled on the floor and who's standing victoriously over you, shall we? Geez. There's a hierarchy, ladies."

"Whatever," Lauren said petulantly.

"Yeah, well, you can 'whatever' this, cheer-reaper." Scout began to clap her hands and stomp her feet in rhythm, her own little cheer.

"Hey," she said, "it's getting cold in here. There must be some Reapers in the atmosphere."

Lauren made some really offensive suggestions about Scout's mom. Did she cheer with that mouth?

"I'm going to ignore those very classless suggestions about my parentals," she said. "Why don't we go back to my first question? Why were you trying to break into St. Sophia's?"

"We didn't just *try*," said the gatekeeper. "We *accomplished*."

"Two feet inside the door hardly qualifies as accomplished, *mi amiga*. Unless you'd like your mouths hexbound as well, I suggest you talk." Scout held up her hands and closed her eyes and began to recite some magical words. But since those words were "abracadabra" and "mumbo jumbo" and "hocus pocus," I guessed she was playing chicken.

"You know why we're here," the gatekeeper quickly answered, her voice squeaking in her effort to get out the words.

"Me and my *Grimoire*?"

"Like you're so freakin' special," Lauren muttered.

Scout squared her shoulders. "Special enough. My *Grimoire* is out of reach, and even if you got me, I'm sure as hell not going to go willingly. Did you two think you could just walk in here and carry me out?"

Lauren laughed. "Um, yes? Hello, hypnosis power?"

Scout moved closer and peered down at Lauren. "Ah, there it is," she said, pointing down at Lauren's neck. I took a closer look. Around Lauren's neck was a small, round watch on a gold chain.

"Have you ever seen those old movies where some evil psychiatrist hypnotizes someone by swinging their watch back and forth? She can do that."

"Huh," I said. "That's a pretty narrow power." Not that it made me any less happy that her hands were bound. These two seemed like the type to write "loser" on your forehead in permanent marker once they'd gotten you down.

"Very narrow," Scout agreed with a wicked grin. "And you know what they say about girls with very narrow powers?"

"What's that?"

Scout paused for a minute. "Oh, I don't know. Honestly, I didn't think we'd make it all the way through the joke."

Lauren did a little more swearing. Gatekeeper girl tried to join in, but she just wasn't as good at it.

"I don't know what that means," I admitted. "How can someone be dumber than a baguette?"

"It means you're stupid."

I thought back to my nearly perfect trig homework. "Try again." But that just reminded me that we had class—including trig—in a few hours. Exhaustion suddenly hitting me in a wave, I worked to get us back on track. "What do you want to do now?"

Scout looked back at me. "Well, we're in the convent, and they're in the convent. That's two too many people in the convent."

Five minutes later, we were dragging two squirming girls through the vault door and into the corridor behind it—and out of St. Sophia's. They were hard to move, not just because they were fidgety, but because every time we gripped them near the shoulders they tried to bite us.

"Isn't there a better way to do this?" I wondered, standing over Scout. "I mean, if you'd knocked them completely unconscious they'd be a lot easier to move."

"Yeah, but we'd be leaving them completely at the mercy of whatever else might roam the tunnels at night. And that would be such a Reaper thing to do."

Lauren growled.

We finally managed it by dragging them by their hexbound feet into the tunnel. But it wasn't pretty, and the swearing didn't get any better. Neither of them—especially not the cheerleader—was thrilled to be dragged through five or six feet of underground tunnel on their backs.

When they were on the other side of the door, Scout put her hands on her hips and looked down at them. "And what did we learn today, ladies?"

"That you suck."

Scout rolled her eyes. I raised a hand. "While we're here, I have a question."

"Go for it, Lils. All right, cheer-reaper and gatekeeper—"

"I'm in the band."

"Sorry?"

"You call her cheer-reaper, I figure you should call me by my title, too. I'm in the band. I play the French horn."

Scout and I shared a grin.

"'Course you do," Scout said. "Okay, cheer-reaper and French hornist, my friend here has a question for you."

"Thanks," I offered.

"Anytime."

I turned toward them. "Have you two seen anything weird in the tunnels lately?"

"Oh," French horn said, "you mean the rat thingies?"

I blinked. I hadn't thought it was going to be quite that easy. "Well, actually, yeah. You know anything about those?"

The French horn player huffed. "Well, of course we do. We—"

She was interrupted by Lauren's screaming. "Shut up. Shut up. Shut up. *Shut up*!" And she didn't stop there. She kept screaming and screaming. Scout and I both hitched back a little, then shared a wary glance. That kind of noise was surely going to attract attention.

"Shut it, Fleming," Scout said, kicking her toe a little, then glancing at me. "That may be our cue to depart."

"They know something," I pointed out.

"I know something, too. I know we're going to attract a lot of unwanted attention if they keep screaming. And then we have to make up some ridiculous explanation about how we heard screaming through the vents in our rooms, and we followed the sound back to the basement, and we found these girls lying on the ground and pretending to be tied up by invisible rope because they're practicing for the regional mime championships."

I blinked at her. "Is that explanation more or less believable than we woke up because two girls who are actually evil magicians tripped a magical alarm wired to a door in the basement we aren't supposed to know about?"

Scout paused for a minute, the nodded. "Point made. Let's go home. Ladies, have a pleasant evening."

Not surprisingly, Lauren stopped screaming. But that just meant the curses were a little less loud than they had been before.

We left a flashlight on the ground between them, then slipped through the door again. When we were both on the other side, we used all our weight to push the thing closed again, muffling the sounds of cursing that were coming from the other side. I took a step back while Scout spun the flywheel and slid the security bar into place, metallic cranking and grinding echoing through the corridor.

"They've seen the rat things," I said.

"And if Lauren's screaming means anything, they've done more than just that. They *know* more than just that, which means the Reapers and the rats are definitely tied together. It wasn't a coincidence that Detroit and Naya saw the slime outside that sanctuary." She put her hands on her hips and looked at the closed door. "I also guess I have to try to ward the door again."

"You can do it!" I said, giving her a chipper thumbs-up.

"Daniel could do it," she said. "And without a spell. Me? He says, 'Go for it, Scout,' and I have to rough out a few lines—hardly have time to pay attention to the meter, to the melody, the rhythm—*ugh*," she said, and the irritation in her voice was really the only part of the monologue I understood.

"So, what does that mean? Dumb it down like you're talking to a girl who's only had magic for, like, a few weeks."

She smiled a little, which had been the point. "You've seen me work my magic. Putting together an incantation is hard work, and wards are harder than most. There's no physical charm—like the origami I used on the thingies—to boost the words. Daniel didn't give me a lot of direction, and he certainly didn't give me time to do it *well*. The ward won't really keep out anyone with any skill, and the hex isn't going to last much longer." She glanced down at her watch. "Fifteen minutes or a half an hour, tops?"

Probably not enough time to find Daniel and get him into the basement, even if he was already in the Enclave. A blast of firespell wasn't going to do much to the door, and opening up the door again to firespell the Reapers into unconsciousness would just be a waste of time. They'd eventually wake up, and we'd still have doors with breach problems.

We needed stronger wards, and we needed them now.

I grinned slowly, an idea blossoming. "Maybe I can do for you what I did for Naya and Temperance."

Scout tilted her head. "What do you mean?"

"Well, if I could funnel energy through Naya, maybe I could funnel it through you. To strengthen the wards, I mean."

"Huh," she said, then looked at the ground, frowning as she considered the possibility. "So you're thinking the trouble isn't that the wards didn't work, but that they weren't strong enough to keep the Reapers out."

I nodded. "I mean, you're the expert on wards so you'd know better than me, but if we pump up the power, wouldn't it make the ward harder to break through?"

"It might," she said with a nod. "It definitely might. Do you need to recharge or whatever?"

"It's two o'clock in the morning."

"I'll assume that's a general yes, so we'll do this and go back to sleep. What do I need to do?"

"What do you have to do to work your magic?"

"Remember the triple I?"

"Um, intent, incantation, incarnation?"

She nodded and held out a hand. I took it in mine. With her free hand, she pressed her palm to a flat spot on the door. She closed her eyes, and her lips began to move with words I couldn't hear. The door began to glow, pale green light filling the corridor.

"Now," she quietly said, her eyes still closed.

I closed my own eyes, and tried to imagine the power around me, the atomic potential in the air. I imagined it flowing through my fingers, then my arm, then across my body. I felt her jump when it reached her, and her fingers tightened on mine.

"You okay?"

"Keep it coming," she gritted out.

"Try not to flinch," I said, "and don't try to fight it. Just let it flow across you and into the door. Let me do the work."

Scout let out a muffled sound, but she kept her fingers tight on mine. She kept the current intact.

A low hum began to fill the air. I opened my eyes a little. The hum was coming from the rivets as they vibrated in their sockets. The green glow was also deeper now, the light more intense as Scout transmitted the magic into the door.

"How's it coming?"

"I think we're . . . almost there. I can feel it filling up. Sealing. Closing up the cracks."

That was great, but it was late, and I was exhausted, and Scout wasn't exactly a finicky magic eater. I could feel her capacity power, like a cavern of magical potential.

And that potential liked firespell.

"Okay, I think we're done, Lily."

I tried to pull back, to slow down the flood of power to a trickle, but it didn't want to stop. Scout's magic kept sucking more power, and I couldn't close that door.

"Lily, we're done here."

"I can't make it stop, Scout."

The door began to pulse with green light. Off and on, off and on, like the world's largest turn signal.

"Lily, I need you to do something. This is starting to hurt."

I looked over at Scout. Her hair was standing on end, a punky blond-and-brown halo around her head.

"I'm trying, I swear."

"You can do it, Lily. I believe in you."

I closed my eyes and pretended the magic was a faucet and I was turning one of the knobs. Unfortunately, that imaginary knob felt like it had been welded closed. "I can't get it!"

"Then we're going to have to do this the old-fashioned way!"

I opened my eyes and looked at Scout. The door was beginning to emit a pulsing noise. Each time it glowed it put out an electrical roar. I had to yell over the sound to be heard. "What old-fashioned way?"

"On three, we pull ourselves apart! Agreed?"

I swallowed, but nodded. "On three!"

She nodded back, and we began the countdown. "One—two—and *three*!"

We yanked our hands apart, but it wasn't easy. It felt like I was pulling back a twenty-pound concrete block. I managed to untangle my fingers from hers, but the power was still pouring out, and it wanted to *move*. Since it couldn't flow into Scout anymore, it pushed her away—and me with it.

I flew down the corridor and hit the floor five or six feet away. I heard the echoing *thump* as Scout hit the floor in the other direction.

"*Ow*."

Very slowly, I sat up, hands braced on the ground to push myself upright. "Oh, crap, that hurt."

"Seriously," she said groggily, sitting up again, a hand on her forehead. It took a moment before she turned her head to look at me. "Are you okay?"

"I've been better. Are you okay?"

She checked her arms and legs. "Nothing broken, I think."

One hand on the wall for support, I stood up, but had to wait until the room stopped spinning. "I have to say, that totally sucked."

Scout tried to flatten down her hair, which was still sticking up in odd angles. "I guess our magics hate each other."

"Or really like each other, since we had trouble prying ourselves apart. Either way, I don't think we should do that again."

"And we also probably should not tell Katie or Smith or Daniel that just happened. Lecture," she added in explanation.

Very, very slowly—my bones aching from the fall—I moved back to the door and reached out a hand to Scout.

"Definitely don't need a lecture," I agreed as I pulled her to her feet. "I do need fourteen or fifteen hours of sleep and a giant cheese-burger."

"Aren't you a vegetarian?"

"That's my point."

When we were both on our feet, we looked back at the door. It still pulsed like a severed heart in a horror film.

"You know, that's really gonna be noticeable if someone comes down here."

"I guess we could try to ward the door upstairs to keep people from coming down."

I gave her an exceptionally dry look. "No way am I going through that again. Got a better idea?"

"Well, the firespell fades over time—I mean, people wake up after they get knocked unconscious with it. You did, anyway."

"I love being a cautionary tale."

"So maybe it works the same way here, too. Cop a squat." Without waiting for me to move, she turned her back to the wall across from the door, crossed one foot over the other, and sat down on the floor.

"We're going to wait it out?" I could hear the grumpy sleepiness in my voice. I felt bad about it, but it was *late*. I wanted to be curled up in bed—or even in a wrinkled blanket on Scout's floor—fast asleep.

"Just until we're sure the green is fading," she said. "If we know it's fading, that means it's going back to normal. And if it's going back to normal, we'll sleep a lot better later."

She had a point. And it would have been pretty irresponsible to just walk away. Adepts were supposed to be a secret, but it wouldn't be long before anyone who saw the door started asking questions.

"Fine," I said, and sat down on the floor beside her. She immediately pulled out her cell phone and began texting.

"Daniel?" I wondered.

"Daniel," she agreed. "We need to tell him about the breach, and we definitely need to tell him the Reapers know about the creatures. That raises all sorts of nasty questions."

"Like?"

"Like whether they're trying to domesticate them to use as some kind of weapon."

I grimaced. "In the interest of my ever sleeping well again, let's pretend that's just not possible."

When the texting was done, Scout put her phone away. She sighed, then dropped her head to my shoulder. "Does the door look any different to you now?"

"Not really. You?"

"Not yet."

"We'll just give it a few more minutes."

If only.

12

There are nightmares, and then there are *nightmares*. You know the dream where you're in class, but you totally forgot to take a shower and stuff? How about the dream where you wake up beside your best friend in the basement of a private school fifteen minutes before classes start?

Long story short, that dream ends with you running through the school in yesterday's clothes in front of pretty much the entire junior and senior classes.

Luckily, the fact that we were nearly late for class kept us from having to explain to the dragon ladies what we'd been doing in the main building so early. But I heard Scout yell "Fell asleep studying!" three or four times before we were back in our rooms.

There was no time for a shower, so I cleaned up the best I could, brushed my teeth, and pulled on my uniform—plaid skirt, button-up shirt, fuzzy boots, and a cardigan. I pulled my hair into a topknot. My only accessory was the classic—my room key on its blue ribbon.

I met Scout in the common room, both of us pulling on messenger bags and hustling through the door. I handed over a smushed granola bar. She ripped into the plastic with her teeth, then stuffed the wrapper into her bag.

"If only the brat pack knew how glamorous we truly were," she muttered, taking a huge bite of the bar. With her wrinkled skirt, untucked shirt, and mismatched sneakers, she didn't look much better than I did.

"Yeah, it definitely looks like you were in a hurry. It's not like you'd wear mismatched sneakers on purpose."

She gave me a dry look.

"Okay, except in this particular instance because mismatched shoes look awesome," I amended. "Truly an amazing fashion choice. You're quite the trendster."

Scout rolled her eyes and started down the hall again. "One of these days, you're going to respect me."

"Oh, I totally respect you. It's your wardrobe I have issues with."

Issues or not, I did a pretty good job of dodging the chunk of granola bar that came my way.

We stood there for a moment, horrified, our mouths gaping, but unable to look away.

It was a Thursday lunch in the St. Sophia's cafeteria.

It was also near the end of what had been a long and unfortunately creative week in the St. Sophia's kitchen: meatloaf with wasabi mustard sauce; vegetable mix with parsnips, whatever those were; and roasted potatoes—the funky purple ones.

Unfortunately, the end of the week meant leftovers. And, unfortunately, leftovers at St. Sophia's meant "stew."

The stew was one of the first things Scout had warned me about (yes—even before the Reapers and soul-sucking). This wasn't your average stew—the stuff your mom made on a snowy weekend in February. It was a soupy mix of whatever didn't get eaten during the week. Today, that meant parsnips and funky potatoes and chunky bits of meatloaf.

I was a vegetarian, but even I hadn't been spared. There was a veggie version of the "stew" that included beans and rice and some kind of polygon-shaped green thing that didn't look all that edible.

And the worst thing? It was only Thursday. Over the weekend, it was actually going to get *worse*. We had three-day-old Sunday stew to look forward to.

I pointed to a green thing. "What do you think that is?"

"It looks like okra. I think the stew is supposed to be gumboey."

I curled my lip. "I'm not sure I'm up for brave food today." I grabbed a piece of crusty bread and a bowl of fruit salad. Compared to my other options, I figured they were pretty safe. And speaking of bravery, I should probably get started on my drawing of the building.

"Hey, I'm going to head outside after class. I need to get my drawing in."

"You still thinking about drawing the SRF building?"

"Yeah. I'm not sure what it'll accomplish, but it's the least I can do. I know I have to stay low-key in terms of investigating my parents, but I still have to do *something*, right?"

Scout shrugged. "I think that's up to you, Lils. You're not even sixteen. You're entitled to believe your parents told you the truth about themselves and their work—that they told you everything you needed to know. I don't think you have any obligation to play Nancy Drew for the Parker family, you know?"

"That's pretty great advice."

"I have my moments."

"Hmm. Well, anyway, did you want to head outside with me?" I bobbed my head toward the window and the strip of blue fall sky I could see through it. "It looks pretty nice out there. Might be fun to get some fresh air."

She shook her head. "Nah, that's okay. I need to get some work done."

"Schoolwork? Did I miss something in class?"

Crimson crossed her cheeks. "No. I'm just working on something."

The words sounded casual, but the tone definitely didn't. I didn't want to push her, but I wondered if this was going to be another one of those locked-door nights for Scout. If so, what was she doing in there? Not that it was any of my business . . . until she decided to tell me, anyway.

"No problem," I said. "I'll see you before dinner."

"Go for it. And if you decide to break into the SRF building to figure out the goods on your parents, take your cell phone. You never know when you're going to need it."

A few minutes later, I stood on the front steps of St. Sophia's, my sketch pad and pencils in my bag, ready to walk to the Portman Electric Company building and begin my investigation. I mean, my sketch.

But that didn't make my feet move any faster. I felt weird about going there—not just because I was trying to be sneaky, but because I recognized I might learn things I didn't want to know.

What if my parents were involved in something illegal? Something unethical? Something that shamed them so much they had to hide it from me? Foley certainly thought it was something that could get them in trouble. At the very least, it was something I wasn't supposed to know about . . . or talk about.

Problem was, my imagination was doing a pretty good job of coming up with worst-case scenarios on its own. St. Sophia's was practically next door to the SRF, and I'd seen the letter in which they tried to convince my parents to drop me off at St. Sophia's. Plus, the SRF did some kind of medical research, and Foley had said my parents did genetic research.

And now . . . the Dark Elite had a medical facility?

That was the rock that sat heavy in my stomach, making me rethink all the memories of my time with my parents. After all, if they'd lied about their work, what else had they lied about?

I shook off the thought. That was just insecurity talking. They were my *parents*. They were good people. And more important, they loved me. They couldn't be wrapped up with the Reapers.

Could they?

I know Foley told me to keep my mouth shut. I know I wasn't supposed to ask questions, to put them at risk. But I had to figure out what was going on. There was too much on the line. That was why I kept putting one foot in front of the other, until I was outside the stone wall that separated St. Sophia's from the rest of the world and walking down the sidewalk toward the SRF building . . . at least until someone stepped directly in front of me.

I looked up into blue eyes.

Sebastian.

He spoke before I could even think of words to say.

"I'm not going to hurt you."

"Get out of my way."

Instead of answering, he took a step forward. This was the closest I'd been to him, and being closer just made the effect that much more powerful. Maybe it was because he was one of the bad guys, but there was something undeniably wicked about him.

But I'd seen enough wicked. I gave him a warning look. "Don't take another step."

"I swear I won't hurt you," he said. "And we both know that if I'd wanted to hurt you, I could have already done it." Ever so slowly, he lifted both hands, as if to show he wasn't holding a weapon. But as long as he had firespell, his weapons *were* his hands.

"Why are you following me?"

"I told you why. Because we need to talk."

"We have nothing to talk about."

He glanced around, gaze scanning the sidewalk like he expected Adepts to attack any minute. And maybe they would. He was in our territory. "Not here. We have to talk somewhere more private."

"You want me to go somewhere alone with you? Are you high?"

"No, I'm not high." His voice was flat. "But I am serious."

"So am I. I also know which side you're on, and it's not mine. Give me one reason why I should do anything other than blast you right where you're standing."

"I'll give you two. First, we're standing in the middle of a public sidewalk. You and I both know you aren't going to do anything here. Second, I've already saved your life once, and I came to your rescue yesterday. I've given you a reason to trust me."

He would play that card. And while I still didn't trust him any farther than I could firespell him, I did wonder what he was up to.

"I'm going to need a better reason than 'you didn't kill me when you had the chance.'"

"Because there are things you need to know about firespell. And if it will ease your mind, I'll use this." He reached into his pocket and pulled out what looked like a flat, gleaming dog tag on a thin chain.

"A dog tag?"

"It's a countermeasure," he said, slipping the chain over his head. When the flat of the metal hit his shirt, he squeezed his eyes closed like he'd been hit with a shock of pain. When he looked up at me again, his stormy eyes seemed dull.

"It neutralizes magic," he said, his voice equally flat. If he was telling the truth, then it was like the magic had actually permeated his personality. Take the magic away, and the spark disappeared.

"It's more effective as a protective measure if you're the one wearing it," he explained, "but I'm guessing you're just suspicious enough to say 'no' if I ask you to put it on."

"I'm *careful* enough," I corrected. "Not suspicious."

"Then both," he said. "I can appreciate that."

I gave him a look that I figured was plenty suspicious, partly because this guy was just likable enough to make me nervous. He wasn't supposed to be likable. Scout might have been the one to pull me into the world of Reapers, but Sebastian was the one who made sure I couldn't get out again.

"Ten minutes, Lily," he repeated.

I took a moment to consider his offer, then blew out a breath. One way or another, I was going to have to get off the street. If Scout—or anyone else from St. Sophia's or Montclare—saw me talking to him, there were going to be lots of questions.

"I'll give you five minutes. And if I don't like what you have to say, you can kiss consciousness goodbye."

"I think that's fair." He glanced around, then nodded toward a Taco Terry's fast food restaurant across the street. The restaurant's mascot—an eight-foot-high plastic cowboy, lips curled into a creepy smile—stood outside the front door.

"Why don't we go over there?"

I looked over the building. The cowboy aside, there were a lot of windows and a pretty steady stream of customers in and out—tourists grabbing a snack, or workers out for lunch. I doubted he'd try anything in the middle of the day in the middle of the Loop, but still—he'd supported Scout's kidnapping and he'd put me in a hospital for thirty-six hours.

He must have seen the hesitation in my eyes. "It's a public place, Lily. Granted, a public place with paper napkins and a really, really disturbing cowboy out front, but a public place. And it's close."

"Fine," I finally agreed. "Let's try the cowboy."

Sebastian nodded, then turned and began to walk toward the crosswalk, apparently assuming I'd follow without blasting him with firespell along the way.

I wiped my sweaty palms on my skirt and made the turn from the school grounds onto the sidewalk on Erie Avenue. I was willingly walking toward a boy who'd left me unconscious, without even a word of warning to my best friend.

But curiosity won out over nerves, and besides—in between his leaving me unconscious and asking me here, he had managed to save my life. In a manner of speaking, anyway.

The only way to find out what was up and why he'd helped me was to keep moving forward. So I took one more step.

We made our way across the street in silence. He held the door open for me, and we maneuvered through the tourists and children to an empty table near the window and slid onto white, molded plastic seats.

Sebastian picked up the foot-high bobble-headed cowboy—that would be Taco Terry—that sat on every table beside the plastic salt and pepper shakers. He looked it over before putting it back. "Weird and creepy."

Not unlike the Reapers, I thought, and that was a good reminder that it was time to get things rolling. "I don't have a lot of time. What did you need?"

"You have firespell."

"Because of you," I pointed out.

"Triggered by me, maybe, but I couldn't have done it alone. You had to have some kind of latent magic in the first place."

He lifted his eyebrows like he was waiting for me to confirm what he'd said. Scout had told me pretty much the same thing, but I wasn't going to admit that to him, so I didn't say anything. Besides, this was his gig. As far as I was concerned, we were here so he could give me information, not the other way around.

"How is your training going?"

If he meant training with firespell, it wasn't going at all. But I wasn't going to tell *him* that. "I'm doing fine."

He nodded. "Good. I don't want you to get hurt again because of something I'd done."

"Why would you care?"

He had the grace to look surprised. "What?"

I decided to be frank. "Why would you care if I was hurt? I'm an Adept. You're a member of the Dark Elite or whatever. We're enemies. That's kind of the point of being enemies—hurting each other."

Sebastian looked up, his dark blue eyes searing into me. "I am who I am," he said. "I stay with Jeremiah because I'm one of his people. I'm one of them—of *us*. But you are, too." But then he shook his head. "But we're more than magic, aren't we? Sure, it's the very thing that makes us stronger—"

"But it also makes us weaker," I finished for him. "It tears you down, breaks you down, from the inside out. I don't know what Jeremiah tells you about that, but whatever superhero vibe you're rocking now, it won't last forever."

"And how do you know that?" he asked. "Have you seen a member of the Dark Elite break down?"

I opened my mouth to retort that I didn't need to see it, that I trusted Scout to tell me the truth. But while that was true, he made a good point. "No. I haven't."

"I'm not saying it happens or not. I'm just saying, maybe you should figure that out for yourself. In our world, there's a lot of dogma. A lot of 'this is how it is' and 'this is how it should be.'" He shook his head. "I don't know how it works for your people, and I'm not saying we're going to be best friends or anything. I'm just offering some advice. Take the necessary time to figure out for yourself what's good and bad in the world."

We looked at each other for a few seconds, the two of us staring across a plastic table, until I finally had to look away. His gaze was too personal, too intimate, even for a secret lunch hour meeting at Taco Terry's.

"Is that what you wanted to talk to me about?"

"Part of it. I also wanted to warn you."

That brought my eyes back to him. "About what?"

"I hear you stepped into the turf war between the vampires. Between the covens."

"I don't know what you're talking about."

"I know you stepped into the middle of something you shouldn't have. But I also know you need to go back."

I lifted my eyebrows. "I am not going back. They nearly tore us to pieces the last time."

Sebastian shook his head. "You need to go back. And you need to ask the right questions."

"The right questions about what?"

He looked away quickly, apparently not willing to share everything. But he finally said, "Find Nicu. Ask him about the missing."

Scout had been kidnapped by the Dark Elite—was that what he meant? Had the Reapers taken more Adepts? "What do you mean, the missing?"

"That's what you need to find out. I can't ask the questions for you."

"If you've hurt someone, I swear to—"

He gave me a condescending look. "I've helped you. I'm helping you again. Remember that."

I lifted my eyebrows. "You just told me to go back to see the vampires while they're in the middle of a turf war."

"For your own good."

I doubted that, but I had questions of my own. Might as well take this opportunity. "While you're being helpful, tell me about the new monsters in the tunnels. Slimy things? Naked? Pointy ears?"

"I know nothing."

I shook my head; he'd answered too fast. "You're lying. I know they have some connection to the Reapers."

"I'm not part of that."

"Wrong answer. You're one of them," I reminded him. "We know the monsters have been in at least two spots in the tunnels. Where are they coming from?"

He looked away. "Just talk to Nicu."

That made me sit up a little straighter. "Nicu knows about the monsters?"

"That's all I can tell you. I have my own allegiances to protect."

"Well, at least you're done pretending to be a good guy."

Sebastian looked back again and leaned forward, hunching a little more over the table. "This isn't a game, Lily. This is our *world*, and we are different from the rest of them. From the rest of the humans."

"No," I said. "We aren't different. We have a gift—a temporary gift. It doesn't make us different. It only makes us lucky."

Shaking his head, he sat up straight again. "We have a temporary gift *now*. Did you know that? That the magic hasn't always been temporary? We've been losing it, Lily. Over time. Slowly but surely, each generation has their magic for a little less time than the generation that came before it. And maybe that's because we're blending with humans. Maybe it's some kind of magical evolution." He shrugged. "I don't know. But I do know we want a different future. We don't want to just give up something that has the potential to help so many people."

"You mean something that has the potential to hurt so many people."

He shook his head. "All of this magic—have you thought about what it could do for humanity? Do you know the things we've *already* done for humanity? All those moments in human history where someone gets some amazing insight—the polio vaccine, the understanding of relativity—you think those moments are an accident?" He shook his head. "No way."

"That doesn't justify what you have to do to keep the magic. If we're losing it, we're losing it. We need to accept that and be done with it. It's not an excuse to use people to keep the magic longer than nature wants you to have it."

"You think no cost is worth the price," he said. "I disagree."

"Your cost is the lives of other humans."

"The cost for our good deeds—for saving millions by our contributions—is a bit of one person. The many are more valuable than the one. We believe that."

I just shook my head. There wasn't much chance I was going to agree with him however well he justified it. I looked up at him again. "Lauren and some gatekeeper girl paid us a visit last night."

His eyes went hugely wide. "Last night?"

I nodded. "You want to tell me why?"

"I don't know," he began, but before I could object, he held up his hands. "I don't. It could be Scout. Jeremiah was interested in her."

"Because she's a spellbinder?"

"Maybe."

"She's off limits. Permanently," I added, when he looked like he was going to object. "I've got firespell, and I know how to use it. Any more Adepts come sniffing around St. Sophia's looking for her or her *Grimoire* or whatever else, and we won't just leave them hexbound in the tunnels."

"You've turned vicious."

"Like you said, this isn't a game."

"At least you're listening to part of it," he muttered. Then he lifted the countermeasure and pulled it over his head, relief clear in his face when he placed it on the table. "I want to show you something. Hold out your palms."

I gave him a dubious expression, which lifted a corner of his mouth.

"You're being guarded by a plastic cowboy, and we're in a restaurant full of people." He put his hands on the table, opening and closing them again until finally, eyes rolling, I relented.

And felt a little bit guilty about it.

I put my hands on the table, palms up. Slowly, he cupped my hands in his long fingers, then curled my fingers into fists. My skin went pebbly, the hair at the back of my neck lifting at his touch.

"You have to learn to control firespell," he said, voice low. "But when you can, you'll harness elemental powers." His hands still wrapped around my fists, my palm began to warm from the inside.

"What are you doing?"

"I'm teaching you." His voice was low, lush, intimate again. Slowly, he began to lift his hands from mine, like he was making a shield over my hands.

"Open your palms."

A centimeter at a time, I uncurled my fingers. There, in each of my hands, was a tiny jumping spark of green. Aware of our surroundings, I stifled a gasp, but raised my confused gaze to his as he continued to shield the sparks from public view.

"You've seen the broad shot firespell can give you," he said. "You've learned how to fan the power out. But you can pinpoint the power, as well."

He tilted my hands so that my palms were facing, and the edges of my hands were against the table. And then, ever so slightly, he began to move my hands from side to side. The sparks followed suit, the momentum pushing them back and forth between my hands like the birdie in a game of badminton.

And just as quickly, it was over. He pressed my hands together again, the two sparks—like they were just a quirk of static electricity—somehow dissipating. He pulled his hands away again. I opened my palms, rustling my fingers as I searched for some hint of the spark.

"The power is yours to control," he said, sliding the countermeasure into his pocket again. "Yours to manipulate. But you must be open to the power and your authority over it. It's not always an easy burden to bear, but that doesn't mean you shouldn't wield it."

He looked at his watch. "I have to go." He slid to the end of the booth and stood up.

"I still don't know what you did. How you gave me that spark."

"The spark is yours. I just brought it out. Remember that. You are different, you know."

Stubbornly, I shook my head. "Not different," I said again. "And only lucky for a little while. We're willing to let it go. Are you?"

He looked away, but I had one more question. "Sebastian."

He glanced back.

"How did you know I was going to be outside?"

He shrugged. "I didn't. I just got lucky."

Without elaborating, he turned and walked into the crowd of men, women, and children waiting for their tacos. The crowd—and then the city—swallowed him up again.

I sat there for a moment just processing the meeting, rubbing the tips of my fingers against my palm. I could still feel the tingle there, and I wasn't sure I liked it. I rubbed my hands against my skirt, as if to erase the feeling. Something about it—about him—just made me uneasy.

"Probably has something to do with the fact that he's my sworn enemy," I mumbled, then slid out of the booth myself. I walked back across the street and toward the school.

I couldn't help but wonder about Sebastian's motivations. He said he was concerned about me—but he didn't really have any reason to be. Was he flirting? I doubted it, and even if he was, no, thank you.

Was it because he'd given me firespell? Had the magic created some kind of bond between us that I didn't know about? I made a mental note to ask Scout about it . . . without telling her why I was asking. I might eventually need to spill Sebastian's interest in me, but I wasn't going to do that now. There was no reason, as far as I could see, to raise the alarm bells.

By the time I returned, my secretly empty sketchbook in hand, Scout was in the common room, ready to head out for dinner.

To be honest, seeing her made me nervous. I still wasn't sure what I should tell her. After all, I'd *willingly* had a meeting with a Reaper. Granted, a Reaper who'd saved my life, but given her experiences, I wasn't sure she'd care much about the difference. I didn't want to keep a secret from her, but I also didn't want the lecture.

So I decided to let it ride. I kept the dinner convo light, and steered away from all things darkly elite.

Study hall followed dinner, and as soon as we got back to the suite, Scout hied off to her room. She walked in, and with an apologetic glance back at me, started closing her door.

"Everything okay?"

"Yep. Just some work to do."

Okay, this was, what, the second time this week she'd locked herself in her room? "What are you working on?"

"Just some spells. Nothing personal. I just need quiet and . . . you know . . . to concentrate."

"Okay," I said. I watched her disappear into her room, trying to figure out what I was supposed to do. Was I supposed to worry about her? Give her privacy? Break down the door to make sure she was okay? I mean generally, I'd be all for having time to oneself, but this girl had been kidnapped. I didn't want to leave her alone if she was in there being held at spell-point by a Reaper.

"She's fine, you know."

I glanced back. Lesley stood in her doorway, the bow to her cello in hand.

I didn't want to talk about Scout within earshot, so I walked over to Lesley's room. "What do you mean?"

She plucked a tiny piece of lint from the bow. "She did the same thing earlier. She seems fine, though."

"Huh," I said. "Did you notice anything odd?"

"She has a nose ring. And her hair is dyed two colors."

Okay, Lesley did have a point there.

"But I'm not sure how you are."

My eyes widened. "What do you mean?"

She tilted her head to the side and gave me an up-and-down look. "You look weird. What's going on?"

Was she really that astute? Or was I sending out some kind of "I just had a secret meeting with a Reaper" vibe? I shrugged and hoped it looked nonchalant. "Nothing. Just. You know. Being me."

She didn't look convinced, but when she shrugged, I figured she was moving on.

In any event, time to change the subject. "So, I'm gonna work on my drawing for studio. How's yours coming along?"

Lesley shrugged. "I'm done."

"Already? We don't have class again until next week."

"I'm not running secret missions at night. I had time." She turned on her heel and headed back into her room. "And now it's time for practice," she said and shut the door behind her.

You had to admire that kind of focus.

Since Amie's room was empty and Lesley's cello-playing made a pretty good soundtrack to creativity, I grabbed my sketchbook and started drawing. Sebastian might have interrupted my afternoon plans, but he wasn't going to take over my evening.

13

Scout's room was empty when I woke up the next morning. I showered and pulled on my plaid, grabbed my bag, and headed to the cafeteria. I found her at the end of a long table, surrounded by empty chairs. There was a tray in front of her, and a half-eaten muffin on the tray. A couple of notebooks were open beside it.

I plucked a box of chocolate milk and a carrot-raisin muffin from the buffet, then took the seat across from her. "You got an early start."

She glanced up from the notebook. "Yeah. Sorry—was I supposed to wait for you?"

I pulled out a raisin from the muffin and dropped it on the tray. I liked carrots, but raisins were just weird. Like little wrinkly fruit pebbles. No, thank you.

"Well, we didn't have a contract or blood oath or anything, but you usually wait for me. Should I ask what you're working on, or is it secret, too?"

She blew out a breath. "Not secret. Just a spell."

Three more raisins hit the deck. "I see," I said, although I really didn't. "How's it coming along?"

"I'm not really sure."

Since she wasn't playing chatty, I finished cleaning out my muffin and downed the bit that remained. When the bell rang, we grabbed our books, dumped our trash, and headed out to pretend to be normal high school juniors.

. . .

I thought about Sebastian pretty much all morning long. I didn't mean to; he just kept popping into my head. I felt pretty weird about that. I was talking to Jason, after all. And when I got a text message from Jason with the deets about our first official date, I felt that much worse.

"FOR OUR DATE SATURDAY—HOW ABOUT LUNCH?" he asked.

"LUNCH WORKS," I texted back.

"ANY PREFS?" he asked.

I thought about it for a second, but decided I wasn't picky. As long as we got out of St. Sophia's, I'd be happy. "UR PICK," I told him.

"IF I COULD, I'D PICK YOU," he said. I swooned a little.

And speaking of secrets, since I'd been interrupted yesterday, I still had art studio homework and Sterling Research Foundation business. Mom and Dad business.

After morning classes, I invited Scout to head outside with me. She said no again, and since she was pretty well focused on whatever spell she was working on, she didn't seem that worried about the fact that I was leaving her alone at lunch again. And this time, I really did plan to be alone. I put a couple of sketch pads and my watercolor kit into my bag, firmed up my courage, and headed out.

The sky outside was overcast, like a gray blanket had been tossed over the city. And because of the clouds, there weren't any shadows. It made everything seem a little weird—a little flatter than before. The St. Sophia's flag hung limply above the school, no wind to stir it up.

I started down the street, walking past the bank and slowing when I reached the STERLING RESEARCH FOUNDATION sign. For a couple of minutes, I stood outside and made myself focus on the architecture. The shape of the windows. The lines of the building. The little details that the original architect had put into it. Because I really did have an assignment to do, I made myself think about shapes and shades, and not about the stuff that might lurk inside it.

The information.

But I was here, and I had a chance. I made a split-second decision, then brushed my fingers against the SRF sign, like that little touch could give me luck. And then I walked inside.

A bell rang when I pulled open the front door. The receptionist, who sat behind a long wooden desk, glanced up. She looked pretty young, with short, curly blond hair and blue eyes. The nameplate on her desk read LISA. She took in my plaid skirt and St. Sophia's hoodie, then smiled kindly.

"Hi there. You must be from the school down the street?"

I nodded, walking slowly toward the desk so that I could get a sense of the reception area. Although the building was squat and old-school on the outside, the interior was bright and modern, with lots of sharp lines and edgy furniture. There was a closed door behind the reception area, and another one on the left side of the room behind an L-shaped sofa.

I reached the desk, then tugged on my satchel. "Yeah, I am. I'm Lily. I'm in an art studio, and we're supposed to study a building in the neighborhood. Would it be okay if I draw yours?"

"Oh, sure, that's fine."

"I just didn't want you to think I was snooping around or anything." *Although I totally am*, I silently added.

"It's no problem. I'm Lisa, so if anyone gives you any trouble, just find me, okay?"

"Sure," I said. "Thanks a lot." I felt a prickle of guilt that she was being so nice. It's not like I had bad intentions, but I wasn't being exactly truthful, either.

After we exchanged a smile, I began walking to the front door. But then I stopped, and I didn't know what I was going to say until the words were out of my mouth. "Um, if you don't mind me asking, what kind of things do you research here?"

"Oh, we don't actually do research. We're a foundation—we sponsor other people's research."

Nerves lit through my stomach. I was getting closer, and I knew it. "Oh, yeah? That sounds cool."

"It's very interesting," she agreed. "We fund scientific research projects all over the world."

Of course they do, I thought, then smiled again. "Thanks again for your time."

"Anytime," she said, then looked over at her computer monitor again.

That was when Lisa's phone rang. "Wow," she said after she'd picked it up. "You finished faster than I thought you would. I'll be right up to get it." The handset went down, and she slid out of her chair and from behind her desk, then trotted to the stairs, where she disappeared through a second-floor door.

I glanced back at her desk.

Crap. You only live once, right?

When the upstairs door closed behind her, I made my move. I skittered behind her desk, put a hand to the door behind it, and peeked inside.

It was an office, and a nice one. My heart thudded when I read the nameplate on the desk: WILLIAM PERRY.

Someone named William had signed the letter to my parents on SRF letterhead—the letter that encouraged them to send me to St. Sophia's and not tell me what they were working on. If this was his office, he was an SRF bigwig—the head of the foundation, maybe.

I wasn't sure how much time I'd have before Lisa came back, so I glanced around to see what could be checked quickly. There were framed diplomas on one wall, and the opposite wall held a desk with a tall credenza behind it.

There was a computer on the desk.

"Bingo," I quietly said. I peeked back into the hallway to make sure the coast was clear, then moved in for a look at the computer monitor.

None of the programs was on, but the guy had a really messy desktop. There were icons everywhere, from files to Internet links to random programs. I scanned them quickly—I surely had only a moment before she came back downstairs again—and decided on his e-mail program.

When it loaded, the first message in the queue was from Mark Parker—my dad—and the subject line read, "DNA Trials—Round 1."

My hand shaking, I opened it.

"Dear William," it read. "To follow up from our last call, we're beginning to pull in the data from the first round of trials. Unfortunately, we're not seeing the DNA combinations we'd hoped to see. We're still hopeful some adjustments in the component samples will give us positive results in this round, but adjustments mean more time. We don't want to push the schedule back any further than necessary, but we think the investment of time is worth it in this case. Please give us a call when you have time." The message was signed "Mark and Susan."

Somehow, over the thudding of my pulse in my ears, I heard the clacking of Lisa's footsteps in the lobby. I closed the program, ran away from the desk, and held up my paintbrush.

She looked inside Perry's office, worry in her expression. "What are you doing in here?"

I smiled brightly and held my paintbrush up. "Sorry. I pulled this out and dropped it. It rolled in here. I didn't mean to pry."

"Oh," she said, clearly relieved. "Well, let's get you back into the lobby."

When I was back in her safety zone, she took a seat behind the desk and gave me a thin smile. "Good luck with your drawing," she said, but she didn't sound very enthused. I might have had an excuse for being in the office, but some part of her wasn't buying it. Time to get out.

"Sure. Thanks again for your help. Have a nice day." I practically skipped out of the building, even though the urge to run back into the room was almost overwhelming. My parents had been on the computer in Perry's office, talking about research—and clearly not the philosophical kind.

I walked outside, heart still beating wildly, and headed to an empty covered bus stop bench. I took a seat and took a moment to process what I'd seen.

Fact—my parents knew Foley. She admitted they knew each other, and I'd seen a letter they'd written to her.

Fact—that letter had been written on SRF stationery. That meant my parents were connected to the foundation, and that connection was strong enough that they got to use the letterhead.

Fact—my parents had talked to William Perry about "DNA" and what sounded like experiments. That meant my parents and Perry were still in contact, and they were giving him updates about their work. Whatever that was.

Conclusion—my parents weren't just philosophy professors, and they were definitely researching *something*.

But what? And even if you put all those facts together, what did they mean? And what did they have to do with my being at St. Sophia's?

And then the lightbulb popped on.

There was one more fact I hadn't considered—Scout and I had snuck into Foley's office one night to return a folder stolen by the brat pack. While we were there, we found the letter from William to my parents. He'd also written something like he'd "inform Marceline."

William knew Foley, which meant that if I wanted more facts, she was the next person on my list. And although she'd cautioned me about digging too deeply, it could hardly hurt to talk to her about things, could it? After all, she was in the middle of the mystery just like I was. Realizing my next step, I walked out of the bus stop and back toward the convent. The school bells began to ring just as I reached the front door of the convent, but I ignored them.

I wasn't going to class.

I walked through the main building and into the administrative wing. Her office was at the end of the hall, MARCELINE D. FOLEY stenciled across the open door in gold letters. A sturdy-looking woman stood inside, dressed in black, clipboard in hand. One of the dragon ladies.

I made eye contact with Foley, who sat behind her desk, and stood a few feet away while she and the woman finished their discussion—something about tuition billing issues. When they were done, the woman walked past me. She looked at me as she passed, but didn't offer a smile, just a tiny nod of acknowledgment.

My stomach knotted, but I made myself walk to the threshold of the door. I stayed there until Foley looked up at me.

"Ms. Parker. Shouldn't you be in class right now?"

"I need to talk to you."

"About?"

"My parents."

Alarm passed across her face, but only for a second. And then she looked like the headmistress once again. "Come in, and close the door behind you."

I walked inside and shut the door, then sat down in one of the chairs in front of her desk, my bag across my lap.

"I know you told me to think hard before I asked too many questions about my parents. But like we talked about, I know they're connected to the Sterling Research Foundation." I paused, gathering my courage to make my confession. "I went there a few minutes ago. I'm going to draw the building for my studio class. I went inside to ask permission, and kind of got a glance at a computer."

"Kind of?" she repeated, suspicion in her voice.

I ignored the question. "I found an e-mail from my parents. It was to William, the head of the SRF, and it was all about their research. Something about DNA results and trials and what they were going to do in the future."

Foley waited for a moment. "I see," she said. "Anything else?"

"Anything else? Isn't that enough? I mean, I've confirmed they're not doing philosophical research. Or not just doing philosophical research. They talked about DNA, so I guess that means genetic research." I stopped. "They've been lying to me."

"They've been protecting you."

I shook my head. "They're in Germany, but even if they were here right now, I'd feel so far away from them."

"Lily." Her voice was kind, but stern. "I am not privy to the details of your parents' work. But I know that they're doing important work."

"What kind of important work?"

She looked away. A dark knot of fear began to curl in my belly, but I pushed it down. "They work for the SRF?"

"The SRF funds their research."

"Why did the SRF give them advice about sending me here?"

"It suggests the SRF rendered advice about protecting you from the nature of their work or the circle of those who also engage in it."

That knot tightened, and I had to force out the words. "Why would they do that?"

She gave me a flat look.

"Because it has something to do with the Dark Elite."

Her lips pursed tight.

My legs shook so badly I had to lock my knees to stay upright. The Dark Elite were doing some kind of medical procedures. My parents were doing some kind of DNA experiments. Were they part of the Dark Elite?

"Do they know I have firespell?" I asked, and I could hear the panic in my voice. "Do they know I'm involved now?"

She sighed. "They receive regular updates about you and your safety."

"And that's all you're going to tell me?"

"That's all I *can* tell you. That's all I'm *allowed* to tell you," she added, as I started to protest. "Just as there are rules of engagement for you as an Adept, there are rules of engagement for me as—"

"As what?"

"As the headmistress of this school," she primly said.

I shook my head and glanced over at one of the walls of books as tears began to slide down my cheeks. "This really sucks."

"Ms. Parker—"

"No, I'm sorry, but it *sucks*. They're my parents. I know less about them than half the people on this block in fricking Chicago, and the stuff I do know is all lies and secrets and half-truths."

Her jaw clenched. "I believe it's time for you to return to class, Ms. Parker, before you say things that you'll regret and that will result in demerits and punishment."

I opened my mouth, but she was up and out of her chair before I could say anything.

She tapped a finger onto the desktop. "Regardless of your concerns about your parents, you are at *my* institution. You will treat this institution and this office with respect, regardless of the circumstances that brought you here. Is that understood?"

I didn't answer.

"Is. That. *Understood?*"

I nodded.

"Life, Ms. Parker, is very often unfair. Tragedies occur every second of every minute of every day. That your parents saw fit to protect you with certain omissions is not, in the big scheme of things, a substantial tragedy." She looked away. "Return to class."

I went back to the classroom building. But I walked slowly. And before I even made it out of the admin wing I ducked into one of the alcoves and pulled out my phone. Sure, I was equal parts mad at my parents, worried for their safety, and sad about whatever it was they were doing—and that they'd lied to me about it—but mostly I felt very, very far away from them.

"ARE YOU OKAY?" I texted my dad.

I sat with the phone in my hands, staring at the screen, wondering why they weren't answering. Were they hurt? In the middle of doing evil things . . . or debating whether to tell me the truth about those evil things?

Finally, I got a message back. "WE'RE GREAT. HOW ARE CLASSES?"

I gazed down at the screen, trying to figure out what to ask him, what to say, how to form the right question . . . but I had no clue what to say.

How do you ask your parents if they're evil?

I closed my eyes and rested my head against the cool stone behind me. You didn't ask, I finally realized. You held off until you knew the right thing to say, until the question couldn't be delayed any longer. You held off so you weren't creating unnecessary drama that was only going to cause trouble for everyone.

Tears brimming again, I set my thumbs to the keyboard. "BORING. TTYL."

"LOVE YOU, LILS," he sent back.

Nobody ever said growing up was easy.

14

Scout could see something was wrong when I walked into class. But it was Brit lit, and Whitfield, our teacher, watched us like a hawk. She took it as a personal insult if we weren't as enthralled by Mr. Rochester as she was. So she skipped the notes and conversation, and instead pressed a hand to my back. A little reminder that she was there, I guess.

When we were done with class for the day, we headed back to the suite, but I still wasn't ready to talk about it.

"SRF?" she asked, but I shook my head. I was still processing, and there were things I wasn't yet ready to say aloud.

We did homework in her room until dinner, and she let me pretend that nothing had happened, that my afternoon hadn't been filled with questions I wasn't sure I wanted the answers to.

I took what Foley said about real tragedy to heart. I knew what she meant, totally got her point. But if my parents were members of the Dark Elite, how could things get worse than that? If they were helping some kind of medical work or research for the DE—if they were trying to help people who were hurting kids—how was I ever supposed to be okay with that?

I had no idea. So I kept it bottled up until I could figure out a plan, until I could figure out the questions to ask, or the emotions I was supposed to feel.

Eventually, we went to dinner. Like I predicted, you know what was worse than Thursday lunch at the St. Sophia's cafeteria?

Friday dinner in the St. Sophia's cafeteria.

We stood in line, trays in hand, for a good minute, just staring at the silver dish of purple and brown and white and orange mess, grimaces on our faces.

Without a word, Scout finally grabbed my tray, stacked hers on top of it, and slid them both back into the stacks at the end of the line. "I'm not saying I wouldn't like to be a few inches taller with, like, crazy long legs, but there's no way I hate myself enough to put that stuff in my body again."

I didn't disagree, but my stomach was rumbling. I'd skipped lunch for my SRF visit. "So what now?"

She thought for a second, then bobbed her head. "Mrs. M," was all she said, and away we went.

I had no clue what that was supposed to mean. I still had no clue when she dragged me into Pastries on Erie, a shop a few blocks down from St. Sophia's. (Thank God for Friday nights and a respite from the convent . . . at least during the daylight hours.)

One entire wall of the bakery was filled by a long glass case of cakes, desserts, tarts, and cookies of every shape and size. A dozen people stood in front of it, pointing to sweets behind the glass or waiting to make their orders.

"Pastries?" I wondered quietly. "I was hoping for something a little more filling."

"Trust me on this one, Parker," she whispered back. "We're not buying retail today." She waved at the tall teenager who was dishing up desserts. "Hey, Henry. Is your mom around?"

The boy waved, then gestured toward a back door. "In the back."

"Is she cooking?" Scout asked hopefully.

"Always," he called out, then handed a white bakery box over the counter to a middle-aged woman in a herringbone coat.

"Din-ner," Scout sang out, practically skipping to the beaded curtain that hung over the door in the back of the bakery.

I followed her through it, the smell of chocolate and strawberries and sugar giving way to savory smells. Pungent smells.

Delicious smells.

My stomach rumbled.

"Someone is hungry," said a lightly accented voice. I looked over. In the middle of an immaculate kitchen stood a tall, slender woman. Her hair was long and dark and pulled into a ponytail at the nape of her neck. She wore a white jacket—the kind chefs wore on television.

"Hi, Mrs. M," Scout said. "I brought someone to meet you."

The woman, who was dropping sticks of butter into a giant mixer, smiled kindly. "Hello, someone."

I waved a little. "Lily Parker."

"You go to school with our Scout?"

I nodded as Scout pulled out a chair at a small round table that sat along one wall.

"Cop a squat, Parker," she said, patting the tabletop.

Still a little confused, I took the seat on the other side of the table, then leaned forward. "I thought we were going to dinner?"

"Keep your pants on. Now, Mrs. Mercier is Henry's mom. She's also part of the community."

That meant that while Mrs. Mercier wasn't an Adept, she knew Adepts and Reapers and the rest of it existed.

"And," Scout added, "she's one of the best chefs in Chicago. She was trained at some crazy-fancy school in Paris."

"Le Cordon Bleu," Mrs. Mercier said, walking toward us with a tray of flatbread. "And she enjoys feeding Scout when her parents are out of town. Or when St. Sophia's serves stew."

"And when you add those together, you get pretty much always," Scout said matter-of-factly, tearing a chunk from a piece of bread. "Warm, warm," she said, popping it between both hands to cool it off.

"Which is pretty much always," Mrs. Mercier agreed, smoothing a hand over Scout's hair. "I have three boys. Scout did a favor for my youngest, so I do favors for Scout."

I assumed that favor was why she'd become a member of the community.

Scout handed me a chunk of bread. I took a bite, then closed my eyes as I savored it. I think it was naan—the kind of flatbread you found in Indian restaurants—but this was hot, fresh, right-out-of-the-oven naan. It was delicious.

"Anything particular you'd like to sample tonight?" Mrs. Mercier asked.

Scout did a little bow. "You're the expert, Mrs. M. Whatever you've got, we'd love to sample. Oh, and Lily's a vegetarian."

"You're in luck," she said, glancing over her shoulder at the stoves behind her. There were pots and pans there, which must have been the source of the delicious smells. "We made dal with potatoes. Lentils and potatoes," she explained. She put a hand on my shoulder and smiled kindly. "Is that okay with you?"

"That sounds really great. Thank you."

"You're quite welcome. Any friend of Scout's is a friend of mine."

Mrs. M plated up a heaping mound of rice topped by the saucy lentils and chunky potatoes, and brought us glass cups of dark, rich tea that tasted like cinnamon and cloves. She pulled up a chair as we ate, crossing her long legs and swinging an ankle, arms crossed over her chef jacket, as Scout filled her in on our last few weeks of adventures. The dinner was amazing—even if stew hadn't been our only other option. And it felt *normal*. Just the three of us in the kitchen of a busy bakery, eating dinner and catching up.

It was clear that Mrs. M loved Scout. I'm not sure what specific thing had brought them together—although I assumed the youngest Mercier had been targeted by a Reaper and that Scout had helped. That was, after all, the kind of thing we did in Enclave Three.

When we were done with dinner, Mrs. Mercier walked us back to the front of the bakery. The workday was over, so the bakery was closing up. The OPEN sign on the door had been flipped, and Henry stood in front of the case, spraying it with glass cleaner and wiping it down.

Mrs. M gave Scout a hug, then embraced me as well. "I need to get a cake ready for tomorrow. Take back some snacks for yourselves and your suitemates, if you like." She disappeared into the back room, leaving me and Scout staring at a good twenty feet of sugar-filled glass cases.

"Holy frick," I said, trying to take in the sight. I wasn't really even hungry, but how was I supposed to pass up a choice like this? I thought of my dad—it was just the kind of decision he'd love to make. He probably would have spent ten minutes walking back and forth in front of the case, mulling over flavors and calories and whether such-and-such would be better with coffee or wine.

A stop at a doughnut place usually took twenty minutes, minimum.

Scout looked equally serious. Her expression was all-business. "Your mission, Parker, should you choose to accept it, is to select an item from the bakery case. It's a difficult choice. The perils are many—"

"You are such a *geek*," Henry said, the glass squeaking as he wiped it down.

"Whatever," Scout said, tossing her head. "You're a geek."

"Mm-hmm," he said doubtfully. He put his bottle of cleaner and a wad of paper towels on top of the bakery case, then walked around behind it. "All right, doofus. What do you want for dessert?"

Scout leaned toward me. "Whatever you get—I'm eating half of it."

"Good to know," I said, then pointed at a sandwich made of two rings of pastry stuffed with cream and topped with almonds. "I'll take one of those."

"Excellent choice," Henry said. "You have better taste than some people."

Scout snorted.

Henry packed it in a small white box, taped it closed, and handed it over with a smile. Then he turned to Scout. "And you, little Miss Geek? What do you want?"

"I am not a geek."

"Okay, Dork. What do you want?"

This time, Scout stuck out her tongue, but that didn't stop her from pointing to a small tart that was topped with fruit and looked like it had been shellacked with glaze. "Tartlet, please," she told Henry. He boxed one up for her, and after teasing her with the box for a minute or two, finally handed it over.

"You kids have a great weekend," he said, as Scout and I headed for the door.

"You, too, geeko."

The door chimed as we walked through it and emerged back into the hustle and bustle of Chicago. Couples heading out to dinner and tourists getting in some final shopping hurried up and down Erie. Even though the workweek was officially over, the city didn't seem to slow down. I wondered what it would take for Chicago to be as quiet and calm as my small town of Sagamore . . . and I bet freezing winter winds and a few inches of snow probably did that just fine.

"They're good people," Scout said as we crossed the street.

"They seem great. The youngest son—"

"Alaine," she filled in.

"Was he a Reaper target?"

She nodded. "He was. He went to school with Jamie and Jill. They tagged him when he was pretty far gone—depressed all the time, not interacting with his family. And how could you *not* interact with that family? They're awesome."

"They seem really cool," I agreed. "And Mrs. M clearly loves you."

"I love her back," Scout admitted. "It's proof that sometimes people come into your life you didn't expect. That's how a family is made, you know?"

Having been dropped off by my parents at a school I wasn't crazy about—and having met Scout on my first day at St. Sophia's—I definitely knew. "Yeah," I said. "I get that. You and Henry get along pretty well."

"Ha," she said. "Henry's a secret geek. He just doesn't want to admit it. He watches every sci-fi movie he can find, but wouldn't tell his friends that. He plays baseball, so sci-fi isn't, you know, allowed or whatever."

We walked quietly back down the block, pastry in hand.

"Are you ready to talk about whatever it is you're not talking about?"

I trailed my fingers across the nubby top of the stone fence around St. Sophia's. "Not really."

"You know I'm here for you, right?"

"I know."

She put an arm around my shoulders. "Do you ever wish that sometimes the world would just stop spinning for a few hours to give you a chance to catch up?"

"I really do."

She was quiet for a second. "At least we have dessert."

That was something, I guess.

It wasn't until hours later, when Scout and I were in her room, listening to a mix of music from the 1990s, that I finally felt like talking.

"Jump Around" was blasting through the room. Scout sat cross-legged on her bed, head bobbing as she mouthed the rhymes, her *Grimoire* in her lap. Since my plans to sketch the SRF still hadn't worked out, I sat on the floor adding details to a drawing of the convent, filling in the texture of brick and jagged stone while I picked at my pastry. And Scout had been right about that—maybe it was the whipped cream (the real kind!), or maybe it was the sugar (lots of it), but it did help.

I finally put my sketchbook away, put my hands in my lap, and looked up at her. "Can we talk about something?"

She glanced up. "Are you going to break up with me?"

"Seriously."

Her eyes widened, and she used the remote to turn off the music. "Oh. Sure. Of course." She dog-eared a page of her *Grimoire*, then closed it and steepled her fingers together. "The doctor is in."

And so, there on the floor of her room, I told her what I'd seen in the SRF, and what I'd learned in my follow-up visit to Foley's office.

And then I asked the question that scared me down to my bones.

"They're doing some kind of secret genetic research that they had to stick me in a boarding school and leave the country to work on. And we know the Reapers were using the sanctuary for some kind of medical stuff. What if—"

Scout held up a hand. "Don't you even say that out loud. Don't even think it. I don't know your parents, but I know you. You're a good person with a good heart, and I know they raised you to care about other people. Otherwise, you'd be hanging out with the brat pack right now instead of resting up for whatever is coming down the pipeline tomorrow—doing the right thing. The scary thing. I don't know exactly what your parents are doing right now, Lily. But I know one thing—they are not helping Reapers. There's no way."

"But—"

She held up a finger. "I know you want to say it so that I can disagree with you. But don't. Don't even put it out there. There's *no* way. It's a coincidence, I'll admit, that we've run across two mentions of medical or genetic hoo-ha this week, but even coincidences usually have rational explanations. And you're not thinking rationally. Your parents are not like them. You know that, right?"

It took a moment—a moment while I thought about all the stuff I didn't know about my parents right now—but I finally nodded. She was right: Whatever questions I had about the details of their work, I knew *them*. I knew my dad had floppy hair and loved to make breakfast on Sunday mornings and told horrible, horrible jokes. And I knew my mom was the serious one who made sure I ate green vegetables, but loved getting pedicures while she read gossip magazines.

I knew their *hearts*.

She must have seen the change in my face.

"Okay?"

"Okay," I said.

"Little more enthusiasm there, Parker."

"Okay."

"You're probably going to find out your parents are in Germany working on some kind of top-secret new mascara or something. *Ooh,* or spy stuff. Do you think they'd be doing spy stuff?"

I tried to imagine my dad playing Jason Bourne, or my mom playing a secret operative. "Not really. That's not really their bag."

"Mascara, then. We'll just assume they're working on mascara."

My phone picked that moment to ring. I snatched it up, wondering if my parents' timing was truly that excellent. But it was Jason. Still pretty excellent.

"Hey. How's your Friday night going?"

"Pretty uneventful," I told him. Which was mostly true. "What's happening at Montclare?"

"Poker night. Except none of us has any money, so we're playing for Fritos. Which Garcia keeps eating—*Garcia.* Lay off my stash, man. How am I going to go all in with four Fritos?"

In spite of myself, I smiled a little. Scout rolled her eyes and flopped down on her bed. "Ugh. Young love makes me totally nauseous."

I stuck my tongue out at her.

"So, about tomorrow. How about I swing by at noon?"

"Noon works. What should I wear?"

"Normal Lily stuff. Minus the plaid skirt. I mean—you should definitely wear a skirt or some kind of pants, but you don't have to wear your plaid skirt since it'll be a Saturday—"

"You've been hanging around with Michael too much."

He chuckled. "Anyway, you two girls have fun. I'll see you tomorrow, okay?"

"Okay. Good night, Jason."

"Good night, Lily."

I hung up the phone and cradled it in my hands for a few seconds. Guilt settled like a rock in my stomach.

Scout rolled over and looked at me. "Oh, cripes. What now?"

I wet my lips. Might as well finish the confession since I'd started it.

"Remember the other day when I went out to draw over lunch?"

"Sure. Why?"

"Well, I didn't actually end up drawing anything. I kind of got distracted."

"Distracted by what?"

"Sebastian Born."

Scout sat up straight, blinking like she was trying to take in the statement. "I did not expect to hear that."

"He found me on the sidewalk. He said he'd wanted to talk to me."

"About what?"

"About firespell. He feels responsible, I think, that I have magic. I told him I didn't want to talk to him, that we weren't friends. But then he asked me to go somewhere and talk."

"Well, you're not going to do it. You're certainly not going to go somewhere and talk with him—" Her face fell as realization struck. "Oh, Lil. You already did it, didn't you?"

"We walked across the street to the taco place."

"Taco Terry's?"

I nodded.

"You met with a Reaper at a Taco Terry's?"

I shrugged.

She looked down at her lap, brow furrowed while she thought it over. "I don't know what to say."

"I don't either."

"I'm not sure if I should ring your neck for going, or congratulate you for the opposition research." She gave me a sideways glance. "I want more info before I decide whether I'm totally peeved."

"He gave me a speech about being a Reaper. About how it's not as bad as people think. About how magic can be a force of change in the world, even if it means sacrificing people."

"You don't believe that, do you?"

I gave her a flat look. "I think the sacrifice argument would be a little more believable if they could point to anything decent they'd actually done in the world."

"Fair enough. But what was the point? Was he trying to sway you to their side or something?"

"I don't know. I feel like he's playing some kind of game, but I don't know all the rules. But I think he definitely believes there's—I don't know—merit to what they're doing."

"That's the Dark Elite ploy," she said. "That's how they build their Reaper army. 'Think of all the wonderful things we could do with all this magic!' But when was the last time you saw any of those things?"

I nodded. "He also showed me how to do something."

"Something?"

"He showed me how to spark my magic—how to create this little molecule of energy."

"And he showed you this at the Taco Terry's?"

I nodded.

She shook her head. "That is just . . . bizarre."

We sat there quietly for a minute.

"Are you totally peeved?"

It took her a really long time to answer.

"I'm glad you're safe. And I could sit here and yell at you about not being careful, but you did exactly what I'd do." She looked over at me. "You didn't just go with him because he's hot, did you?"

I gave her a flat look.

"Hey," she said, holding up her hands. "I'm not blind. Just because he's completely evil doesn't mean he doesn't have that tall, dark, and handsome vibe. At least tell me you took the opportunity to interrogate him."

"Tried," I said, "but didn't get much. He denied knowing about Lauren and—what's the other girl's name?"

"The French hornist?"

I nodded.

She tilted her head up, eyes squeezed closed. "Joanne or Joley or something? Let's just say French hornist."

"Anyway, I asked him about them. He confirmed our *Grimoire* theory."

Scout paled a little. "They're looking for me?"

"They are. Or at least your spell book. But I think I put the fear into him."

There was some pretty insulting doubt in her expression. I batted her with a pillow. "I can be fierce when necessary."

"Only because you have a wolf at your beck and call."

"He's not at my beck and call. And we're getting off track. Sebastian denied knowing anything about the monsters, but here's the really weird thing—he told me to go see the vampires. He said something about the 'missing,' and said we needed to talk to Nicu to figure out what's going on."

"A Reaper sending us into the arms of warring vampires. Yeah, that rings a little more true."

"What about the missing thing?"

"What about it?"

I rearranged my knees so that I was sitting cross-legged. "Does that mean anything to you?"

"Not really. I mean, other than me being kidnapped and all." Her voice was dry as toast.

"Yeah, that's what I thought, too. He did say Jeremiah was interested in you."

Scout went a little pale. "I gotta tell you, that does not thrill me."

"We're quite the pair, aren't we? They're after you 'cause you're some kind of wonder sorceress, and I'm some kind of crazy, firespell-wielding Adept."

"You know, we could totally turn that into a comic book."

"Who'd want to read about pimply teenagers with boy issues and magic problems?" We looked at each other before bursting into laughter.

A knock sounded at the door. "It's open," Scout said.

The knob turned, and Lesley stood in the doorway, blinking wide eyes at us. "I need to show you something," she said.

"What?" Scout asked.

"I'm not sure, but I think it falls into your jurisdiction."

Without so much as a word, apparently trusting that Lesley had seen something important, Scout gathered up her messenger bag.

"Let's go."

15

"Let's go," of course, was easier said than done when we were being stalked by the brat pack. The three of us emerged into the suite to find Veronica walking into Amie's room, stack of magazines in hand. She wore the kind of grubby clothes that beautiful girls could get away with—flip-flops, blond hair in a messy knot, rolled-up sweatpants, and a tank top.

Veronica stopped, free hand on the doorknob, and looked us over. "What are you doing?"

We bobbled forward as Scout pulled the door shut behind us and hitched up her messenger bag. "We're going to find a quiet place to study. What are you doing?"

Veronica held up the magazines. "Self-explanatory?"

"Excellent," Scout said. "Good luck with that."

"I know something's up," she said. "I don't know what it is, but I know there's something."

"Something like how M.K. sneaks out at night to meet her boyfriend, you mean?" I smiled innocently at Veronica.

She all but growled, but kept her eyes on me. "Are you going to meet Jason?" she asked.

"Of course not," I said, but I could feel the blush heating my cheeks. I'd never been a very good liar, and while I'd been mostly honest—we weren't planning to meet him—who knew what the night would hold?

"What about John Creed?"

There it was again. Veronica was clearly obsessed with Creed. Why not just call the boy and ask him out?

"We'll be studying," Scout repeated. She opened her messenger bag to show Veronica her art history book. "You want to join us?"

Veronica watched us for a minute. "No, thanks," she said.

She didn't say anything else as we headed out the door, but I could feel her eyes on us as we left.

Lesley led us through the Great Hall and then into the main building. When we got there, she led us down into the basement along the route we used to get to the vault door.

"It's down there," she said, pointing down the stairs.

"What is?" I asked, nervousness building in my chest.

"You'll see."

"Do me a favor?" Scout asked. "Could you stay up here?"

Lesley didn't answer, but Scout apparently took her silence as agreement, as she pulled my elbow and tugged me down the stairs.

We found what Lesley had seen when we reached the corridor just ahead of the vault door—a trail of thick, ropey slime that led all the way back to the vault door, which stood wide open. There was no glow from the wards.

"Oh, crap," Scout said.

"You think it's from—"

"Where else would it come from?" She frowned and surveyed the goop. "It has to be the creatures. Maybe the wards didn't hold."

"Temperance faded after a while," I pointed out. "Even with the power boost, the wards might not have held forever. Maybe those Reaper girls broke through them again, and the rat thingies followed them in."

"And then the rats ate the girls?" she asked hopefully.

"Or they're working together."

Scout froze. "That would be very, very bad. Reapers are awful. Reapers with minions are far beyond awful."

"What's the other option?"

"Maybe they just skipped in after the girls."

We both looked up. Lesley stood at the end of the hallway, arms crossed over her chest.

Scout gave her a look of disapproval. "We told you to wait upstairs."

Lesley lifted her nose, and with a voice I'd never heard her use before, gave that attitude right back to Scout. "I am not a child, so don't talk to me like that."

It took Scout a moment, but she backed off. "You're right," Scout said. "I'm sorry—but that doesn't mean—"

Lesley cut her off with a hand. "I told you I'd help you," she said. "And I'm not going to leave just because things get slimy. Literally."

It took Scout a moment to respond. I understood why—even after I'd taken firespell, she hesitated to bring me into the fold. She'd worried about my safety; after all, if a Reaper thought I had information about Adepts, they might use me to get to them. It was probably the same fear she had for Mrs. M and for her friend Derek, who worked at a bodega near the school.

"It's dangerous," Scout finally said, "to know too much."

Lesley took a step forward. "I know what people think about me. That I'm weird. That I study or practice my cello, but can't do anything else." She shook her head. "Just because I'm not a social butterfly doesn't mean I'm not smart or capable. I *am*," she insisted. "And I'm loyal. I just want a chance to be something more than the weird girl, even if you two are the only ones who know it."

We stood quietly for a minute. I'm not sure what Scout was thinking, but I was impressed. How many friends did you have who offered themselves up—to danger, to the unknown—because they wanted to help? Not because they wanted anything in return, or because they'd get credentials or fame out of it, but because it was the right thing to do?

"And the danger?" Scout asked.

Lesley rolled her eyes. "Take a step back."

"What?"

"Take a step back."

We did as she asked, and just in time. Without any more warning, Lesley twisted on one heel and kicked so high she would have knocked the ring out of Scout's nose if she'd been standing any closer.

Scout's jaw dropped; mine did, too.

"How—where?"

"I'm a black belt."

Scout extended a hand. "You are *so* in. Welcome to the community."

Lesley waved her off. "First things first. What do we do about this—stuff?"

"The trail ends at the corridor," I pointed out, "so it looks like they didn't get any farther than that. Maybe they peeked in, didn't find what they wanted, and left again."

"That's something," Scout said. "First of all, let's get some help." She pulled out her phone. "I'm going to tell Daniel what's up. He'll have to come through and re-ward the doors since they found a way to break through our spell. And we're probably going to have to clean up the slime."

Lesley raised her hand. "Could we lead the brat pack down here first?"

Scout gave her a pat on the back. "You're good people, Barnaby."

Things I didn't sign up for when I hopped the plane to O'Hare to attend St. Sophia's School for Girls: firespell; werewolves (but still lucked out there); brat packers; Reapers; snarky Varsity Adepts.

And slime. Lots of slime that had to be mopped up by Lesley,

Scout, and me. 'Cause what else would a sixteen-year-old girl rather be doing than mopping goo off a basement floor?

But we had to erase the evidence. Someone else finding the trail would only lead to questions Scout didn't want to answer. Besides—if we had to come back down to battle anyone, it was a safety hazard. The stuff was really slippery.

We'd found a rolling bucket and mop in a janitor's closet a few corridors away and pushed it down to the slimy corridor. Scout and I swabbed down the slime, and Lesley used an old towel to dry down the floor.

It took twenty minutes to clean it all up, but when we were done you could hardly tell it had been the sight of paranormal activity.

Scout put her hands on her hips and surveyed our work. "Well, I think it looks pretty fabulous."

"At least it doesn't look like the room got slimed. What's next?"

Scout looked at Lesley. "Can you head back upstairs?" Before Lesley could protest at the slight, Scout held up a hand. "I don't mean back to the suite. I mean stand guard upstairs. It's unlikely anyone would find their way down here, but stranger things have happened." When she gave me a pointed look, I stuck my tongue out at her. Not that she was wrong.

"Can you keep an eye on the basement door and make sure we have time to get it closed down again?"

With a salute, but without a word, Lesley headed down the corridor.

Scout watched her walk away. "Okay, is it wrong that I really like the fact that she saluted me?"

"It probably means that you're destined to be Varsity so you can have JV Adepts at your beck and call."

"Do you really think I'd have them at my beck and call?"

Scout had once told me that she wanted to run for office one day. Given the sound of her voice, I had a sense she wanted to head up Enclave Three one day, as well.

"Well, as much as you're at Katie's and Smith's beck and call."

"I'm not at Katie's and Smith's anything. Wait—what is a beck and call exactly?"

"I think that's when you do their bidding whenever they want."

She grimaced. "I guess I am that, then. All for one and one for all, and all that." Her phone beeped, and Scout pulled it out of her bag again.

"Daniel's on his way. Should be here in fifteen."

"So we're camping out in the basement again?"

She blew out a breath, then crossed her legs and sat down on the stone floor. "I don't suppose you brought any cards?"

Daniel's estimate had been a little low. It actually took him twenty minutes to get to us. He came in through the vault door, huffing like he'd run all the way through the tunnels.

"Sorry. Got here as fast as I could." He put his hands on his hips. He wore jeans and a smoky orange T-shirt beneath a thin jacket. He glanced through the corridor. "You got the mess cleaned up."

"Indeedy-o."

"How much? I mean, how far into the building did they go?"

Scout showed him where the trail had led. "They didn't get far," she concluded. "Although I'm not entirely sure why."

Daniel frowned, then paced to the end of the corridor and back again. "First the girls, now the rats and maybe the girls," he said. "They keep returning to St. Sophia's. But why?"

"Same reason they pinched Scout?" I offered. "They want her *Grimoire*?"

He seemed to think about that for a minute, then nodded. "That's the best theory we have right now. Let's assume that's true and build our defenses accordingly." He walked back to the door, then began looking it over. "The wards didn't hold, huh?"

Scout shook her head. "Not even. Can you work it so they're permanent? Like, they'd let Lily and me get through, but not anyone or anything else?"

Daniel pressed a hand to the door and closed his eyes in concentration. "Yeah, I could probably work that."

It looked like he was getting started, but I still had a question. "Aren't we going to go after them, or at least see how far they got? I mean, we can't just let the rats run loose in the tunnels."

He glanced back, only one eye open. "All the Adepts are accounted for, tucked safe and sound into their beds, with the exception of you two." He didn't say "troublemakers," but I could hear it in his voice. "So there's no immediate risk. Not enough that would justify sending you out on a hunting mission."

I couldn't argue with that logic.

While Daniel prepared to fire up his ward, Scout sent a message to Lesley to let her know that her work was done for the night, and that we'd be up as soon as Daniel was done.

His method of magic was quite a bit different from Scout's . . . or anything else that I'd seen. She'd said he was a protector. Maybe they had their own special brand of mojo. After he'd communed with the door, he pulled a short, cork-stoppered clear bottle from his jacket pocket and held it up to the light, checking it out. A white cloud swirled inside it, like he'd bottled a tiny tornado.

Daniel sat cross-legged on the floor, facing the door. He pressed his lips to the bottle's cork, then pulled out the stopper. The mist rushed out. Daniel closed his eyes, smiling happily as it expanded and circled him, swirling around like a magical version of Saturn's rings.

"What is that?" I whispered to Scout.

She shook her head. "I'm not sure."

The rings still circling and his eyes still closed, Daniel put hands on his knees and offered his incantation. "Solitude, sacrifice in blackness of night. Visitor—enemy of goodness and light. Hear the plea of this supplicant, protector of right, and quiet the halls of this reverent site."

For a second, there was nothing, and then the door flashed with a brilliant, white light that put huge dots in my vision. It took me a few seconds to see through the afterimages. By the time I could focus again, the mist was gone and Daniel had recorked the bottle.

Scout squeezed her eyes closed. "Little warning about the flash next time, Daniel?"

He stood up and put the bottle back into his pocket. The door's glow faded back to normalcy. No buzzing, no pulsing, no vibrating rivets.

"That should hold," he said, "at least until they find a work-around. As Adepts, you'll be able to come and go at will. It'll only keep out Reapers—and whatever else they try to drag in here." He pointed toward the other end of the corridor. "That the way back to St. Sophia's?"

Scout nodded, and we all headed off in that direction.

"What was in the bottle?" she asked as we took the stairs to the second floor.

Daniel slid her a glance. "You've never seen sylphs before?"

Scout pointed at his jacket. "That was a sylph?"

Surprisingly, I actually knew what a sylph was—or what it was supposed to be. My parents had given me a book of fairy tales when I was younger. There was a fable about three sylphs—winged fairies—who'd tricked proud villagers into giving the sylphs all of their youth and beauty. I think "Vanity gets you in trouble" was supposed to be the moral of the story. I always got the sense they looked basically like smallish people—not clouds of mist.

As if in answer to Scout's question, Daniel's pocket vibrated a little. "That was *many* sylphs," he said, "and since I can still feel them rattling around, I think you offended them."

They must have been snowflake-small to fit into that tiny bottle, I thought, wondering what else the underground had in store. What other creatures were hiding in plain sight, living among Chicagoans even though they had no idea?

"Sorry, sylphs," Scout half shouted. "I didn't mean to offend you."

"You probably don't need to yell."

"Yeah, well, you're not the one who offended the sylphs, are you? One can never be too careful."

"I'd agree with that if I didn't think you were being crazy sarcastic. I'm assuming you're actually leading me out of this building?"

"Of course," Scout said. "We're taking the bad-girl exit."

Daniel lifted his eyebrows. "The 'bad-girl exit'?"

"Walk and talk, people. Walk and talk."

Lesley was gone when we emerged upstairs, and the main building was quiet. Scout silenced Daniel with a finger to her mouth, and we tiptoed across to the administrative wing where the offices—including Foley's—were located. "We're taking the secret exit without the alarm. This is how some of St. Sophia's *busier* girls, if you know what I mean, sneak in and out at night."

"No way," Daniel said.

Scout nodded. "Welcome to the glamorous world of boarding school. Where the things that go bump in the night are either horrific creatures—"

"Or equally horrific teenagers," I finished.

We followed Scout through the main administrative hallway and into a narrower corridor that led from it. The offices looked dark . . .

"Students," a voice said suddenly behind us.

We froze, then turned around. Foley stood in her open doorway, a candle in one of those old-fashioned brass holders in her hand.

"I believe it's past curfew." She slid her gaze to Daniel. "Mr. Sterling." It took me a moment to remember Foley knew Daniel because he was our studio TA.

"Sorry for marching through your territory," he apologetically said, "but we were on a bit of a mission."

"A mission?"

"Interlopers," Scout said. "There were Reapers at the gates, so to speak. Daniel here warded the door, and now we're escorting him out."

We stood in the corridor silently for a moment, Foley probably debating whether to let us go. Since she didn't rush to call the cops about the man standing in the middle of her girls' school in the middle of the night, I assumed she knew about Daniel's magical tendencies.

Her voice softened. "You're being careful?"

"As much as we can, ma'am," Daniel said. "And—I was sorry to hear about your daughter. She was a good friend—and a good Adept."

I snapped my gaze back to Foley and the grief in her expression. She'd had a daughter who was an Adept? And she'd lost her?

Foley actually seemed to make more sense now. But before I could say anything, her expression went bossy again. She nodded at Daniel, then turned and walked away. "Get back to bed," we heard.

We were quiet for a moment until I looked at Scout. "Did you know?"

She shook her head. "I mean, I suspected, given the fact that she was in the community, but I didn't know she'd had a kid—or lost her."

We both looked at Daniel. His brow was furrowed. "I didn't mean to bring up bad memories. Her name was Emily. She was a green thumb Adept—she could grow trees and vines that practically encapsulated buildings." He paused. "We think it was a Reaper attack."

"I had no idea," Scout quietly said.

Guilt settled heavy in my stomach. "I didn't either. And I was pretty hard on her earlier today."

"We do the best we can with the information we have," Daniel said. "For now, let's focus on the things we can change. Such as getting me out of here."

Scout nodded, then gestured down the hall. "This way," she said. We continued the walk in silence, and didn't speak again until Scout paused in front of an old wooden door.

She jimmied the ancient crystal knob. "There's no light in here, but you can use flashlights when the door's shut."

We stepped inside, shut the door, and pulled out our flashlights. The room was big and mostly empty, and the ceiling arched above it. The floors were made up of old wooden boards, and along one side was a fireplace that took up almost the entire wall. It was made of rough, pale stones that were still stained with soot. A simple wooden chair, the kind with rails across the back, sat beside the fireplace.

I shivered. There was something creepy about this place—the empty chair in the otherwise deserted room. I could imagine Temperance living here alone, waiting for someone to conjure her up. I shivered, then wrapped my arms around my shoulders.

"What is this?" Daniel whispered.

Scout walked to a corner of the room and began feeling around on the floor. "Not sure. I think it was the original kitchen for the nuns before they built the new wing. Mostly no one comes in here anymore."

"Except bad girls," I pointed out.

"Except that," Scout agreed. She lifted up a ring, then pulled open an old door that was set into the floor. "Root cellar," she explained when we walked over. She pointed down into it. "There's a door to the yard, and from there you can just walk out the front gate. No alarms or anything."

Daniel headed into the cellar, disappearing into darkness. I followed him down, and Scout followed behind me.

The root cellar looked exactly how you'd expect a root cellar to look. It was dark and damp, and it smelled like wet soil and plants. The ladder into it was wooden and rickety, as was the door that led to the side lawn. Had the folks who'd changed the convent into a school with fancy classrooms failed to find the rickety door—or had Foley left a secret exit for any Adepts that needed it?

Yet another question, but I was already full up for the night.

The evening was cool, so I tucked my hands into my hoodie pockets and followed Daniel and Scout to the street.

"Thanks for the help," he said. "I might find some Varsity kids and ask them to take a walk through the tunnels. I think you've already had enough close calls for the week."

"I couldn't agree more," Scout said. We said our final goodbyes, and Daniel took off at a jog toward the street, then turned and headed out of view.

"This has been quite a week," she said as we headed back up the ladder and into the building. "First teethy monsters, then vampires, and now Reapers."

I stopped. "What did you say?"

Scout glanced back, then blinked. "What?"

"Just then. What did you say?"

"Oh, uh, teethy monsters, vampires, Reapers?"

"Teethy monsters," I repeated. "You said it the other day—the rat things had fangs. And vampires have fangs, too, right?"

"Yeah, but so what?"

I frowned. "I'm not exactly sure." I was on the edge of *something*. . . . I just didn't know what.

She pointed toward the door. "Come on. You can sleep on it and let it percolate in your dreams, or something."

"Actually, I have a better idea."

"And that is?"

"I think we need to go visit the vampires."

16

"You want to *what*?"

"I want to go see Nicu," I said. "Monsters with fangs, monsters with pointy little teeth. I mean, I know it's kind of a long shot, but my gut tells me something's going on there. Besides, Sebastian said we needed to talk to Nicu." I shrugged. "Maybe this is why."

Her look wasn't exactly friendly. "So now you're following Sebastian's advice?"

"I'm following the only lead we've got."

She was quiet for a moment. "The vampires weren't exactly friendly the last time we saw them."

"And they may not be friendly this time, either. But what other choice do we have? I say we visit the coven and skip the turf war bit altogether."

"Oh, you just want to traipse into a coven of bloodsucking fiends and beg them for help?"

I shook my head. "Not beg, but definitely ask. Do you remember what Marlena said about Nicu's coven being weak? What if that wasn't just talk? Sebastian said something about the 'missing.' What if the Reapers aren't just targeting Adepts?"

Her expression softened. "You think they're taking vampires, too?"

"I don't know," I admitted. "But if we find the vampires, and if we offer to help them . . ."

"They might not make breakfast out of us."

I nodded. "Exactly."

She whistled. "That's risky. And even if it doesn't get us eaten, we don't know where the coven actually is."

"No," I said. "We don't. But we know who probably does."

Fifteen minutes later, we were in the back of a dark green cab with GYPSY printed on the door in white cursive letters. We were heading for Buckman's, one of those old-fashioned multilevel department stores a few blocks from St. Sophia's. I wasn't entirely sure why we were meeting at a department store, but when the girl with the map tells you to jump, you ask how high.

The cab ride was short, probably not even a mile. But I stared out the windows the entire time, taking in a view of Chicago I hadn't seen before—I hadn't yet been aboveground in the dark. We drove past soaring skyscrapers, including two that looked like a pair of concrete corncobs, cars stuck into parking spaces right against the edge like tiny steel kernels. We crossed an iron bridge over what I assumed was the Chicago River, and then we passed the marquee of the Chicago Theater—

"Oh, my God," I said, turning to stare as we passed it by. "Did you see that?"

"What?" Scout asked.

"In the theater sign—in the marquee. There's a circle inside a Y behind the word 'Chicago.'"

"Folks say that Y is supposed to stand for the branches of the river," said the cabdriver, glancing up at his rearview mirror to look at me. "You see 'em all over the city, including over by the theater. Kind of a weird deal, I guess, that they're on buildings and such, but there you are. Probably somethin' to do with politics. It's Chicago, after all."

Scout and I exchanged a glance. I wondered if she wanted to speak up—to tell the driver that the symbol wasn't just on the buildings for decoration, that it represented the places where Adepts had fought for the soul of Chicago. But if she wanted to, she didn't say anything.

We pulled up outside a tall, squarish building, a clock extending out over the sidewalk.

"The shops are closed, ya know," the cabbie said as Scout pulled money from her messenger bag.

"We're just meeting our parents," she said, passing the money over and opening the car door. "They went to see a show."

That seemed to work for the driver, who took the money with a nod and watched in the rearview mirror as we scooted across the bench and out of the car.

We found Detroit outside beneath the clock. She was wearing a brown vest over a long-sleeved shirt, brown suspenders connecting the vest to a pair of wide-legged pants with lots of pockets. The map-making locket was around her neck, and she had an old-fashioned, silver-tipped walking stick in her hand.

"Thanks for meeting us," I said when we reached her.

"No problem. It's in everyone's interest to deal with the monsters, and if vampires are the way to do it, that's the way we do it." She shrugged. "What exactly is the plan?"

"We're going to talk to Nicu," I said, offering up the explanation I'd come up with in the cab (the one that didn't involve a Sebastian-related confession). "There's no way the rats could move around the city without intersecting with the Pedway at some point. And if they've been on the Pedway, the vamps know about them."

"So you want to talk to Nicu," she said. "But why Nicu instead of Marlena?"

"He seemed a little friendlier," Scout put in, after giving me a silencing glance. "So we're trying him first."

Apparently buying the explanation, Detroit nodded, then walked toward the building and peered inside one of the glass doors. She knocked on the glass.

"I am now officially confused," Scout said.

"Me too. What are we doing here?"

"The Pedway runs through the basement," Detroit explained, as a guard in a tidy blue suit and cap walked toward the door.

"Closed," the guard mouthed, pointing at his watch.

Detroit, apparently undeterred, flashed the guard a peace sign. It took a second, but the guard nodded, then began the process of unlocking the door with a key from a giant loop.

"He supports peace?" Scout wondered.

"I made a *Y*," Detroit explained, showing Scout the sign again. "It's recognized by the community. And Mr. Howard here is very much a member of the community. So be nice to Mr. Howard."

But Scout was too busy with her new trick to be mean—she'd made a peace sign and was staring down at her fingers. "Genius," she said, eyes wide with excitement.

"You'll have to teach that to Derek and Mrs. M," I pointed out, and she nodded back.

Mr. Howard held open the door while we moved inside. Once in, he locked it tight again. "You on the hunt for Reapers tonight?" he asked politely.

"Not quite," Detroit said. "But we appreciate the help, sir."

Mr. Howard nodded, then gestured toward a set of elevators. "Basement level, if you're headed into the Pedway."

"Thank you," Detroit said, and we were off again.

"Seriously, I want to go see Derek right now just to show him this. I know it's not a big deal, but it's like having a secret handshake. Haven't you always wanted to have a secret handshake?"

"Not that I can recall right at this minute," I said, as we followed Detroit through displays of makeup and perfume. "But I'm excited you're excited."

The main lights were off, but it was clearly a department store— floors of merchandise around an atrium in the middle. Although the *stuff* in the store was modern, the rest of it was old-school fancy. I stared up at the atrium. Fancy gold balconies ringed the floors above us like architectural bracelets, and the entire thing was capped by a pillow of frosted glass. The floor looked like marble. This place must have been really interesting in its heyday.

We followed the marble path to the elevators. There were two of them; both had brass doors engraved with flowers.

"They really spared no expense back in the day, did they?" Scout asked.

"I was just thinking that."

When the elevator arrived, we stepped inside. Detroit mashed the button for the basement. The one-floor trip was short but jarring. The elevators were definitely old-school, and the jumpy ride felt like it.

We emerged into an area with lower ceilings and signs for restrooms and customer service areas. A giant sign reading PEDWAY hung on a corridor in front of us.

"Does it ever feel like we spend at least thirty percent of our Adept time just traveling around?" I wondered aloud.

"Oh, my God, I was just thinking that, too! We are totally psychic today."

"You two are definitely something today," Detroit said. She flipped open her locket, then projected the map hologram against one of the walls of the corridor. This chunk of the Pedway was actually much nicer than the last one I'd seen—the floors were fancy stone with glittering chips in it, and long wooden flower planters lined the sides. The ceiling above us was a single, long, glowing rectangle, like a superhuge fluorescent light.

The Pedway diagram looked like a subway map, with red marks in the shape of droplets—blood, I assumed—at certain points along the way.

Detroit scanned the route, then nodded. "Yeah, a couple more blocks, and we're there." She snapped the locket shut again, then turned on her heel and started walking, her giant pants making a *shush-shush* sound as she walked. The outfit wasn't exactly covert, but then again, walking into a home of vampires probably wasn't all that stealthy, either.

We walked in silence for a couple of blocks, occasionally going up or down a small ramp but generally staying in the basement level. After a few minutes, the scenery changed to "disco office chic." The floors became orangish industrial carpet, the walls dark brick.

Detroit stopped in front of a glass door with a long handle across the front—the kind you might see in a strip mall office. She looked back at us. "This is it. You'll probably want to be ready with the fire-spell and stuff."

When we nodded, she pushed open the door. A set of old mini-blinds hanging on the inside of the glass clanked against it like an office wind chime. A haze of gray dust swirled through the air.

I glanced around. We'd walked into an abandoned office, the fabric-covered cubicle walls still standing. But instead of separating the room into little mini-offices, they made a maze that led farther back into the building. Bass from music being played somewhere in the back echoed through the room, vibrating loose screws in the cubicle walls. I didn't recognize the song, but "paranoia" kept repeating over and over and over again.

"Vampires nest in old offices?" Scout whispered.

"Vamps nest in whatever space they can find in the Pedway," Detroit explained. "It's lined with parking garages, offices, stores that sell to the business folks who grab lunch, whatever. When an office clears out, it gives the covens an opportunity to split. That's what Nicu did."

After a glance to make sure we were ready, we began to wind our way through the maze. It ringed around in what felt like a spiral, finally dumping us into a giant circle surrounded by more cubicle walls . . . and filled with vampires.

Rugs and pillows in various shades of gray were scattered on the floor, and similar fabric was draped over the cubicle walls. The vamps, still in their dark ensembles, lounged on the pillows or stretched on the rugs, but the best seat—a clear plastic armchair in the middle of the room—was reserved for the head honcho.

Nicu.

He wore a long, military-style coat and pants in the same steel gray color, and one leg was crossed over the other. He held a cut-crystal goblet in his hand, and there was no mistaking the dark crimson liquid inside of it. As I looked around, I realized the only color in the room was that same dark red that filled glasses in the hands of other vampires. That explained the coppery smell in the air.

My stomach knotted, and I moved incrementally closer to Scout, squeezing my hands into fists so the vampires couldn't see them shaking.

Nicu gestured at us with his glass. "What do we have here?" he said, that heavy accent in his voice. "Little rebels without a cause?" The vampires snickered, and he didn't wait for our answer. "Tell me this," he said. "If you reject the Dark Elite, what does that make you?"

"The huddled masses?" one vampire suggested.

Nicu smiled drowsily. "Indeed. And there can be no mistake that you have walked of your own accord into our nest, yes?" He glanced from Scout to me, the question in his eyes.

Out of instinct, I nearly nodded, but Scout held up a hand. "Don't answer that," she warned. "If you say yes, you agree you came here willingly. That means you came here to give them blood. We're here for information," she told him. "Not trickery."

Nicu barked out a laugh. "You enter our home, you have already caused me trouble, and yet you seek to ask a favor? Danger lurks where you tread." As if to prove his point, he took a sip. The drink left a crimson stain around his lips, which he licked away.

The vampires began to rise and shift, some of them moving around us, encircling us—and cutting off our escape route again. I swallowed down fear, but opened the channels of my mind enough to let the energy begin to rush around. If I had to use it, I wanted to be ready.

One of the vampires—a woman in a high-necked dress—moved toward us in a spiral that became tighter and tighter.

"Backs together," Detroit whispered, and we formed a triangle. I put my hands out, ready to strike, and assumed Scout and Detroit were doing the same with the magic at their disposal.

But it wasn't until I heard the *yelp* that I looked back. Detroit was wielding the walking stick—the end tipped in silver—like a weapon. And from the look of the crimson line that was beginning to trace down the female vampire's arm, she'd gotten too close.

The vampires pulled the wounded female back into the main cluster and tended to the wound on her arm. The rest began arguing with one another, their voices high-pitched. I couldn't make out what they were saying. Some of it, I think, was in another language. But some of it was more animal than human, like the yelps of fighting cats. We huddled closer together, our shoulder blades touching.

"Silence!" Nicu finally yelled out, gesturing with his goblet, blood slipping down the sides from the movement. It took a moment, but the room finally quieted. It didn't still, though—we'd agitated the vamps, and they slithered around as if waiting to be set loose on us again.

Nicu scowled, but nodded at us. "Get on with it."

"We've been seeing things in the tunnels," I said. "Creatures. Not quite human, not quite animal. They're naked. Pointy ears. Slimy skin. Lots of teeth."

"And?"

I swallowed, but made myself say it aloud. "And they're terrorizing the tunnels. Someone nearly helped them breach St. Sophia's tonight. The Reapers—the ones you call the thieves—believe you know something about them. Something about the missing?"

Nicu went silent. A vampire from the far side of the room, a tall man dressed in long black layers, rushed to Nicu, the fabric of his clothing swirling as he moved. He knelt at Nicu's side and whispered something.

Nicu looked away. When he finally began to speak, his voice was so quiet I had to lean forward to catch the words.

"One of our children is missing," he said, thumping a fist against his chest. "One of *my* own."

Scout and I shared a worried glance. "One of your vampires is missing?"

He nodded, then looked away, a red tear slipping down his cheek. "For two months now. We have heard nothing from her. Seen nothing of her. Her lover is bereft, and we fear she is . . . gone."

"And you think the thieves were involved?"

"Who else would do such a thing?"

"Marlena? One of the other covens? We heard you were fighting."

Nicu swiped at the tear on his cheek and barked out a laugh. "Vampires do not steal from other covens. We may not agree on all things, but we have honor enough."

I nodded in understanding. Vampires might not do it, but Reapers definitely would. And if we were right about the sanctuary, they weren't above kidnapping someone to take what energy they could. But could that even work with vampires? "Do you know why they would have taken her?"

Nicu shook his head, but the vampire at his side prompted him with more whispers.

"We have heard rumors," Nicu reluctantly said.

"What kind of rumors?"

Nicu met my gaze again, his eyes now fully dilated—sinking orbs of black. "Rumors that the thieves are unsatisfied with their lot. There are rumors . . ."

Pausing, Nicu held his goblet out, and the man at his side took it. Hands empty, he sat forward, elbows on his knees, and stared at us with terrible eyes. "There are rumors the thieves are no longer satisfied with their short human lives. They seek our blood and our secret."

I frowned at him. "Your secret?"

"The secret of vampire immortality."

I looked down at the fabric-covered floor, working through Nicu's theory. He thought Reapers had kidnapped a vampire to take the vampire's blood, thinking that if they had the blood, they had the immortality, and they could use that power to keep their magic forever.

But then I thought of what Temperance had said about the sanctuary, and I thought of the monsters. I came up with a different theory. A very, very bad theory.

A cold chill sank into my bones.

"I don't think it was just the blood they were worried about," I said, looking up at Nicu again. "And I think I know what happened."

All eyes turned to me. I ignored my nerves and went for it. Vampires or not, Nicu and his band had a right to know.

"We discovered a new sanctuary, a new building where the Reapers are doing some kind of work. Medical work. And the creatures that we saw in the tunnels had similarities to vampires. Claws and"—I made myself get the last word out there—"fangs."

Scout turned to stare at me, horror in her eyes. "Lily, no. That's not possible. They couldn't have—"

I just shook my head, and let them reach their own conclusions.

"You think they took one of mine—used one of my children—to build some kind of abomination? Some kind of monster?" Nicu shook his head and waved a hand through the air. "You are no longer welcome here."

"But we need to find them—to figure out how—"

"No!" Nicu said, standing at his throne, his jacket falling around behind him. "You are no longer welcome. Return to your domain, and never speak of this evil again."

We didn't waste time arguing.

We hurried back through the Pedway. Scout texted Daniel to let him know what we'd discovered—that one of Nicu's vampires was missing, and the missing vampire might have somehow been used by

Reapers to build the monsters that were trekking through the tunnels and trying to sneak inside St. Sophia's.

Had Lauren and her gatekeeper friend been attempting to breach the doors just to let in the rats? Once inside, what were they supposed to do? If they started attacking schoolgirls, their existence was definitely out of the closet. And Scout and I would have to battle them back, which meant our magic was out of the closet, too.

Maybe that was the point. Did the Reapers hope the move would make us rejoin the Dark Elite? Like we'd go back to the mother ship for safety once we were outed as Adepts?

Frankly, I wouldn't have put it past them. That sounded like the kind of plan Reapers would come up with. It also sounded like the kind of plan Sebastian might have known about. I made a mental note.

We reached the pretty portion of the Pedway again, walking quietly along until Scout held up her hand. We stopped, and before I could ask what she'd seen, she put a hand to her lips. We stood in the middle of the Pedway, soft jazz playing above us, waiting . . .

That was when I heard what she'd heard: movement and hard-soled shoes on the Pedway in front of us.

"Hide," Scout said, shooing us all toward half walls that extended out on each side of the hallway. She and I squeezed behind one; Detroit ducked behind the other. We all peeked around the walls.

Vampires.

It was Marlena and her minions, sauntering through the Pedway like a queen and her entourage. But that wasn't all.

"Oh, crap," Scout said. "They've got Veronica."

17

"What are we going to do?" I asked, watching two of Marlena's minions drag a cursing Veronica down the Pedway. Her hair was falling down and her cheeks were streaked with tears and mascara, but it didn't look like she'd been bitten.

On the other hand, total brat drama had now become Adept drama.

"What is she doing down here?" I whispered.

Scout sighed heavily. "She probably followed us into the basement one night, then decided to play Nancy Drew. She's been watching us like a hawk this week."

"And she probably thinks we were with John Creed," I realized, the puzzle pieces falling together. "She's been interrogating me about him all week. She thinks we're buds because he and Jason are friends."

"Nothing to do about it now," Scout said, taking a step into the Pedway. I followed, and Detroit did the same.

The vampires began to hoot, the minions' grip on Veronica tightening as she began to demand that they let her go.

Marlena stepped around her vampires, this time wearing a tweed dress, fur wrap, and those old-fashioned stockings with the dark line up the back. She put her hands on her hips. "Did you lose something, darlings?"

"Let her go," Scout said. "Or you get magic and firespell and a silver-tipped walking stick, and you get knocked back into the nineteen forties where you belong."

Marlena hissed. "This is not a game, little one."

"I am so sick of people telling me that," I muttered, raising my hands. I relaxed and let the power begin to flow, letting it collect in my hands so that I could toss it out if necessary.

"Did you invade St. Sophia's?" Scout asked.

Marlena arched a darkly penciled eyebrow. "We hardly have need for that, *iubitu*. Not when she is wandering through the corridors alone."

"Bingo," Scout muttered.

"Let go of me!" Veronica screamed again, yanking at her arms as she attempted to break free.

Marlena had apparently had enough. She turned and slapped Veronica across the face, leaving a red welt across her cheek. "Silence!"

Veronica's howls turned to silent weeping. Scout took a precautionary step forward.

"Marlena, if you have issues with us, you need to let her go. She's not one of us, and has nothing to do with this. She will only bring attention to your kind."

Marlena's expression faltered for a second, but then went stone-cold again. "Liar."

"She's a normal," I confirmed. "You keep her down here, and things get very, very ugly for you."

"Uh, ladies, speaking of ugly, we've got a problem." We turned to see Detroit looking behind us.

I hated to turn around, but I wasn't exactly in a position to run. Slowly, I glanced back as well.

Vampires. An entire crowd of them, moving in from behind us.

But these were a different kind of vampire. They were Nicu's.

Nicu stepped through them to the front of the horde. He nodded at me and Scout and Detroit, then took in Marlena.

"They are children," he said. "Let her go."

"She is mine. My catch. My bounty. My prize." She rolled the *R* in 'prize' like an opera singer, and the sound sent a chill down my spine.

"She is not part of this world, and your bringing her into it will not help." He inched closer, as did the vampires behind him.

"When it's time," I whispered, "I'll grab Veronica. You two jump to the right, and then we make a run for it."

Detroit nodded, but Scout looked worried.

"Firespell," I reminded her. "If they get me, I take them out."

She blew out a breath and nodded, then turned her attention back to the vampires and the turf war we'd gotten stuck in . . . again.

Marlena put her hands on her hips. "You choose children over your own kind?"

"They have offered their help. They have come to us with information and have treated us as equals. In this, yes. We choose children over those who would forsake us."

In the silence, Nicu and his vampires took another step forward, then another, until they were directly behind us. I wasn't thrilled about the proximity, but I trusted him a lot more right now than I did Marlena.

"Then let us decide this once and for all."

"Not liking the sound of this," Scout said.

"Detroit," I whispered, hoping the myths about vampires were true, "when I give the word, point the locket at the vamps holding Veronica."

"Got it," she said with a nod.

"On one," I said, leaning forward just a bit to prepare myself for the steal. "Three . . . two . . . *one!*"

Detroit popped open her locket, light flashing into the corridor as she aimed it toward Marlena's vampires. They raised their hands to their faces, hissing at the light, releasing Veronica. I jumped forward and grabbed her, then pulled her back behind the half wall, Detroit and Scout behind me.

I dumped Veronica onto the floor, looking her over for wounds. She was quiet now, shock obviously setting in. In the vacuum behind us, the covens of vampires rushed together, Nicu's vampires scratching and clawing as they fought for the right to exist, Marlena fighting back the vampires who'd tried to escape her.

Nicu ran through the fray to reach us, stopping as he stared down at Veronica. She looked up at him with wide eyes, and his own widened in surprise.

I glanced over at Scout, who shrugged.

A second later, Nicu blinked, then looked at me. "Run," he said. "As fast as you can. Get her to safety and then find the monsters. Dispatch them."

We ran.

Detroit led the way back to the Enclave. Scout and I each had an arm around Veronica, half walking and half carrying her through the dark tunnels, the light of Detroit's locket guiding the way. Detroit used Scout's phone to send a message to Daniel. By the time we arrived at the Enclave, we found Katie, Smith, Daniel, Michael, Jason, and Paul waiting. The twins must have still been off on their own mission.

The mood wasn't exactly light, and seeing Veronica didn't help. But Daniel stayed calm. He directed Katie and Smith to help Veronica, then clustered the rest of us together.

"The vampires are missing one of their coven," he said. "The Reapers have, perhaps, used the sanctuary to build these monsters. They have put Adepts and vampires, the Pedway and St. Sophia's—the whole city—at risk. This ends tonight."

Scout and I looked at each other, but nodded. We knew what needed to be done. We had to find them, and we had to take them out.

"We'll deal with the girl," he said. "You start at the sanctuary. God willing, it will still be empty of Reapers. Either way, destroy the monsters."

"We'll do it," Jason said.

"You've got to," Daniel advised. "If you can't, we're all in trouble."

. . .

Jason took the lead, and Paul was at our back. The rest of us—Michael, Scout, Detroit, and me—were clustered into groups in the middle.

This time, we needed speed, so we decided to try the shortcut, hoping the vampire squabble had played itself out. We didn't see anything out of the ordinary until we made it to the Pedway. But when we emerged from the janitor's closet—one careful Adept at a time—things got more interesting.

The hallway was empty but for five scratched and bleeding vampires—Nicu and four others.

"Is she okay?" Nicu asked.

If he'd developed a thing for Veronica, I was going to be totally freaked-out.

"She's fine," I told him. "She's being cared for."

"Will you erase her memory of these events?"

I looked over at Scout, who nodded. "She's not the type we'd trust in the community. She might use the information against us. One of the other Adepts will work their magic, and she'll have no memory of what transpired. It won't hurt her," she added, at the obvious heartbreak in Nicu's eyes.

Did love at first sight really operate that quickly?

"Then that's the way it must be," he said, resigned.

"And your coven?" I asked him. "Are you okay?"

"We have survived the night," Nicu said, "so we are now a coven in our own right."

Oh, awesome, I thought. We'd actually helped the vampires establish themselves. I really hoped that didn't bite us in the butt later.

"Good night, Adepts." Nicu placed his hand over his heart, and then the entire group of them—all at once—bowed to us.

Detroit worked her magic on the stairwell doors, and we popped back into the tunnels again. If the rats were back, there wasn't any sign of them.

"You think that means they're gone?" Scout asked.

"I think that means they don't shed slime all the time," Jason said. "At least, that's my guess."

"And even if they were here," Scout said, "the Reapers could have cleaned up after them. Who knows?"

When we reached the sanctuary, we peeked around the alcove and into the final corridor. The doors were closed, the lights off.

But there was a trail of slime that led from the corridor into the sanctuary.

"And they're back," Michael muttered.

"Honestly," Detroit said, "I'm a little glad to see the slime. I was beginning to worry that I'd imagined it all."

"No such luck," Scout and I simultaneously said. Scout glanced over at Detroit. "The trip wires," she said. "Got anything for that?"

"As a matter of fact, I do." After searching her pants pockets, Detroit popped another black pill into the hallway, letting the magic smoke illuminate the trip wires. Then she unzipped a long pocket along her knee and pulled out a child's spinning top.

"Quick invention," she said, "but I think it will work." She crouched down and put the top on the floor, then gave it a twirl. It wobbled, but began to spin, whirring as it gathered speed and moved down the hallway toward the double doors.

And as it spun, it began to spindle both the magic smoke and the trip wires the smoke had revealed. In a few seconds, the hallway was clean, the top glowing with newly bundled magic.

"Seriously, I think that's the coolest thing you've done so far." Scout's tone was reverent.

"Glad you like it," Detroit said. She walked down and collected the top, then held it out to Scout. "I thought you could have it. You can unspindle the trip wires. Make them your own."

With her eyes gleaming like it was Christmas morning, Scout accepted the gift.

"All right," Jason said. "Now that the coast is relatively clear, let's get this show on the road." He stopped in front of the double doors and glanced back. "Everybody ready?"

When we nodded, he pushed them open. One by one, we tiptoed inside.

"Lily," he whispered. "Lights."

I pulled the power and sent it upward. Long rows of fluorescent lights above us stuttered to life.

We were in a hallway—the kind you might see in a hospital. Wide corridor, pale green walls, doors on the right and left . . . and a long trail of slime leading back toward other rooms.

"Stay here," Jason said, then began to move forward, peeking through the rooms on the right-hand side of the corridor. When he reached the second door, he stopped.

"What is it?" Scout whispered.

He beckoned us forward, then walked inside. We followed him . . . and gaped.

Temperance had thought the sanctuary was a clinic. But this didn't look like any clinic I'd ever seen. The center of the room was lined with counters topped by pieces of medical equipment. And the walls were covered by whiteboards. Some with lines and lines of formulas, others with writing—theories about vampires and immortality and magic.

And how to keep it forever.

We stopped and stared at the last board.

Photographs had been stuck there with magnets—photos of Reaper works in progress. The rats, from tiny nubbins to full-grown creatures. For a second, I felt a little sorry for them.

"We were right," I said. "They were doing experiments, and vampires were their model."

Hands on her hips, Scout gazed at the pictures. "What were they trying to do? Build some kind of forever-magic superbeings?"

"Maybe," Jason said. "Or maybe just figure out if there was a source for the immortality."

"Maybe it has something to do with the slime," I suggested.

"Maybe the slime served some kind of purpose. Like, I don't know, some kind of immortality elixir or something."

"That is totally rank," Scout said, her face screwed into a look of disgust. "But I wouldn't put it past them."

"Temperance must not have known what these were," Detroit said. "If she had, she'd have known this wasn't a clinic."

"I'm sure she did the best she could," Scout said.

"We'll let our guys figure out the details," Jason said. "Scout, take pictures of the whiteboards so we can turn them over. Lily, as soon as she's done, erase them. *All* of them. We're not helping them preserve whatever 'science' they've done here."

We followed his directions. Scout walked slowly around the room, snapping photos with her camera so we had proof of what the Reapers had been up to. I followed behind her. Each time she snapped a photo, I used my sleeve to wipe off the writing.

When the room was clean and Scout's phone was tucked away again, we headed back into the hallway. The rest of the rooms on the mazelike floor were either research labs, or more like the medical facilities Temperance had described. There were needles, bandages, and monitors just like she'd said, but not for healing. For experimenting.

The whole place had an awful vibe. And then we rounded a corner . . . and walked right into the nest.

The rats had taken up an entire corridor, the walls and floor coated with slime. Dozens of them slept in a pile in one corner.

Home sweet home, I thought.

Detroit screamed.

Chaos erupted.

Jason immediately shifted, his giant silver wolf taking the attack. He pounced on the back of a rat, which began squealing and screeching and trying to throw him off.

I looked over at Michael, who stood in the middle of the room, eyes wide with fear. I pulled him away, then planted him beside the wall on the other end of the corridor. "Stay here, okay?"

He nodded, but pointed at Scout. "I think she needs help."

Scout was throwing what looked like marbles at the rats. Each time they made impact, they sent a shock wave through the creatures—their skin wobbling in circular ripples just like on a slow-motion camera. Unfortunately, while the shock waves moved the rats back a few feet, they didn't stop coming.

I looked around the room—and found the same problem all over. Everything we were doing was working, but only to a point.

"This isn't doing much good," Paul yelled, tossing one rat over his shoulder. "It's not killing the rats!"

That was when the gears clicked into place. Scout's spell might have worked before, but normal combat wasn't going to do the trick. "That's because they're not really rats!" I yelled over the din of battle. "Scout, what takes out vampires?"

"The usual stuff!" she yelled back. "Fire, stakes, garlic, crosses, silver, and, you know, dismemberment."

I decided to leave that one to Jason. "Remember they're related to vampires!" I called out to everyone else. "So hit 'em where it hurts!"

I went with my best weapon. Firespell wasn't exactly fire—it was Jamie who had that power—but it was as close as I was going to get. There was too much chaos to try an all-out burst of it—too high a chance that I'd hit an Adept. But Sebastian had said I could use it in pinpoint fashion. Might as well try that now.

I maneuvered around until I had a clear shot at one of them, then squeezed my hands into fists. I opened myself to the power, but instead of trying to throw it all back out again, I lifted a single hand, my fingers cupped, and visualized sending that single burst of magic into one of the creatures, the way Sebastian had taught me.

And then I let it go. It still warped the air, but it was focused—the firespell moving in the air in a tight spiral that ripped toward the monster and hit him square in the chest.

He went down . . . and he didn't get back up.

Sebastian might have been evil—but he definitely had some firespell skills. And maybe because it was kind of like fire, vampires weren't immune to it.

Together, the four of us used our magic to knock out the rats one by one. It wasn't easy—there were so many of them, we hardly had time to get one on the floor before the next one attacked. Even with my focused attack, I'd gotten too close to their claws and had burning scratches up and down my arms and legs as I fought back the army.

I finished up the knot closest to me, then glanced over at Scout. She was using a pencil from her bag—a make-do wooden stake—to take out a rat in front of her. It worked, and he hit the ground, but the rest of them were beginning to surround her.

"Scout!" I yelled over the sounds of fighting and squealing monsters. "Duck!"

She did, and I threw out another dose of firespell, which put the creature lurking behind her on the floor. Then she popped up again, gave me a thumbs-up, and knocked out the one in front of her.

"Lily!"

At the sound of Detroit's voice, I glanced back, expecting to see her encircled by monsters. But there was a pile of them at her feet, her silver-tipped walking stick between both hands like she was wielding a sword. For an Adept who wasn't supposed to be a fighter, she was definitely holding her own. But she used the stick to point into the other corner—where Jason was quickly getting surrounded.

I couldn't see Jason's entire body, just bits of bloody fur as he leaped and rolled with the monsters.

"Jason!" I ran forward toward the melee, my hands outstretched, spiraling the firespell at each monster that jumped forward to attack him.

One of them jumped out at me, but I tossed firespell in his direction. He was too close for a shot and the bobbling air nearly bounced back to knock me down as I moved toward Jason, but I shimmied and sidestepped it.

I became a dervish, spinning and tossing firespell at anything and everything that stood between me and him. I finally reached him and helped him claw his way out of the pile. When the path was clear, he sat back on his haunches, tongue lolling as he caught his breath.

I couldn't help but smile down at him. "Good dog."

He might have been in wolf form, but the look he gave back was all Jason Shepherd. He shifted back, scratches on his face and arms, and looked around. "Thanks," he told me. I nodded and squeezed his hand.

We stood, chests heaving, in the middle of a room full of dead rats. Whatever genetic engineering the Reapers had done, they really hadn't done much for their postmortem longevity. They were beginning to *smell*.

He glanced around. "Everyone okay?"

Scout wiped at her brow with the back of her hand. "I'm good."

"I'm tired, but fine," I added.

Michael and Paul gave waves from their corners of the room.

Detroit looked up. "I'm—I'm not" was all she got out before pulling up the knee of her pants. There was a giant bite on the outside of her calf; blood was everywhere. Jason reached out to grab her before she went down, but didn't quite make it. She stumbled backward into the wall—and into some kind of emergency button.

A piercing alarm began to ring through the sanctuary.

Jason let out a curse. "That might alert the Reapers," he yelled over it. "We've put the monsters down, and now we have *got* to get out of here."

Detroit slid onto the floor. "I'm not sure I can make it out."

"You just need a little help," he said soothingly, then scooped her up and into his arms. "I'm taking the lead, and I'm going as fast as I can. Stay close behind in case we missed anything."

He began running down the hallway. Michael snatched Detroit's walking stick and took off behind him. Scout and I followed through one corridor after another . . . at least until she stopped short. I watched Jason, Paul, and Michael disappear around another corner.

"Scout, come on! Reapers might be coming, and we need to *go*." I tugged her arm, but she wouldn't move.

She pulled her arm free. "I can't go, Lily. I've been in the missing vampire's position—being hurt and alone. And what they've done is awful. We can't leave it intact and let them continue the work. We just can't."

"Scout, we have to go. Detroit's injured and—"

"You don't have to be here. I've been working on a spell. I can plant it alone and get out afterward. You don't have to be here."

That, I realized, was what she'd been working on in her room. Getting rid of the sanctuary had been her plan all along.

"I was one of them, Lily. I know how they work—how much it hurts, how bad it feels." She slapped a hand to her chest. "I'm an *Adept*. I make a promise every day to help the people they try to hurt. To stop them from doing it. I can't leave this place here for them to use at will. I *can't*."

Tears began to brim in her eyes. "I can't."

We looked at each other for a moment, before I nodded. "Then I stay. And I help."

She shook her head. "You should go. You used up all your fire-spell."

"I think Sebastian taught me how to make my own power."

Her eyes went even wider. "Lily—" she began, but I shook my head.

"I've already kind of tried it, and I think it will work. You need it, and that's all I need to know to try again. What's your spell supposed to do?"

"Implode the sanctuary."

Well, that would probably do it.

"Won't that take down the buildings on the street?"

She shook her head. "It's a pinpoint spell. It'll wipe down the interior, but leave the architecture—the hardware—intact. It's like cleaning off your hard drive—the hard drive's still there afterward, right?"

I still wasn't crazy about the idea—one wrong move, and we single-handedly brought down whatever building happened to be above us—but she was right—we couldn't just leave this place intact. Decision made, I nodded back at her. "Okay. What do we do?"

She reached into her bag and pulled out one of the tiny houses from her shelf. "We have to set this spell. Then I give the incantation, and we run."

"Can you take down a building this big?"

"I don't know. I haven't actually tried it. And even better, I'm only going to get one shot."

An idea bloomed. I reached out my hand toward Scout. "Then we make that one shot count. Give me your hand."

"You want to help me trigger it?"

"It worked last time."

"It *hurt* last time."

"And it's probably going to hurt this time, too. But if that's what we need to do, it's what we need to do. And we're in this together."

"You're the best."

"I know. But mostly I want to get out of here. Preferably in one piece."

She nodded, then walked into the room and put the tiny house on one of the tables. When she made it back to me, we let the door close in front of us. Scout offered her hand. I gripped it tightly in mine.

Before we could begin, Michael ran back around the corner. "What are you doing? We need to *go*."

"Michael," I said. "*Run*. Tell Jason to get out of the building, and tell everyone to huddle down at the other end of the corridor. We'll be right behind you. We promise. But for now, we've got to take care of the sanctuary. Go *now*."

I saw the hitch—he wasn't sure if he should leave us.

Scout looked back at him. "Do you trust me?"

His face fell. "Scout—"

She shook her head. "I have to do this, Michael. And I need you to trust me. Okay?"

He ran to her and whispered something in her ear. She threw her arms around his neck and gave him a fierce hug, then pressed a kiss to his cheek.

"*Run*," she said, and Michael took off. I trusted Scout just like he did, but that didn't mean I didn't still cross my fingers for luck.

Scout moved back, took my hand, and closed her eyes. "Your cue is 'night.' When I hit that, fill me up."

"Let's do this," I agreed, and then she began.

"We are bringers of light."

I closed my eyes. Instead of pulling in power from the world around us—power that I'd had trouble controlling the last time—I imagined a spark blooming of its own accord. Bright and green, shaped like a dandelion.

"We are fighters of right."

I opened my eyes. There, in front of me, hovered a tiny green spark. Small, but condensed. A lot of power in one tiny ember.

"We must pull this place in, and make safe the *night*."

I pulled the spark into both of us. It bloomed and blossomed and spilled outward. I opened my eyes, and through the window in the door saw the tiny house explode into shards of light.

And then it began.

Like a tornado had suddenly kicked up in the Chicago underground, all the stuff in the building—doors, walls, tables, medical implements—was sucked behind us.

Scout and I yanked our hands away from each other. It definitely hurt—my fingers burning like I'd stuck them into a roaring fire—but we were still on our feet.

And then we ran like the rats were still after us.

We hurdled spinning lamps and dodged computer gear, pushing ourselves against walls to avoid the doors that came hurtling toward us.

Scout stumbled over an office chair, and I grabbed and pulled her along until she was on her feet again. And the sound—it was like a freight train roaring toward us.

The walls began to evaporate, drywall and wiring sucking back toward the center of the spell. Finally, we turned a corner, and there were Jason and Michael, holding open the double doors that led out of the sanctuary.

It was getting even harder to run, like we were swimming through molasses. The nightmare flashed through my mind, the door I hadn't been able to reach.

But this was real life, and I wasn't about to go down in a sanctuary in some nasty tunnel. I pushed forward like I was racing for the finish line. We made it through the doors just as they were pulled off their hinges and into the current.

We ran to the other end of the corridor and hunkered down in the threshold of the tunnel with Jason, Michael, Paul, and Detroit, and then we watched it happen.

All of the stuff—everything but the concrete support columns—was sucked backward into an ever-tightening spiral. It swirled around and closed in, becoming a sphere of stuff. And then, with a *pop* and a burst of light, it was gone.

There was silence for a moment as we stared at the husk of the sanctuary—a place the Reapers could no longer use to hurt anyone, or try to further their own magic.

"Now that," Scout said, "was a good spell."

18

Maybe needless to say, we slept in Saturday morning. There was something about working serious magical mojo that pulled the energy right out of you.

After checking in with Scout and reading a message from Daniel (Detroit was doing fine, and Veronica's memories of the capture had been ixnayed by Katie, who had manipulation power), I finally managed to pull on jeans and a hoodie so I could scrounge through the cafeteria for some breakfast. I nabbed a tray and loaded it with energy: juice, yogurt, and muffins for me, and a plate of eggs, bacon, and toast for Scout. I ignored the stares as I carried the tray back through the Great Hall. They thought I was weird, and I might have been. But I'd also worked my tail off keeping them safe, and I deserved a little weirdness now and again.

When I got back, I went directly to Scout's room. We chowed down without speaking, finally mumbling something about being tired when we'd cleared the tray of pretty much every crumb. Although I was still contemplating a trip over to Mrs. M's for a post-breakfast.

And that was pretty much how the rest of the morning went, at least until we made the transition to my room.

After all, it was Saturday, and I had a date.

With a werewolf.

I know, I know. I play the unique, totally hip, magic-having, brilliant, always-together teenager.

Of course, the "teenager" bit is the most important part of that sentence. That was the part that made me change clothes four times, flipping through skirts and jeans and tops and scarves until the floor was pretty much covered in fabric. Scout read a magazine on my bed, generally not helping.

She'd suggested I wear a "potato sack."

What did that even *mean*?

The sun was out, so I settled on skinny jeans, a tank, and a half-cardigan. I shooed Scout out of my room and locked the door behind us, then settled the key around my neck. I was getting used to wearing it, and there was something about the weight of it that was kind of familiar.

Outside my door, Scout yawned again, back of her hand at her mouth. "You wanna go to dinner when you get back?"

"Sounds like a plan."

She nodded, then began to trudge toward her door. "I'll be in my room. Wave at the gargoyles for me."

I snorted. "Yeah, 'cause they're gonna wave back?"

She arched an eyebrow.

Right. We were at St. Sophia's.

But it was also a weekend at St. Sophia's, so the buildings were pretty quiet as I walked to the front door. Some of the girls' parents picked them up for a weekend visit home; some of them headed outside to explore the city.

Me? I was going on a date with a werewolf.

He stood at the edge of the grounds in jeans and a tucked-in, button-up shirt in the same spring blue as his eyes. In his hand was an old-fashioned picnic basket.

"Hello, Lily Parker," Jason said, leaning forward and pressing his lips to mine. "Happy Saturday."

"Happy Saturday."

"Our goal for today," he said, "is to pretend to be normal for a few hours. So I thought we'd spend our time outside. In the sun. And not underground."

I smiled grandly. "Great minds think alike." I nodded at the basket. "What's that?"

"We're having a picnic."

"A picnic?"

He held out his hand. "Come on. We only have an hour."

I looked at him for a minute, trying to figure out what he was up to, before taking his hand. "An hour before what?"

"For lunch. Then we have an appointment."

"All right, bucko. But this better be good."

"Bucko? We aren't going on a date in nineteen seventy-four."

I rolled my eyes, but couldn't stop the grin. Taking my hand in his, he led me down the sidewalk.

Our picnic spot was a square of grass in a long, narrow park that ran between two buildings off Michigan Avenue. It was like one row in a checkerboard, squares of grass alternating with fountains and plazas with benches. Jason pulled his fleece blanket out of the picnic basket and gallantly held out a hand.

I took a seat and waited for him to unload the basket. The first thing he pulled out was a glossy white box. He unfolded the top, revealing two brownies topped with a dusting of powdered sugar.

I pulled a chunk from one of them and took a bite. "Wow. That's really good."

"I made them myself."

I slid him a suspicious glance.

"Did I say 'make'? I meant to say I bought them at a bakery on the way over here."

"I figured. I mean, how would you have the time to bake? And you live in a dorm room, right? Do you even have a kitchen?"

"I have matches and a mug warmer."

"Rebel."

"And with a cause, too. Just stick with me, kid. I'm going places."

I shook my head at the joke and pulled out another piece of brownie, trying to avoid splattering my jeans with a snowfall of powdered sugar.

For nearly an hour, we sat on the blanket in the grass, and ate our lunch. We joked. We laughed. We talked about our hometowns and the people we went to school with.

For nearly an hour, we pretended to be teenagers who had nothing more to do on a weekend than finish up homework, spend the night at a girlfriend's house, or figure out what to wear to class on Monday morning.

We just . . . were.

And the more we sat in the grass on that beautiful fall day, the more we laughed.

Every time Jason laughed, his nose crinkled up.

Every time Jason laughed, my heart tugged a little.

If I wasn't careful, I was gonna fall for this boy.

And yet something was . . . weird. Maybe it was the fact that I'd seen Sebastian. Maybe it was the fact that I'd seen Jason in wolf form. Maybe he was just tired. But there was something in his eyes. Something darker than I'd seen before. Scout had said once that the summer had been long, that the Adepts were tired.

Maybe fighting the good fight was wearing on him, as well.

But I pushed the thought aside. There would be enough worry when darkness fell again. For now the sun was enough.

When lunch was done, the trash was tossed and the blanket was packed away again. Taking my hand in his, Jason led me toward our "appointment" on the other side of the river. As we crossed the bridge, I walked beside the railing, my eyes on the water beneath us.

"They dye it green for St. Patrick's Day, you know."

"Yeah, I saw that on TV once. It's cool that it runs right through downtown."

On the other side of the bridge, we took a set of steps down to a small riverside dock. I looked over at him. "What are you up to?"

"We're taking a ride," he said, then gestured to his right. I glanced out across the river, where a longish boat topped with dozens of chairs was gliding toward us.

"River tour," he added. "We're going to take a little trip."

"I see. Thanks for keeping me posted."

"Anytime, Lily. Anytime."

When the boat pulled up, we waited while the passengers stepped off; then Jason handed the captain two tickets. We took seats beside each other at the front of the boat, and when the coast was clear, the captain motored us into the river. We headed away from the lake, deeper into the forest of steel and concrete. I stared up as the towers drew nearer, growing larger. Some looked like pointy pinnacles of glass. Others were round, like giant sugar canisters.

"They call them the corncobs," Jason said, pointing to those twin, curvy towers that were full of parked cars.

"They look like it," I agreed, neck stretched upward as I watched them pass.

"Here, lean back against me," he whispered, rearranging himself so that his body supported mine. I leaned back, my head against his chest. He wrapped his arms around me, and we floated down the Chicago River, the world around us. For the first time in a long while, I felt safe. Secure, like even if the world was full of ghosts and monsters and evil motivations, they couldn't get to me. Not now. Not while we floated on inky blue water, the riveted steel of bridges above us, orangey red against the bright blue sky.

"I was thinking about the Sneak," he whispered. "I think we should go together."

My stomach felt like tiny birds had taken flight, and I was glad he couldn't see the silly grin on my face. "Yeah," I said. "That sounds good."

He squeezed me tighter. "Life is good."

For once, in that moment, it simply was.

But moments like that don't last forever, do they?

. . .

We were back on land, walking toward St. Sophia's when he pulled me toward the alley and the garden of thorns. I figured he wanted a quiet place to talk. I hadn't expected him to unbutton his shirt. Blushing, I looked away, but I got enough of a view to see that he had the body of an athlete.

"You can look," he said with a chuckle. "I need to show you something."

I glanced back, my eyebrow arched suspiciously.

He held up two fingers. "Completely PG. I promise."

I looked . . . then gaped. Across his chest were three foot-long scratches. They were well-healed now, three ripples of pinkish skin, the scars of an attack.

Instinctively, I reached out my hand to touch him, before curling my fingers back into a fist. "What happened?"

"Initiation," he said.

I wasn't sure if he meant it was a badge of honor for joining the werewolves, or it was a mark of how he'd become one. But then I remembered that he'd told me being a wolf was hereditary.

"When a wolf is old enough, he or she spends a night on a kind of journey. Like a vision quest. He—I—went into the woods. Some of the night is gone—the hours passed, but I don't remember what I did. Some of it I remember, but a lot of those memories are just random sounds and images."

"What sounds and images do you remember?"

He shook his head. "I'm sworn to secrecy."

"Seriously?"

His expression was grim. "It's one of the rules. My parents don't even know what went on. Just me and"—he looked down at the scars on his chest—"me and the wolf who did this."

"Initiation," I repeated. "That seems kinda harsh."

"You're thinking like a human. Think about puppies. They learn by play fighting, biting, clawing. That's different from the way humans learn." He shrugged. "Same goes for werewolves. The world is a violent place."

"Did you"—I paused, trying to figure out how to ask the question— "did you learn anything while you were out there? Have a vision, I mean? See part of your future or whatever?"

"I guess you could say I understood what it meant to be who I am." His eyes seemed to cloud, like whatever he'd learned, he wasn't thrilled about it.

"Is it magic?" I wondered. "I mean, they call you an Adept, and you're a member of Enclave Three . . ."

His expression darkened. "I'm an Adept because I'm something *else,* something other, and something powerful. Not because I have a talent." He looked away. I could tell that something was bothering him— something about being a werewolf—but I still wasn't sure what it was.

What had he wanted to show me? The scars?

"What is it?" I asked.

"I need to tell you something. And it may mean something to you. It might not—but I need to tell you."

My stomach rolled. Scout had tried to warn me about Jason; she hadn't been specific, though. Now I wondered if I was about to get all the gory details. Did he have a girlfriend? Was he a Reaper in disguise? Had he seen me talking to Sebastian? I gnawed the edge of my lip. "Okay. Go ahead."

"It's a curse," he said.

We were quiet for a moment.

"I don't know what you mean about a 'curse.'"

He shook his head, and he wouldn't make eye contact. "It means it's not a gift, or magic. I'm not some kind of romantic mutant. I'm not a superhero." He looked up at me, and his eyes shifted in color—from sky blue to chartreuse—just like those of an animal in the night. His voice dropped, became a little growlier.

"There was an ancient king named Lycaon. He was cruel to gods and men alike, and he was punished by both. The gods punished him by turning him into a wolf—but only halfway. So he wasn't really a wolf, and he wasn't really a man. He had to live in between the two worlds, never really a part of either. Humans punished him for that."

I reached out and took his hand, slipping my fingers into his. "So that's where it all started?"

Jason nodded. "With Lycaon and his sons. They were my ancestors and the cause of it all. I bear the curse every day, Lily, of someone else's guilt."

"You told me you ran away when you found out you were a wolf. Is that why you left?"

"Part of it, yeah." He looked up and away, out toward the city.

He was quiet a long time.

"Why do I get the sense you're not telling me all of it?"

It took a minute for him to look back again, and when he did, there was sadness in his eyes. "I like you, Lily."

I looked away, expecting the worst.

"I'm not human," he finally said. "I know you saw me transform, but it's not a full moon. If you're there, you'll get hurt."

"Hurt?"

"As the moon grows larger, my control gets weaker. I can be around friends, at least until the moon is full. That's when we run."

"Friends?"

His eyes shifted from blue to green and back again, and my heart tripped in time. "I have feelings for you, Lily. I shouldn't. Not when I could put you at risk. There will be a girl. A wolf my parents will choose for me."

My head began to spin.

"That's the real curse," he said. "Not the fact that I transform, not even the fact that I lose control when the moon is full. The curse is the loneliness. The separation. Never really being anything except a wolf, because being something else—being human—puts everyone else at risk."

We were quiet for a moment.

"I need you to say something."

"I don't know what to say. I don't know what you want me to say."

He dropped his forehead onto mine. "Tell me it doesn't matter."

I blinked back tears, but what could I say to this boy? This boy with the spring blue eyes? "I guess the lesson I've learned over the last few weeks is that life is rarely what we think it's going to be. So you do the best you can. Right?"

"Does that mean we're still on for Sneak?"

I was quiet for a minute, considering my options. Best-case scenario, we just spent time together and didn't waste time worrying about the future.

Worst-case scenario? I fell for a boy I couldn't have, and lost my heart completely.

But I wasn't even sixteen yet, and the future was a long way off. With all the crazy in the world—especially in my world—why not enjoy it, right?

"Yeah," I finally said. "We can go to Sneak."

With a victorious groan, he pulled me tightly into his arms, his body smelling of sunlight and springy cologne. "I knew there was a reason I liked you."

We held hands as we walked back to St. Sophia's, but we didn't speak a word. He stopped in front of the gate and embraced me again, then dropped his head to press a kiss to my lips.

After he left, I glanced back at the school. I wasn't ready to head back inside. I looked out over the city again and spied the familiar orange moon of a coffeehouse down the street.

"There's nothing a little overpriced latte can't fix," I quietly said, then headed back down Erie toward Michigan Avenue, trying to clear my head.

He was cursed.

Let me repeat that. He was *cursed*. And when the full moon came, if I was around, he'd rather rip me into shreds than kiss me. It did tend to discourage dating humans, I guessed.

Why did stuff like this have to happen just when things were looking so promising? When I was starting to like a boy with blue eyes who, at least until a few minutes ago, hadn't been trying to kill me. There was a pretty big nasty in the closet, and the burden fell on me to deal with it. What was I supposed to do? Tell him it didn't matter?

Or worse—lie to him? Tell him we'd find a solution that thousands of years—and probably thousands of wolves—hadn't revealed.

Tears stung at the corners of my eyes.

I crossed the street at the light. I'd dealt with getting dropped off in Chicago, with firespell, with a best friend with a magical secret, with constant doubts about my parents.

This was the straw that broke the Adept's back.

It might be time to skip the latte and go straight for the triple hot chocolate.

"We keep running into each other."

I glanced up. Sebastian stood in front the coffeehouse, orange paper cup in hand. He wore jeans and a dark blue fleece jacket that almost perfectly matched the color of his eyes.

I swiped at the tear that had slipped down my cheek as casually as possible. "I assume it's not a coincidence you're a block from St. Sophia's?"

Frowning, he held up his cup of coffee. "It is, actually. My parents have a condo." He gestured toward the tower above the coffee place. "I was visiting."

It took me a second to remember that Reapers, whatever their motivations, were people, too. With parents and condos and lives beyond evening battles.

But still . . . "We aren't going to be friends, you know."

His eyes seemed to darken. "I didn't expect that we were."

"Good."

"Friendship is a lot simpler than what we are."

I looked over at him. "*We* are not anything."

"Then why are you still standing here?"

I looked away.

"The world isn't black and white, Lily. Ambivalence rules the day."

I looked up at him. "Meaning what?"

"Meaning what I've been telling you. Meaning things are rarely as simple as they seem. Sometimes you don't figure out how the story is supposed to end until you've read it."

"And what are you supposed to do until you get to the end?"

He looked out over the city, pride in his features. He was undeniably handsome—dark hair, dark brows, dark eyes. He had the bones of a fallen angel—and apparently the same wickedness. But he had helped me, had given me undeniably helpful information. "You're supposed to do the best you can with what you've got. Or you're supposed to get it." He looked down at me. "There's no fault in that, Lily. That's what life's about."

But that was where he was wrong.

"No," I said. "That's not what this is about. Not *this*." I cupped my palms together, closed my eyes, and blew into my hands. When I opened them again, the spark was there, the tiny star of pure green power.

I looked up at him and saw the surprise in his face. I guess he hadn't expected me to catch on so quickly.

"This isn't a weapon. This isn't a strategy. It's the thing that holds the universe together. The stuff that keeps us moving. You want me to doubt my friends. You want me to doubt what they do, the battle they fight."

I opened my palms and let the spark free. For a moment, I watched the spark flitter and float, then mouthed the words "come back." The spark spiraled in the air, and then with a slow, arcing descent, landed on my palm again.

When I spoke again, my voice was quiet. "I'm not sure why you're talking to me. And I'm not sure I trust you. But I do know right from wrong. I don't need a boy or a girl or an Adept or a Reaper to tell me that. You try to drown people in the sea of their own misery." I swallowed. "And we try to bring them back."

"It's never that simple."

"It *is* that simple," I said, eyes on the spark, which floated—as if waiting for a command—just above my palm. "We may not have magic for very long. But this isn't a force for destruction."

I looked up at Sebastian, expecting to see disdain or disagreement in his expression. But instead, there was something soft in his eyes.

He looked down at his clenched palm, and then opened it. In his curled fingers sat his own small spark. Suddenly, it jumped out to meet mine, the attraction of opposite forces. Like long-separated lovers, the sparks entangled, then rose into the air and floated through the currents across Erie Avenue.

"So that you don't forget the world isn't black or white," he said. "It's gray. And someone tells you otherwise, they're lying." He reached out, and with a finger, brushed a lock of hair from my face. "You deserve more than lying."

And then he turned and walked away.

I stood there for a moment imagining the world—the city— spinning on an axis around me.

What if it wasn't so easy to pick out good from bad?

How were you supposed to know who the bad guys were?

I looked across the street at the Portman Electric building, and let my gaze take in hearty brick and simple landscaping . . . and the letters of the Sterling Research Foundation sign.

More important, how do you know who the good guys are?

As I crossed the street and walked down the block, I found a tour group standing in front of the convent's stone gate. The tour leader wore a long black coat and a black top hat, a stuffed raven perched on his shoulder. He stood atop the stone wall, arms outstretched, his voice booming across the sunlight. The tourists kept looking between him and the convent—back and forth—like they weren't quite sure what to believe. I stopped a few feet away to listen in.

"And in 1901," he said, "the convent was the sight of a mysterious disappearance. The door to a room shared by four of the nuns rattled in the howling winter wind, so it was locked every evening when the nuns retired for their rest. But the lock was on the outside of the door, so once the nuns went to sleep, they stayed in the room until they were released the next morning.

"One evening, Sister Bernadette went to sleep with her sisters. They said good night to each other, said an evening prayer, and fell asleep. But when the other sisters awoke the next morning, Sister Bernadette was nowhere to be found! Her bedsheets were tousled—and still warm. But the bed was empty—and the door was still locked from the outside! Sister Bernadette had disappeared in the night, and she was never seen again."

The tourists offered sounds of interest, then began snapping pictures of the convent.

A few weeks after my initiation by firespell, his ghost story didn't sound so unusual. I had a few ideas about where Sister Bernadette might have gone . . .

The man in black noticed I was heading for the gate and waved his hand at me. "Young lady, are you a student at St. Sophia's School for Girls?"

The people taking the tour turned to look at me. Some of them actually looked a little scared, like they weren't entirely sure if I was real. Others looked skeptical, like they weren't entirely sure I wasn't a plant.

"Um, yes," I said. "I am."

"Mm-hmm," he said. "And have you seen anything mysterious in the hallowed halls of St. Sophia's?"

I looked back at him for a moment and kept my features perfectly blank. "St. Sophia's? Not really. Just, you know, studying."

At his disappointed look, I continued through the gate. I glanced up at the black stone towers and the monsters that stood point on the edges of the building's facade. These were the gargoyles Scout had referred to, with their gnarly dragonlike faces and folded batlike wings. They perched on the corners of the building as clouds raced behind them, their bodies pitched forward like they were ready to take flight.

"They're definitely St. Sophia's appropriate," I murmured, "but they aren't exactly pretty."

Okay, maybe I imagined it. Maybe I was tired, or the run-in with Sebastian had finally scrambled my brain.

But just as the words were out of my mouth, and before I'd taken another step forward, the gargoyle on the right-hand corner of the building tilted its head and stared down at me with an expression that was none too amused.

Frankly, he looked a little irritated.

My jaw dropped. I wasn't sure if I was more surprised that he'd moved—or that he'd been offended because I didn't think he was pretty.

"Sorry," I mouthed back.

Within the blink of an eye, he reassumed his position, and looked just the same as he had a moment ago.

Surely I hadn't just imagined that?

On the other hand, I thought, walking toward the door again, stranger things had happened.

It was St. Sophia's, after all.

Chloe Neill was born and raised in the South but now makes her home in the Midwest—just close enough to Cadogan House and St. Sophia's to keep an eye on things. When not transcribing Merit's and Lily's adventures, she bakes, works and scours the Internet for good recipes and great graphic design. Chloe also maintains her sanity by spending time with her boys—her favorite landscape photographer and their dogs, Baxter and Scout. (Both she and the photographer understand the dogs are in charge.) Visit her on the Web at www.chloeneill.com.